By Amy Lane

Published by Dreamspinner Press
www.dreamspinnerpress.com

Published by DREAMSPINNER PRESS
www.dreamspinnerpress.com

CROCUS

AMY LANE

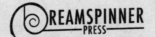

DREAMSPINNER
PRESS

Published by
DREAMSPINNER PRESS

5032 Capital Circle SW, Suite 2, PMB# 279,
Tallahassee, FL 32305-7886 USA
www.dreamspinnerpress.com

Crocus
© 2018 Amy Lane.

Cover Art
© 2018 Reese Dante .
http://www.reesedante.com
Cover content is for illustrative purposes only and any person depicted on the cover is a model.

Mass Market Paperback ISBN: 978-1-64108-070-5
Trade Paperback ISBN: 978-1-64080-636-8
Digital ISBN: 978-1-64080-635-1
Library of Congress Control Number: 2017919616
Mass Market Paperback published April 2018
v. 1.0

Printed in the United States of America
∞
This paper meets the requirements of
ANSI/NISO Z39.48-1992 (Permanence of Paper).

To Mate, because I get mad at the weirdest things at the weirdest times and he just nods and goes, "Okay, so what'd I do now?" Nothing. He's the person I love best, and when I'm hurt, he takes the heat. That's all. And to Mary, for reading it. And to my daughter with depression, because I will worry about her forever and ever, but I am proud of how strong she's been.

ACKNOWLEDGMENTS

"CPS" IS a vaguely mentioned shadow agency in a lot of books—mine is no exception. But they are underfunded and they face daily horrors, and we need people like them in so much of the world. Thank you for protecting those who don't protect themselves.

AUTHOR'S NOTE

THERE'S NOT really a train station in Forresthill like the one I described. The one I described is in Colfax, which is a much bigger town. But I needed a train station in Forresthill, and since Colton is a fictional place too, and so is Dogpatch, I just threw the whole area into Amy-land and made it a thing. Forgive me.

CLOUDS OVER THE SUN

"OLIVIA?"

Larx regarded his oldest daughter with surprise. She'd been planning to come home at the end of the spring semester to deal with her pregnancy, it was true, but—

"Sorry, Daddy," she said, her lower lip trembling. Oh God. Her eyes, limpid brown pools on the happiest of days, were shiny and filling with tears even as she stood on his porch.

"Come in," he ushered belatedly. "It's cold out there!" February in Colton, up in the Sierra Mountains, was snow season. "How did you even get—"

Olivia turned and waved, then gathered her suitcases and came inside, shivering in shirtsleeves. The unfamiliar SUV in the driveway backed out, and Larx was left with his daughter and what appeared to be everything she'd taken to her dorm in August.

Stunned, he started moving bags into the house. His hair—still wet from the shower—became brittle in the chill. He was dressed in sweats and a hooded sweatshirt, the better to tuck into masses of weekend paperwork without interruption.

Which was where he'd been when his oldest daughter once again decided to turn his life upside down.

"You're moving back home," he said, stating the obvious.

"Yeah." She turned to him apologetically. "Dad, just leave those in the foyer—"

"So everybody can trip on them? No—I'll take them to your room."

Her piquant little face screwed up into a grimace. "I was hoping… you know. Remember when Aaron's daughters came for Christmas, and they stayed at his house since he moved in here?"

Larx gaped at her. "That is making one hell of an assumption."

Larx and Aaron had gotten together during a tumultuous autumn—but the relationship and the love had stuck, and stuck hard. Aaron and his son, Kirby, had moved into Larx's little house right before Thanksgiving, building a super special space-age chicken coop for their beloved birds. Aaron and Kirby's house was about five miles away on conventional roads, but only about two miles by the forestry service track that ran behind both properties. Aaron's daughters had stayed there over Christmas—one under extreme duress—but for the most part Aaron checked on the place once a week to start the heater and make sure nothing leaked and (Larx suspected) to read his phone in the bathroom in complete peace since there were only two bathrooms in Larx's house and five people living there.

Yes, it was vacant.

Yes, it was available.

But it was *Aaron's*, and Larx was just so damned grateful to have Aaron in his life that he didn't want to impose.

But then, thinking about having one more person using the bathroom in the mornings—one who, by all accounts, was suffering terribly from morning sickness—felt like a burden Larx's crowded little house shouldn't be made to bear. It had been hard enough over the Christmas break, but this was… forever?

"Daddy!"

"We'll ask him," Larx said, numb.

"Where is he?" she asked brightly, turning around and walking backward.

"He's at work today—"

"The boys?"

"Kirby took Kellan to go visit Isaiah. Watch out for the—"

By the grace of God, Olivia avoided Toby, who'd picked that moment to dart across the room. Toby, always a skittish sort of cat, disappeared behind the entertainment center, where she'd probably stay for the next two days.

"How are Kellan and Isaiah doing?" Olivia asked, turning around to negotiate the furniture.

"Still broken up," Larx said shortly. Kellan, the boy Larx had taken into his home in October, had been heartbroken. But Isaiah, who had sustained a brutal knife wound, was busy recovering—both physically and emotionally—and Larx could see how he'd be reluctant to share the darkness in his heart with the boy he loved.

That didn't mean Larx didn't hurt, every day, picking up the pieces.

But Aaron's youngest—Kirby—had adopted Kellan as a brother pretty much from the beginning. He'd been the one to make Kellan keep sending letters, and to explain how having hope for a friendship was so much better than being a bitter, snarling asshole because he was in pain.

Kirby's words. Larx had been hampered by his own compassion—or that's what Aaron told him after Kirby had gone off in Kellan's face and snapped the boy out of his funk.

"Aw, Dad, that's too bad," Olivia said softly. For a moment her attention was focused on something besides her own problems, and her brown eyes showed kindness and sorrow. "I know you were rooting for them."

"They're still friends," Larx said, trying to keep his own opinion out of it. His own opinion was that they were still very much in love. "But, honey, you haven't said—"

"Where's Christiana?"

"At her friend's house, so she can whine about her girlfriend and eat ice cream."

"She didn't break up, did she? She would have texted me!"

Larx had always been proud of how close his girls were—but at this point he sort of wished that closeness swung both ways, because Christiana should have told him her sister was coming home!

"No. Jessica was feeling neglected since Christi started dating Schuyler. This is sort of friend time."

Olivia's relentless movement stopped. Her expression closed down, and she bit her lower lip. "That's nice," she said hollowly. "That's… really mature, actually. You know. So, uh, Christiana."

She started backing away from him, once again not watching where she was going.

"Livvy, what's wrong? Shit, Livvy! Don't trip over the—"

And she did. She tripped over the half-grown shepherd/retriever mix sprawled between the kitchen and the living room. Dozer startled and leaped up, barking his head off.

Olivia screamed, fell backward on her ass, and burst into tears.

Larx scrubbed his face with his hand and leaned forward to give her a hand up. "Honey," he said, hefting her to her feet. "Why don't we start at the beginning?"

The beginning, apparently, was born in a relentless shower of tears. It took him an hour—an uncomfortable, unhappy hour, during which time he made her hot chocolate, gave her space while he made her lunch, stacked her boxes in the hall, and took her overnight bag to Christiana's bedroom, where she'd slept when she'd been home for Christmas, and then held her and rocked her and actually sang to her to calm her down.

By the time she'd calmed down enough to maybe, perhaps, tell him what was going on, she fell immediately asleep, facedown on the couch while he was stroking her back.

Larx was in his empty house with his despondent daughter and a table full of paperwork he'd *just* started an hour before.

And a brain that wouldn't stop buzzing.

Olivia had zoomed into the house at the beginning of Christmas break too. She'd zoomed into the house, run to the bathroom, hugged everybody, petted the dog, sat down at the table, and told Larx she was pregnant.

Larx had hugged her and cried and told Aaron, pretty much in that order.

And Aaron had taken it like a champion. No freaking out about how Olivia wasn't the most stable bee in the bonnet, no wondering what they were going to do after she had the baby and they might end up being responsible for it while they helped Olivia juggle her school schedule—nothing.

Just "Oh—we're going to be grandparents."

And Larx, reeling from the news himself, had been counting his good fortune every day.

He would be doing something hard, yes—but he'd be doing it with a helpmate, and damn, after all those years of both of them going it alone, that seemed like such a blessing.

But the more Larx talked to Olivia, the more she texted him constantly throughout his day, the more concerned he got. He couldn't put his finger on the source of his worry—he didn't have a name for it.

All he knew was that every time he tried to pin her down on a plan for the next year, she either cried or ran away, or, worse, got hysterical and angry on the phone and hung up. As long as he'd been parenting, he'd prided himself and his girls on their ability to talk to each other, to work out any problem, to discuss things rationally.

Rational had not been on Olivia's plate since Christmas. Hell, if Larx thought hard about it, since even before that.

Larx didn't know much about mental health issues, but what he did know made him want to take her to the nearest psych ward for an evaluation. But every time he tried to bring it up—something along the lines of "You're getting a little, uh, extreme in the mood department, honey," she lost it—anger, tears, or simply avoidance—and now she'd avoided herself right back home, where three more people lived than had been living when she left.

Larx sat in the sudden silence of his little house in Colton, California, and tried to put his own breath into perspective. Not too loud, not too soft, just there.

That's what he needed to be as a father right now. He hoped.

Because otherwise he was as lost as his butterfly daughter, and he didn't have a Larx to turn to.

HE STOOD with a sigh and walked into the kitchen, thinking more coffee was in order. He'd brought home an entire stack of behavioral referrals that needed his signature and some sort of follow-up, as well as minutes from the last board meeting that he wanted to add remarks to, *and* he was in the middle of trying to reorder textbooks, which was harder than it sounded.

America's textbook industry was still very much dominated by Texas, and Larx was damned if he would okay a science textbook that spent more time on creationism than evolution, because he had a brain.

And because his students' brains were still developing, and he would really very much appreciate it if they didn't develop into complete idiocy under his watch.

Ugh. What was the world thinking?

He'd been looking forward to six or so hours to catch up on his paperwork. The boys, Christiana, Aaron—they were all due back in the late afternoon, when they would make dinner together and play cards and maybe fall asleep in front of a movie as a family, and Larx had planned to enjoy that too.

He had, in fact, been dreaming about some time leaning against Aaron George's solid chest for the past week. Both of them had been busy—heinously busy, in fact.

The last time they'd tried to have sex, Larx had fallen asleep with his hand on Aaron's solid erection and his head on Aaron's shoulder.

For the first time in nearly ten years, they both had somebody in bed and in their lives whom they loved and wanted to be with, and that was as good as sex got?

No. Absolutely not.

Larx was not going to let this stand.

Or he hadn't been, until Olivia had danced in through the front door with all her stuff and moved her ass back onto his couch before he was ready for it.

With a sigh, he put his elbows up on his ginormous stack of paperwork and buried his face in his hands.

His phone, sitting on the table next to him, buzzed, and he was damned grateful.

Hello, Principal—are you being a good boy and getting your work done?

Larx groaned. *Sort of. Olivia showed up on the doorstep this morning.* Oh hell. He didn't even want to *ask* Aaron about using his house.

Is she visiting for the weekend?

No.

The phone rang. "Are you kidding me?"

"Sorry, Aaron." He sighed and sipped his tepid coffee, then took a deep breath. "I don't know what's going on. She came in talking a mile a minute, tripped over the dog—"

"Is Dozer okay?"

Larx had to laugh. "Your dog is fine, Aaron."

"He's your dog," Aaron protested weakly. Yes, the puppy had been a gift for Larx when his oldest cat passed away, but Aaron—big, solid, strong—had apparently been waiting for Dozer for most of his life.

Larx wasn't going to argue that the dog was definitely Aaron's, but it was true. Dozer—a mixed breed somewhere between a Labrador retriever and a German shepherd—was fine with Larx, answered to him just as well as he did Aaron, appreciated the hell out of the full food bowl, gave plenty of sloppy, happy kisses, and pranced about on spindly legs and feet the size of dinner plates.

But when Aaron came home, Larx watched the dog melt, roll to his back, offer up his tummy in supplication, and beg for pets.

Larx couldn't object or be jealous—he felt the same way. Except Larx wanted Aaron to pet more than his belly.

"That dog's your soul mate from another life," Larx said now, scratching Dozer behind the ears. "Yes, you are. Yes, you are. But you can't have him. He's mine."

"Wow. Just wow."

Larx chuckled, because the distraction had been welcome, but now… now grown-up things. "She's asleep on the couch," he said softly. "Aaron… she's not sounding…." He took a big breath. His ex-wife had suffered from depression after a miscarriage, and he remembered coming home from work bringing dinner once so she didn't have to cook or clean up because she'd been so sad. She'd yelled at him—didn't he think she was capable of cleaning her own kitchen? Then she'd burst into tears for an hour, while Larx had fed the girls and tried to calm her down.

It had been like standing on the deck of a ship in a storm—and Larx had that same feeling now, with his daughter, when his children had always been the source of peace in his heart.

"Pregnancy?" Aaron asked hesitantly. They were so new. Larx hadn't spoken about Alicia more than a handful of times. Nobody talked about depression or mental illness.

Nobody knew what to say.

"Yeah." Larx didn't want to talk about it right now. He just couldn't.

"Baby…." Aaron's voice dropped, and considering Larx had gotten him at work, where he had to be all tough and manly and shit, that meant he was worried.

"Later," Larx said gruffly. "Just not, you know…."

"When the whole world can hear. I get it." Aaron blew out a breath and then took the subject down a surprising path. "Larx, do you have a student named Candace Furman?"

Larx stared at the paperwork in his hand, shuffling back to where he was right before Olivia had knocked.

"Yeah. Not one of mine, but... huh." He reached over to his laptop and accessed the school's portal site. "Hm...."

"That's informative. Want to tell me what you're looking at?"

"It's sort of privileged, Deputy. Want to tell me why you need to know?"

Aaron's grunt told him he was being annoying, but Larx couldn't help it. He didn't want to just divulge information on a kid if it wasn't necessary. It went against everything he'd ever stood for as a rebellious adolescent.

"I just got.... It was weird. We got a domestic call to her house—her parents answer, and it's all great. 'No, Officer, we have no idea why somebody would call in screaming or a fight in the snow.' We take a look inside, house is okay—but really clean."

"Like somebody just swept up all the pieces of all the things?" Larx hazarded.

"Yeah. Either that or just... unhealthily antiseptic. And Candace and her sister—"

"Shelley," Larx supplied since he had the file open on his computer.

"Yeah. Anyway—the girls are fine. 'Yessir. Nossir. It's all okay, sir.' But they've both got these... like, girl masks on?"

"Makeup?" Larx said, trying to picture it.

"No… like… face goop. Like… whatwazit? Mrs. Doubtfire stuck her face in the cake 'cause she didn't have her makeup on?"

It took Larx a minute to process all that. "A facial," he said, blinking hard because the movie was that old, and the antitrans messaging had been so strong that Larx forgot he too had been part of America who'd laughed their asses off at a man in a dress with flammable boobs.

"Yeah. That. And that shit could be hiding anything, right? Their eyes were red, but then, for all I know the facial goop did that. So I'm not sure if they're hiding shiners or if their neighbors just got hold of some bad weed—"

"Did you knock on their door?" Larx asked. Between him and Aaron, they really did know most of the town. "Who's their neighbor?"

"Couple of brothers," Aaron said thoughtfully. "Just moved at Christmas. Youngest one goes to Colton High—"

"Jaime Benitez," Larx said promptly. "Junior." He pressed the right link and there was the master schedule. "He and Candace are in some classes together."

Aaron grunted. "Well, the older brother had been lighting up pretty hard—but it doesn't seem like Jaime's the type to indulge."

"You didn't bust them?" Larx asked curiously. He'd done his share of weed in college—but Aaron had been off fighting and bleeding for his country when Larx was in college. This was something they'd never talked about.

"Hell," Aaron muttered. "Unless they're growing to distribute, it's mostly legal. Not for minors, of course, but both boys were functional, polite, and their eyes were clear. Roberto—who's twenty-one, by the way—actually produced a prescription for anxiety without being asked. I could have made a stink about it, but I couldn't see the point."

"I love you so hard," Larx breathed. "Seriously. I can't think of a sexual favor good enough for you. I'll have to make something up."

"I'm sorry?"

Larx couldn't articulate it. It wasn't that he'd smoke it now unless it was prescribed, and he didn't want his kids—or his students—indulging without cause. But something about knowing Aaron, for all his law-and-order propensities, didn't push rules just for the sake of there being rules made Larx even prouder of him.

"Just you're a good guy. Jaime Benitez is getting good grades. He's part of the local service clubs, including one where he tutors eighth graders in trouble. Nice boy."

"In your class?" Aaron wanted to know.

"Senior year, like Kirby. Christiana is sort of—"

"Special," Aaron said fondly. "Yeah. I know."

Well, Larx's youngest was the girl with the flower—her brightness and sparkle was coupled with a quiet good sense. Irresistible. She was also razor-sharp, which was why she was taking Larx's class in her junior year.

"So what about Candace?" Aaron prompted.

Larx sighed. "She's… well, she *was* a straight-A student, but no involvement in anything."

"Nothing?"

Aaron might well be surprised. It was a small school in a small town. Activity involvement wasn't mandatory, but if a kid wanted any sort of social life, being part of a club or a sport was pretty much the only thing going on after school.

"No—that's odd. And that's probably why I can't place her. Her sister's in grade school, so I wouldn't know her. But Candace is just… not involved."

"Was," Aaron prompted, and Larx rested his chin on his fist and looked woefully at his paperwork. Ye gods, the pile wasn't getting any smaller.

"Yeah. *Was* getting straight As. Is no longer. Is veering off into C and D territory. And I have in front of me, waiting for a signature, her very first referral for behavior."

He stared at it, wondering how the pieces fit.

"What'd she do?" Aaron asked patiently.

"Well, it says she got to class late and then ran out a few minutes after the bell rang. It was her first-period class, and when she came back—looking pale—the teacher asked if she was okay. Apparently she laughed hysterically and told the teacher to fuck off."

"Uh…."

Larx sighed. "Yeah. That's why I'm up to my eyeballs in paperwork, Aaron—so I can look for kids like this and ask them what happened. I'm on it."

"That's my boy," Aaron praised softly. "Good. Keep me in the loop, okay? I don't know if the girls were being abused, and frankly I didn't have enough evidence to so much as make them wash their faces. I don't know the story behind the boys living together without parents, and I don't know why one of them would be anxious enough to get a prescription for a ton of weed. These are things I would like to know before I go venturing in there with CPS and the DEA to make sure everything is kosher, you understand?"

"Got it, Deputy." Larx looked at both kids' files again and wondered at the puzzle. "Aaron, I'm serious. You're a good man. These kids—there's pieces missing here. Yanking them away from their homes, dragging them into the fray—I'm not sure if that's the best thing here."

Larx was starting to know Aaron's grunts—this one was the respectful disagreement grunt. "Some stuff needs to see light, Mr. Larkin," he chided gently. "If something's festering in that girl's life, it's our job to make sure she's okay."

Of course.

"Roger that." Larx tilted his head back and pinched the bridge of his nose.

"Have you eaten?" Aaron asked.

"Uh…." He'd gotten a sandwich for Olivia, but he'd put off getting his own.

"Eat, Principal. Work on your paperwork. And maybe take a nap on the couch before I get there. Save up your strength." He gave a chuckle that was absolutely filthy. "You're going to need it."

Larx whined. "But… but Olivia—"

"If hearing us have sex gives her reason to move out, more's the better," Aaron intoned darkly.

Oh shit. "She… uh… she sort of hinted… never mind."

"My house. Yes. We'll move her tomorrow."

Larx groaned and rested his forehead on the paperwork on the table. "God. You're the perfect man. Where's the rub? Where's the flaw? There's got to be

something here that makes me want to smack you—
where is it?"

"Mmm…."

Oh yeah. That conversation they *weren't* having
because of all the conversations they *were*.

"Understood." Larx sighed. "I'll see you when
you get home."

"Eat, dammit."

Larx smiled, reassured. "Sure. Take care of what's
mine."

"Always do."

"Love you."

"Thanks for the info."

Aaron signed off, and Larx's text pinged thirty
seconds later.

Love you too.

Yup. Too good to be true.

Larx's worry about his daughter—and about Aaron's input into the situation—doubled down in his
chest.

Please, Olivia—please. Don't make me choose
between you two. Please.

TEMPERATURE DROPPING

AARON FOUND Larx asleep at the kitchen table, a rumpled pile of referrals under his cheek as he snored.

Kirby and Kellan were working quietly around him, chopping vegetables for a salad and tending to a stew Larx had apparently started in the Crock-Pot.

"Hey," he said softly. "How was Sacramento?"

Kirby winced, his *Oh, honey, you stepped in it* expression so much like his mother's that Aaron's heart clenched a little.

"Sucked balls," Kellan said morosely.

"We don't want to talk about Sacramento," Kirby agreed. "Olivia's here. She's upstairs. Crying."

"Excellent. Christi?"

"Will be home in a few," Kellan said, his face lighting up just a bit. Christi did that to people. "I didn't tell her about Olivia." He finished chopping the bell pepper on the board in front of him and wrinkled his nose. "I'm… uh… she brought all her stuff."

"Wonderful," Aaron said brightly, just in case Larx woke up and heard him. "She's staying in our house for… uh… the foreseeable future. It'll be good. We won't have to keep checking up on the place. Hell, we were going to have to furnish a nursery anyway. Maybe Tiff's old room?"

His eldest had shown up for Christmas ready to piss Aaron off and flounce out of his life forever. Her plan backfired, however, when her grandparents weren't able to fly out from the Midwest and rescue her.

Backfired.

All over the family.

Tiffany had been insufferable—rude to Larx, rude to his kids, bitchy to her brother and sister, and a surly, judgy nightmare to Aaron himself. By Christmas Eve, Aaron had taken pretty much enough. He'd had Kirby go fetch Maureen, his middle child, from Aaron's house where he'd put up both girls for the holidays.

And hadn't told Tiffany that Kirby wasn't coming back.

And then he and Maureen and Kirby had blocked her on their phones.

At three o'clock Christmas afternoon, Tiffany had knocked humbly on Larx's back door, shivering with cold from the two-mile walk through the snow.

Aaron hadn't wanted to let her in at first. Larx had been the one to scowl at him until he opened the door.

He'd had his speech planned and on the tip of his tongue even as he'd slid it open. Not one more bitchy word about Larx, not one more sly innuendo about being "suddenly gay," and not one more demeaning put-down of her brother and sister for wanting to be part of the new family unit.

And especially not one more goddamned word to Kellan about how he'd get over Isaiah, or to Christi about how her girlfriend Schuyler was "just a phase."

But as he'd opened the door, his little girl tumbled into his arms.

"You were going to leave me alone?" she sobbed. "On Christmas?"

"Well," he mumbled, remorse swamping him, "you were doing a really good job of convincing us that you didn't want any company."

She'd cried.

She'd said she was sorry.

She'd apologized to everybody in the house, even Larx's family, who all looked distinctly uncomfortable.

Then she'd sat docilely at the table and eaten Christmas dinner with everybody and opened her gifts, which had sat forlorn under the tree that morning while everybody else was ripping into theirs.

Aaron wasn't sure if her repentance had been sincere—but he'd been grateful for it anyway. God, not having his kid there for Christmas had sucked. It had been Larx's idea to block her number, and Aaron had been grateful. Larx was right—she needed to see what life would be like if she succeeded in pushing all the people in it away.

Aaron couldn't imagine how bleak it had looked from the living room of the house she'd grown up in, when her family was somewhere else.

Larx's vision was just so clear when he was looking at kids—even his own.

Which was why the situation with Olivia was so damned painful.

Aaron knew very little about depression or anxiety or bipolar disorder—at least on a personal level.

But he encountered people all the time in the course of his job.

The guy with gin oozing from his pores was often depressed and self-medicating. Aaron had steered a lot of guys coming to in the drunk tank to the county's spare mental health services center. He couldn't do much—couldn't fix their lives, couldn't fix the world, but he could at least tell them their pain was real.

And hopefully keep them away from guns—that was key. The kid on the violent bipolar upswing was often not dangerous—until he grabbed a spare pistol from Dad's stash and went haring off into the woods in search of adventure.

He was aware that a lot of the people who ended up on law enforcement radar had mental health issues—but very often he could do very little to help them.

And he wasn't sure what to do with his boyfriend's daughter.

Because Larx was right—she wasn't doing well.

Aaron hadn't wanted to say anything during Christmas break. Tiffany had been damned unpleasant, and Olivia—for all her fluttery excitement about Christmas and her unplanned pregnancy and the new members of her family and the damned dog—had at least been trying to be part of the family.

But at one point, Aaron had gotten up early to turn the thermostat on so they didn't all freeze to death at four in the morning, and Olivia had been sitting, back to the wall in the hallway, wearing shorts and a tank top.

Her lips had been blue, and Aaron noticed that she hadn't washed her hair probably since she'd arrived and her teeth were a little gunky.

And as he'd chivvied her up and made her go back into the room where Christi was sleeping, Aaron realized that all the fluttering, the shrill laughter, the puppyish excitement over *all the things* seemed to be masking a sadness she didn't want the world to see.

Aaron saw it then—and too often in his job, he saw where it ended.

By the time she'd left for school again, she'd brushed her teeth, washed her hair, and hadn't caught her death of cold, so Aaron had hope she'd pulled herself together. But the sight of her huddled in the hallway, without so much as a blanket to keep herself warm, had haunted him.

He hadn't told Larx.

Larx loved his kids with so much of his heart—if he couldn't see Olivia's pain, Aaron wasn't sure how to be the one to point it out.

"Fine with me," Kirby said now, pulling Aaron back into the room. "Tiff's old room it is."

Aaron laughed. "Maybe Mau's—she'll be going off to the Peace Corps after you graduate anyway."

"Why not yours?" Kirby asked, laughing wickedly, but Aaron paused, thinking about it.

"Actually, my room would make a good suite," Aaron said thoughtfully, sitting kitty-corner to his exhausted boyfriend. "That's not a bad idea. And it's connected to the study, and we could convert that into a baby room." He smiled at Kirby. "Good idea, son!"

Kirby didn't return the smile. "Wow, Dad. That's… well, permanent."

Aaron frowned. "Well, I'm not planning on moving, you know?"

To his surprise, Kirby thought about it. "I like it here. I don't want to move," he said—which he'd been saying from the very beginning, those first frantic weeks when Aaron and Larx had gotten together and come out and the kids had bonded over keeping Kellan sane after Isaiah had been wounded and forging a new family in the heat of extraordinary events. "I guess it's just in my head—there's your room, and it's sort of inviolate. I mean… it wouldn't change my life, you know? But it would *feel* permanent."

"Yeah, like they were married," Kellan said softly. Then he brightened. "Which would be a good thing. But it would… I don't know. It would be important."

Aaron scrubbed at his face with his hand. The day had been long and difficult, and dealing with Candace Furman and her religious zealot parents had scoured his nerves raw. He wasn't sure how much they followed local news, but his and Larx's coming out that fall had been pretty dramatic, and he'd gotten the feeling they were going to bless their threshold with chicken's blood when he left, in order to cleanse the hated gay from their home.

He wished his churning gut could be cleansed with a little chicken's blood. He had plenty of the beasties outside, and frying one up for dinner to ease his mind wouldn't bother him in the least.

Talking about important things right now was so beyond his capabilities.

"Well, if it's important, we'll give it more thought," he told Kirby, smiling to make it positive. "But I do think helping Olivia move in and find her bearings will be our weekend project for a couple of weeks, so prepare yourselves."

"Fine with me," Kellan grumbled. "Isaiah doesn't want me there right now anyway."

Aaron gave him a sympathetic look. "Are you sure that's how he feels? Or is he just being macho about not wanting you to see him suffer?"

Kellan gave a grunt that indicated he might not have thought of that. "Men are assholes," he muttered. "I don't mind being gay, but I think falling in love with someone like Christi, who actually talks about her feelings, would have been so much easier."

Aaron hmmed, not wanting to comment. His late wife had communicated, it was true—but so did Larx. Often, if Larx wasn't talking, it was because he hadn't framed his thoughts for *himself*, and he didn't want to bother Aaron with them until he had.

Aaron was the one who got stopped up with feelings—need, fear, hurt—and couldn't articulate the things in his chest, not even to Larx.

Gently, he slid his fingers through the lock of hair falling over Larx's forehead. "Larx? Baby? Time to wake up. The kids are setting the table."

But in spite of his gentleness, Larx only had one way to wake up.

He shot up like a rocket, the kitchen chair kicking out behind his legs.

"I'm up! I'm sorry! Why are you here? What time is it?"

The late-afternoon gravitas shattered, and Kirby and Kellan both chuckled.

"Gee, Larx, that was a fun trick," Kirby snarked. "Good thing you don't sleep with a knife under your pillow—my Dad'd be history."

Larx squinted at him. "Who's teaching history?"

Kellan and Kirby cracked up, and Aaron stood, grabbed his elbow, and steered him through the house. "You are, Larx. Tomorrow. Ready to teach history?"

"But I'm a science major!" Larx moaned. "How do I teach history? I don't even know where Sumeria *is*!"

Aaron chuckled, some of the melancholy draining from his soul. "I think Sumer used to be in the Middle East, but don't worry. We won't quiz you." Aaron continued to steer until Larx wandered up the stairs, hand gripping the rail to pull himself up. "I just want a few minutes alone with my favorite science major. Is that so bad?"

"Mm… will there be kissing? I need there to be kissing."

"Sure. I'll add it to the agenda."

"I think you need to add oral and a rim job to the agenda," Larx grumbled. "I think that would be a list I could actually follow!"

And that did it. Aaron cracked up and followed a mostly awake Larx into the bedroom. He shut the door behind them and did the little lock, not because he was planning to go full-frontal balls-out with the family making dinner downstairs, but because he wanted privacy.

When he turned Larx in his arms to kiss him, it was so their bodies could touch for comfort, and for no other reason.

Then Larx opened his mouth and moaned.

Suddenly oral and a rim job wasn't a fantasy, a tossed-off comment meant for comedy. Suddenly they were actual acts, actual *things* that Aaron and Larx could perpetrate upon one another until their eyeballs rolled back in their heads and the kids couldn't look at them in the morning because they'd heard the sounds coming from the room.

It had only happened once, but Aaron had no regrets.

With that end in mind, he plundered Larx's mouth, slid his hands under the waistbands of Larx's sweats and boxers, cupped tight handfuls of runner's ass, and squeezed, parting Larx's cheeks and kneading with pure carnal intent.

Larx rucked up Aaron's shirt and groped his chest without any finesse whatsoever, pinching Aaron's nipples delicately, then harder when Aaron ground up against him in a frenzy.

They were both deliciously hard.

Aaron backed up until his thighs were against the bed and sprawled backward, Larx on top of him, while they continued to make out like teenagers.

Larx rippled his body, back and forth, up and down, grinding their erections together through their clothing, and Aaron kept kissing, kept kneading, kept himself from ripping both their clothes off and pulling Larx's cock down the back of his throat and sucking until he tasted come.

The way Larx was bucking against him, though, oral might be optional.

Aaron kissed his way to Larx's earlobe and tugged gently with his teeth. "Thought of this all day," he panted.

"I thought of rimming you," Larx confessed, and Aaron's whole body heated. That hadn't been in his repertoire when he'd been married to Caro, but Larx had it down to an art form and Aaron lived to be his canvas.

"Nungh!" He arched hard against Larx's groin, and Larx bit the side of his neck. Aaron slid his hands under Larx's waistbands again, fully intent on stripping off his sweats and setting a parental record for quickest, hottest, dirtiest sex before dinner that the kids wouldn't know about, when there was a hard knock at the door.

Larx moaned softly in his ear and then raised his head. "Yeah?"

"Daddy? There's an Olivia in my room, and it won't move so I can set down my stuff!"

This groan, Larx made out loud. "I don't even believe this! I didn't know you were home, Christi-lu-lu-belle, but I'll try to make the Olivia move!"

"Thanks, Daddy."

"Go down to dinner, sweetheart. Help the boys. I'll be right there."

"Okay." Her voice was a little wobbly, and Larx grimaced at Aaron.

"Is there anything else you need, baby?"

"We can talk later," she said weakly. "Don't worry. It can wait."

And then they both heard the patter of her slippered feet as she ventured downstairs.

"That didn't sound promising," Aaron grunted.

"For what? Family peace or our sex life after everyone goes to bed?"

"Yes. Those things." God—Larx was *right on top of him*, silver-sprinkled dark hair carelessly

tousled, wicked dark eyes glimmering, tight runner's body poised—*poised*—for intense erotic
acrobatics.

And Aaron was going to let him go get lost in
the family melee with long painful talks with his
teenaged daughters, and there might never be sex
again.

"There will be sex," Larx promised doggedly.

Aaron tried to let him down easy. "Baby…."

"No." Larx rolled off him and scowled, no longer
sleepy or pliant, but no longer a nuclear sexual-fueled
heat generator either. "There *will* be sex, if I have to
wake you up midblowjob. You and I spent ten years of
our prime living like monks. That's a *crime*, Deputy.
Especially for someone with your body. And now that
I'm someone with your body, I'm not breaking that
law another damned night."

Aaron stood and adjusted himself in his khakis.
"You'd really do that?" he asked, making sure. "Wake
me up with a blowjob?"

Larx had a sharp nose and chin, and when he
smiled wickedly, he really *did* look like an evil imp
from hell. "Don't doubt it for a minute."

Aaron grinned back. "I am so in."

Larx winked and opened the door and then ventured into the girls' room—because apparently there
were some dooms you couldn't put off—leaving Aaron to change. When he was done, he went downstairs
to maybe talk to Christiana, because he, too, had practice calming down teenaged girls.

That was the nature of the tag team, he realized—
but that didn't mean he wouldn't like a cage match
with his partner once in a while.

CHRISTIANA, AS it turned out, had a problem he could deal with—a painful one, especially for a teenager in her first relationship, but something doable.

She also had, as it turned out, two brothers who were totally okay with dispensing advice.

"Dad's right," Kirby said, shoveling in a giant mouthful of fried potatoes. The boys had made a veggie egg scramble and chips for dinner—and Aaron wasn't going to complain about one luscious, butter-soaked mouthful. "If Schuyler doesn't understand you having other friends, that's her problem. I mean, it comes down to she trusts you or she doesn't."

Christi tried to still her wobbly lip—but she seemed to be listening. "She may break up with me," she whispered.

"We could be a club," Kellan said brightly. "You and me and Kirby—the junior lonely hearts."

"You and me are seniors," Kirby said dryly. "But don't let that stop you from posting my single status all over the school."

Kellan squinted at him. "You don't *want* a relationship. Man, I don't even know which way you swing!"

Kirby gave an evil smile. "I'm pansexual. I'm waiting for a mythological creature to sweep me off my feet and into his or her secret love bower."

"A mythological creature named Pan?" Christi hazarded, some of her depression evaporating.

Aaron's son nodded irrepressibly. "You'll know him or her when you see him or her."

"Can't we say 'them' these days?" Kellan speculated. "I'm pretty sure the issue of nonbinary gender blew pronoun use out of the water. Or at least that's what Mr. Nakamoto said, but he also said he was too lazy to reinforce that when Merriam-Webster keeps spazzing out on Twitter, so I'm not sure which way we're leaning these days."

"It's leaning toward a whole lot of leftovers if Larx and Olivia don't get a move on," Aaron told him, glad to change the subject. Hey—the only thing coming out as bi had taught him was that he'd been a fool to let so much time lapse when he could have been *having sex* with Larx!

"You'd better save some for me," Larx said, entering the kitchen and sitting down. He gave an overbright smile—a father's smile. He was covering for something he didn't want to talk about in front of the other kids, and Aaron knew it.

"What about Livvy?" Christi asked. "Should I make her a plate?"

"I'll make her one," Aaron forestalled when Larx looked like he was going to pop up again. "Sit down and eat, Principal, and allow my son to shock you with his definition of pansexual."

Larx and Kirby exchanged a droll look before Larx said, "Isn't that when a mythological creature named Pan comes out and sweeps you into his love nest for hot no-strings fornication?"

"Or *her* love nest," Kirby said, holding up his palm for a five. "But otherwise, well called, sir. Could you clear that definition with Mr. Nakamoto?"

Larx returned the five with evil intent. "Absolutely not. You have my permission to mess with my vice-principal and best friend, but I am under strict orders not to participate in the torment."

"Understood." Kirby smirked. "Would you like to hear my definition of 'demisexual'?"

"Does it involve Demi Lovato or Hercules?" Larx asked guilelessly.

"*Yes!*" Kirby crowed, and Aaron laughed along with the rest of the table as he put together a small plate of potatoes and apple slices, leaving the eggs behind.

As he recalled, his wife had loathed eggs when she'd been pregnant. Something about the texture. But the salty carbs of potatoes would be a comfort, so he went with that.

He kissed Larx's cheek. "I'll be back in five." Then he disappeared up the stairs.

"Olivia?" He knocked on the door with his free hand.

"I'm really not hungry" came the muffled reply.

"You may not be, but the baby needs to eat. I brought apple slices and peanut butter and potatoes, hon. Shouldn't be a hardship."

"Sure." She didn't sound happy. "Thanks, Aaron."

She'd washed recently, and her teeth were clean, and she was even wearing a tatty old sweatshirt that Larx used when he was gardening—but she still didn't look good.

Her eyes had that sunken look, surrounded by shadows, that people had when they'd been crying for hours, and her nose was starting to chap. When he opened the door, she was huddled in the corner of the room, on the bed, looking like she was keeping watch for monsters.

Aaron sat on the bed, putting the plate directly in her hands.

She stared at it glumly for a moment before taking the fork he offered and digging into the potatoes and swallowing convulsively. "These are good," she said, but without passion. "Dad cook these?"

"Kirby and Kellan. I think they like showing him up sometimes."

That got a quirk of her full-lipped mouth. He was used to seeing her smile—seeing that mouth now, flat and chapped and colorless, seemed wrong somehow.

"Olivia, have you thought about seeing a doctor?" he asked baldly.

"Prenatal care, once a month," she returned by rote.

He sighed. Oh God, how he hated this. "Not that kind of a doctor."

That got a reaction. "No. No. Why would I? It's just hormones. Not a big deal. I can manage."

Aaron grunted. "Honey, you're not eating—"

"I'm taking vitamins. I'm drinking a smoothie every morning. I have to! I don't need a shrink, Aaron. I'm fine."

Oh yeah. This was not going well. "I should have seen one," he said, just to get her to stop talking and start eating. "When my wife died. Instead I drank and almost let my in-laws take my kids. That was painful. Shrink would have been better."

Her smile then was ghastly—the most terrifying thing Aaron had ever seen.

"I got this," she said, patting his knee. "Me and my baby are going to be fine."

You can't make yourself eat just for your kid, Olivia. You can't take care of yourself because you think the baby will make it better. You need to have happiness. You need to find joy in your life some-where. Whatever is going on in your heart and your head right now aren't good for anybody, including your unborn child.

But Larx was the talker, and not even Larx seemed to have the words.

"Glad to hear it," Aaron said softly. "I... I real-ly love your father, you know? And his sun rises and sets by you and your sister. Don't... I mean, the house is crowded, and I know that's got to be weird. But don't think his love changed just because it got louder, okay? There's nothing you could say or do that would make that man not love you."

It was a near thing for a moment—her face threat-ened to crumple, and she couldn't catch her breath. But she fought it, her expression the perfect blankness of a doll's. "That's kind of you to say," she whispered. Then she took another bite, and Aaron fought not to scream and shake her.

He sighed and stood, the silence and all the words neither of them were saying becoming so oppressive he couldn't breathe.

"If you could take the plate down when you're done," he requested nicely. "You'd think the fu—uhm, ants would have all died off with the snow, but I swear those little bastards march all the way here from town just to jump on a plate we leave in a room."

This was mostly a lie—they really *had* all died off in the snow but were probably going to come back in legion during the spring. Telling it had the desired effect of watching Olivia try a real smile and nod.

Aaron left the room and closed the door, lean-ing his forehead against it and muttering to himself.

"Good talk? Yeah, good talk. Jesus, George, get it to-fucking-gether. She's a girl, not a bomb."

Except she *was* a bomb—a time bomb of depression and triggers and hormones and shit not even Aaron knew about and probably Larx didn't either.

They were going to have to try harder to defuse her before she went off.

LARX HAD shooed the kids off to watch TV and was doing dishes with Christi when Aaron got downstairs. From the sober way he shook his head and the way she seemed to be keeping her voice from quavering, they were having a deep, dark conversation.

Well, Aaron hoped one of those worked out.

Kirby and Kellan opted for a movie, and Aaron was lost and dozing on the couch when Larx finally came to sit down.

Aaron sighed and wrapped his arm around Larx's waist, rested his head on Larx's shoulder, and fell asleep again.

The next thing he remembered was being hustled off to bed from an empty, darkened living room.

"Wha' happened?" he mumbled.

"We fell asleep and the kids deserted us."

"That's no' fair. Ingrates."

"Everybody had a day, Deputy. Now off to bed with you."

Aaron whimpered. "Sex?"

"Maybe." Larx shoved at his backside like sex was the carrot dangling from the stick. "It all depends on what you're doing after I change for bed."

"Dammit."

Sleeping. Sleeping was what he'd be doing. He stripped down to his boxers dispiritedly—it had been that kind of day. After crawling into bed on the side against the wall—so Larx didn't kill himself if he popped out of bed like jackrabbit on speed—he turned his face to the wall and pulled the blankets up to his shoulders before closing his eyes to Larx's nightly ablutions.

Things got blurry then.

Darkness, sleep, oblivion….

Lips trailing from his nape down his spine.

Quiet, healing unconsciousness….

Hands shoving at him until he lay on his stomach, legs spread.

The kiss of cool air as his shorts were peeled down.

A wicked tongue along the base of his spine.

A yearning, an ache in his groin.

He started to turn over, but an insistent hand kept his shoulders pinned, and he ended up with his knees pulled up under his hips and his bare ass spread wide to the world.

A warm washcloth, nubbly and rough in his private place. Larx's tongue, dragging down his crease.

He squinted in the darkness, but Larx wasn't there to ground him, just a pair of firm hands parting him, wiggling at his cock, pulling him for better access.

Aaron couldn't put words to what was happening. All he could manage was actual pleasure and some moans he couldn't control. And then, oh God, there was a tongue at his back door, and the moans weren't the only things he couldn't get a handle on.

"What are you… oh hey…. Larx?"

Larx licked him faster, wicked tongue moving, clever hand stroking, and Aaron was as vulnerable and as susceptible to pleasure as he'd ever been in his life.

Finally, words.

"I thought you said blowjob?"

Larx pulled away long enough to say, "Rim job? You're complaining?"

Aaron gave a hard shudder. "No. No—carry on." He fumbled under his pillow for the lubricant and passed it behind him, and that was the last conscious thing he did for a while as Larx treated his nether regions like his own personal playground.

He was shaking—honest-to-God shaking—and shoving a pillow in his mouth to keep himself quiet before Larx positioned himself at Aaron's entrance and thrust carefully in.

And now Larx was the one making noises.

"Oooooh…," he breathed, and Aaron beat at the mattress with his fist as the pleasure overtook him. Oh man. Oh *wow*. This thing right here, getting fucked like this, this hadn't been something he had ever done until recently either, and oh!

He couldn't believe he'd lived without it.

Larx groaned softly, seated deeply, and Aaron had just enough left of himself to whisper "Fuck me now!" before burying his face in the pillow again.

And Larx must have loved him because he did. Slow at first, making sure Aaron was good, stretched enough, comfortable enough, to really enjoy it. But Aaron screamed "Faster!" into his pillow, and Larx took the hint, harder, faster, his hard, capable body slamming into Aaron's more solid one with every confidence that Aaron could take it.

Ah! Oh, relinquishing himself, giving himself as Larx took charge—that was a thing Aaron had never known before, and as orgasm roiled up from his stomach and shuddered through every muscle and every pore, he wondered how he'd lived so long without it.

Behind him Larx grunted, and then he must have shoved his palm in his mouth because his muffled roar as he stiffened behind Aaron and poured his climax into Aaron's body was particularly subdued.

But his body was screaming, hot and sweaty, draped over Aaron's back in the chill. From his stretched backside, Aaron could feel Larx's come trickling as Larx softened, and the raw, visceral trace of their sex shook him again.

Oh damn, how he'd needed this.

"I'm awake now," he mumbled, and Larx's chuckle reassured him.

"That's good, 'cause I might do the man thing and roll over and pass out."

"Bastard."

"You're welcome."

Larx did roll over—but then he busied himself with his boxers and a T-shirt, and Aaron found his so he could do the same. They resettled in bed, shivering because Larx always turned the thermostat down too far, and Larx cuddled up against his chest.

And Aaron and his big mouth couldn't let things rest.

"Larx?"

"Mm?"

"Olivia…."

Larx sighed. "I'll push a little more tomorrow," he said quietly. "But I can't promise…. If she doesn't start eating, I can take her to the hospital. That's all I've got."

"She ate tonight," Aaron told him. "I had to remind her about the baby."

"Good." Larx's troubled sigh echoed through their darkened bedroom. Aaron hadn't brought any of his stuff in here—he'd liked Larx's old rock band posters and the color scheme. His own bedroom had been navy and tan, which wasn't a bad combo, and Aaron sort of missed the picture of his kids, but other than that, Larx just added so much color to his life.

The knowledge that Larx's things were around them comforted him right now.

"Her... her mom let them down so bad," Larx whispered after a moment of just their breaths. "I... I don't know if that's what's got her so knotted up now, or if...." He grunted. "I'm going to just start googling the fuck out of depression. Let's see what I can turn over."

"Can you consult the school counselor?" Aaron prodded gently.

As expected, Larx resisted. "I'll look stuff up," he said. "We're not... spill-our-guts-on-authority-figures people, you know?"

"No, I had no idea."

"I can hear your eyes rolling in the dark, you know."

"Understatement, I has it. What would you tell a kid with the kind of symptoms your daughter has?"

Larx whined. "I'd tell her to go see a professional, but that's not necessarily—"

"Really, Larx?"

"And *you've* seen a counselor how many times in your life, oh great widower and father of three?"

Aaron made a noncommittal sound in his throat.

"That would be man-speak for not once. Don't think I don't know cop statistics," Larx accused.

"Did you google those too?" Aaron asked, uncomfortable in the extreme. Yes. It was common knowledge in the profession that cops would self-diagnose themselves right into eating their own guns—but Aaron felt a protective surge that didn't want Larx to worry.

"It's a very handy tool."

"I should have made you go see someone after that thing in the school," Aaron admitted—guilt speaking, of course. "You don't just get shot and have it be okay."

"Did you?" Larx asked, referring to an incident years ago, before they'd begun seeing each other.

"Augh! You're insufferable!"

Larx growled, and then, like it sometimes did, the fight just bled out of him. "Neither of us are good at it," he said softly. "Depending on others for help. But... but you're also right. About needing to get Olivia to see someone. I mean... you and me, we *had* to be self-reliant. We grew up thinking men didn't see shrinks and we could deal with our own shit. But that's not how we raised our kids. It's just...."

Aaron stroked the hair back from his temple, seeing a few strands of silver glint in the moonlight from the window. "I get it. Finding words. I... I didn't have any myself."

Larx sighed, living up to his promise and beginning to fall asleep. "We'll move her into your house next weekend," he mumbled. "Let's see if she can perk up a little in the meantime."

He was asleep that soon, and Aaron shortly after—but they both knew this wasn't over.

It was just not something they could fix, even after some great sex and conversation.

SNOW FLURRIES

"She just showed up?"

"Yes, Yoshi."

"Just, on your doorstep. 'Hey, Dad, all my problems are here but six months early!'"

"Yes, Yoshi. Just like that."

"Like, no warning?"

Larx dragged his hands through his hair and concentrated on the lunch Aaron had packed for him. Peanut butter and jelly on whole wheat with mandarin oranges and chips. It wasn't leftovers, which Larx actually preferred, but it *was* a lunch, made for him before he flew out the door, complete with a bottle of water to remind Larx to hydrate.

Yoshi Nakamoto, Larx's best friend and reluctant vice-principal, had bought him a soda at the machine out of pure pity.

Yoshi loved Larx too.

And right now Yoshi's bird's nest of fine black hair and his chia-goatee were looking damned well-groomed compared to the mess Larx was making of himself.

"No warning." Larx grimaced. "Well, in retrospect there was some warning. Remember when Delilah died?"

"Your old cat?" See—as sarcastic as Yoshi was, some people would expect him to blow off the ancient Siamese goddess that had held Olivia together when Larx and his girls had first moved to the tiny fleaspeck of Colton after Larx's hellific divorce.

But not Yoshi—Yoshi had loved that cat too, and the drop in his voice showed it.

"Yeah. When she passed away before Thanksgiving, Olivia got upset—"

"Well, she'd had the cat for, what? Seven, eight years?"

"Something like that." Larx closed his eyes, hearing again that hysterical, fingernails-on-a-chalkboard pitch Olivia had hit when Larx had told her over the phone. "But… I mean, grief, yeah. We all were sad. But Olivia didn't sound right. And she sounded strained over Thanksgiving—which is when she said she got pregnant, and you know? No details. 'Dad, I went out and did someone stupid and now I'm pregnant.' And it's not like a father in the picture is necessary. But… but Olivia is more responsible than that. I didn't push her over Christmas because…." He let out a fractured sigh.

"Hard to know," Yoshi said wisely. "You're not judging, but a helper with a baby would be damned…." Yoshi waved his hands wildly.

"Helpful," Larx supplied, rolling his eyes.

"Well, *yes*. Because right now her helpers are you and Aaron, Grandpa, and I'm not giving you bullshit about getting old. I'm giving you bullshit about almost having your kids out of the house and being able to have sex at will!"

"God, Yoshi—anybody could hear us!" Larx ducked his head like a naughty schoolboy.

"Oh right!" Yoshi's turn to roll his eyes. "It's the middle of fifth period. Not even the teachers are awake right now. Most of them dropped off right after that one suck-up in the middle of the classroom who couldn't stay awake after lunch."

Larx chuckled. "Yeah, sure. So nobody can hear us. Look—I can raise another kid if I have to. But I don't want Olivia to have to live with that. I… I don't even *know* what she must be thinking right now, given how her mother treated her and her sister."

Larx had gotten pulled out of his old classroom in Sacramento because he'd come out to a troubled student as bi, hoping it would give the student faith. Instead, Larx had been put on leave, and his wife had kicked him out of the house. As Larx's leave had progressed, he'd realized during his visitations that Alicia had been neglecting their children, taking her own prejudice out on their kids. Larx had gotten custody and fled into the hills, to a small town where nobody would have heard of him and his girls could start fresh.

They'd survived—they'd *thrived*—but now, with Olivia's presence in her room all weekend, crying, not eating, all of it, bearing down on his shoulders, he wondered how much of what his daughters endured had been festering away in their hearts, waiting for something like this to set it off.

"Well, maybe it's not your job to know what she's thinking," Yoshi said, pursing his lips. "Maybe it's your job to get her to someone else who can know what she's thinking."

Larx groaned and tilted his head back. "Heard that song all weekend, Yoshi. Believe me, I'm working on it." He sighed. "Now about calling those kids in…."

"I so much like your personal problems better." Yoshi sulked. "Do we have to cold-call random students to our offices?"

"Yes, Yoshi—when we know they're having trouble with the law, I think that falls within our purview. Besides, Candace's grades have dropped damned dramatically. Something's up. If I hadn't been tipped off by Aaron, I was definitely tipped off by her referral. Hang tight—let's see what she has to say for herself."

Yoshi grunted. "Let me talk to her. I actually had her last year. She was timid and shy, and you will scare her."

Larx tilted his head. "Are you saying you're snuggly?" No. Yoshi was about as snuggly as a porcupine.

"I'm saying I have Hello Kitty stickers in my drawer, asshole, and those are like the secret to teenage girls everywhere."

"Sexist."

"Shut up. Besides—you had the misspent youth. That kid with the pothead brother will trust you way more than he'll trust me. I have *square* written all over me."

Larx let out a laugh. "*That* I can agree with. Okay—let's go get a student runner, and we can do our jobs!"

Yoshi shook his head in disgust. "Seriously? This is in our job description? I've seen the movies, Larx. We're supposed to be faceless bureaucrats who tell the good hardworking teachers they can't take the poor minority kids to the tech fair."

Yoshi routinely brought bagels to his AP class in the morning and let the word get out so he was feeding half the school—often the half with parents too proud to ask for free lunch.

"Well, Yosh, if that's our job description, we should both get fired. Now scoot! The somnolence of fifth period only lasts so long."

"Good word, Larx. You almost sounded like a grown-up."

"Fuck off and get out of my office."

Yoshi flipped him off on the way out the door.

Fifteen minutes later, Larx was sitting on his desk while one of the sweetest kids he'd ever met was curled up in the visitor's chair, arms wrapped around his shins, big brown eyes open and alert in an elfin sort of face.

He was gazing at Larx with a sort of worship.

"So, the sheriff—"

"Sheriff George," Larx prompted.

"He said he came by, and he just wanted you to make sure I was okay."

"Well, yeah, Jaime. Your brother—"

"Berto," Jaime supplied, the same way Larx had.

Larx winked at him. "Berto, he had a pretty big prescription for anxiety medication—"

"His pot," Jaime said without blinking. "He grows it in the back. He's got a permit."

"Yeah. He had a giant prescription for stash, and you're a minor, and he didn't want to get Berto in trouble because you guys seem to be good kids, but I wanted to make sure you're okay."

Jaime grinned. "In Sacramento they just would have arrested us both, legal or not—you know that, right?"

Larx grimaced. "Well, yeah, some places. It's the you being a minor thing, Jaime—"

"I don't do that shit, erm, stuff, Mr. Larkin. I tried it once, 'cause Berto seemed to do so much better, but I didn't like it at all."

Okay then. "Good," Larx told him. "Good. Keep it like that—seriously. If you need it, you need it, but if you don't, you can buy yourself a whole lot of trouble using it."

Jaime shrugged. "Looks like I bought myself a whole lot of trouble as it was."

Ah… an opening. "Were you the one who called the police?"

The kid looked supremely uncomfortable for someone with his feet on his chair under his ass. "Look, Berto lights up, and I go outside so I don't get dizzy. Berto set up a little shed with a space heater for me, and I do homework and shit. He says he's going to learn how to make brownies and stuff—we can't afford the dispensary, but, you know…." He grimaced.

"Not saying a word. But edibles can be really powerful. Anyway—so you're outside in the shed and…."

"And I hear… well, it sounds…." Jaime grimaced again. "It sounds like a horror movie, where the heroine is running away from someone and she doesn't want him to catch her, and then he does and…."

Larx frowned, trying to put the kid's discomfort together with the story.

And then felt like a fool when he did just that.

"He hit her?"

Jaime nodded unhappily. "I didn't see it—and I don't know the people there very well. There's two grown-up men and two kids, and I'm not sure which kid—I went running out and saw two people heading toward Candace's house, one a big guy with his hand over the girl's arm. The girl was quiet with the guy, but I could swear before that she was screaming. So I wait until they're out of sight and then I run in the house, and me and Berto have a long, uh, discussion over whether or not to call the cops, and I'm like, 'What the hell's the prescription for if it doesn't get you a free pass to call the cops when a girl's getting hurt,' and he groaned and said 'Go ahead' while he tried to clear out the smell. The house was freezing before the cops got there, I'll tell you that, and it was still damned strong. But the sheriff seemed like a good guy—I mean, he made sure I wasn't using and then…."

Jaime had gotten animated during the central part of the story, but now his face fell.

"I still don't know what happened to the girl. I should have… I don't know. Run into the snow, I guess?"

Larx smiled his best, sweetest smile. This kid weighed ninety pounds soaking wet, and at fifteen years of age was still about five feet four inches tall.

"Going into the woods to deal with a domestic dispute is not the way to go, Jaime. I'm damned grateful you didn't. But I have to ask you—why doesn't your brother medicate in the shed?"

Jaime shifted uncomfortably again. "He, uh… he got beat up. Really bad. In Sacramento. And he… he still has nightmares. But he wanted to move up here—and his friends, uh… didn't want him to."

Larx rubbed the back of his neck. "Jaime, I used to work in your old district. Did you know that?"

Jaime sent him a quick glance, then looked away. "No, sir. I didn't."

"Your brother got jumped out of his gang so he could get you out of a shitty neighborhood, didn't he?"

Jaime nodded and pulled his knees tighter. "I was so scared," he confessed painfully. "I thought it would all be shitty white people. And there's a lot of white people, but so far, everyone's been really nice. But Berto—he… he still has nightmares, you know? And I had to… had to call about this girl, because if he's still having nightmares, I hate to think what's going on with her, but… but…." He bit his lip.

"But you're a little guy, and you were probably wearing those tennis shoes anyway, weren't you?"

Jaime shrugged. "Snow. Nobody tells you about this shit."

"What's your brother do for work?" he asked kindly.

"He's, like, labor—he works for all the shops. He's their loader/unloader. Some guy with a pottery shop who makes these weird sculptures gives him a ride to work every day."

Larx rubbed the back of his neck a little harder. "Tane?" he asked, shaking his head. "Tane Pavelle?"

"Yeah! He's really intense, but he seems okay. I think he's related to my science teacher."

"He's her brother," Larx said, fighting the urge to roll his eyes. He was also Yoshi's boyfriend, although they were scrupulous about nobody in the town knowing. Yoshi had come out that fall just as spectacularly as Larx had, but Tane was not nearly as comfortable in the spotlight as Aaron. Yoshi had quoted him as saying he didn't want those fucking people to know a damned thing about him—and apparently that meant Yoshi too. "He's in good company. Tane *is* intense, but he's also a good guy."

Jaime smiled guilelessly. "That's good. I mean, I trusted Berto—he's older, and our folks moved back when he was twenty and left us here. But after…." He shuddered. "He almost died. So it's good to know he's got a friend."

Oh, this kid. *This* kid was why Larx taught in that district for so long. Because most of those students in the "big scary districts" that caught every bad news story ever were a lot like this kid. Bright, willing to hope, willing to work so damned hard with just a little approval.

Larx couldn't look at his feet in his ripped-up sneakers anymore. He let out a sigh and scowled. "Jaime, my, uh"—*boyfriend's kid*—"How's this. I know a few guys who might have some old waffle stompers for you. Let me take your size down and see if we can't keep your toes on before April, okay?"

Jaime smiled, embarrassed and relieved. "That would be *so* exciting. You have no idea how excited I would be about not freezing my feet off. I'd absolutely love to not freeze my, uh, feet off for the rest of the winter. Did you say April?"

Larx grimaced. "Well, usually by the end of March, but sometimes mid-April. Sweaters. I think between Aar… uhm, my friend's kid and I—"

"Aaron? Deputy George?" Jaime's bright eyes didn't waver.

"Yeah."

"You're dating, right? 'Cause I got here and all the kids were, like, 'Our principal's gay and he's dating the deputy sheriff but you gotta be cool about it 'cause he's, like, a hero.' And I was, like, 'Hey, I got a cousin who's gay, and if I could make the whole world leave *him* alone by saying he's a hero, I would, so this guy's got no worries from me.'"

Larx scrubbed at his face and tried not to lay his head in his arms and laugh until he couldn't breathe. "So, uh, glad you approve. Anyway, my boyfriend's kid is about to throw out a whole bunch of stuff he outgrew last year. Give me a day or two and I'll see if you—"

"And Berto?" Jaime asked hesitantly. "He's bigger than me—more like Deputy George's size. But he's working in tennis shoes, and he's dropped shit, erm, stuff on his toes, and we spent all our money moving here over Christmas." For the first time, he looked dispirited. "There's no place I could work here. I had a job at the animal shelter cleaning cat boxes— didn't pay much, 'cause I didn't have a work permit, but it paid something. I'll be sixteen in April, but…." He shrugged. "No place to work here. All the places, they're family run. I'm afraid to even go into the pizza place or the burger place, you know?"

Larx nodded. He knew. Olivia used to say that her life was incomplete and she'd never graduate college because she hadn't run the gauntlet of being a fast-food maven, but until she'd shown up on his doorstep Saturday, he really hadn't thought that was true.

"Okay. Tell you what. Give me a day, maybe two, and we'll see what we can scare up for a couple of ten-derfoots who don't know snow, okay?" Jaime smiled gamely, and Larx felt compelled to add, "And I'll ask around town for a job." And before the boy could open his mouth to say thank you, Larx finished with, "And my daughter just ran screaming back home, but once we get her settled and okay, I'll see about having you and Berto over for dinner. It'll be crowded and nobody in the house can cook, but the dog loves company."

And that did it. Jaime's expression melted. "The dog?" he asked hesitantly. "You have a *dog*?"

And so did Larx's heart. "Yeah. A dog. We'll try to move Olivia this weekend. Dozer would love an-other friend to play."

And then he remembered what he was there for. "Oh! And about Candace?"

Jaime's whole body seemed to shrink. "Yeah?"

Larx thought about it carefully. "Jaime, domestic disputes are scary things, even for the police. So, call them—but call them secretly if you can. You seem like a good kid, and I bet your brother is one too. But... but there's probably more guns per household here in the country than there was in the city, you know what I mean?"

Jaime loosened a little and sobered. "You mean don't let nobody see I'm the one calling the cops, and maybe don't tell anybody at school either."

"Yeah. Are you the only neighbor?"

Jaime shook his head. "No—we're not even the closest one. She just happened to come out our way, I think. I don't think it was for me—she doesn't even talk to me in school."

Larx nodded. "Okay. So by all means call the police if you need to, if you hear anything. They're not going to give Berto a hard time—at least Deputy George won't, and if you get someone who does, call me—and I am more worried about the danger to *you* than anything else, okay? Untrained personnel get hurt in these situations. Call in the professionals and keep your head down." *Trained* personnel got hurt in these situations too, but Larx wasn't going to stress over that in front of this kid.

Jaime seemed to ponder Larx's advice for a minute. "I can call you?" he asked suddenly. "When things get weird?"

Larx nodded and wrote his number on a Post-it. "Don't go spreading that around," he said, although there were probably forty kids who had that number. "And my daughter texts me about twelve thousand times a day, so if you could maybe...." He winced.

"Not be part of that noise? No, I get it. Not so much emergencies only, but... uh... concerns. Like, right before Christmas our power went off, and Berto had to walk into town to find someone who could tell us how to fix it, because we didn't know anybody's number. So this way I got your number, and you could help us out."

Killing him. This kid was *killing* him.

"Yeah. Sure. Like that. Do that for me. My family would be happy to give you a better welcome to the neighborhood."

"Thank you, Mr. Larkin. Like, *thank* you. You're the best. Let me know if there's anything I can do for you—wash your car, walk your dog—anything."

This kid was in three different clubs already. He was dying for a chance to belong here.

"Keep your grades up," Larx said softly. "And there's scholarship workshops for sophomores and juniors on Saturdays, starting in March. Show up for them—even if it's just junior college, they can help you get a start when you graduate. Deal?"

Jaime nodded, and Larx shook his hand. "And if anybody asks, *that's* what the principal wanted to talk to you about. Scholarship Saturdays. There will be posters up with times and rooms and stuff. Okay?"

Oh yeah. That grin was what teacher's dreams were made of.

"Sure, Mr. Larkin. It was a *great* talk. You totally sold me!"

Larx opened the door and ushered him out. "That's good to hear. Come to my science room before class, or see me in the parking lot after school. I should have some gear for you tomorrow."

"Deal!"

Jaime bounded out, so full of hope and promise Larx almost couldn't bear it. He and Yoshi needed to talk about Candace, because Jaime's report was frightening, but Jaime—damn. Larx carried that conversation close to his heart for the next hour, smiling, humming to himself as he did paperwork. Most teachers went into education hoping they could make a difference—and it was hard work. Shoes and a scholarship program rec were such easy things. Not that Jaime's life was easy—not by a long shot. But Larx had things in his arsenal to make his life better, and *that* felt damned good.

So he was very satisfied with himself, right up until Yoshi walked in, looking like death, and turned around and closed the door behind him.

"Oh God," Larx muttered.

"Did you have a good conversation? You look very pleased with yourself. I bet *you* had an *amazing* conversation, didn't you?"

"It was peachy," Larx said, eyes on Yoshi like a snake's on a hawk. "So amazing. It lifted me up where I belong."

"Are you feeding that kid yet? Clothing him? C'mon. You can admit it, Larx. You're practically a breast. You're probably a barn-raising away from getting him a brand-new home and a new car. Tell me. Tell me now. I need to have something good in my life."

"Uh, your boyfriend's giving this kid's brother rides to town in the morning?"

Yoshi nodded. "Unexpected, but not a complete surprise. Tane does things like that. He'd be just like you, except he scares people and likes it that way. So that's interesting. When's this kid coming over for dinner?"

"Next weekend. Why do you have that kill-things expression on your face? Was there something that Hello Kitty won't fix?"

Yoshi collapsed into the chair Jaime had occupied not an hour before. "So bad, Larx. So… so bad. That situation in Candace's house… so, so bad…."

Larx took a deep breath and girded his loins.

Ah. So Jaime had been a decoy. Life's *real* curveball had been thrown at Yoshi, and it had knocked him on his ass.

DRIFTS

AARON LISTENED to Larx on speakerphone as he made his usual patrol rounds, but Larx was—for once—skirting uncomfortably around the point. Whatever had gone on with Candace, it was a big deal, but Larx wasn't getting to it.

"So, Yoshi is pretty sure the girl is being abused," Aaron clarified, "but he's not sure how—"

"He's pretty sure how," Larx corrected, "but he's got no proof. We're going to have to ask the school psychologist to talk to her to see if she'll confess to anything."

Aaron made a confirmation noise, his stomach balling up unhappily at what Larx was implying. Right before he could ask the hard question, he rounded the curve of the highway before Olsen Road and remembered his first move on Larx that October, when he'd stopped to beg his son's favorite principal not to risk death by running on the side of the road.

For a moment—just a second—he missed the joy he used to feel when he knew Larx might be running alongside the road.

He was brought to the present with a thump when he saw the young man in jeans and a hooded San Diego sweatshirt sliding along the icy shoulder. The poor guy had no gloves, no scarf, and tennis shoes, and he looked thoroughly out of his depth.

"Hold off, Larx. I'll get back to you. We might have a stranded tourist or something."

"Drive safe."

"See you at home."

Aaron stopped slowly and rolled down the passenger window. Unlike Larx, who'd been most adamantly *not* in search of help on this road, this guy looked like he needed a friend.

"Hey there," he called, trying not to sound too cop-like. "Can I give you a ride somewhere? Did you leave a car behind you?"

The kid looked frightened for a moment, although he was most definitely out of high school. "I did. I, uh, left my car in a snowbank. By a tree. I, uh… don't have chains. I…." He swallowed and for a moment looked ready to cry. "I don't know how to get chains. And I have no idea where I am. All I know is that GPS said there's a high school on this road and it looks like it might be a school for bears, because this place is, like, wild fucking kingdom!"

Aaron chuckled kindly. "I'm sure it looks that way to someone from San Diego." He put the SUV in park and leaned over to open the door. "Would you like a ride to town? I know the tow place—they can get your car out of the snowbank and probably find a place to put you up for the night while they fix it."

The kid gave a shaky nod. "Is that okay? You don't have to put me in the back, do you? Because I hate these roads. I really fucking hate them. And I don't want to be trapped in the back of your cop-mobile when you start sliding around on them."

Wow. This kid could make coffee nervous. "The front's fine," Aaron said, nodding slowly. "Let me see your hands for a minute. Now pull up your sweatshirt and turn around. Just checking, okay?"

The kid did the dance on the side of the road, his boxers pulled up past the waistband of his sagging jeans, but other than that, harboring no deep dark secrets and no weapons.

"Fair enough," Aaron said. "Hop in."

He'd cranked up the heater before the kid had even slammed the door shut.

On closer inspection this kid didn't look bad—he had hipster's scruff and streaky dark hair past his ears and over his forehead, but he also had big blue eyes that seemed to be widened in a perpetual state of shock.

"So, I'm Sheriff George—pleased to meet you." Aaron put the SUV into gear and stepped gently on the gas, the snow tires digging in deep and the chains digging in deeper so the car gave a gentle acceleration over the slippery road.

"I'm Elton," the kid said. "Elton McDaniels. Thanks so much for stopping."

"I take it your car is up a little ahead?" Aaron scanned the road in front of him, but snow had come in during the afternoon and gotten thicker since.

Belatedly Aaron wondered if the tow truck could even get the thing out before dark fell.

"Yeah. I… I sort of panicked. I knew the high school was ahead of me, but I saw the road and thought, 'This is it! This is my last chance to turn back!' and while I was deciding, the car decided for me."

Aaron bit his lip so he didn't smile. "Well, cars will do that," he said diplomatically. "Why would you want to turn back?"

"I don't know what I'm doing here," the kid said wretchedly. "I… there was this girl." He covered his face with his hands. "This is so dumb. *So* dumb—"

"Oh shit," Aaron muttered. "Talk about dumb. Kid, *this* is your car?"

The kid nodded and scratched the back of his bare head. "It's, uh, not in great shape."

"Kid, are you okay?" Aaron pulled to a halt and looked at the car in dismay. A Datsun B-210—from way back in the day, before electronic everything—was wrapped around one of the bigger pine trees off Olson Road.

"My neck's a little sore," Elton confessed. "And I've got a seat-belt bruise. And my stomach's bruised. And I've got a headache." He fingered his forehead, and once he pushed his hair back, Aaron could see a bruise forming. "And…." His voice grew a little wobbly. "I still don't know where in the fuck I am."

"Oh Jesus." Aaron closed his eyes and tried hard not to freak out on this kid like a parent. If this was *Kirby's* car, he'd be losing his shit. "Okay, Elton. We've got a small hospital about half an hour away. I'm going to call in and take you there, okay? Then I'll call the tow-truck place, but the snow is getting sort of thick, and they might not be able to get to your car until tomorrow, and maybe not until the day after that if tomorrow's as bad as the weather prediction. Do you have someone you could call?"

The kid made a sound perilously close to a whimper. "No. My folks don't know I'm here. I left school, you see? I… I know it's stupid. She's totally an adult, and it was only one night, but I thought we had something, right?" Elton rubbed his stomach and closed his eyes. "But she wouldn't talk to me afterward, and I thought I'd connect with her again after Christmas, but she just up and left school."

Aaron's head started to pound. "Elton, what were you doing, looking for the high school again?"

"The only things—and I mean the *only* things—I know about this girl is that she's from this tiny town and has a sister. And her dad works at the school." He blinked. "And her cat died right before she came to the party where we hooked up."

Welp.

Aaron let out a sigh. "Okay, Elton. Let's get you to the hospital, and I'll see if we can get someone to come sit with you while they're doing the tests."

"Why would you do that?" Elton asked, but he sounded too close to real tears for Aaron to take exception.

"Because being in the hospital sucks, kid, and it's worse when you're alone. Now here, let me call in."

FORTY-FIVE MINUTES later, Aaron excused himself from Elton's bedside where he was being held for observation and debated. On the one hand, he should call Larx.

He should *really* call Larx.

But on the other hand, Larx wasn't the one who'd had the one-night stand and gotten knocked up either.

Debate, debate, debate....

"Olivia?"

"Hi, Aaron." She sounded drowsy, like she'd been napping. "What's up? Is my dad okay?" Her voice sharpened. "Is he hurt again?"

Larx had been the one to get grazed by a bullet that fall, but apparently they were all carrying scars.

"No, hon. But someone else you know is in the hospital for observation, and he's alone, and he's scared, and he apparently drove for fourteen hours to get from San Diego to here, only to crash his car on Olson Road."

"Oh no," she said, her voice small.

"Oh yes. Olivia, unless you tell me—right now—that this kid has done something to harm you, something to harass you, something to make what's going on in your life miserable, I'm going to have to ask you to put your grown-up pants on and get over here. Your dad can drive you if he needs to, but this kid's had a hell of a day, and he could really use a friendly face."

When she spoke next, he could hear the tears in her voice, and for a moment he was afraid. Larx, who was so good at facing his responsibilities, at doing the grown-up thing when it was called for, had been so proud of his daughters owning up to their own lives.

If Aaron had to tell him Olivia chickened out here, it would kill him.

"Christi just got home," she said softly. "I'll be there in an hour. Is he okay?"

"He's got a mild concussion and some bruising. They need to make sure nothing's internal." Aaron tried to keep the exasperation out of his voice. "They weren't sure he was coherent, but I'm thinking he's just sort of naturally that way."

"Oh yeah," she said, and he heard the echo of the happy, pretty girl he'd watched grow up in the town where he lived. "Elton's sort of got the mind of a poet, and he doesn't have a filter for it. He's really smart, but his teachers are always sort of surprised."

"Well, he surprised the heck out of me," Aaron said shortly. "It sounds as though you like this boy."

"I didn't want to…." Her voice choked. "I was on the pill, Aaron. This wasn't his fault."

Aaron closed his eyes and counted to ten.

"What are you thinking?" she asked nervously.

"I'm trying not to speak like your father," he muttered.

To his shock—his *utter* shock—she laughed. "Oh give it the fuck up, Sheriff George," she said. "That's one of the things you and my dad have in common. It will *kill* you not to try to parent me. I dare you."

Aaron glared at the white wall of the corridor. "I can't now. *You* sound too much like your father. I'll leave it for him to do."

"You haven't told him, have you?" she asked, the horror in her voice telling him everything he needed to know about what a close call he'd almost had.

"Are *you* going to?"

He heard defeat in her sigh. "Yeah. Yeah. Let me come out, talk to Elton. Explain that it's not his fault, any of it. He didn't do anything wrong."

"No," Aaron murmured. "No, he didn't. But I think he'll be happy to hear it from you. I mean… fourteen hours, Olivia. He drove in the snow. I don't even think he knows what snow is."

"I'll be there," she promised. "Give me an hour. I…." He heard her grunt, like this had just occurred to her. "I should shower and dry my hair."

"Understood. I'll be here until you get here," he told her. "Maybe grab a sandwich on your way out of the house."

"I'll make one for Elton too," she said. "He doesn't like institutional food. Conformity freaks him out."

Aaron crossed his eyes. "Of course it does. See you soon."

"Yeah. Uh, Aaron?"

"Yeah?"

"Thanks for calling me. I… my dad thinks I've got it all together. Thanks for giving me a chance to tell him… I… I sort of fucked up with Elton."

Aaron leaned against the wall, grateful it was the end of his shift. He could sit by Elton's bed and use his tablet to fill out some of his paperwork.

"Nobody has their shit together all the time," Aaron told her gently, meaning it. "I'm surprised your father hasn't told you that."

"The thing with Dad…." She cleared her throat. "The thing with Dad is that he's sort of larger than life, you know? I mean, sure, he'll tell you he's lost his shit before, but he's always had a plan. He's always seemed to know exactly what to do. Even when he was trying to feed us something godawful because he hadn't learned to cook yet, there was always a can of refried beans, some cheese, and some tortillas, you know? He just didn't want plain. He wanted *awesome*, and he got it a lot. So… so when I really screwed up…."

Aaron pinched the bridge of his nose. "I hear you. Shower, honey. Get over here. I'll stay until you're here. Bring some jammies if you want—they'll let you sleep on a cot." Aaron glanced over his shoulder to where Elton was playing with his IV tube and scowling suspiciously at the bag hanging from the stand. "I think they'll be relieved you're there."

AN HOUR later, Aaron looked up from his tablet where he'd been filling out his paperwork and greeted Olivia at the door of Elton's room. Elton himself was dozing, the almost-blue circles under his eyes a testament to a really long day with a fairly climactic end.

Later, Aaron would say the look on Olivia's face at that moment was a signal of all that was to come.

The tenseness around her eyes and mouth that had aged her since Christmas eased up, and she bit her lip, a softness in her chin telling him all he needed to know about her "random hookup" and what had followed.

No matter what her state of mind now, no matter how she'd felt when the relationship began, she cared for this boy. She cared a lot. All that remained to see was why she'd pushed him away.

Aaron stood and opened his arms, like he did for Christiana and his own daughters, and Olivia rushed into them without hesitation. It was a gift, he thought, from her father, that she could accept affection so easily—at least from father figures.

"How's he doing?" she asked quietly.

"He's sore and tired." Aaron shrugged. "Hurt."

Olivia grimaced. "Okay. My job. I need to fix that. I'll wait until he wakes—"

"Olivia?"

That quickly, her attention was diverted. "El? You okay?"

She wiggled out from Aaron's arm and snagged the chair he'd been sitting in so she could pull it close to the bed. Aaron stepped in and lowered the rail so she could talk to him intimately—he got the feeling they were at that stage.

"You've got snow here, Olivia. What in the fuck is snow doing in California?"

She hmmed and stroked his hair back from his eyes. "What in the fuck is a desert dweller doing in the mountains?" she chided. "Seriously, El—what were you thinking?"

The hurt on his face was hard for Aaron to see. "I was thinking I missed you. We hung out for months and… and one good night and… *bam*. No you. Wanted you back."

"Aw, Elton," she whispered. "I'm sorry. I didn't mean to hurt you. I… I put off, you know. Being with you. 'Cause…." She swallowed. "I wasn't in a place to be with anyone, you know?"

Elton nodded, then grimaced, and Aaron moved back toward the door, torn between going to get him a nurse with some pain meds for his head and staying here and watching through this intimate window to get a glimpse of what was going on inside Larx's daughter.

"You kept saying," Elton said. "And I didn't press, and then, Thanksgiving and you were so sad and—"

"And I… I just wanted to make the pain go away," she finished, her voice choking. "And you were so kind. But I didn't want to pull you down with me. And then things got complicated. I'm so sorry. I know I hurt you, but I thought you'd get over me. I just… I didn't want to keep hurting you, because I'm… I'm not good inside."

Elton raised a shaking hand to her cheek, and Aaron took his cue to go get the nurse. It wasn't until he felt the cool air hit his own cheek that he realized *he* was crying too.

Oh, Olivia. Why couldn't you say something?

AARON HAD pulled himself together by the time he got back with the nurse, and Elton squinted up at him as she added some painkiller to his IV.

"Olivia, I thought your dad worked at the school?"

Olivia sniffled and wiped her eyes with her sleeve, smiling a little when Aaron offered her a Kleenex. "This isn't my dad—he's more like my stepdad. But he's nice too."

"Your stepdad. But… but you don't live with your mom…."

Olivia's mouth twisted in amusement, and she raised her eyebrows at Aaron, mouthing "Five… four… three… two… one…."

"I don't understand," Elton moaned.

"He's my dad's boyfriend," she said, holding her face carefully neutral, and Aaron suddenly knew what that cost her.

"Oh." She had her back to Elton, but Aaron saw the sudden comprehension his face. "Oh! Oh! I get it!"

He looked confused again. "Why didn't you tell me? That's sort of cool!"

Her shoulders relaxed, and she turned toward him again. "That's sort of cool that you think so," she said. She took a step toward the bed and squeezed his hand. "I'm going to go talk to Aaron for a minute, then I'll come ba—"

"I'm going to get to meet him, right?" Elton asked. He smiled apologetically at Aaron. "You were awesome, Mr. Sheriff George. I mean…. Dude. You've been great. But. You know. I've heard about her dad all year."

"I'm new," Aaron said, liking Elton more every time he opened his mouth. "And yes." He looked at Olivia with meaning in his eyes.

"Yeah," she said, nodding back. "You'll get to meet Larx. It'll be fun."

"A laugh riot," Aaron muttered just as his phone buzzed in his pocket. He stepped in to hug her and took a sec to ruffle Elton's hair—gently. "Hang tough, kid. I gotta get home before the snow's too thick." He hugged Olivia again. "Call us before you start home— especially if you're bringing Elton with you. We'll fix up my house—you guys can have some privacy."

She nodded, biting her lip. "Thanks, Aaron. You… you're really really like my dad, you know that?"

Aaron grunted. "It's the dad thing. It takes over our personalities sometimes." He checked his phone and winced. "And I really gotta go."

He took a step toward the door and turned back to her. "Olivia?"

"Yeah?"

"I don't keep secrets from your dad. I'll tell him a friend from school wrecked his car coming to see you, and you know what he's going to say?"

She nodded. "Yeah. Tell him what you need to."

"As long as we're clear."

She nodded, and he left just as Elton muttered, "But what does that mean?"

Well, as much as he'd love to be a fly on the wall for the rest of that conversation, it wasn't his place, and it wasn't Larx's either.

He hoped Larx felt that way too.

He hit speakerphone as soon as he was outside and had warmed up the SUV. "Larx? You're home, right?"

"Yeah—all of us except Olivia. Christi said she took off in her car—"

"Uh, yeah. Don't worry about Olivia. She's safe. I'll talk to you when I get home. Do you need me to bring dinner?"

"We're on it, Deputy—eggs, chips, and—" He changed the pitch of his voice. "What are we doing for a green again?"

There were a few moments of absolute silence.

"Uh...," Larx said into the phone, as though at a loss.

"Sautéed green beans with bacon," Aaron shot back, because *bacon*.

"Microwaved brussels sprouts with fakin!" Larx crowed, like his answer was better because his was healthy.

"No," Aaron said in numb horror, relieved when Kirby and Kellan echoed the sentiment behind him.

"God, no! Larx, please!" Kirby wailed.

"Larx—it smells like chicken farts!" Kellan voiced, and then, on the heels of that, came Kirby's voice again.

"Dude, you are getting *way* too friendly with our chickens."

"Shut up! You know what I mean!"

"He means it smells like raw sewage," Kirby said resentfully.

"Not with butter and Bac-Os!" Larx told him, all enthusiasm. "Trust me! A little garlic salt, it's practically parmesan wine sauce!"

"No, it's not," Aaron muttered.

"No, it's not!" the boys wailed.

"Can we use the butter powder, Dad?" Christiana chimed in, because apparently Larx had them all on speaker now. "It's better for us, even if it's higher in sodium."

"Suck-up," Kirby told her bluntly.

"No, no, she actually has a point," Kellan said, and Aaron called out "Traitor!" because that boy had been his last best hope.

Larx cackled and told them to get to it, and then Aaron could hear the change of venue as he moved from the kitchen into the quieter living room. For a moment, as Aaron peered through the darkness and the thickly falling flakes of snow, he could picture Larx tucked into the corner of the couch, his feet pulled up under him, one arm wrapped around his knees as he tried to hide in the shadows of his own house. Olivia had called him "larger than life"—but then, Larx had always tried to make himself dependable to her. She never got to see Larx tired, vulnerable, second-guessing his every move as he tried to pilot his ship of family through the reefs and shoals of real life.

That was Aaron's job now.

"So," Larx said into the sudden quiet. "Where'd Olivia go?"

"A friend of hers came up to visit from school and plowed his car into a snowdrift," Aaron said. "She's staying overnight in the hospital to keep him company."

"Oh."

That was a very dangerous sound.

"Yes."

"A friend."

"Yes," Aaron answered promptly.

"A *male* friend?" Larx clarified.

"I believe I said."

The next sound Larx made was a very careful breath in through his nose and out through his mouth.

"Was this a specific *kind* of male friend?"

Aaron knew this was deadly serious, but he fought the urge to chuckle, because Larx had not originally been a patient man—and sometimes his white-knuckled grip on his fly-off-the-handle self was damned entertaining.

"Yes, Larx. *That* male friend. He's a sweet kid, actually—he got lost because all he knew about Olivia was that her father worked at Colton High. She...." Aaron hated to be the one to tell him this. "She sort of treated him badly. If nothing else, he deserved an answer to why she bugged out after Thanksgiving."

"Mm." The sound lost a lot of Larx's original starch.

"'Mm' what?"

"Not a bad kid?" Like Aaron's opinion really mattered.

"You'll like him," Aaron promised. "He's sort of a doofus, actually—but a sweet doofus. He wasn't stalking her—I think he was just worried. I guess they'd been friends all semester and she…."

Oh God.

"She what?"

For a moment Aaron peered into the darkness and drove, making sure he had total control over his vehicle on the icy roads and his tongue on the suddenly slippery terrain of his relationship.

"She said the reason she put off having a relationship in the first place was that she wasn't feeling right. Like she was depressed all semester, and then Thanksgiving, and—"

"The fucking cat," Larx muttered.

"Yeah. The cat died and she wasn't home. And, you know…."

"Comfort," Larx said. "With someone safe. I get it."

"And kind," Aaron felt compelled to add. "Larx, he's really sweet. I think… I think if Olivia can get her head on okay, he'll be a good person to have in her life, no matter what capacity."

"That's very diplomatic of you, Deputy," Larx said dryly. Then he heaved a big sigh. "Thanks for telling me. I mean, you could have just told me it was Olivia's business—"

"I told her I'd tell you," Aaron said, absurdly proud. "I don't keep secrets from you. I couldn't from Caro; I won't from you."

Larx hmmed. "Okay. That's reassuring, actually. Except you *do* manage to be pretty tight-lipped when there's danger, but we're working on that, so that's okay."

Oh thank heaven. "You're not mad?"

"Mad?"

"That I called Olivia and not you?"

Larx snorted. "So I could go get a shotgun and make that varmint marry my helpless little girl?"

And Aaron had to laugh. "Guess not," he said softly. "Larx?"

"Yeah?"

"You know how you said you loved me because I wasn't going to torture the guy with the ganja prescription?"

"Yeah?"

"I love you because you knew why I called Olivia first without even asking."

"This is good," Larx said, sounding pleased. "This is promising."

It was Aaron's turn to snort. "Promising? Like me moving my chickens in wasn't sort of a promise?"

"Well, yes. You did come with a trousseau, Deputy, but there were particulars to work out."

"Shit!" The SUV bucked and tried to get away from him, and Aaron steered it back on track. "Larx, how about we save the rest of the convo for when I get home. This snow is getting thicker by the minute, and I need to watch the road."

"Love you," Larx said. "Stay safe."

"Love you back."

Aaron peered into the darkness, being very careful to take care of Larx's property the whole time.

FRIGID DARKNESS

WITHOUT THE shadow of Olivia hovering over the dinner table, Larx felt himself relax for the first time in three days.

He chatted with the kids, made time for a moment or two with Christi, and then, finally, when he and Aaron were doing dishes together, he had a breath to talk.

"Nice?" he asked for the fiftieth time.

"Adorable," Aaron said, sounding totally serious. "He's like a wombat—a creature of no hostility, a great deal of fuzz around his chin, and considerable cuteness. They may forget to pay the gas bill, but they'll love that kid warm by sheer will."

Larx let out a brief laugh and then sobered.

"What aren't you telling me?"

Aaron looked uncomfortable then, focusing all his attention to the dishes in the sink. "Larx, she was depressed before this happened. To the point of putting off a relationship with the wombat of her dreams. And now she's pregnant and still not even close to happy. How's she going to take care of a baby when she's too depressed to take care of herself?"

Larx set the cup he was drying down with a *thunk*.

She'd slept for three days.

His whirlwind, his butterfly—she'd been in hibernation.

He was starting to be afraid she couldn't break free of the stasis she'd been locked in for days.

"I'm…." He let out a breath. So many years— his girls, his classroom, his high school—he'd been the one people came to. The girls depended on him to have a plan—"What's for dinner, Dad? When can we turn the heater on? Can we have a cat—or three?" The students depended on him to have a plan—"What are going to do today, Larx? What's the assignment, the lab, the lecture?" The teachers depended on him to have a plan for *everything*—"Where's the money gonna come from for the field trip? Who's running snack bar at the basketball game? Who has student activities this year?" All these plans, all the damned activity he'd spent his life immersed in, and he had no plan for this.

"I'm…." He inhaled and exhaled again, trying to clear his mind. "I should just… just take her in. Call the mental health department, take her in for an evaluation. She's… she's reasonable. I tell her I'm worried, she says, 'I'll put your mind at rest, Daddy!' and…." He shuddered. "Except it won't be like that, will it? Because she'll go in, and they'll tell her something is wrong, and we both know how this goes. It will get worse—and it will get messy. It always does before a person gets help. And… and she's lost."

She was lost and in pain, and Larx didn't have a plan.

"I don't have a plan," he muttered, trying to breathe. Him and Aaron—equals. He had to pull his own weight. Aaron didn't sign on for this. He'd looked grandfatherhood in the eye without blinking, but this was different. This was Larx's kid, and she was about to demand a lion's share of his time, and more than that, if she was going to have this child and *not* be up to taking care of it, that would put him and Aaron on deck, and that was a whole lot different than being Grandpa, and Larx wasn't sure he knew what to do with that. Larx was *just* getting good at captaining the school ship and *just* getting used to coming home and knowing there was another grown-up there who cared about him and Christiana, and now Kellan, and Larx loved Kirby too, and what was he going to do if Aaron decided to take his kid and his chickens and bail out of this madhouse and—

Aaron's hands, warm, wide-palmed, and grounding, settled on his shoulders.

"What are you thinking?" he asked softly, nuzzling Larx's temple.

"I…. God help me, Aaron, I don't have a plan."

"Of course you don't." Aaron wrapped his arms around Larx's shoulders and pulled Larx back against his wide, strong body. "Who's got a plan for this? My kid showed up for Christmas wearing Class-A Bitch Body Armor—I didn't have a plan for that. It took a week and a half to come up with something that wouldn't result in jail time."

Larx couldn't laugh. His brain was chasing around in circles as he tried to put it all into perspective—Olivia, sad and in pain, a wombat boyfriend, a baby on the way—and all he got was an image of an injured wombat, wailing in a hole.

"Daddy!" Christi called from the living room. "Are you guys coming to watch TV?"

"Dad's having a moment," Aaron called back. "Start the show without us."

"Having a moment?" Larx repeated, feeling indignant. "What's that mean?"

Aaron's arms tightened. "It means life threw you a curveball and you're sizing up the pitch before you swing. Now come on. You were telling me something about a student when I called—finish. It might be important."

Larx grunted, his mind focusing on the conversation.

"Yoshi called her into his office today, and as soon as the door closed behind her, she backed up against it like he was the boogeyman."

"Yoshi?" Aaron adored Yoshi—but so did Larx, and anybody could see Yoshi was as frightening as his beloved Hello Kitty sticker collection.

"Yeah—so, that's an alarm. Yoshi has her open the door and sits her down, then sits behind his desk and pulls up her grades, and the first thing he notices is that all the classes she's suddenly doing not so great in have male teachers. Then he notices that she's put on a little weight—which girls do—but it's in the breasts, and her chin is rounded, and in the middle."

"Uh-oh," Aaron said, because these were pretty obvious tells.

"Right? And then Yosh asks if there's a reason her grades went down, and he thinks she's going to break down. He's fully prepared for her to lose her shit on him, but she doesn't. She stands up and says her stepdad's ex-law enforcement, and he says she doesn't have to answer any of Yoshi's questions."

Aaron blinked. "Uh… is he?"

"Sort of," Larx told him. "He's done security for things like the fairgrounds or rock concerts—apparently he has a Taser and a badge, and she seems to hate both things. But Yoshi doesn't lose his cool—that's why he took her when I got Jaime Benitez—"

Larx blinked.

"Hey—do you and Kirby have old snow boots we can give him and his brother? They're new here and sort of on a shoestring and—"

"Not a problem," Aaron said, sounding unfazed and rock-solid and totally normal, draped over Larx's back as Larx leaned against him. "Both of us do. We usually give to the charity drive, but we weren't sure if Kellan needed a pair, and then we got him some for Christmas, remember?"

"Yeah," Larx said, one thing falling off his list and—maybe—making room for his *What to do about Olivia* list. "That would be great. Before we go to bed, could you guys put them in a bag by the door, along with—"

"Coats and any long johns we might have. I hear you. Are you having these kids over for dinner?"

Finally Larx's desperation lifted a little. "Yoshi said the same thing."

"Mm… that's because we know you, Principal Larkin, and once you take a kid under your wing, they're protected from the elements for life. So, if I promise to get the boots for Jaime, will you tell me what you and Yoshi decided to do about Candace? She's clearly being abused by someone in her life…."

"We think it's the stepfather, but yeah." Larx and Yoshi had come to the same conclusion. "And she might even be pregnant—which is awful enough, but she's scared, and she's not talking. So we called the school psychologist to come talk to her tomorrow, and she's going to get pulled out of class again, and we've called social services so they can be there for the interview—but it's going to be messy, and her sister is going to need to be removed from the home, and the CPS office is about thirty miles away, so we can only hope they get here tomorrow before school is out, especially if the sister is involved. So Yoshi let her leave his office thinking that was the end of it—he was just worried about her grades, but tomorrow—" Larx shuddered.

"Yeah." Aaron's lips cruised the back of his neck. "Tomorrow's gonna be hard," he said softly. "And then Olivia is going to get home, and it's going to be harder." He kissed the join of Larx's shoulder then—with an open mouth.

Larx's brain shut down. Shut. Down.

The Olivia thing, which had been churning in his stomach for three days, was tabled. She was with her wombat now, and he couldn't fix it. The Candace thing, which had sat like a stone on his shoulders, was tomorrow's nightmare—still difficult, but Larx had made a dozen phone calls, and he and Yoshi had planned for half a dozen scenarios. They were as prepared as they were going to get.

Aaron had plans to put boots at the door, so Jaime and his brother might not freeze to death during the dreariest month of the year.

Dinner was done. The dishes were dry.

And his entire body was telling him he had a different agenda.

He moaned breathily.

Aaron turned him around and, by bending his knees a little, tucked his hands into Larx's back pockets.

"Go upstairs," he whispered into Larx's ear. "We're going to watch TV in your room until the kids bang on our door and tell us good night. Can you deal with that, Principal?"

Larx had to fight tears. "Yes. Oh God, yes."

Aaron's throaty laughter actually gave Larx wood. "And then we'll do something where saying 'Yes, oh God, yes,' is a requirement."

Larx buried his face against Aaron's throat. "I… I… uh…."

"It's okay, Larx. You don't have a plan for once. Well, for once *I've* got a plan. It'll do until you get a better one. How's that?"

Larx nodded hopelessly. "It's good. I like this plan."

"Good. Go put on your pajamas. I'll round up boots and calm the troops."

Larx practically whimpered as he beat a retreat upstairs. He was in bed under the covers, flipping moodily through channels, when Aaron came in and started getting ready for bed. *Lucifer* was on, which is what the kids were watching downstairs, so he settled in for that, relaxing even more when Aaron crawled in next to him. For long, soul-drugging moments he did nothing but follow the television and run his palm dreamily over Aaron's mildly furry chest, stopping every now and then for a desultory pinch of the nipples.

Aaron's indrawn breaths started to get harsher, and Larx—whose brain had been pleasantly off—began to remember that his body could be very much "on."

The show continued, and Aaron began to trace his fingertips very gently down the side of Larx's bare arm.

Larx's turn for the indrawn breath to mean more than just oxygen.

Moment by moment, touch by slow, teasing touch, the storm brewed between them. The show ended, and they locked eyes, both of them listening to the sounds below.

The TV shut off; Kellan fed the cats, calling "Kiss kiss kiss kiss kiss!" which was a phrase he'd brought himself and they both found endearing. Kirby let Dozer out for a run, and at the sound of the back door sliding open and Kirby calling to the dog and cursing the cold, Aaron lowered his head to Larx's neck and began a slow lick to his collarbone.

Larx started to shake, the desire in his stomach exploding to *now* just that fast.

Christiana—it must have been—turned off the lights, locked the front door, and called Dozer in, because he didn't obey Kirby worth a damn.

Then... oh then... they heard all three kids on the stairs, calling, "Night, guys! Night, Dad! Night, Daddy! Night, Aaron!" in a soft chorus.

Aaron pulled his head back, and he and Larx both said, "Night, guys! Sleep tight!" through the door.

Aaron ducked his head again, this time aiming for Larx's nipple.

Larx pulled in another harsh breath, knotting his fingers in Aaron's thick blond hair and kneading, slowly kneading, at Aaron's rhythmic tugs.

The hall light disappeared under their door and Christiana's door closed, and Aaron surged upward, claiming Larx's mouth with aggression.

Larx answered back the same way.

They couldn't be loud. The kids weren't asleep just yet; the house was still in the breathless quiet of lights-out. But all Larx wanted to do was devour the man in his bed, eat him alive, take him into his soul.

Aaron apparently felt the same way, but Aaron was a man of action. He shoved at Larx's waistband until his shorts slid down and without finesse wrapped his hand around Larx's erection. After a few terrible moments of fumbling with Aaron's briefs, Aaron unfurled in Larx's hand, hardening, thick, and oh, hot. So hot.

They moaned into each other's mouths and squeezed in tandem, both of them stroking, bucking against the other, the soft rustling of the covers and their hushed, ragged breathing the only sounds in the room.

And still they kissed. Aaron's tongue in his mouth fed his soul; Aaron's hard chest against his other hand kept him grounded, grounded and sane when the rest of the world felt like it was spinning beyond control. And still that silky, hard grip on his cock—augh!

They both started bucking in rhythm, and Larx's precome spilled, scalding and slippery, making Aaron's grip on him a delirium of pleasure and pressure.

Aaron whimpered and Larx felt him, just as hot, just as slick, spurting into Larx's fist.

Close. They were so close.

The kiss never faltered, never failed, and together they stroked and thrust, rocketing toward a quick and dirty climax, shuddering with desire ramped slowly, relieved quick.

Larx's hit first, and he bucked hard, letting out a soft whine, a chuff of air into Aaron's mouth, and then Aaron did the unthinkable.

He moved, taking Larx's cock into his mouth and presenting Larx with his own. Larx had it down his throat just as Aaron swung his leg over Larx's head, and the feeling of the crown, already spitting come, shoving down his throat caused his climax to roar like wildfire, taking control of his limbs with it.

Aaron's spill of spend in his mouth was salty and bitter and everything Larx had craved without knowing it when he'd gone up to bed that night.

He swallowed as fast and as hard as he could, smiling to himself as Aaron's leg lowered, resting limply on Larx's ear.

Larx gave his cock one more long, leisurely slurp and sighed happily when Aaron did the same.

"We should probably move," Aaron murmured.

"This could get awkward if we fall asleep this way," Larx agreed.

Aaron was the one who shifted back, and they both pulled up their underwear in the general reshuffling of people and blankets. Just when they were about situated again, Dozer gave a soft whine and a scratch at the door, so Larx had to get up and let him in, closing the door behind him.

He crawled back into bed, made sure his phone was set up to charge, set an alarm, and then snuggled back into Aaron's arms.

"Aaron?"

"Mm?"

"I'm glad we did that."

"Me too."

"I mean… the world's still really confusing—but that?"

"Felt really good."

"Yeah. Made it all better."

Aaron chuckled, insufferably pleased with himself—but deserving of bit of pride. "'s my job, Principal."

"You're good at it, Deputy."

"Love you, Larx."

"Love you back."

Larx's eyes closed against the darkness, and for a moment—a very brief moment—he was at peace.

AARON'S BODY wrapped around Larx's like a giant bear rug, and Larx didn't want to move, but there was the noise… the insistent noise. Not the alarm, the other thing. That… thing. Larx batted at the thing and grabbed it, pulling it to his ear and poking at it futilely.

"S'op," he muttered.

Aaron took it from his hand and hit the right flashing light, holding it up to his ear so he could talk.

"S'Larxwho'reyou?"

"Principal Larkin?"

The voice was young, breathless, and frightened, and Larx struggled against the blanket of sleep that bound him so tightly. "Ulhn, Jaime?" Yah! A name! That was a triumph!

"Yeah, sir. This is Jaime Benitez—you remember me?" There was something wrong with the kid's voice—it was tight and it stuttered.

Like the kid's teeth were chattering.

"I 'member you," Larx slurred. "Why you cold?"

"'Cause that girl," Jaime whispered and chattered. "She came back. She came back and went to hide in my shed, and I remembered what you said and tried to circle around and go in the house."

Larx tried hard to focus.

They'd had plans for Candace and her sister that morning. The school psychologist, CPS, the whole nightmare of investigating to see if the girls—or Candace alone—were being sexually abused in their own home.

They hadn't told Candace that, of course. They'd just sent her back to her room—but then, maybe her stepdad didn't need any more than that. Maybe he'd come after her because she'd been pulled out of class. Oh Lord.

Larx swung his feet out of bed, suddenly awake. "Jaime, where are you?"

"In the woods," he chattered. "Beyond the cabin. I'm freezing. But she's in the shed, and some guy banged on the front door of the house and he's yelling at Berto and… he can't yell at Berto, Mr. Larkin. Berto—he's not so good with people yelling."

Larx tried not to moan, just in sympathy. "Hang on there, Jaime. Me and Sheriff George, we're on our way—we'll call someone else too. Help's coming—I swear it. Help's coming."

"Okkkay—what should I do?"

Larx had pulled on yesterday's jeans by then and was working on a hooded sweatshirt to go under his fleece-lined flannel jacket. "Does the shed have any hiding spots?" Larx didn't want this kid in the middle, but the danger of freezing to death in the next hour was very real.

"Yeah. A couple—it's even got a cot."

"Go there—I know what I said about staying away from Candace, but you can't stay outside. Knock softly on the door and tell her you need to hide too. And then both of you hide. Stay away from the windows, don't let her stepdad see you, and don't come out until you hear us, okay?"

"Got it," he whispered. "I'm going in now—I gotta. I won't be able to move in a minute."

"Okay. Keep the line open, but put the phone in your pocket, okay? That way we can hear what's going on but you have your hands."

"Thanks, Mr. Larkin. Come quick, okay?"

Larx had his hand on the door and looked up in time to see Aaron—dressed in tomorrow's uniform, freshly pressed—lacing his boots and damned near ready to go.

"As quick as we can," he vowed, and then he put the phone in his own pocket so he could get his boots.

Before he trotted downstairs, he knocked softly on Christiana's door. "Christi? Sweetheart?"

"Daddy?"

He opened her door. "Honey, somebody needs our help. Aaron and I are going out to make sure he's okay—could you start some coffee and some hot chocolate, just in case? Put the chocolate in a thermos and then go back to bed, but it sure could come in handy."

"Yeah, Daddy. You and Aaron be careful."

"Will do, sweetheart. Thanks for being awesome."

Her appearance at the door was almost wraithlike, and he tried hard not to startle. "Was taught by the best," she said and kissed him on the cheek.

As he ran out the door toward Aaron's SUV, bag of snow boots and extra jackets in hand, he wondered if he'd really taught her anything. He certainly seemed to have let her sister down—he was pretty sure Christiana had learned awesomeness all by herself.

Larx held tensely on to the Praise-Jesus handle while Aaron negotiated the roads. Aaron's driving skills were impeccable—it was Larx's knowledge of exactly how treacherous the snow was that made him nervous. That and the fact that Aaron was talking on the radio, calling for Sheriff Mills, his boss, to join him on the small, quasiresidential stretch of road where Candace Furman and her family as well as Jaime and Berto Benitez lived.

Larx held his phone to his ear through most of it—he'd heard Jaime telling Candace that he needed to use the shed too, and then showing her where to hide under the cot, or in the closet. From what he could glean, Candace had taken the cot, and poor Jaime got the closet because he was smaller. But each one of them took a blanket from the cot, and Jaime made sure hers was tucked well and good under the cot, so the shed looked abandoned, and they could both get back to crouching in fear of their lives.

"Eamon's coming," Aaron said into the silence. "And he called in two more units. We might be the first one there, but we won't be without backup."

"Good," Larx said. "You guys go take care of Mr. Furman, and I'll go to the shed and—"

"And stay in the goddamned car," Aaron snapped. "Jesus, Larx. You're coming to calm the kids down once we get them. You're not going in there."

Larx gaped at him, indignant. "What do you mean, I'm not going in there—he called me for help!"

Aaron cleared his throat. "I've got Kevlar, Larx. Specially fitted—for me. I do not have a vest for you. I know you want to help the kids, baby, but you can't help them if you get gunned down. You told Christiana you'd be back. I'm not letting this play out any other way."

Larx gaped at him for a moment, trying to separate his urgency from his common sense—and it was rough going for a minute. He wanted to help, *dammit*.

But Aaron was trained. Aaron had a gun and a Taser at his hip, and Kevlar and a tactical pen and probably three other things Larx didn't know about.

"Unless I'm needed," Larx said after a moment, and the entire SUV lightened with Aaron's sigh of relief.

"I'll call you in," he said.

"Or, you know, something obvious, and the kids need me."

"Larx!"

"I'm not running out into the middle of a firefight and shouting, 'Hey, hit me! Hit me!'" Larx defended. "I hate guns!"

"Do I have to remind you—"

"And besides, do you remember when you almost got run over?"

"You got *shot*!"

"You've gotten shot before!" Larx sallied, wondering when this had become something they should have bonded over.

"And do you know why I wasn't dead? Because I had *Kevlar*! And do you know why *you* weren't dead?"

Larx grimaced. "Pure dumb luck?"

"Pure dumb luck." Aaron pronounced the words like a prison sentence. Which they apparently were. Larx was being sentenced to the SUV until Aaron let him out. For a fulminating moment, Larx remembered he'd spent most of his life bucking authority, but then Aaron slipped and slid up the driveway of Jaime Benitez's house.

Every light inside was blazing, and to the far right of the house, back against the tree line, sat a small outbuilding, without a single light and no appearance of life. The house—a small, square, plain affair, probably two bedrooms, one bath, a living room, and a kitchen—was lit up in every window, and ominous crashes and raised voices carried through the windows of the SUV.

"Please, Larx," Aaron said one more time.

Larx grimaced. "Unless I see something," he promised.

Aaron nodded. "That's fair. Stay safe." He paused and smiled faintly before opening his door. "Take care of what's mine."

And like that, Larx couldn't hold his authoritarianism against him. "Backatcha."

Aaron strode across the snowy yard like nothing could hurt him and he had every right to be there. Larx had to believe in him, right?

Aaron paused at the front door at the moment, then spoke into the radio clipped to his collar. He waited a moment before looking up. Larx saw the red lights flashing across the snowscape and turned in time to see Eamon Mills, Aaron's boss, sheriff of Colton County, drive up. Aaron waited for Eamon to get out and Kevlar up before knocking on the door.

Larx's heartbeat roared in his ears for a moment as he realized they suspected the absolute worst in that house.

The door closed behind Aaron, and Larx was stuck watching the shadows ghost over the windows, wondering who was inside.

When he heard voices coming from his pocket, he almost screamed.

"No!" Jaime whispered harshly. "Don't go out. Larx! Tell us what's happening, or she's gonna bolt!"

"Tell her to stay put," Larx ordered. "Deputy George is in there now." He watched with relief as Eamon walked through the door, Kevlar on, hand on his weapon.

The next voice was muffled and hysterical. "He's crazy! He'll kill them!"

"Stay put!" Larx barked, his hand on the door handle. "Stay put. He doesn't know where you are. Don't make yourselves vulnerabl—"

The shot broke the front windshield, and Aaron's headrest exploded.

Larx spilled out of the SUV, crouching on the ground in the snow, the house at his back and obscured as several shots more split the air.

"Larx!" Jaime cried, and Larx tried desperately to reassure him, looking across the yard at the small shed and hoping—God, hoping—he was doing the right thing.

He was not surprised when the door opened and he saw a figure—warmly dressed, thank God, in a heavy snow parka and boots—burst from the shed and go running into the woods. Larx tried to think, since he couldn't see in the dark, and his heart fell when he realized she wasn't going toward the small nest of houses on this little road, but rather back into the woods.

"She's gone!" Jaime wailed, and Larx snarled, "Lay low, Jaime—get on the ground, under the cot—she's got gear and you don't!"

His voice sounded abnormally loud in his own ears, and that's when he realized the shots had stopped. Keeping low to the ground, grateful for his own snow parka and comfortable, warm fleece-lined boots, he found the worn path between the house and the shed and made his way as quickly as he could, wary of the slippery packed snow underneath his tread.

He got about halfway across the yard when he heard his name and turned.

Sheriff Eamon Mills was in his sixties, African American, with a low, deep voice and a head full of silver to vouch for an eventful, well-lived life. Larx had never seen him look worried—until now.

"Larx—he's hit. He's down. Shooter is secured, ambulance is coming, but boy, he's asking for you."

Larx's brain fogged out for a moment.

He was still standing there, blinking, when Eamon said it again. "Larx, he's got his vest on, but he needs you."

Larx nodded and started back toward the house, his entire body cold. Jaime's whimper through his pocket brought him back to earth with a thump.

"The girl ran off," he said. *They need you calm. They need you calm. They need you calm.* "Jaime's under the bed—is Berto—?"

"He's fine."

"He's fine," Larx told his pocket. "Jaime, Berto's fine."

Jaime's hysterical sobs told them both that the boy was *not* okay, even if his brother *was*.

"I'll have an officer get him," Eamon said, patting Larx's back and pulling him into the room. "We've got about two minutes before there's more help here than we know what to do with."

Larx grunted and looked inside.

And tried not to throw up.

In the corner of the room, a man lay handcuffed—and dead, judging by the blood pool underneath him. Mr. Furman, the evil stepfather—probably—but Larx didn't care. Aaron sprawled in the far corner from him, slumped with his back against the wall, his legs out, eyes closed. A picture of the ocean in a shattered frame sat next to him, and he had an emerging goose egg on his forehead, with a tiny trickle of blood, but his Kevlar was squashed against his stomach, flattened, and he was having trouble breathing.

Larx fell to his knees next to him as Eamon squatted next to the slightly built young man in the corner of the room who was rocking himself back and forth and whimpering.

"Eamon, he's... he's under treatment for PTSD," Larx said, waiting until Eamon looked at him and nodded.

That's all Larx needed before turning back to Aaron.

"Jesus," he muttered, stroking Aaron's cheek with his knuckle. "That was not how this night was supposed to go."

Aaron grimaced. "Does this mean… the wedding's… off?"

"You need to propose to me first, asshole!" Larx snapped, furious—and even more so when Aaron grinned weakly.

"See? Now you're pissed, right? Not—" He caught his breath, and Larx knew enough about Kevlar to know he had cracked ribs, possibly some internal bleeding, and maybe even a punctured lung. "Not thinking I'm dead."

Larx squeezed his hand. "If you were dead, I really would be pissed," he said, fighting for his own breath. "If you were dead, I'd be… I'd be…." He started to shake, angry all over again, because he hadn't even been shot and this felt like going into shock and he wasn't going to do that when Aaron needed him. "I have to tell your kid you got shot, goddammit. I have to do that. You had better be fucking okay."

Aaron nodded soberly. "You'll take good care of him till I'm home. Trust you."

"Your dog will never forgive me." The sob surprised him. He wasn't that guy—not the guy who cried in a crisis. But this hurt—his chest was on fire, and he was a deep breath away from vomiting fear and grief all over the ground. He took the deep breath and viciously suppressed the urge to lose his shit.

"Who took care of the bad guy?" he asked, in an effort to *not* talk about their home, their happiness, the things they held most dear. "Just so I know."

Aaron grimaced. "Eamon. Motherfucker had his gun out. I was talking him down, and I don't know. Just fired. Out of nowhere. Eamon took him down."

"Good," Larx said fiercely. "Better him than you."

"Kids?" Aaron took another gasp. "How're kids?"

"Jaime's fine." Larx heard noises and looked up in time to see paramedics rush into the room. Aaron gasped again, and this time some blood trickled out on the exhale. Time to get him looked at. Fixed. *There is no other option. Oh God. Oh God. Oh God. There is no other option.*

"Over here," he called, putting a little bit of cop in his voice when he could have sworn he had none. "That guy's gone. This guy's got a punctured lung and possibly some internal bleeding. You're going to have to cut the Kevlar off, but you may want to wait until you're at the hospital—oh." Larx stared at the girl who had doctored his arm in the fall, suddenly adrift. "Mary-Beth." She'd been one of his students six years ago, and now he was having trouble thinking of her as an adult, an adult who would take his lover—his *Aaron*—and make sure he was okay. "Mary-Beth. He's… he's bleeding. His lung…."

"Sure thing, Mr. Larkin," the girl said. Small, powerfully built, with blonde hair back in a no-bull-shit ponytail, she ventured in first, one hand carrying her field kit, the other hand behind her as she guided the wheeled stretcher in. "You've got to move, okay? We're gonna take good care of him, okay?"

She'd been there. She knew about them. The whole world knew, but she *knew*.

"Aaron, I'll be there, okay? I'll be in the ambulance—"

"Larx," Eamon called. "I'm going to need your help with this boy and the girl from your school."

Larx closed his eyes and almost—almost—dropped the weight of the world he and Aaron agreed to carry on their shoulders side by side.

"No…," he whimpered.

Aaron had the nerve—the motherfucking audacity—to roll his eyes. "Ambulances suck. You'll be there at the hospital after surgery. When they tell you I'm a big baby and I get a week off."

He coughed then, and more blood, and Mary-Beth took Larx gently by the elbow and pulled him aside. "He'll probably go straight into surgery when we get there, Mr. Larkin. By the time you get his kid and get to the hospital, he'll be out."

He nodded. "We'll be there when he's out."

And then she and her coworkers got to work.

Larx watched anxiously as they slid Aaron onto a backboard and then lifted the backboard onto the gurney, and listened, underneath it all, to his labored breathing, and even as the fear *oh God oh God oh God oh God* tried to seep into his heart, his bones, freezing him to the ground, filling his head with every possible grief, he became increasingly aware of the chaos around him.

"Go, baby," Aaron choked. "I'll be fine."

Larx nodded and wiped his face. "You'd better be," he warned, even as they hustled him away. They had him out the door before Larx could make himself turn to Eamon.

"What—Jaime." He swallowed. "Jaime. You're okay?"

The boy looked worse for the wear—body shaking, lips almost blue—but he launched himself into Larx's arms without words, and Larx pulled the boy into his hug with sublime gratitude. He had someone to take care of, and he might just be able to pull his shit together.

He needed to pull his shit together.

Aaron needed him to pull his shit together. His entire family needed him to pull his shit together.

Helping this kid might just help him do that.

But sometimes helping someone meant letting them go.

Berto wouldn't come out from the corner of the room. No amount of coaxing on Jaime's part could persuade him that Larx was a good guy and that the world was safe again.

Larx whispered in his ear, "Jaime—does Berto have any medicine he can… you know, eat?"

Jaime grimaced. "No—that shit's expensive, and we don't know how to make our own yet."

Dammit—the boy had said that yesterday. Larx took a deep breath and tried to think—but Aaron was the best part of his brain and Yoshi wasn't here and—

"Berto," he said, putting his back against the wall and sliding down next to Jaime's brother. "I'm going to call Tane—would you like to stay with him?"

Berto probably had Jaime's delicate, porcelain-doll features once—until his nose had been pummeled sideways and his cheeks scarred with brutal blows. The look he sent Larx was desperate. "Yeah. I…. Tane and I get along," he whispered. "I… I'm sorry." He closed his eyes and trembled. "I don't know you. Jaime says you're nice, but I don't know you… and I hate…." His breath caught. "God, I hate hospitals."

Larx nodded. "I'm going to get hold of Tane's, uh, friend—"

"Yoshi?" Berto said wistfully. "'Cause Tane talks about him. I… I wanted to meet him, 'cause Tane doesn't talk about anybody."

"Yeah. Yoshi's my best friend in the world—you know how I know he's my best friend?"

Berto shook his head and wiped his eyes with the back of his hand. "How?"

"'Cause he's gonna call me a prick before the end of this phone conversation. Want to bet on it?"

A tiny smile pulled at the corners of Berto's mouth. "Not for any money."

Larx nodded. "Can I squeeze your shoulder?" he asked, very conscious that Berto's stress levels might be way too high for that.

"I… I miss touch," Berto mumbled.

Larx put his arm gently around the young man's shoulder and pulled out his phone. "Yoshi?" he said when the receiver clicked.

"Larx? You prick! Do you have any idea what time it is?"

"Yoshi, I'm going to need you to wake Tane up. And I might need your car too." Suddenly the good feeling, the drive he had from helping out Berto and Jaime disappeared, and he was left with the hollow ache in his chest that Aaron was not where he was supposed to be. "Yosh, Aaron's in the hospital, and his SUV is sort of shot up, and Berto Benitez needs Tane and I need a ride. How fast can you get to Berto's house?"

"Tane! Yes, now! Jesus Christ, get your ass in gear!"

Larx pulled the phone away from his ear as Yoshi raged and apparently threw on every warm thing he had. By the time he got back on the phone again—judging from their noises—Yoshi and Tane were on the way over.

"Five minutes," Yoshi said tensely into the phone. "We're taking separate cars—Tane'll get Berto and Jaime, I'll get you."

"Please," Berto whispered in Larx's ear. "I'm a mess. Don't let Jaime see me like this."

Larx nodded. He knew that feeling too. "Yosh, we'll take Jaime to my house so I can fetch Kirby and take him to the hospital, okay? Does that work? Do we have a plan?"

Jaime and Berto both nodded at him, and he wanted to laugh. He had a plan, it was great—and it was all a lie.

Because Aaron—goddammit, Aaron *wasn't there*.

TANE PAVELLE didn't look a thing like his sister.

Nancy was a plump, rosy-cheeked fortyish soccer mom who taught biology at Colton High—she, Yoshi, and Larx had been the three cynical musketeers pretty much since Larx had moved to Colton. She had a wicked smile, a sharp tongue, and a way of making the most dire situations a matter of simple tactical planning.

While she'd been going to college and planning lessons and cutting her teeth at an inner-city school before she and her husband moved up to Colton, her little brother had been going out, getting high, and getting into trouble with the law.

Tane had cleaned up since then—served his time, come out, started working as an artist—and, of course, met Yoshi.

When Nancy had moved up to Colton, Tane had followed her, and when Tane had moved up, Yoshi had followed him. Yoshi had never disclosed the details of that move, but Nancy had told him once, after graduation, when they'd all had just a beer too many out at Larx's house. Apparently when Tane had moved, he'd expected Yoshi to take the quick way out of Tane's life, and Yoshi had simply showed up on his doorstep, suitcases in hand, saying, "I got a stupid job at your sister's stupid high school, so we might as well live together because I can't live without you."

On the one hand, it was the most romantic fucking thing Larx had ever heard.

On the other, it was so very Yoshi.

They had lived together, quietly, for the last six years, and until the tumultuous events of the past autumn, Larx and Nancy had been two of maybe five people who knew Tane and Yoshi were even roommates.

But after Yoshi had come out—very publicly—Tane had gotten a little less… intense. Larx had seen him at the staff Christmas party. He'd even been granted a smile.

A midsized man, rail thin, with skin baked brown by sun and kiln, Tane's uncombed white-blond hair looked almost supernatural compared to the rest of his complexion. He was missing a top molar on each side, and when he gritted his teeth like he did when he was displeased, the effect was almost chilling.

But when Yoshi spoke, his razor-thin face relaxed infinitesimally and he looked, somehow, like he could find a modicum of peace.

Tane wasn't smiling or at peace tonight.

He stormed into the little house, blazing with lights and filled with law enforcement personnel, Yoshi at his heels. They spotted Larx and Berto in the corner of the room with precision.

"Berto," Tane said, voice gruff from yelling over the roar of the kiln and not dealing with people—but not from unhappiness with the young man on the floor next to Larx. "How you doing?"

"Guy just barged in here," Berto said, not looking at him—or anyone. "Looking for his sister. Shot the deputy. The nice one. Got taken out."

His eyes darted to the coroner's team, who was zipping Berto's attacker up in a body bag. "Right here. Got blood all over my rug, Tane. I can't… can't fucking deal!"

Tane nodded and reached into his pocket for something; then his eyes darted around the room, and he grimaced. He sank down in front of Larx and Berto, nudging Larx's knee.

"I got gummis," he said quietly. "One of these'll chill him out enough to get him out of the house, but we need to not catch any flak for it."

Larx was pretty sure Eamon wouldn't give a flying fuck—but Percy Hardesty and Warren Coolidge had been partnered together this night. Warren wasn't bad, but he wasn't bright, and he tended to follow the lead of anyone he was with. Percy was an asshole, pure and simple, and he was likely to raise a bloody stink if he knew they were giving edibles—no matter how legal—to a cooperating witness.

Especially one with the last name of Benitez who had come up from the big city with a rap sheet.

Larx squeezed Berto's shoulder and murmured in his ear. "Tane's going to help you, okay? I'm going to make sure nobody gives you shit."

He pushed up on Tane's shoulder because he was tired and worried and his body hurt, and then he called Eamon and Yoshi over to where he stood, their legs a forest of protection from prying eyes.

"So you brought your own car?" he asked Yoshi, almost hoping that no, Yoshi had come in Tane's old Explorer and he wouldn't have to be a passenger as Yoshi—who had been born and raised in the Bay Area with no snow whatsoever—tried to negotiate the roads outside.

"Yes, Larx, the Escort is outside." Yoshi rolled his eyes to let Larx know his fear for his life wasn't appreciated in the least.

"We need to go get Kirby," Larx said, very aware of Tane making the hand-off behind him and hoping all the other activity in the room masked the sound of the cellophane. "And settle Jaime with Christi and Kellan." Larx closed his eyes and tried not to think of Aaron, alone in the hospital while he was triaged and assessed for surgery with nobody there for him. "And we need social services for Candace Furman—"

Eamon shook his head. "Sorry, Larx. We couldn't find her. I know you've got other things on your mind, but it's dumped about four inches of snow in the last half hour. Whatever tracks she left—"

"She's not a very big girl," Larx muttered, voice dead in his chest.

"Yeah—they're covered by now. We're going to have to get dogs up here and conduct a house-to-house looking for her. You need to get on your way."

Larx closed his eyes. "On his way" meant getting closer to Aaron, and that was the one place he wanted to be.

"Yeah," he croaked through a dry throat. "Can Jaime pack a bag?"

"He did that while you were calming his brother down," Eamon said softly. "And I think Tane has given him whatever he was going to give him, so you can go now."

Tane tugged on Larx's pant leg, so Larx knew that was true.

"Let's go," he said, turning toward Tane and Berto first. "I'll send him home after he's dropped me off—"

Tane shook his head and rolled his eyes. "He can crash at your place. You'll have kids to deal with. He's good with 'em. Right, Berto?"

Berto gave a smile that only wobbled a little. "Jaime adores him," he said dreamily.

"All righty then," Larx murmured. "You ready, Jaime?"

Jaime dropped to his knees and pulled Berto into a hard, fierce hug. Larx didn't hear what they said—if anything—but he was left in not the slightest bit of doubt that these kids clung to each other in love.

Berto was the one who turned away, looking at Larx in mute appeal. "Take him… I… I can't…."

Larx reached for the young man's shoulder as he stood, devastated, and took a deep breath. "Eamon, we've got to go," he said, voice shaky. "Aaron's SUV got… uh… decommissioned—you may need to have it towed."

Eamon tilted his head, an expression of outrage on his face. "You were *in* that thing when it happened?"

Larx shuddered, numb to it now. It had been terrifying, right up until Eamon had told him Aaron was down.

"Not for long," he said. "Yoshi—the Escort?"

"We can have someone run you over in a unit," Eamon told him gently. "Yoshi's Escort—"

"Won't have flashing lights and a strange officer to tell Kirby his dad is hurt," Larx said brutally. "We've got to go—now—and I need to tell my kids." He felt it pushing at him. Kirby's fear, the thing he'd had to live with. Christiana and Kellan, who hadn't done this before, who might be strangers to the kind of strength they would need.

Eamon nodded slowly. "I'll see you at the hospital, Larx—"

Larx shook his head. "Tell me when you find Candace?"

Eamon's grimace spoke volumes. He was the man in charge—and for a moment, he'd forgotten too. "I'll keep you apprised," he said shortly. "You do the same. He's my boy too."

Deep breath. Nod. Deep breath. Step. It was how Larx made it to the SUV to pull out the snow gear for Jaime. He handed the boy the parka, which he put on wordlessly as they trudged to Yoshi's small car, looking forlorn in the snow. Jaime crawled into the back and burrowed into the jacket.

"So are you going to be there, Mr. Larkin?" Jaime asked, voice shaking. "You said you were going to the hospital—"

"I'll stay at the house," Yoshi said as he started his crawl through the deepening drifts of snow. He had good tires—and heavy chains—and Larx knew he didn't take snow lightly. In the back of his mind, Larx wondered when he'd realized he loved Tane enough to move to a place with snow.

"Really?" Jaime asked, his voice full of wonder. "You know Mr. Larkin's house?"

Larx had to laugh. "Mr. Nakamoto is my bestie," he said fondly. "The dog loves him almost as much as it loves Aaron.... Deputy George—"

"Aaron," Jaime said softly. "I hope he's okay. Berto looked...." He started to wobble. "He looked really bad, Mr. Larkin. I'm glad he had a friend there to take over, but... but I really miss my brother."

Larx pulled in a deep breath and tried to remember the things he'd told Aaron back when he'd been hurt. "I know you do. You guys have a lot of love between you. You'll feel that at our house. And someone will stay with you—Mr. Nakamoto, yes, but Christiana and Kellan may too. We'll switch off, I'm sure." Larx thought restlessly about how long it would take to get through triage and be X-rayed and whether or not he'd have a chance to see Aaron before surgery. "I... my other daughter is staying at the hospital with a friend. Don't worry. The house will have people.

"I should call his daughters," Larx mumbled, and then, "No. No. Tiff still hates me. She'll need to hear it from Kirby. We'll see how surgery goes. Fuck. I wish she didn't hate me." He'd been okay with it during Christmas—he'd figured, hell, four out of five was damned good odds, and he was going to take Maureen and Kirby's affection and call it a win. But Aaron was hurt, and he'd want to talk to his kids, and it would be really rockin' if his daughter didn't make that horrible. *Please, let her make it not worse than it is.*

"Larx," Yoshi said sharply, and Larx wondered how long he'd been sitting, eyes closed, mumbling about Aaron's oldest daughter and her unreasoning hatred. "Larx, we're here."

Larx opened his eyes and turned to Jaime as they got out. "You and Yoshi get the couch," he said with a small smile. "Hope you brought PJs." Then, "Fuck, Yosh—we were going to give Berto boots, and I just brought the bag with me, and you're going to have to have Tane come and get them and—"

"Larx!"

Larx's head snapped back like Yoshi had slapped him.

"Look, Larx, I know you're trying to hold it together here, but I'm going to give you a little hint. You can't do it if you hold everything. You got me and Jaime here. Achievement unlocked. Now go talk to your kids, and we'll figure shit out from there. He's going to be all right, okay? He's got to be, because I can't believe otherwise and neither can you. So go in there and deal with your family, and we'll get Berto his snow boots some other time."

Larx smiled faintly. "You're good at this, Yosh. You should have had kids."

"Why would I want kids when I get to raise you? Now go. Be a grown-up. We'll be right behind you."

Larx had enough presence of mind to calm the dog down as he opened the door. Dozer, used to Aaron getting late-night calls sometimes, was well-behaved when he greeted the strangers. Jaime, exhausted and scared and sad, pretty much sat down just inside the entryway and wrapped his arms around Dozer's neck and took the ever-present tongue full in the face.

Well, therapy was cheap and easy if you didn't mind walking it in the snow to poop.

Larx's house was so familiar that his feet made his way to Kirby's room before his mind knew what he was doing. But then he got there, and all the lessons of the past year hit him, and he realized they needed to do this thing as a group or not at all.

He knocked on all the doors in turn. "Guys. Guys, I need you up. Come out into the hall, family meeting. It's important."

He wasn't sure what he was expecting—grudging teenagers, irritated frumpiness, clueless innocence—but all three of these children had known loss and fear.

None of them took a full night's sleep for granted.

They gathered around him, rubbing sleep out of their eyes and staring at him, sober and attentive. Christi had haunting dark eyes and dark hair like Larx's late sister, and Kirby looked like his mother, with pale brown eyes and pretty oval of a face, but with hair a little blonder. Kellan was smaller than they were but with broad shoulders and hazel eyes—together, they made his heart swell.

His kids.

His family.

"Guys," he said, keeping his voice steady, "Aaron is going to be okay, but there was an incident, and he's in the hospital right now. I'm going to take Kirby with me, and you two can come too if you want—"

"Of course we want," Christi said, lower lip wobbling. "Aaron? He's going to be okay?"

Larx nodded, strengthened because he needed to reassure her. "He was wearing his Kevlar, but he took one at close range. Nothing penetrated, but—"

"Broken ribs," Kirby said, his voice mechanical. "Possible punctured lungs and internal bruising or maybe bleeding. He may need surgery."

"He's probably in surgery already," Larx said, stomach knotting with the worry, with the *hurry* he'd put on hold so he could be everybody else's grown-up.

Kirby blinked as though coming out of a trance. "You'll be there, right, Larx?"

Larx wrapped his arms around the boy's shoulders and pulled him in like he would Christi. "Course. Wouldn't be anywhere else. Go get dressed in a minute, but first." He turned to the others. "Guys, there's a boy downstairs. Yoshi's with him, so if you decide to come with us to see Aaron, he'll be okay. But his brother saw the whole thing, and his brother's not okay. Berto's with Tane, trying to calm down, but Jaime's had sort of a crappy night. Even if you come with me, you need to say something nice to him. Welcoming, okay?"

"He can sleep in my room," Kellan said quietly. "I'll get dressed and show him where it is. He can borrow my clothes too—I know him. He'll be okay with me."

Larx ruffled his hair and then pulled him into a hug. "You're so awesome. Do that. We'll meet downstairs in five. I want to get there when they know about surgery."

Kirby reluctantly disengaged from the hug, and Christiana rushed in. "Daddy?" she said, lip still wobbling. "Daddy, he *is* going to be okay, right?"

Larx nodded. "Yeah, baby. He's got to be. Look at us. I mean, you and me thought we were doing fine, but look how much we needed an Aaron in our lives, right?"

She nodded back, her chin crumpling. "I'll go get dressed and show Jaime where the cat food is and tell him about the chickens. Is he going to school tomorrow?"

Larx shook his head. "No. And we all might not either. Olivia's got your car, so you guys can come back after we know for sure what's going on."

Christi's usually open expression grew irritated. "Is she going to be happier now that her boyfriend is here?"

Larx sighed. "No. I think… I think she's been really sad for a long time, hon. I think the boy might help, but there's going to be a lot more to go."

Christi let out a grunt. "Well, I hope she can get her shit together, Dad. I mean… I'm always glad to see her, but she's starting to piss me off."

Larx let out a little bit of a laugh. "You sound like Lila," he said softly, remembering when his late sister used to give him a good kick in the ass. "It means you love your sister very much. Don't change."

LARX TOOK five minutes in his room finding Aaron's favorite sleep pants and old T-shirt, so he wouldn't be forced to wear the hospital pajamas, and then rooting around for the paperback he'd been reading before he fell asleep on the nights he didn't just crash.

As he was lying across the bed, trying to weasel the book out from between the end table and the frame, he inhaled the smell of the two of them: Aaron's aftershave, his deodorant, the smell of their lovemaking earlier that night.

"Goddammit," he murmured. "Goddammit, George. You had better fucking be okay." With a heave and an "Aha!" he loosened the book and fished it out from the tiny space between the bed and the wall.

He scrambled up, made a small bundle of the pajamas and the underwear and the book, and ran downstairs, where his children hadn't disappointed him in the least.

They were all dressed and pulling on snow boots and grabbing jackets—and giving Jaime last-minute instructions on how to live in their home like family.

"Here," Christi said, hopping on one foot as she finished getting her boot on. "I'll show you where all the pet food is. We should be here in the morning, but if we're not, the big fat furry floofy things are going to be all over you, and Uncle Yoshi hates cats, so you're going to have to save him."

"I do not hate them," Yoshi complained good-naturedly. "They just want to kill me."

"They love you, Yoshi," Kirby told him. "They love you so much they want to sleep on your face!"

"True story," Yoshi said to Jaime. "Go with her. They've got stupid mash-eating birds outside that need instructions too."

"Here's sleeping bags and stuff," Kellan said, coming out of the laundry room with his arms loaded. "I'll make up your bed, but Jaime can sleep in my room. The cats come in sometimes, and he might need them."

"Go show him where the room is," Larx said gently, "but don't be too hurt if he wants to sleep in here with someone familiar."

Kellan nodded and went trotting off, and Yoshi stopped smiling. "Don't worry. They all welcomed him—tomorrow won't be too bad."

"Someone should be home before you have to leave for school—"

Yoshi gave a humorless shake of his head. "Didn't you check your phone? Tomorrow's a snow day—the text went out right before you called me."

Larx squeezed his eyes shut really tight. "Right before I called you I was watching… uhm… EMTs…" *work on Aaron and hustle him off into the night.*

"Doh." Yoshi scowled. "I'm as tactless as the damned kids," he complained. "So, snow day. We don't have to worry about anything except—"

"Except Candace Furman wandering around in a fucking blizzard," Larx said grimly, because while Aaron was sucking up most of his functionality, the part of him that worked for kids was not on complete hold. "Let me…." His voice threatened to break. "Let me see to my family, and then you and me and Eamon will have a talk if they haven't found her by then."

Yoshi groaned. "God—Larx, she's out tonight? It's freezing out there!"

"She was dressed in snow gear," Larx told him. "And even more—I think it was survival gear. Like

Red Cross or something. In fact…." He looked over toward the sliding glass door, where Christi, Kellan, and Jaime were all herding through. "In fact, if you get a chance to talk to Jaime, see if you can get some info from him about where she might be going, what specifically she was wearing, anything she said. Anything we can give Eamon to help find her—she was running, Yosh. Not sure if she'd planned it or if the school intervention tipped her off, but she was getting the fuck out of Dodge."

Yoshi nodded. "We've got to find her," he agreed. "But first…?"

"Way ahead of you," Larx muttered. Then he raised his voice. "Kids, I'm going out to warm up the car. Get your asses in gear, okay?"

Christi burst in through the sliding glass door just as Kirby finished with his impossibly complicated lace-ups.

"Jaime?" Larx called the kid over and put his hands on the boy's slight shoulders. "Jaime, you're welcome here. Don't worry if you forget to feed somebody. Yoshi knows the routine. Someone will be here in the morning, and there's plenty of food, so make yourself at home. As soon as Yoshi knows something about Berto, he'll tell you. But I need you to feel safe here, okay? Nobody here will be mad at you if you break a dish or track mud in on the floor. The sheriff knows our house and stops in frequently, so if you see lights, don't freak out. You can stay here as long as you need to while your house is getting fixed up and Berto is calming down. So relax. Sleep if you can— anywhere you want, bedroom or living room. Yoshi is comfortable here—he's your friend too. Are we good?"

Jaime nodded and gave Larx a hug because apparently Larx invited that. "Thanks, Mr. Larkin," he said hoarsely. "Go be with your family. You've been a good friend to me and Berto tonight."

And like that was the blessing he needed, Larx finally made it out the door.

THE OTHER HALF OF
YOUR BRAIN

LARX HAD conveniently forgotten about the drive to the hospital in the middle of the blizzard with the kids in the minivan offering commentary.

If he was lucky, by the time he actually hit fifty he would block that moment of time out, because he was pretty sure he aged at least two years while the car was in slow, torturous, slippery-slidey motion.

When they arrived, the kids didn't exactly fall to their knees and kiss the earth, but—as Kirby said sourly—that was only because the earth was covered with snow.

But the bitching about the drive helped channel their anxiety as they spilled into the hospital and made their way to the waiting room. The nurse brought them right in behind the doors to the waiting room for surgery, and Larx tried to keep his heart out of his throat and in his chest where it belonged. They were greeted immediately by a practical nurse, who informed them that yes, Aaron was in surgery, and then told them soberly that he should be out within the hour.

"Trauma surgery goes pretty fast," she said. "The body's not ready to be shut down like that so we mostly go in, tie things off, and go."

Larx tried not to laugh hysterically. You'd like to think being a surgeon was one of those things that didn't come with a hurry-do-your-best caveat, but apparently the world really was in the hands of people just like him.

He and the kids huddled in a corner, quietly. Kirby, to his relief, leaned his head on Larx's shoulder while Kellan held his hand, and Christiana sat on Larx's other side.

She was texting furiously.

"Olivia?" Larx asked after about fifteen minutes. He wouldn't tell anybody, but he was dying to do something—even if it was just play a game on his phone—but both sides were taken.

"Yeah. I asked her if she wanted to come visit Aaron, and she said she would, but Elton John—"

"That's not really his name," Larx chided dryly.

"I don't care. It's a stupid name. It's the name of the bad boyfriend pick in *Emma*, and I'll never forgive her for getting knocked up by a guy named Elton. Anyway, Elton McJohnson—"

"Christi!" he warned.

"He used his Johnson, Dad—she's pregnant, you can't argue—"

"Aaron said he was a very sweet boy." Larx let out a strangled laugh. "He called him a wombat."

Christi was one of the best people Larx knew. But she was still human.

The laugh *she* let escape was the epitome of evil.

"Heh… heh-heh… heh-heh-heh… wombat. Oh, Dad. We're going to have to run with that."

Larx pinched the bridge of his nose. "Honey, the wombat—I mean Elton McDaniels—may be living in Aaron's house *with your sister* and the baby for a little while. Nothing's been set in stone, but anybody can see where this is heading. It would be… I dunno… politic to not call the poor kid Wombat Willie before we get to know him."

His daughter gazed at him with worship in her eyes. "Wombat Willie," she said, the thrill of ecstasy in her voice.

"No," he said staunchly. He was not going to let this happen.

"Wombat. Willie."

"Christiana, please—being awful to this poor kid is not going to help anyth—"

"The wombat. With the willie. That knocked my sister up." She nodded, eyes closed in happiness. "It's the most beautiful thing I've ever heard."

"May I remind you that the young man has a concussion and is in Critical Care and I haven't even met him yet?"

"Daddy wants to meet Wombat Willie," Christi voiced as she texted. "But first—" She bit her lip and looked at Larx beseechingly. "—we need to make sure Aaron's okay."

Larx let out a slow breath. She was doing the same thing he'd been doing for the last two hours—warding off the terrible fear that this person, this terribly important person they'd let into their lives—might possibly leave them without anybody's permission.

"He'll be okay," he said, with the same *oomph* in his voice that he usually reserved for those days when he hadn't tried this lesson plan before and wasn't sure it really did what he hoped it did.

"Yeah, Daddy," Christi said wisely. "He's got to be. We need an Aaron in our lives."

Larx tightened his grip on Kirby's hand. "We do." Kirby returned his grip, and his breath shuddered against Larx's shoulder. Larx turned toward him for a moment. "Kirby, you will never be alone, you know that, right? Your room will be your room until you bring your kids to the house and they sleep there. Don't ever doubt it."

"I'm not," Kirby said softly. "It's the only reason I'm not losing my fucking mind."

Larx let go of his hand and pulled the boy's head against his chest and looked back at Christi.

She was begging him with her eyes not to get serious on her. "So, how is Wombat Willie?" he asked, silently asking poor Elton McDaniels's forgiveness.

Christi gave a watery smile. "His head hurts, but he's not slurring his words. She thinks they may let him go tomorrow after they take some X-rays."

Larx gave a groan. This kid was Olivia's age. "We're going to have to call his parents," he said, hating where this was going. "Tell her to ask if she wants us to do that for him."

Christiana grunted. "God. That's gonna suck. 'Hi, welcome to the family, we're sorry your son's got a concussion, excuse us, our other dad got shot.'"

Larx's whole body felt too weary to laugh at that—but a bitter chuckle escaped anyway. "Wow. This has been the strangest year."

"You are telling me," Kirby said, his voice muffled against Larx's chest. Their shoulders all moved, together, like it was choreographed, and then they fell silent again.

Christi spoke a few moments later. "She said she'll call them in the morning. The roads are impassable anyway—they won't be able to get here for another week."

"So Yoshi's sleeping at our house and we're all sleeping here. There is something fundamentally wrong with that," Larx mumbled, closing his eyes. He was surrounded by warm kids, he was bored, and his brain wanted to shut down and shut out the worry over all the people—*all* the people. Aaron, Olivia, Candace Furman, Wombat Willie.

For fifteen minutes he took the narcoleptic's way out and slept.

That's what he was doing when he got a tap on his shoulder. The relieved-looking doctor—the same graying, wiry, practical man who had taken care of Kellan's boyfriend—*friend*—Isaiah, had pulled up a chair and was waiting patiently for the lot of them to wake up before he spoke.

"Oh God," Larx mumbled, for once waking up fully cognizant of his surroundings. "How is he? He's okay, right? You wouldn't look like that if he wasn't okay. Please tell us he's okay."

"Yeah," the doctor said, nodding. "Yeah. He had some internal bleeding—we had to tie off some puncture wounds and set his ribs, inflate his lung and insert a breathing tube, as well as a whole lot of shunts to let everything drain. But I can say with 98 percent certainty I got everything. He's coming out of the anesthesia now. He's been asking for you."

Larx swallowed and nodded. "I wanted to be here before he went under," he confessed, feeling wretched.

"We took him straight from the ER to the OR," the doctor said. "You wouldn't have seen him then anyway."

Larx swallowed past the bitter regret he'd tried to keep at bay. "Just as well. Had to gather the troops." He squeezed Kirby and Christiana as they lay against him and reached out to ruffle Kellan's hair. Not children, but definitely his kids.

The doctor smiled faintly. "Excellent. They'll be good for the morale. Kids, how about you go in first while I talk to Larx here, okay? Follow the nurse back."

Larx squeezed Kirby's shoulder and nodded for the kids to go in and then turned to the doctor, his stomach cramping with anxiety.

"What?"

"You know what," the doctor said quietly. "We went through this with Isaiah too, but with a lot less trauma this time. We both know the biggest risk here is infection. It might not happen—we were in and out of there as quickly as possible. He's healthy and strong, and I have all the hope in the world—but don't forget to pray, Larx. To whatever God you've got. I've got skill, but I'm not too proud to take whatever help I can get."

God can kiss my ass—it was Larx's first thought, always, when someone told him that. Thoughts and prayers were great for politicians, but the world ran on science and good works.

Except… this was Aaron.

Larx could sacrifice a little bit of pride for Aaron.

"Me and the kids will do our best," he said, trying not to shake.

The doctor grimaced. "Like I said—take it seriously. But I've got faith. You need to as well."

I have faith in Aaron. "I hear you," he said numbly. "Can I go back there now?" It was the wail of a child, and he knew it. Maybe the doctor knew his adulthood had been stretched to the limit.

"Sure. Send the kids out when you get there."

Aaron was holding his son's hand, natural as breathing, and smiling faintly as Kirby gave him instructions for how not to die in recovery.

"So they've reinflated your lung, and you need to breathe normally—not too deep and not too shallow, because oxygenation is really important when your internal organs are traumatized. We learned that in chemistry, okay?"

"One more thing I can thank Larx for," Aaron murmured, voice weak. There was a tube in his lung, reinflating it, and talking probably hurt.

"Hey!" Christi said brightly. "We'll get to donate blood!" Her face fell. "Except me. I'm always low on iron. But the guys will. It'll be totally awesome—I'll tell you if they pass out."

Aaron chuckled weakly. "Take pictures. I wanna see."

"Time to go, guys," Larx said, swallowing hard. "Tell Aaron you love him and you'll see him in the morning."

Because that was how it had to go, right? There wasn't any choice here. The other option was fucking unworkable.

Kirby went first, and Larx could see by the way the boy's chin trembled that he'd need Larx most of all when Larx came out. Christi next, uninhibitedly burying her face in Aaron's throat and then pulling back to kiss his cheek. Kellan next, shyly, but he grasped Aaron's hand and kissed his cheek too.

"I'll see you in the morning, right?" Aaron asked, voice still a shallow, breathy imitation of what it usually was.

"You'll have to," Larx said, injecting false bounciness into his tone. "The roads are shit, and I'm not driving them again until county gets out there with salt and the plows. I should have made everybody pack jammies, because I think we're doing cots in the waiting room—or in Wombat Willie's."

Aaron's laugh sputtered without the air behind it, but Christi let out a quiet burble that helped make up for his weakness. "You love it, right?" she teased. "It's going to stick. The entire family will be calling him that before the baby's born. It'll be beautiful."

"You'll feel bad," Aaron breathed. "But that's—" Breath. "—a mistake—" Breath. "—you'll have to make."

His eyes were closing.

Larx turned to the kids. "Guys—a minute?"

"We'll go ask the nurses for those cots," Kellan said, voice gruff. "I know which cots won't screw up your back—I slept there a lot when Isaiah was here."

"So you've got an expert," Larx said quietly. "I'll be out soon."

The kids retreated, and Larx was left alone, finally, with the man he'd been missing like a lung, a heart, a kidney, his frontal lobe, ever since he'd bailed out of the SUV and walked confidently into the darkness.

"Wombat Willie," Aaron mouthed. "She's diabolical."

"I'm saying!" Larx took his hand gently and, mindful of the IV tube in his arm, pulled his knuckles up to his lips.

"How you doing?" Aaron rasped.

Larx closed his eyes and fought the temptation to say it was all hunky-dory.

"I am not okay," he said, surprising himself. "This is not okay."

Aaron nodded, eyes closed. "But are *we* okay?" he asked, and his voice made Larx ache.

"We will always be okay," Larx whispered back. "As long as there's enough of you to stitch back together, I will always be here when you wake up. It's not great, but it's better than living without you."

Aaron's smile was a little dreamy, a little drugged. "Anything's better than living without you," he whispered.

And a part of Larx spoke up. This would be it. The perfect time to say, *Hey! Push him! He can quit his job in law enforcement so you don't have to worry!* But Larx hadn't gotten in the back of the ambulance because there were kids who'd needed him. He was just as guilty as Aaron about being more to the world than just a lover and a father.

"Amen," Larx whispered, kissing his knuckles again. And for a few heartbeats, his lover's hand in his, he did what the doctor ordered.

He closed his eyes and prayed.

A NURSE woke him up about a half an hour later.

"We're moving him out of recovery in an hour," she said softly. "When we get him into ICU, we'll move your family there so you can be with him. Right now there's a bunch of kids in the waiting room settling down for a slumber party, and a young woman who really needs to eat asking for you."

Larx groaned. "God. Olivia. Do we know how her boyfriend's doing?"

"That sweet-looking woodland creature who keeps asking us if the telemetry robots have AI?" the nurse asked dryly.

"I haven't even met him," Larx confessed. "But he sounds like a treat!"

Aaron made a sound that pulled him away. "Be nice," he whispered.

Larx kissed his forehead. "You're nice. I'm Larx."

Aaron smiled, eyes still closed. "You're nice."

"I love you," Larx said rawly. "No scary surprises between here and ICU."

"Roger that."

Larx turned reluctantly and followed the nurse out into the waiting room, where the kids were, indeed, bunked down like refugees in a horror movie.

Olivia huddled, wan and thin, on the end of the empty cot, her nose buried in her phone.

"Hey," Larx said softly, not wanting to wake the others if they could get sleep. "Want to see if the cafeteria is open?"

Olivia looked up and shrugged. "Okay, Daddy."

The sharp-eyed nurse spoke up. "Honey, if you were mine, I'd have you on IV fluids. They've got turkey and gravy tonight. I'd make it a priority."

Olivia nodded meekly and swung her legs over the cot. Larx looked up at the nurse, who had taken her place behind the counter at the admitting window. "If anybody wakes up looking for me, tell them where I am?"

She nodded soberly. "The taller boy—the one who looks like Deputy George?"

"Kirby—his son."

"He wanted to make sure you were coming back here."

Larx sighed. "Hold up, Olivia."

He squatted over Kirby's cot. "Kirby—son?"

Kirby's eyes shot open with alacrity. "Larx? Is my dad okay?"

"He's fine. I'm taking Olivia to the cafeteria to eat—I didn't want you to wake up missing me."

Kirby nodded, eyes closing. "Thanks, Larx. Just… thanks…."

He drifted off to sleep, and Larx nodded at the nurse. Then he looked grimly at his oldest child, who stood waiting in the doorway like she knew the hammer was about to fall.

"Have you eaten?" he asked as they made their way down the beige hallway. What time was it? They passed a clock. Four? It was 4:00 a.m.? Holy hell, how did that happen?

"Not breakfast," she said.

"Dinner?" He recognized evasion—he was a master.

"No." Her shoulders slumped with defeat.

"We're eating. Sausage, biscuits and gravy, and fruit."

She nodded meekly, but it didn't assuage the anger building up in his chest, and she could feel it too. Larx had never spanked his girls—not once. But he'd yelled a few times—and each time, he'd been terrified. Afraid. He'd yelled when Olivia had tried driving home without her lights on. He'd yelled when Christi had used the pressure cooker without him there the first time and had nearly blown the stove up. He'd yelled when both girls had gone "exploring" in the middle of fire season without telling him.

His daughter was in danger—every parent sense he had was screaming that something was desperately wrong. He'd tried to be gentle, tried to be positive, but his hold on his temper was thin and sad this inky black morning, and he knew the lid was going to come off.

It had to.

It was the only thing he could think of to wake his girl up.

"Is Aaron going to be okay?" she asked quietly in the elevator.

"I hope so," he said softly. "They had to operate—broken ribs, perforated kidneys, a punctured lung. Lots of bruising. He's going to be here for at least a week until they're sure he's going to heal." He swallowed and shuddered, trying not to let his own fear seep through. "Kevlar is good, but the gun was small, or...." He knew this. He'd looked up statistics. A .22 at close range was still a formidable weapon.

"He was so nice tonight," she whispered. "He brought Elton in, called me up. Told me I needed to be a grown-up about everything. Elton thought he was my dad."

Larx could still feel Kirby's head resting on his shoulder. "He loves you girls. I love Kirby and Mau."

"Not Tiffany?" she asked slyly, but he couldn't play that game. Not now.

"I have hopes for her," he said bluntly. "Whatever is going on in her head, it can't be pleasant. We should cut her some slack."

Olivia grunted like he'd gotten her where it counted, and he wiped his palm across his eyes.

"Is that what you want?" he asked after a moment of letting some of his mad slip away. "Do you want me to cut you some slack? Let you keep sleeping in your room? Tell your young man that you're just not feeling it right now and he should come back in a few months?"

"No," she whispered. "No."

Oh God. He felt like he'd smacked her. With a sigh he lifted his arm, and she leaned against him like a reluctant cat. They were quiet as the elevator doors opened, and they followed the smell of cooking food to the cafeteria.

It didn't look bad. He made her take the sausage and some fruit, and he took biscuits and gravy because he needed the high-carb comfort.

Together they sat at a small table near one of the even smaller windows and looked out into the night, where the snow continued to drift down with purpose.

He ate a few bites and sank into the food—it was everything wrong with a person's diet, and he need-ed that buttery biscuit in the fat-filled gravy with the salty sausage pretty much more than he needed his next breath.

Then he needed to talk. "There's a girl out there in that," he said, staring into the blackness. "Someone she should have trusted—her stepfather or someone else—abused her, and scared her, and she decided that taking her chances in that was better than staying at home. It's cold out there. Freezing. And she ran out of a woodshed and into that madness and didn't look back, not once."

"Oh God," she whispered.

"It's bad," he admitted, letting his fears out, since he had food to protect him. "I'm worried. I didn't know her well—she was Yoshi's—but Yoshi's at our house with a boy whose brother saw Aaron get shot, saw the guy who shot him die. Both boys are terrified and traumatized and… and Jaime was just so glad for the kindness of strangers, you know."

She nodded and bit her lip. Tears tracking her cheeks, but no sobs.

"Aaron," he said, not sure how he could make her see—it was all connected. "He… he put himself out to make sure your boy got help. Made sure you knew he was here. And this boy has parents who are worried for him. All these people… have people worried for them. And so do you. But you might as well be out in the snow, Olivia. You might as well be seven hundred miles away. Because you're right here, and you won't tell me anything, and you're not eating, and it's hurting the baby."

That made her sob, hard, but God, it needed to be said.

"And I don't know what to do for you. I don't know how to reach you. And… and it was one thing when Aaron could say, 'It's okay, Larx, we'll get to her.' But he's not here—he's *hurt*—and I'm…. God, I'm freezing, Livvy. I'm just shaking with terror. I… I had to *pray* for him. I had to trust some outside force to make sure he doesn't get infection, or start to bleed again, or that there wasn't anything the doctor missed. I had to have faith in the universe that he's going to be okay. I have to hope and trust that that little girl is going to be okay. But you're *right here*. You need to tell me why you're not okay!"

She nodded, and he handed her a napkin. He wanted to cuddle her, like when she was a little kid, and just let her cry herself out. But he'd done that. He'd done that over Christmas. He'd done that when she showed up at his doorstep. The tears weren't stopping. He needed words or there was nothing he could do.

"I…." She took a deep breath. "I… last year, Daddy. I got really sad. And I went and saw a doctor—got assessed. And they said it was depression—but…." She took another breath. "But really bad. And they asked if my family had a history of depression, and I remembered Mom."

He swallowed and nodded.

"And… and it hit me. Like when I was being treated, and when I was talking to my shrink. Oh my God! I'm just like Mom!"

"No," he whispered. No. Oh God, no.

"I am! I'm selfish—I only think about what's inside my own head. I don't think about how it affects other people."

"Depression does that," he said, panicking. "It's not you, honey—it's not because you're selfish—"

"But I am!" she cried. "I am. And I didn't want… didn't want to make you and Christi listen to all of it. To the therapy and the… oh God, Daddy. I hate group. I hate it. I can talk to people one-on-one, but I hate group therapy. I stopped going. I stopped, and then I stopped taking the medicine because it felt like cheating. And I came home over the summer and I was happy. I was like, 'Hey! I just needed a new start! Like a reboot!' But I left again and…." The sobs rocked her body. "I… I got so sad. And I met Elton. And he's…."

For just a moment, he saw a sunshine glimmer of the daughter he knew peeking out from the terrible storm that ravaged her. "He's really nice," she said on a big inhale. "He's really nice. But I was so sad. I didn't… I didn't want a relationship. I told him we could try when I got my head together. And… and then… the fucking cat…."

Thanksgiving. Alone. And the fucking cat died.

Larx closed his eyes. "She thought her job was over," he said, voice cracking. "You needed to tell her… tell us… you still needed our help."

She nodded, face crumpling, and he stood. God, so much else to say. So much to work out. But she'd told him. And he would have been an idiot to not know how hard it had been. He held out his arms and let his little girl cry.

EVENTUALLY THEY ended up eating ice cream at five o'clock in the morning while she told him about Elton, who said his major was philosophy but seemed mostly to be majoring in whatever his friends were taking.

"Philosophy?" Larx said skeptically, remembering his own college days. "That usually meant a BA in inhaling and a master's of agriculture in growing your own."

Olivia let out a cross between a cough and a snort, then covered her mouth. The wicked expression in her eyes let him know he wasn't far off in the slacker assessment, and the disapproving father in him wanted to knit its grizzled brows.

In the back of his head, though, he could hear Aaron's dry voice asking him how close *Larx* had gotten to getting a degree in philosophy. The answer had been a semester of slackitude and a few baggies of righteous shit.

He asked the one question he'd always told himself would matter in this situation.

"Is he a good person?"

She nodded, and her hands fell away. He saw again that sunshine glimmer. "He's the best, Dad. He deserved better than to have me just take off like that. I just...." She bit her lip. "I've been so lost for what to do."

Larx took a deep breath, and for a moment he really thought he was going to put together a game plan for how to fix his daughter's life at five o'clock in the morning after a really fucked-up day.

Then his phone buzzed—he looked at it and grimaced, and not just because the battery was at 10 percent.

"Kirby woke up—Christi says he's crying."

Olivia's lower lip wobbled. "Sorry, Daddy. This... this isn't the best time—"

He waved away her apology. "We'll pick up later," he promised, standing up and taking his dishes to the bus tub. "Right now, we both have people who need to see us."

She nodded. "Oh! Daddy, do you need a power pack? I've been charging mine all night." She reached into her jacket pocket and produced a little charger with a cord, and for some reason... for some reason, it gave Larx hope.

"Thanks, sweetheart," he said, his voice thick. "This... seriously. Give me the plug and I'll charge it when I'm through."

She fished that out of her pocket too, and they went back to the elevators. She got off on her floor, but not before giving him a quick kiss on the cheek. He plugged his phone in and walked wearily to the waiting room, appreciating the dimmed lights like he hadn't before. When she was sixteen and had first gotten the cell phone, she'd once lost it for a month and pretended it was just never charged. They'd worked on her habits—putting the phone in her backpack every time. Charging it every night. Having a charger ready for emergencies and checking on it every week. For a while they'd even had a calendar, like they had when she'd been a kid.

And now, in the middle of all this other stuff—this painful, grown-up, terrifying other stuff—she'd produced evidence that things could get better.

It was like she'd pulled a bunny out of her pocket, but even more astounding.

It was magic.

AWAKENINGS

OH GOD.

Aaron kept his eyes closed, but he recognized the sound, the smell, the discomfort.

He was in the hospital.

He'd gotten himself *shot*.

He remembered being in recovery, the kids visiting, the few quiet moments of just *knowing* Larx had fallen asleep with his head on Aaron's mattress.

That had been nice. Just having him there, no angry words, no recrimination. Not that Larx had ever done that—or Caroline, his late wife, either.

But there was the fear of it—the fear of knowing that he'd let somebody down.

Aaron couldn't remember much about the visit with Larx, but he knew Larx saying "I'm not okay" didn't equal *them* being not okay. Good.

Aaron thirsted, suddenly, for a permanence to them. Yes, they were living together—they could live together happily for the rest of their lives, and nobody would blink.

But he could easily move into his old house, just a few miles away on the forestry road—he and Larx passed it almost every day when they went running. One day he and Larx could come to an impasse, and Aaron would simply have to leave, heartbroken, and not be a part of his life anymore.

The thought made him gasp aloud from pain.

"Oh, hey!" The chirp of the cheery nurse told him that shift change had happened and it was probably after six. "You look like you're in serious need of some morphine."

"I wouldn't argue that," he mumbled after doing a quick internal assessment. Yes, things hurt. Yes, he was going to have to put a cap on that if he was supposed to think. "This isn't recovery."

"Nope—this is ICU, and you're here for another forty-eight hours before you get shifted to Critical Care. But you know what the bennies are here, right?"

Aaron saw the cots already made up. "Sleepover visitors."

"Yeah, but no kinky stuff. Your boyfriend looks like a screamer." The nurse—in her sixties and old enough to be his mother—gave him a bawdy wink, and he had to chuckle. His mother never would have told a joke like that, and he wondered loopily if this woman would adopt him.

"He's just naturally loud," Aaron told her, trying to be stolid and loyal. Truth was, if they were in a house, alone, with no kids in sight, sound, or phone distance,

Aaron was the loud one—but it had taken them a couple of tries to figure out how much louder. Larx had accused him of trying to summon moose by the herd.

"Not tonight he's not," the nurse said gently. "He took the kids to go get ice cream for breakfast—one look at the roads, and I don't think they're going anywhere until the plows get here."

Aaron puffed softly. "Oh God. The girl. In the house. I gotta talk to Sheriff Mills…."

His eyes struggled to open, and he tried hard to stick to that one thought. They'd been working on a faulty assumption—that Candace Furman's stepfather had sexually assaulted her. When Aaron had knocked on the Benitezes' door, he'd gone in expecting her stepfather to be the one in the room.

That hadn't been the case, but Eamon had come in, things had escalated, and *boom!* Aaron's world had exploded, and the last thing he remembered was the picture on the wall falling on his head.

And then Larx talking to him, coolly assessing his wounds, and trying so hard not to lose his shit. God, Aaron was proud of him. When Larx had been hurt, Aaron hadn't been nearly that capable. But then, Larx's practicality let him teach high school students without completely losing his mind. Aaron had firmly believed that even before he'd seen Larx running without his shirt and been smitten.

He was falling asleep again, but he managed to say the one thing that could get them through this without heartbreak. "Larx. Gotta talk to Larx."

NATURAL LIGHT was coming through the small prison window above his bed, and he had a grim and uncharitable thought about whoever designed this hospital. If he was actually going to die of his wounds here, he'd love to have something to look at besides the plain white wall with the exhausted man slumped against it.

His exhausted man.

Oh Lord, he hated to wake him up for this.

"Larx?" he whispered, and Larx's body popped right up, his eyes bright and alert, proving that he'd only been dozing. If he'd been getting real sleep, he would have stood up, plowed into a wall, and said something truly amusing and incoherent.

Dimly, Aaron wished Larx had been truly asleep. He loved those mornings when there was nothing to do but wake up and run his hands over Larx's chest. Besides the fact that it was a really nice chest, Larx made delicious sounds, decadent humming ones in the back of his throat, half-muffled chuckles, little gasps. Even if they didn't end up having morning sex—and given how early the kids got up, the answer was usually no—just having him there, in Aaron's arms, was all the heaven Aaron thought people ever got.

"Whassup?" Larx mumbled, walking across the room to the chair by Aaron's bed. "You need drugs?"

Aaron assessed again. "No," he said soberly. "Not for a little while. I gotta stay awake. Eamon... is Eamon coming?"

Larx grunted and checked his phone. "Yeah. He says it'll take two hours for the plows to get through, and then we'll have a big meeting."

Aaron grunted. Who knew how conscious he'd be *then*. "Wasn't her stepdad," he slurred. "Killed stepbrother. Stepdad is still out there... out there with gun."

Larx made a sound like he'd been hit, and Aaron missed the memories of those other good sounds. "Oh no. *She's* still out there, Aaron. One of the things we were going to do when Eamon got here was quiz Yoshi about where she might be going. But wherever it is, it's got to be someplace that'll give her shelter and hopefully food."

Aaron groaned. "Oh God, Larx. We've got to get her."

Larx's hand on his was gentle. "We'll get her," he promised. "We will. But you're sitting this one out, Chief. This ain't TV where you get shot in one frame and do a running tackle in the next."

Aaron's entire body ached under the softening effect of the morphine. "Believe it or not, I know that," he muttered.

Larx let out a faint bit of laughter and stroked his hair back from his brow. "Not warm," he said, voice relieved. "We may be able to get you out of here before spring."

"What's your house like in the spring?" Aaron asked wistfully. Larx had a garden—Aaron remembered passing by the front and seeing flowers in flowerbeds and ragged stone borders up the walkways and in front of the house.

"Mud everywhere," Larx laughed.

"Flowers."

"Mm… yeah. We've got rose bushes, and bulbs. There should be buttercups and pinks and crocuses when it gets warmer."

Aaron closed his eyes, seeing that yard again as it had been in other springs. "Morning glories. You have morning glories growing over the carport."

"Some years," Larx agreed. "Do you want me to plant some this year? I think I pulled off all the vines in the fall so the carport wouldn't rot."

Aaron nodded. "Just like flowers. Stupid. Grown man."

Larx laughed a little. "Grown men need pretty too. And kind."

And you. "How're the kids?" He didn't want to get maudlin. He was doped up and in pain. When he said romantic things to Larx, he wanted to be in full control, so Larx knew he meant them and they were important.

"Kirby is hurting," Larx said softly. "He's... he was able to deal before this by superstition. Someone told him it would all be okay when he was little, and he believed them. He had that ripped away—can't lie, Deputy, it was rough."

Aaron lifted his hand—was hard, everything felt like lead—and he cupped Larx's cheek. Larx's usually bright brown eyes were swollen small with lack of sleep and—he could see it now—with tears.

"Rough night," Aaron pronounced. "You need some sleep."

Larx nodded, but he didn't get up to go lie down.

"Put your head down here, like before," Aaron begged. "Eamon will be here soon enough."

Larx smiled tiredly. "Word." And then he did. Total surrender, like he did sometimes, just did what Aaron asked, stopped thinking, stopped trying to always participate, stopped working to make people happy and the world a better place.

Just stopped.

Rested his head on Aaron's bed. Let Aaron do the comforting, stroking his hair softly before they both fell back asleep.

Aaron dreamed of spring, of helping Larx dig up his garden, flowers in the front and veggies in the back. Or warm red earth under the pine trees, and the smell of roses and buttercups and pinks.

Of life.

THE MORNING stillness eased into the sort of hushed activity of a beginning day in the hospital. Aaron heard the kids first, talking about going to get food, and heard Kirby saying something about ice cream at five in the morning.

"That's weird," Christi mumbled. "Livvy said Dad took her for ice cream at four."

Aaron grimaced, eyes still closed, and flexed his fingers to make sure Larx was still there. He was about to tell them to fetch some bacon and eggs for him, since he'd been running on sugar in the wee hours of the morning, but a familiar clearing of the throat stopped him.

"I'd say that means you should fetch your father some protein and some caffeine, both at the same time, don't you think?"

"Eamon," Aaron breathed, smiling as he opened his eyes. His lungs still hurt. Talking still hurt—but oh, it was good to see his boss again.

"Deputy." Mindful of Larx, still sleeping at Aaron's side, Eamon moved to his other side and pulled up a seat.

"Not sure who had the rougher night," Eamon said softly. "Yours was over when you got shot—he still had shit to do."

Aaron nodded. "Thanks, by the way."

"For what?"

"Getting the guy before he could take the head shot." Aaron remembered that much, sprawled on the floor, trying to breathe. He remembered the gun aimed at his head, his astonishment when he heard the shot and realized the intense, twentysomething young man who'd shot him had gone down.

Eamon shrugged like he hadn't saved Aaron's life. "Well, we all have our uses."

At his side Larx yawned and swallowed, then sat up in bed and rubbed his eyes. "Ezomo?"

Aaron couldn't chuckle, not really, but *this* was how Larx was supposed to wake up: completely disoriented and not even a tiny bit coherent.

Eamon's tired chuckle served double duty, and Larx scowled at him while checking his mouth for drool. "Nungh. Timeizit?"

"Almost nine," Eamon said. "You got to sleep in!"

Larx squinted at him. "You sleep at all?"

Eamon shook his gray head with a bit of weariness. "Not so much. In fact, I may steal one of those cots for an hour before we get a move on, if that's okay."

Larx nodded and squeezed Aaron's hand. "I may send the kids home when Womb... uh, Olivia's, uh, boyfriend gets released."

"He's okay?" Aaron mouthed.

Larx shrugged. "Still haven't met him—I'll need to make the rounds. But...." He frowned like he was thinking and stared at Eamon. "Okay. Plan. I talk to Livvy and Wombat Willie—"

Eamon burst out laughing.

"Shit. I will *kill* Christiana for that. That kid doesn't have a chance. But if they're ready to go, I'll send the kids all home in the minivan, and I'll go with Eamon to help find Candace. That's what you were going to ask, right?"

Eamon yawned and nodded. "Yeah—Larx, we're going to need you to start asking around the school. We think she had a plan, but her mother's hostile, her little sister's not allowed to talk, and her stepfather...." Eamon shook his head. "He's wandering around the backwoods with a gun, and that is a bad goddamned thing."

Larx and Aaron met eyes. Yes, all three of them had seen the damage brought on by someone not in their right mind holding their gun like a savior. Larx hadn't ended up in the hospital—but he could have just as easily ended up in the morgue.

"Let me square my kids away," Larx said decidedly, "and I'll start making calls." He grimaced at Aaron. "I always thought... you know... me and you would play chess or something when this happened."

Aaron rolled his eyes. "Words with Friends," he breathed.

Larx shot him a telling look, and Aaron managed a smile.

"I'm fine," he insisted. "Go be a grown-up."

Larx shook his head, an unfamiliar expression tightening his jaw. He swallowed another yawn before kissing Aaron's cheek while avoiding the cannula and squeezing his hand.

"I'm going to go wrangle idiot children and let Eamon get some sleep. You rest up, Deputy. By the time we get you home—if it's still standing, 'cause remember, Yoshi's been there all night!—you're going to think the hospital's a dream vacation."

Larx left, and Aaron watched him go. He hated feeling helpless, hated that Larx was leaving—but God. He really loved that man.

Eamon cleared his throat. "All done making gooey eyes at your boy's ass?"

Aaron smiled impishly. Painkillers, pain, exhaustion—sort of took the formality out of dealing with your boss.

"Yup."

"Look, I'm going to tell you a little secret about situations like this. I'm tired, I'm cranky, and like Larx, I'm worried sick, so you'd better listen to me. Are you listening?"

Aaron nodded dutifully. His own father had been a pale, stern man with high expectations and low communications. Eamon looked nothing like Herbert George, but Aaron really did think of the guy like a father.

"Listening," he mouthed.

"Good. So, about ten years before you came to Colton, I got shot. I was in surgery for four hours and in the hospital for two weeks, and my wife was an angel of light the whole time."

Aww. That was lovely. Georgina Mills—loveliest woman on the planet.

"And I thought, 'Geez, I sure am blessed to have a partner in my life who respects my choice to go out and get my ass blasted to kingdom come all in the name of the greater good, and my life is truly a thing of wonder.'"

Oh, Aaron loved this story. He nodded and smiled, thinking how nice it was that he had a partner like that too!

"And then, about two weeks after I got home, as I was stumbling through the house and trying to remember my ass from a hole in the ground, that woman tried to kill me with a baking pan and asked for a divorce."

Aaron blinked.

"Yeah, not what you expected to hear, is it?"

No, no it wasn't.

"You promised him a happy ever after and then walked out of the car and got shot—and more than that, you left him ass-deep in kids he had to tell. And whatever is going on with Olivia and that kid you keep calling Wombat Willie is making a tic jump out in his jaw. And you left him in the middle of this, you son of a bitch, and not only that, he's got to worry about your sorry ass too. Now I was lucky. She hit me with the baking pan, and that opened up the stitches and she saw the blood and started to cry and my ass was forgiven. But I'm telling you right now—it's coming. I'd tell you to be ready for it, but I got no idea when he'll blow, and I'd hazard that you don't either. He'll be all good one minute and freaking out the next. So be ready. Be ready to *forgive*. Because you almost did the worst thing you could do to that man, and you're going to have to have that conversation more than once."

Aaron gaped at him. "But… but we…."

"You think you had it. You *think* you've had that conversation." Eamon sighed and grunted, most of his weight resting on his knees from his elbows at this point. "Whatever you think you've had, you haven't had it for real until you get home and you don't look like shit. Once you look healthy, he'll remember you almost fucking left him. So be ready, okay? Figure out what you're going to say to keep that boy in your life."

Aaron yawned. "Gonna say... love him."

Eamon shrugged. "Georgina needed a better package than that." And then it was his turn to yawn. "I'm going to nap. You concentrate on healing so you're ready when he turns around with a garden hoe and takes after your weenie-wounded ass like all the hounds of hell."

And with those words of reassurance, Eamon went to the cot in the corner of the room, took off his boots, and settled in like the kids had, pulling the thin blanket over his shoulders and dropping off to sleep like the old soldier he was.

Aaron watched him for a moment before closing his eyes again himself. Well, if Eamon was right and Larx's real meltdown would be saved for when Aaron's lung wasn't threatening to collapse, it was better to rest up now. It wasn't like he had anything better to do—like go out with Larx and help find a girl lost in the snow.

BLIZZARD

WOMBAT WILLIE... erm, Elton Johnson... oh, holy Jesus on crackers, Elton *McDaniels* was actually not a bad guy.

"So, dude!" Elton sat up in bed, eyes wide. "That nice cop with the blond hair that I thought was you— he's in the hospital too!"

"Yeah," Larx said, blinking. "He had surgery this morning—he'll probably be here for another week or so." The boy had a lot of brown scruff on his chin and wide blue eyes—and a sort of sweetness in his smile that reminded Larx a lot of Olivia. Oh Lord—if these two kids ended up together, they were going to need a grown-up handy to remind them to keep themselves and the baby out of the rain.

"Poor dude. I get out today." Wombat... Elton nodded. "I...." He looked around the room disconsolately, but Olivia wasn't there. Larx had sent her back down to the canteen to make sure Kirby was okay. He didn't want that boy left alone after the way he'd broken down on Larx's shoulder when Aaron had been moved from recovery to ICU. Something about knowing they were in it for the long haul had broken the boy, and Larx was going to be worried about him for a long time.

"About that," Larx said delicately. "Uh, right now our house is *really* crowded." Elton's face fell. "But Aaron's house is about two miles away, and Olivia was going to move in there anyway, until after she had the baby and she had a plan for her education. So, uh, we realize you and Olivia might need some time and some space to talk and plan and"—*fuck like lemmings because, Mister, you knocked my little girl up and you don't seem at all repentant so I'm going to assume your interests are carnal*—"whatever else you need to do. And we thought you and Livvy might like to use the house."

Elton's face lit up. "Me and Olivia?"

"You'd need to be prepared, though," Larx warned. "You may get unexpected houseguests. Like the kid we've got right now—Jaime. A guy got shot in his house last night, and he and his brother are going to need to fix their place up again before they go back to live there. I haven't asked Aaron yet, but, you know, extra room is extra room."

Elton shrugged and waved his hands. "Totally cool. Like, hippie-in-a-commune type cool. I mean, what else you gonna do? Let them live in the dead-guy house? Naw—I get it. Like, you guys got the space and all, but just 'cause Livvy and I sort of flaked out, you don't want to punish the rest of the world, right?"

Larx felt a little corner of his tired, wrinkled heart
fill up. Yes, he was sort of a space cadet, but Wombat
Willie here wasn't an awful person.

Larx hated to piss on his parade.

"Elton, look—I want… I want you to be happy,
and my daughter to be happy, and the grandbaby to be
happy and all the good things. You know this, right?"

Elton nodded, his eyes impossibly wide. Oh wow.
Olivia must have had a hard time saying no to this
one. If this kid had been chasing *Larx* in college, Larx
would have been completely beguiled.

"Olivia—we need to get her some help. She's depressed, Elton. And it's bad. She wants to have the
baby and I'm not going to argue with that—but you're
barely a kid yourself, you know?"

Elton's lower lip started to wobble. "Yeah. But she's
sad, and she needs help. I mean…." He bit his lip like he
was trying to trap it and keep it from getting away. "I'm
not a good student, Mr. Larkin. My parents were paying my tuition and I was trying, but… but there always
seemed like something more interesting than school going on. And then I met Olivia, and she made me want
to try, because she was so smart, right? But more than
that—paying attention wasn't her thing, but she wanted
so bad to make you proud, right? So I thought, 'Hey, this
pretty girl thinks school is a good thing, and I'll do my
best in it!' So she's already making me be my best. And
if I can be a good student 'cause she makes me want that
for myself, I think I'd be a bitchin' dad. Just sayin'. Lots
of playing with us. I can find a job with my dad's company or fixing video games or something—I'm not worried
there. If I gotta feed the little goober and keep Olivia in
medication, I'll do things right, trust me."

He smiled awkwardly. "I mean… I'm sort of a train wreck *now*, but… you *do* trust me, don't you, Mr. Larkin? That I'll do my best? That I can be there for her, even if… you know…." And his voice broke. "Even if she never loves me like I love her?"

And Larx's heart broke a little.

"Yeah, Elton." Larx sighed. "I trust you. And call me Larx. Everybody does."

Elton nodded, still sad, and wiped his eyes with the back of his hand. Larx stood and got him a box of Kleenex, and then did what his dad instincts were screaming for him to do.

Hugged the kid.

"Welcome to the family, Wombat Willie."

Elton nodded into his shoulder and sniffled. Well, he'd had a rough two days. Larx could relate.

Larx pulled away, and Elton sniffled again.

"Why do you people keep calling me that?" he asked, and Larx gave a half laugh.

"Young man, I'm going to wait to tell you the answer to that question until you are feeling very much better."

At that point Olivia came into the room, followed by Kellan and Christie, and Larx held up both hands.

"Okay, kids, here's the plan. Olivia, how confident are you feeling in snow right now? The plows have hit all the roads—I texted Yoshi, and he says our road is clear but his is not. You guys ready to go home?"

There were a lot of tired nods, and Larx felt bad. Snow day, and they were probably all going to use it wandering the house in their pajamas and eating crackers and Yoshi's famous potato leek soup.

"Good. Then Olivia is going to drive you all home. She and Elton will spend the next few days moving her into Aaron's place and deciding if Elton is going to stay here for the rest of the semester or go back to San Diego—"

"Stay here," Elton said promptly.

"Baby…," Olivia whined, but that soft jaw went unexpectedly hard.

"No. You can't make me go back for my own good," Elton told her. "You can't. I'm going to stay here and we're going to make things right before the baby comes. I want to help."

Larx swallowed—well, he'd just done the impossible and stood up to Olivia. There was a chance—just a chance—this wouldn't end tragically.

"So you're going to move into Aaron's house as soon as he's feeling up to it and then call Elton's parents and talk," Larx said firmly. Both young people nodded, so he was going to have to take that on faith. "I really mean it about your parents, Elton. Tell them to maybe wait to come up here until the roads are better, but they deserve to know where you are."

Elton grimaced. "They don't expect to hear from me until tomorrow—can I wait until then? My head still hurts, Mr. Larx, and my father can *yell*."

Larx smiled slightly. "Sure, Elton. The good thing about being way out of town is you can fake a bad connection on a moment's notice."

"Dad does it with my grandparents all the time," Kirby said brightly, and Larx grimaced. Shit.

"Kirby, while we're planning…."

Kirby let out a sigh. "Could you? I…."

"Not a problem." Larx nodded so he could pretend he meant it. "Which one should I call first?"

Kirby sighed. "Call Tiff first, because Dad always calls Maureen because she's easier. If you call Tiffany first, she can't get mad like you're trying to hide something."

Larx shrugged. Sound advice from a kid who had apparently been keeping his sisters away from each other's throats since he was a very small child. "Should I call your Aunt Candy?" He had, as of yet, not spoken to Aaron's sister, although he had seen pictures. The laughing woman with the long blonde hair and the flowing dresses looked like she'd worked hard not to fit in with Aaron's supposedly straitlaced parents, and Larx approved.

Kirby's face relaxed just a tad, hearing her name. "I'll call her. But... but you're good to remember. Thank you, sir."

He said it so formally, like those hard moments in the waiting room hadn't happened. "My pleasure, young George," Larx said dryly, waiting for Kirby's rolled eyes.

Good. Kirby and Larx had bonded, Kirby was fragile, and they would never mention Kirby coming unglued again.

"So that's our plan," Larx told them. "You guys go home with Olivia when Elton is discharged—"

"And you're taking Christi's car?" Olivia asked, which made sense because it was smaller and lighter and had probably been a nightmare to pilot to the hospital the night before, chains or no.

Larx grimaced. "I'm actually going out with Eamon to try to find a missing girl."

All of the children in the room stared at him, even the grown ones.

"Uh, Daddy? Why would you be going with the sheriff?" Christi spoke up first, because she was always fearless.

"The same reason I was with Aaron last night," he told them truthfully. "Because there are students involved, and I've got the best contacts for them. The… the young man who shot Aaron invaded the Benitez home because he was trying to find his sister. He had a gun, and Jaime was afraid, so Jaime hid in a little outbuilding while his brother dealt with the freaked-out stepbrother. While that was going on, the girl hid in the outbuilding with Jaime, and when the shots started, she took off."

"Why didn't somebody go after her?" Elton asked, but his daughter and Kellan and even Kirby were looking at him in horror.

"Because somebody told Larx my dad got hurt," Kirby said, eyes big. "Right, Larx?"

Larx grimaced. "Yeah. I was heading toward the kids when Eamon called me." He shuddered and barely managed to keep himself together. "Bad moment. But Candace Furman got away, and Jaime came to make sure Berto was okay. He was and he wasn't—"

"What's that mean?" Elton asked again—maybe because he didn't know the family language yet.

"It means he wasn't shot, but he was traumatized," Kellan told him knowledgably. "It's sort of a club we're all in."

"Babe," Elton said, wonder in his voice. "Your family is, like, badass commandos and shit. No wonder you're afraid I won't fit in!"

Larx rubbed his forehead, right where his eyebrows met when he was scowling. "We really hope you don't have to join this club," he said sincerely. "Dues are really frickin' high."

"Wait," Olivia said, eyes narrowing like they did when she was doing math. "Where's Aaron's unit? I mean, he drove it home, right? He usually drives it, unless you guys are going out in his Tahoe. The Tahoe's still in front of the house, right?"

Christi, Kellan, and Kirby, his bouquet of haiku poems, the teenagers in his home, were staring at him with dawning horror.

"Uncle Yoshi had to drive you home, Daddy," Christiana said. "Where's Aaron's cop SUV?"

Larx grunted. "It got, uh, damaged. I think someone tried to fire warning shots before Aaron got hit—"

"Were you in it?" Christiana demanded.

Shit. "Well, not after the first shot!" Larx told her, feeling beleaguered. "But you guys see, right? Candace Furman is wandering the winter fucking wonderland and her stepfather is out there with a gun and... and a reason for her not to talk."

Larx had never been one to hold things back from his kids, but now, as they all looked at him with a spectrum of emotions from fear to anger, he could see why Aaron was so careful with his words when he was talking to his children.

God.

There were some things you just didn't want your kids to know about days like this.

"Daddy?" Christiana's voice wobbled, and Larx held out his arms. She went in for the snuggle, and he looked at all the kids in the room—even Wombat Elton.

"Guys, it'll be fine. I'll be with Sheriff Mills the whole time. Remember—he saved your dad, erm, Kirby's dad—I mean your Aaron—" *Weak shit, Larx. Pull your ass together.* "Aaron," he finished on a gasp. "Sheriff Mills took care of Aaron. He'll take care of me. Let's give the man a nap while you guys check out, and we'll find the girl, okay?"

"What about the angry stepdad with the gun?" Kellan demanded. "Look, I know I'm new to the party here, but… but I haven't had people before and I… I mean, Aaron's in the hospital and… and you're—"

"Going to be fine," Larx said with all the confidence he could muster. He looked around the room and felt foolish. "Guys. *You* guys. I'm not doing this lightly, okay? I don't have a hero complex. I don't think I'm the guy with the gun and the vest who can save the day. I just have some resources Eamon needs right now. Usually Aaron taps me for this stuff and I give him the info over the phone and we're all good. That's not going to work for us right now. But that doesn't mean I'm throwing on a vest and running in like the last scene from *Platoon* either."

"Hated that movie," Elton said with feeling.

"Word." Larx was standing close enough to offer a fist bump, and the atmosphere of the room lightened up a little when they flamed out together. "No tragic ending. No Larx in Kevlar facing armor-piercing bullets. I'm just going to be calling people and giving Eamon up-to-date info on where we think she is. It'll be easier when I'm in the car—and I'm pretty sure I'll be in the back, in the gross part, where the perps sit."

The girls grimaced, because boys were still disgusting, apparently, and Larx was glad.

Truth was, those cars had reinforced paneling and good reception—Larx could use his phone and borrow a tablet and basically look up everything he'd need to in order to figure out where one teenaged girl, no matter how closemouthed, could have gotten off to.

Eamon was right—he was needed. But he couldn't go with his kids losing their shit either.

"No risks," Kellan said, voice shaking. "No risks. You gotta promise us, Larx. No risks."

Larx nodded. Easy promise. "Guys—I already got shot in October, remember? I'm all there with the no-risks thing. I swear."

But after a round of hugs, Larx excused himself to talk to Kirby's sisters—and had to hide the shakes in his own hands.

God, they'd never forgive him. Nobody in that room would ever forgive him if he went out and got hurt.

It wasn't until right then, as he tried to fit his mind around how he was going to go out into danger, just like Aaron had, that he realized his hands were shaking with *anger*.

He had to crouch in the hallway, wrapping his arms around his knees, biting his palm to control the sheer growl of fury.

Aaron had gotten shot.

Aaron had gotten shot. He'd told Larx to stay in the car, and Larx had agreed, thinking it wasn't a big deal and Aaron was being overcautious, and *Aaron had gotten shot.*

Kellan's words about just having a family, just *now having someone to love him*, and please, please don't take that away, rang in Larx's ears.

God, that kid was brave.

And Larx wasn't. Larx was a fucking coward, because that kid—with all he'd been through this year—had said what all the other kids in the room were thinking, and Larx hadn't been able to tell Aaron this, not a word of it, not a moment.

He was so angry—at Aaron, at himself, at the situation—that he was pretty sure his throat would have closed up with rage.

Breathe. Breathe. Breathe.

Candace Furman needed him to think.

His kids needed him to come home.

Aaron needed him to, for sweet Christ's sake, stop freaking the fuck out.

And Eamon needed him back in an hour—two at the most—with his phone charged and his head on straight so nobody else got shot.

Larx stopped his shaking with sheer force of will.

He had to concentrate. Every joint in his body ached with exhaustion, but he shoved himself up the side of the wall and pulled out the phone. Taking Kirby's advice, he dialed Tiff's number first.

"Ugh… whoever you are, you're waking me up."

Larx bit back a retort. This was probably funny with her friends—typical twentysomething bitching, and Larx had no place to judge.

"Tiffany? Uh, this is Mr. Larkin—Larx—"

"Oh God. Is Dad all right?"

And that fast, she went from demanding, needy bitch to vulnerable girl. Larx's stomach cramped, reminding him that he'd been the one to make Aaron hold off judgment, to try something else with her besides just kicking her out of Aaron's house outright that Christmas.

"He's fine," Larx soothed. "He had... he had an incident super early this morning, but he's out of surgery and recovering well—"

"Incident?" she asked suspiciously. "Wait—that usually means... oh my God, he was *shot*? Didn't he have his vest on?"

"He did," Larx explained. "But vests only protect from penetration, not from impact. The impact broke a couple of ribs, and they punctured his lung and his spleen and his kidneys. The doctor stitched him up fine—he's talking and breathing okay, but his lung's being inflated, and of course they still worry about infection. But right now, prognosis is good. The doctor thinks he can come home sometime next week, but we'll see."

"That's not fine, Larx," Tiffany shrilled. "That's the opposite of fine."

"Yeah, I know." Larx sighed, more naked with Tiffany, a hostile element, than he had been with the vulnerable people he was supposed to be strong for. "It's not fine for any of us. Not for your father, not for your brother, and believe it or not, not for me or my kids either. None of us are fine. But we're all breathing, and I just wanted you to know."

"Great. Thanks a fucking lot. Now I know. What do you want me to do?"

Larx closed his eyes. "You could always text him with 'I love you, Daddy,' but since you never did that even before we started dating, I don't know why you'd start now. Or, hey, maybe a phone call when you don't need money. That would be fucking awesome, but I'm not talking about a miracle here. Maybe—just fucking maybe—you could say you're glad he's not dead. I'm sure he'd be happy to hear that, but don't put yourself out."

He clapped his hand over his mouth. Oh God. He'd *said* that. He'd said that. All that shit you weren't supposed to say because you were the adult and you didn't want to hurt someone's feelings and because you were supposed to exercise empathy before enmity, and God. He'd just flushed all that shit out the window, hadn't he?

A vision of a flushing toilet and a window almost catapulted him to the psych ward, but he pulled himself together.

"What in the hell do you know about it?" she snapped. "Who died and made you a part of my family?"

He actually gaped at the phone.

"Uh, Tiffany?"

"What?"

"I'm going to hang up now before you realize what you just said. Your father loves you—he does. I called you to honor that, because he'd want you informed. I offered to do it for your little brother, and he's a bit of a mess, so he took me up on it. He seemed to feel you'd take it badly. Go figure. Maybe—and don't take this the wrong way—maybe you might want to talk to somebody about the chip on your shoulder, but right now? Your family needs you to either grow the fuck up or keep your anger to yourself. Your dad getting hurt was not personal to you, any more than him falling in love with me was. They are things that happened because he's Aaron, not things that happened because he's Tiffany's dad. So tell him you love him, then stay off the phone. He'll be fine."

Larx hung up and closed his eyes. When he opened them, he realized Kellan was standing there, one of those awkward expressions on his face that told Larx he'd been listening to more than he should have.

"Oh God," Larx moaned, scrubbing his hands through his hair. "How much of that did you hear?"

"So much," Kellan said, nodding. "You've got it on speaker—you don't like the heat against your ear, either, do you?"

"There used to be a thing about brain cancer," Larx said weakly.

Kellan and looked sideways. "You were pretty awesome. You need to know that. And good call on her bullshit being hers. Whatever makes her that awful, I don't think it has anything to do with Aaron or her mom. Kirby and Maureen are... you know. They're all okay inside. Maybe she heard something or saw something, or maybe she's just one of those people who has vinegar in her soul."

Larx smiled at him, some of his anger healing, and reached out to ruffle his hair. "Vinegar in her soul—that's good."

"Mr. Nakamoto had a thing on metaphors last month. I really liked it."

Kellan used to have a problem with any class Isaiah wasn't leading him through by the teeth. Maybe living with his principal made him think school was better—or maybe it was hugs, every day, and people who smiled at him instead of yelled.

Maybe it was that he was growing up and realizing school was a choice, and so was cleaning his room.

"Mr. Nakamoto is a good teacher," Larx said wistfully. "He's wasted as my VP, but I can't give him up."

Kellan shrugged, some of his usual restlessness showing in the way he moved his body. Time for Kellan to go home and take his Adderall, feed the chickens, and chase the dog around the snow for a while. "Yeah, well, I lucked out. I get you both. But I came to ask you something—it's sort of… I don't know. Tactical."

Larx grimaced. "Where's everybody going to stay? I figured Aaron's place. I'm pretty sure I said Olivia and Elton can go there."

Kellan nodded, biting his lip. "You're sure, right?"

Larx was tired—but he wasn't *that* tired. "Yeah. Why?"

"I don't know. I mean, we kept airing that place out, and I kept expecting… I don't know. That you'd figure your house was too crowded for me."

And now Larx was really awake. "No. No, Kellan. No, you are not moving out. I meant what I said in October. You. My house. For… well, through junior college, at least. Adopted child."

He shrugged again, and Larx was starting to hate that gesture. "Yeah, but… you know. Jaime now—"

"Is that why you offered him your room? Like… you were getting ready to be kicked out?" Oh *hell* no.

"It's just… it's been really nice," Kellan said, nodding. "Just… having somewhere good to live. And

I… you know. Wanted you to know I got it. I can't take all of it. So—"

Larx hugged him, suddenly, almost angrily. "You are special," he said quietly, adding an extra squeeze. "And not because you're gay, and not because Isaiah got hurt. You were special to me because you are just like me, and *I* needed to be special when I was your age. You are ours—and Jaime and his brother may be with us for a while, but they won't be you. You have your own room. You have your own cat at night—Trixie won't let anyone else touch her. You have a place. Forever. You will bring Isaiah or any other boyfriend to our house for the holidays. When someone says 'Where's your family?' on a form, you will put my address. You. Are. Ours."

Ours.

His and Aaron's.

In the pit of his stomach, a hard knot loosened.

Because no matter how pissed off he was, they were still *they*. The things—the people—they had, were still "ours." That had not changed since October, and yes, October wasn't that long ago—but neither was last night.

When he'd looked at a future without Aaron full-on and realized his heart stopped.

Kellan pulled away and smiled a little. "Were you really like me when you were young?" he asked shyly.

"Someday I will tell you stories," Larx promised, remembering the lost, hyperactive teenager he'd been. Larx hadn't found the love of his life to settle him down then. He'd found a caring principal and a good friend, and that had done it instead.

"Someday," Kellan echoed. "But not now. I guess now I'm supposed to go eat, but Olivia got us through the line and forgot her card."

Larx refrained from rolling his eyes and pulled out his wallet and a chunk of cash.

And synapses he hadn't known were still working started to fire. "Here," he said distractedly. "You go pay for everybody's brunch. I've got to call Maureen and Yoshi. Eamon and I really do have to get a move on."

The phone call with Maureen went much better than the one with Tiffany—as evidenced by the fact that Maureen said something about her sister as Larx was hanging up.

"Larx, I really appreciate you calling me. I know Tiff's being sort of a bitch about it, but she knows it's not your fault."

Larx closed his eyes and tried to drink in the approval from Aaron's *other* daughter. "Mau?" he asked tentatively, wishing he and Maureen had more time together under other circumstances. "Is there… did something happen to Tiffany after your mom died? Did… I don't know. Was there something… extra awful going on there? Her level of hostility—it's just so… not your dad. You know what I mean?"

"Yeah. I don't know what to tell you. There was this really weird week when we thought we were moving in with Grandma and Grandpa, and then Dad said no, we were staying home. Grandma kept laying some weird sort of guilt trip on Tiff about how she had to raise us all because Dad wasn't capable. Sometimes I think it really sunk in."

Oh God help them all. "Well. That's unfortunate." Because he was tired and he had a lot he wanted to say there, but dammit, *time*.

"Yeah. I know. It's not something you can fix—but you called us when shit got bad, and that's important."

Her voice wobbled, and Aaron's most practical child sounded like a young woman—like Olivia, or Christiana—again. "It's really important. Should I come visit? He's going to be... I mean, I could come this weekend, you know?"

Larx sighed. "He'll still be in the hospital this weekend. But as long as you don't mind a crowded house—and that's your house that's getting crowded, not just mine, because God, this week!—I'm sure he'd love that."

Maureen gave a clogged laugh. "Thanks, Larx. I'll call him later and see. I... I guess I take him for granted sometimes. I shouldn't. You just never want to think about your dad out there getting hurt."

"Well, for what it's worth, I don't think your sister wanted that either."

They rang off, and Larx started pacing in the corridor, trying to get the thread of thought back from where it was before he called Maureen.

In a way, it was comforting.

No kids, not his, not Aaron's. No injured feelings. No fear of grief. Just pure high school administration. Doing what he'd always done best—look at students as people.

If he was a scared, lost female person who was running from her abusive stepfather and stepbrother, where would he go?

More importantly, how would he prepare, if he'd been getting ready to go the night before?

What would he have with him besides just a good hat, jacket, and boots?

Where would he be planning to stay?

Oh! And where would he get the money for his plan?

Okay. Okay. Larx had a line of questioning now, and he had a—

His phone beeped in his hand.

With a grunt he went back into Aaron's room to hook his phone up to the charger and recharge Olivia's power station.

Goddammit. He'd been on a roll too.

BY THE time the kids came back from food, his phone was at 85 percent, Eamon was starting to snore, and Aaron had woken up twice asking for Larx.

Larx had come to his side each time, a familiar portion of his heart lighting up. Larx recognized it as the same part of his body that shivered whenever he and Aaron neared Aaron's house as they ran.

Aaron wanted him.

And in spite of all the other crap they were both dealing with, that was still somehow a magical thing.

That magic gave him the strength to kiss Aaron's temple and tell him he'd be back soon before Aaron lapsed back into his healing doze. Olivia and the kids came by to tell them that Elton was all checked out of the hospital, and they'd go get his clothes from the towing company tomorrow, provided there wasn't any more snow.

Larx hugged everybody, shook Elton's hand, and looked at the sky through the hospital door. Yeah. Wombat Boy was going to be running around in borrowed clothes for the next week, Larx didn't have any doubt. He'd tell Olivia to keep the guy away from his boxers, but he had the feeling Kirby and Kellan were going to make more clothes sacrifices to the wombat gods than Larx and Aaron—they were all about the same size.

As soon as they were gone, he shook Eamon awake.

"Sorry, sir," he said quietly. "But it's been two hours. I need to talk to Yoshi and have him search my laptop, but I think I have some ideas for where to look."

Eamon yawned and stretched, scrubbing his face with his hands. "Two hours isn't what it used to be. But thanks for the extra time. I might not crash and kill us both."

"That's reassuring," Larx said dryly. "Let me say goodbye to Aaron one more time—"

Eamon stopped him. "Let him sleep. He knows you want to be here, Larx. Just like you know he wants to be with us. Go call Yoshi—I'm going to use the head to rinse and spit."

Larx nodded. "Toiletries in the hospital bathroom, if it will help."

"Oh thank God. My breath could kill a squirrel in a tree."

Larx gave a rusty chuckle, grabbed his phone, and stepped outside the unit to call Yoshi. It was time to pretend he was a professional again.

WHITEOUT

"OKAY, YOSH, you got my laptop open?"

Larx had started the call in the hallway while pulling on his snow parka and lacing his boots. Kirby and Kellan had gone together for Christmas and gotten him a cashmere scarf—warm, soft, and a muted denim blue, it was such a guy thing—and so practical.

It was going to save Larx's life in weather where you either followed the snow plow or you didn't make it to the store.

"Larx, you just told me your kids are on the way over. Quick, I need to hide the hookers and blow."

Larx choke-snorted even as he made sure his parka was zipped. "The only blow you know how to do is the clarinet—don't lie."

"Oh my God, you even guessed the instrument. Now seriously—I've got the laptop open, but before I go snooping, how are you doing?"

Larx tried to think about his morning, and his brain froze. "Uh…."

"Awesome. Emotional constipation. It'll be like defrosting an engine in Minnesota."

"Yet another thing you've never done—"

"I've read books. You have to start an actual fire under the car to melt the oil enough to travel through the car or you'll fuck up your vehicle."

"I have no idea what that has to do with my brain. Can we stick to shit I actually need done *now*, Yoshi?"

"As opposed to what you'll need me to do next week, when you completely lose your shit over something stupid that's not what you're really freaking out about? Sure. I'm down with that."

"Candace Furman is lost *now*," Larx told him. "Next week she might still be lost, but we'll have less of a chance of finding her."

Yoshi sighed. "That's fine. You be a powder keg. Other men might choose emotional health, but you go ahead and do you. I've got her teachers pulled up, and it's the same story as before—falling grades and no involvement. What do you need me to look for?"

"First off, how's she doing in geography or life science?" Larx had learned that much looking at her profile. "And who are her teachers there?"

"Huh." Oh, blessed Yoshi—he might know where Larx was going with this. "Those classes she is not failing. She's getting a B in one and a C plus in the other—apparently she did some extra credit in life science, but I don't know what the assignment was."

"Good. Now we're getting somewhere. So here's what I want you to do—do you have a pencil and paper? We're going to need to make a list."

Yoshi let out a raucous squawk of laughter. "Oh my God—you just told me to get organized. I might need surgery myself!"

At that moment Eamon bustled out, looking practically daisy fresh after his nap and some mouthwash. He nodded at Larx, and Larx fell in step behind him, like Larx was a deputy or something. Funny how some men could lead an army with just a nod of the head. Aaron was like that too.

"You're a laugh riot, Yoshi. Now here's the list of things you need to do."

"Okay, CSI Colton High, shoot."

Larx took a deep breath and watched his step over the snow. By the time they got to Eamon's unit, he'd outlined about half the list, and by the time he'd hauled himself into the passenger's side, belted in, and shut the door, Yoshi had the rest.

"So text me what you got when you got it," Larx finished off with, "and talk to Jaime first."

"Fine. By the way, that kid and Aaron's dog have a very suspect relationship. It's a good thing the dog sleeps inside, or Eamon would be arresting me for child neglect."

Larx half smiled. "Good. Tell him he's welcome to sleep with the dog on the couch after you go back home."

Yoshi's voice dropped. "Larx? Tane called. His brother's in a... in a really bad place right now."

Oh Lord. "Do we need to take him to a psych ward?" Larx asked, mindful that Eamon was sitting right next to him and tended to take things literally.

"God. No." And Yoshi, cheerful and sarcastic Yoshi, had a moment of complete and total sobriety.

"Larx, look. I've… I've seen one of those places, when Tane and I were dating. Not for Tane, but he told me he spent time in one. They're… if you don't have family, like Tane did, they're not good places. And even though none of us would let that boy twist in the wind, he doesn't know that. Just… just give him some time. Tane knows how to give somebody peace, okay? I mean… I know he freaks you out because he's way intense, but he can get this boy to chill. To stay with the living, if you know what I mean. It's what he was doing in Sacramento when I met him. He took on a student of mine who… who might not be alive today, you know?"

Yoshi's voice, soft and passionate, actually made Larx's chest hurt.

"I hear you, Yosh. You've got faith in him. That's all I need. Jaime's welcome in my house until his brother's good, okay? And you are too. Tell him that. Tell him he won't have to sleep outside with the chickens. Olivia and Wombat Willie are going to move to Aaron's house as soon as the service road gets plowed, and then everybody will have breathing room. Tell him that. And if he likes Kellan's room, he can have a bag on the floor. But in the meantime you've got to ask that kid some questions or we might lose the girl, okay?"

"Yeah. I hear you. Thanks, Larx. He took the love seat last night, and I took the couch—we might do that for a while, but it won't kill either of us. Thanks."

"Not a problem. I'm going to sign off and let you talk to him. Text me the info on the teachers so I can talk to them. Eamon's going to take us to get coffee and then to talk to Candace's little sister and her mother, and we'll get back to you after that. Deal?"

"Deal. Break."

And with that Yoshi rang off, and Larx fumbled in his pocket for the charger so he could plug into the SUV's power supply.

"I don't remember anything about coffee," Eamon mumbled.

"Eamon, do you think we're going to make it anywhere without coffee?" Larx was weary to his bones, and their day had just started. But hey—even Colton had a Starbucks, and it was probably the one business that would be open this morning.

"No." Eamon let out a sigh that was the closest to complaining the man ever got. "You know, in a bigger town, they would have had takeout coffee in the hospital."

Larx let out a matching sigh. "They don't," he said glumly. "I asked."

"Been asking for years."

"Bastards."

"Yeah. Okay, pity break over. Get back on the horn, boy. We need something to hit Candace's mother with, because she was not talking last night."

Larx remembered the dead body on the floor, facedown. "Was she close to her stepson?" he asked, curious.

Eamon grunted. "I'd say more terrorized by him. That family gives me the fuckin' creeps—I know you and Yoshi were going by the book, but next time you get that freaked-out about a kid, call me first. CPS is so far away, and this thing got bad quick."

Larx grunted. "It was just... you know. Aaron was called out there for a domestic call Saturday night, asked me to look up the kids. Jaime was fine, but he and his brother had heard raised voices in the Furman house. Berto got freaked-out, so we figured her grades slipping was a sign of other shit. Yoshi called her to his office Monday, and he didn't like her vibe. We set up a meeting with CPS and the school psychologist for tomorrow… wait. Today. And… and Jaime called me…. God. Last night. Monday night. And…."

Recounted like that—Saturday, Sunday, Monday—what was today?

"Holy fucking Jesus, Eamon, is it only Tuesday?"

"Yeah. Yeah, Larx. It's only Tuesday. Your life went to hell that quickly. You need to keep up."

Larx tried to hold his breath—but even more, he tried not to lose his grip. "So quick," he breathed. "It…. Olivia showed up Saturday, and my life was stable, and now it's…." He'd left Aaron in the hospital and sent his kids home to Yoshi. He couldn't put it all together in his head.

His heart might explode.

"He'll be home by Sunday," Eamon said practically. "And you can put your life back to where it was."

Larx closed his eyes. "Olivia and Wombat Willie are going to move into Aaron's house, and me and Aaron are going to be grandpas."

Eamon cackled. "That is the most excellent news! I can't wait to give George shit about that. Grandpa George. Oh my God—it even *sounds* like Dudley Do-Right!"

Dudley Do-Right. Deputy Dudley Do-Right. "He'll make a good grandpa," Larx said, the humor helping to hold him together. Good. Between Yoshi and Eamon, Larx might not lose his shit. His shit might stay completely contained in the same bag that held his panic and his fury. He could do this. He could function. He could compartmentalize.

Aaron probably did this shit every day.

"Yeah," Larx reaffirmed, feeling stronger. "He's going to be a good grandpa." Larx saw Aaron holding his son's hand at his own hospital bed. "He's a great father."

"Yes, he is," Eamon said gently. "And you'll find your way to be okay with this. He's not going away."

Larx nodded and pulled his shit together—he'd already established he had the bag for it. "I'm going to call her teachers. You make a giant, swimming-pool-sized coffee your priority, and I'll get you some ammunition so you can talk to her family."

A half an hour later, Larx was so over talking on the phone he almost couldn't open his mouth to talk to Eamon—except Eamon had bought him not one but two giant mochas, and he was sort of indebted.

"Okay," he said on an exhale as Eamon idled in the Starbucks parking lot and munched doggedly on a breakfast sandwich. "Here's what we got."

Tessa Palmer, her life science teacher, had given her the extra credit for writing a paper on how to survive in cold weather. Her plan had involved a basic backpack of power food, grease in tuna cans, flannel long johns, good boots, a packet of hand and feet warmers, and a shovel.

"Was she carrying that?" Eamon asked sharply, breathing on his Venti coffee black. "Could you see?"

Larx shook his head. "I couldn't—but I had Yoshi ask Jaime some things, and this is what he remembers…."

First off, Jaime had been freezing in the outbuilding—but he'd grabbed a blanket for himself and one for Candace off the small cot in the corner. Candace had kept the blanket when she left, shoving it in her pack and thanking him hurriedly as she ran. In return for stealing his blanket, she'd shoved a power bar in his hand while they were waiting to see what would happen. Yoshi said Jaime had blushed about that, like the gesture had been a thank-you or a kindness, and Larx had a moment to think about the goodness that could linger in even the most traumatized kid.

Second, Jaime remembered that as she'd squeezed under the bed, a scraping sound had terrified him in the quiet of the shed. When Yoshi questioned him further, he thought it could be a shovel.

Third, Candace had begged Jaime to protect her little sister. Larx passed that on to Eamon and got "Well, yes—the girl and her mother are being supervised in their own home, but the stepfather—we had nothing on him, Larx, and his son was going to the morgue. So she's safe for now, but we need to sort this out quick."

Larx grunted. "You know something? I'm not a stupid guy. Just tell me the job I need to unfuck the world, and I'll apply for it. Counselor? Lawyer? Judge? Social worker? Which one is it? Is it too goddamned much to ask that kids feel safe in their own goddamned homes?"

Eamon regarded him impassively. "You done?"

Larx scowled and took another sip of his second giant mocha. "No, but the rant is tabled until it's more useful. So, okay—stepdad is wandering the woods with a gun, kid is wandering the woods with a shovel, hand warmers, and power bars. Why hand warmers?"

But Eamon knew this one. "So she can melt water on the run. I bet she has an aluminum flask. She packs it with snow, tucks it next to a hand warmer, and she has water. Not to mention, if she keeps them both near her core, she has another heat source—depending on which ones she got, those things last a couple hours."

"God, she was smart," Larx muttered. "I mean—smart. Her grades were tip-top until this semester, but nobody knew because she kept to herself."

"I wonder if her little sister's the same," Eamon mused.

Larx remembered that Eamon and his wife had no children. Eamon was in his sixties, and he'd met his wife about twenty years ago—perhaps they had simply decided not to. "I doubt it," Larx responded. "Kids... find a niche. If one of them is 'the nice one,' the other one's going to be 'the pain in the ass.' If one of them is the clean freak, the other one is going to need a hazmat detail to clean her room. Part of it is establishing an identity, but part of it, I think, is just that people are different. Kids want their parents to know that no matter how many times you call them by each other's names, they are not interchangeable people."

"You've done that?" Eamon asked, amused.

"I just started calling them both together so I didn't have to worry about it." Larx shrugged. "I do that with students too. The rule is, you look them in the eye and say a name—any name—and that kid has to respond. So you look at Jessica and say, 'Andrea, what's the answer to that question?' and Jessica says, 'I'm Jessica and I'm pretty sure it's X.' Or, 'Kirby, put the dog out.' 'This is Kellan, putting the dog out, sir.'

The first kid who splits hairs has to pass out papers or gets oatmeal for breakfast, depends on the venue."

Eamon chuckled. "Understood. So, if Candace is an A student, Shelley is probably not."

"Until this semester, if patterns hold true."

"Yeah. Maybe call the middle school when we're done here and on our way to interview the little sister."

"Yes, sir—but I've got one more teacher I talked to, and it's important."

Eamon hmmed, and Larx kept going.

"It was geography, Eamon. And apparently she was doing a whole lot of research into the local forest and train routes."

"Well, we've got the local bus and train stations monitored," Eamon told him, somewhat exasperated. "What else do you want me to do?"

"Except she's smart, remember? I don't think she's heading for the local ones. You don't ace geography so you figure out how to make it to Main Street and hop on a bus."

"By God, you do not. Any ideas?" Eamon was looking at him like he held the keys to the kingdom.

"I'd have to see a map first," Larx told him. "Does your tablet get Wi-Fi?"

Eamon took the tablet and entered the password. "Knock yourself out."

Larx pulled the map up and adjusted it for size, putting the closest outlying towns on the edge of the screen and Candace's parents' house in the center.

"Okay—she's got a hike ahead of her," Larx said thoughtfully. "The easiest town to access is here—"

"No bus stop," Eamon said promptly. "If she's smart enough to survive so far, she's smart enough to know that."

"Truth." Larx studied the map some more. "So we've got Foresthill, which has a train stop, and Dogpatch, which has a bus station."

"Foresthill is closer," Eamon reminded him.

"Yeah, but Dogpatch is easier. Not so many hills or snow pitfalls or cliffs." He hmmed. "What do you want to bet she has a compass?"

"No bet." Eamon gathered all his wrappers and put them in a trash bag in the front of the cruiser. "What do you want to bet she's got a hunting knife?"

Larx paused. "I hope so. If her stepfather's out there with a gun, I don't want her to be defenseless."

Eamon sent him a long look. "What happened to 'children and guns are a bad combination'?"

"I didn't say arm the psychopaths, Eamon! I just said don't let the sexually abused fourteen-year-olds wander the snow without a knife!"

Eamon grunted. "You know, I like police work. There are a lot of absolutes in police work. There's law and not the law and—"

"And good cops know the gray areas too. Don't bullshit me, Eamon. You wouldn't like Aaron so much if he didn't see the human factor in between the by-laws." Larx swallowed, because the mention of Aaron had come out so easily. "How did he get shot?" he asked, even though he knew this. "Why was there a gunfight in the living room of Berto Benitez's house? Aaron was in there alone for a minute—what happened?"

Eamon sighed. "What happened?"

"Yeah. How'd it go so wrong?"

Eamon pinched the bridge of his nose. "You're the first person to actually ask that. Everybody else, we said, 'Suspect with a gun. George arrives first, Mills second, suspect opens fire.' You are the first person to ask me how it went wrong."

Larx shivered. "Eamon?"

"It's like there was a black man in the room, Larx. Because there was. Me. The guy was yelling at Berto—saying the shit you'd expect from a racist asshole, and then I walked in, and that kid's hostility level jumped through the roof. I said, 'Son, just calm down'—doing my best Morgan Freeman, I swear to Christ—and Braun Furman just swung around with his gun drawn. Aaron shouted his name just as he fired or I'd be toast, because it was close quarters and he was aiming at my head. Those were the shots that took out Aaron's unit, by the way—you're welcome."

"Jesus."

"But Aaron was shouting to draw his attention, he swung back around, and we both shot at the same time. Aaron lived. Braun Furman didn't."

Larx frowned. "Aaron shot?" Aaron hadn't thought he had.

Eamon frowned back. "I… you know, I'm… oh God. I'm not sure. His arms were out until Furman was down. I guess we'll have to wait for forensics. Does it matter?"

Larx thought about it, shivering some more. "I hope he did," he concluded, surprising himself, going back on everything he thought he'd believed. "I hope he defended himself. I… I don't ever want him to hesitate because he's thinking about what I would do instead." Larx smiled at Eamon a little. "You either."

Eamon sighed. "You were asking which job you needed to unfuck the world?"

"Yeah?"

"Law enforcement ain't it. Our job is to catch the fucked-up. But you—you figured out the fucked-up was happening and are trying to stop it. I'd put my money on you and Yoshi any day."

Larx gave him the side-eye. "Do you have any idea how screwed up that is?"

Eamon's laughter was sort of a miracle, and it rolled through the car as he turned the ignition. "Let's go talk to that little girl's mom."

THE PLOWS had just cleared the roads as Eamon pulled up to the same neighborhood that had seemed so terrifying the night before. In the daylight, Larx could see Berto and Jaime's little house and the crucial outbuilding across a snow-covered yard and up a hill from the perfectly maintained log-cabin-style house where Eamon parked.

Berto and Jaime's house looked old—a classic small ranch house, probably bought to fix up, with yellowing stucco, chipped on all the corners—but Larx could see signs of life: new gutters, bright and shiny, new roof tiles, unstained raw boards replacing some of the weathered, warped boards on the porch. Old, but with new life—the potential for one, anyway. There was also a small greenhouse, hastily erected— with what were probably exactly five marijuana plants as well as some cooking herbs and maybe a flower or two—attached to the back of the house.

"Did you keep the greenhouse going?" Larx asked, thinking of poor Berto, pulling the tatters of his safety around him in the house that night.

"Yeah," Eamon said. "I went in after cleanup—Tane asked me to. That kid—he's going to need a lot of help. He was sort of fragile to begin with, you know?"

Larx sighed and tilted his head back. "I do now. I didn't before. I... I hadn't met Jaime before Monday. Without Aaron's call, I wouldn't have known him. Wouldn't have known Candace either. Just luck." God. "If I'd been their teacher—"

"You wouldn't have been Isaiah and Kellan's when they needed you. Don't go second-guessing yourself, Mr. Larkin. I can tell you the one thing I know for sure about your place in all this."

"What's that?"

"I wouldn't have had Nobili in my car looking for a missing teenager if I told him there was money under the seat." Nobili—Larx's predecessor—seemed remarkably unlamented, and not just by staff. "He wouldn't have called that kid to his office in the first place—and he damned sure wouldn't have been a friend to Jaime or Berto. You just keep on doing what you're doing. Like I said—law enforcement isn't what's gonna unfuck the world."

It was all he had.

Together they got out of the car, zipping up their coats and pulling on their gloves for the trip from the SUV, past the two cold troopers doing watch in the driveway, to the front door.

The thin woman with hurriedly twisted dyed pink hair and dead eyes did not look happy to see them.

"Did you people kill my husband now?"

"I don't know," Larx snapped. "Has he molested any more fourteen-year-old girls?"

Candace Furman's mother gaped at him. "What in the hell—?"

Larx scowled at her but spoke to Eamon. "You didn't tell her? Nobody told her what this was about?"

Eamon shook his head. "No, sir. We were waiting for CPS—and they're on their way—but, well, officers in the hospital, dead racists with guns, and snow."

Larx took a deep breath and tried some compassion. "Do you care about your daughter, ma'am? Even a little? Because we're trying to find her, and at this point, knowing whether she had enough money for a bus ticket or a train ticket could mean all the difference in the world."

"My husband will find her," Mrs. Furman replied, and Larx tried hard to remember what her name was from the file he'd read.

"That's our biggest fear, frankly," Larx said, dropping his voice. "May we come in?"

The woman regarded them both with unfriendly eyes. "That thug killed my stepson," she snarled. "Why is he even still working?"

"Because he's an elected official, ma'am. Unless there's an investigation by the US Marshals, he's not obligated to turn in his gun or any of the things you see on television. Now, your stepson shot an officer—and damned near shot me, since I was sitting outside in the police unit. The officer made it because he was wearing a vest, but your stepson opened fire on two peace officers in close quarters. There was no good way out of that situation the minute he pulled the gun. We are sorry for your loss, but your daughter is out there—aren't you the least bit afraid for her?"

Marie. That was it. Marie Furman dropped her eyes to the brown-haired blue-eyed girl standing a little behind her. The girl was small-boned, like her mother, and sported the same narrowed eyes and tightened lips. Larx remembered his and Eamon's conversation about one daughter getting the good grades and the other acting out.

Larx could see rebellion in the young one—he thought they could work with that.

"God will help us find my baby if she's meant to be found," Marie Furman muttered.

"But maybe God wants you to help!" Larx protested. "Lady—your daughter is afraid and in pain—"

"Then she shouldn't have run away!"

Larx shook his head. "Sometimes there are bigger things out there than we know of. Sometimes we think we're looking at our kid, and it's really like looking at a seal in the ocean. The seal is cute, and it's familiar, and underneath there's frickin' Jaws ready to come up and eat it. Your kid's shark was…." This was going to be rough. "Ma'am, she had all the behaviors of a victim of sexual assault—"

"Are you calling my daughter a slut? My baby does *not* get nasty like that!"

"We don't think it's her idea, Mrs. Furman. We think she was forced. She had all the behaviors—in fact, if last night hadn't happened, we would be having a very different conversation today. Your daughter was *planning* to run away. Do you understand that? The only way she could have survived last night's storm is that she was *prepared*. She was wearing all-weather gear, flannel long johns, and knew how to build a snow shelter—"

"She was just a little girl—"

"She taught me how," Shelley blurted.

Larx smiled at her. Thank God. "Yeah? Was it warm?"

"It was weird. She insulated it—like, an old sleeping bag on the bottom and a small fire—like those fires in a can? She used a cat food can and grease. Wanted me to play in the shelter like a fort."

Larx and Eamon exchanged a hopeful glance. "Warmer than you expected, wasn't it?" Larx suggested.

"Yeah." Shelley moved closer, looking at him earnestly. "She didn't like Braun. Said his breath smelled like the cat box."

"What about your stepdad?" Larx asked. Above them, in grown-up land, Mrs. Furman made a sound of protest, but Eamon cleared his throat.

"He spanks us." Shelley's voice dripped resentment. "Sometimes with sticks. But Braun—he's who she didn't like the most. Told me to stay away from him. She'd find a way to hide us." Shelley sent her mother a fierce look. "I told her I'd stay safe until she came back."

Marie Furman backhanded her, rattlesnake quick, and Shelley went flying backward. Larx went to pick her up, and Eamon snapped cuffs on Marie before the little girl could even stand.

"She's lying," Marie Furman snarled, struggling against the restraints. "Her stepbrother was a good man, like his father!"

Larx grunted. "I'm done with you," he said, high on hope and fury. "Eamon, can we hand her off to the patrol car and get CPS here if we have to teleport them? I'll stay here with Shelley—I have some more questions I want to ask."

"Where are we going?" Shelley asked, wiping the blood off her split lip with more poise than Larx would have had.

"Well, that's going to depend on Child Protective Services when they get here," Larx told her frankly.

"So we don't have to live here anymore?" Hope and fury—Larx recognized the sound.

"No. But we still need to find your sister." They could find her, he thought, able to breathe for just that moment. She'd prepared—even better than Larx had hoped for. "Shelley, while Sheriff Mills gets your mother to the nice police officers waiting outside, do you think you could show me your sister's room?"

"Wait until I get back inside," Eamon cautioned. "You need to stay in this room—understand me, Larx?"

Larx nodded. "How about we sit at the table. Shelley, go fetch me some crayons and some paper, okay?"

Shelley ran off even as her mother protested.

"You can't stay in here with her! Aren't you that gay teacher? You're not allowed near little kids!"

"I'm a principal, Mrs. Furman. Being near kids is my job. And you just—" He shook his head. "How could you just do that?" he asked, baffled. "That's your daughter—how does she even respect you if you just haul off and hit her like that?"

Mrs. Furman's gaze was flat and unfriendly, and Eamon tugged her toward the door. "Don't ask," Eamon said softly. "You can't fix this, Larx. Work on getting information from the little girl."

Shelley came running back in, paper and crayons in hand, and Eamon took Mrs. Furman out to the chilly police car.

Larx realized his hands were shaking. Maybe they'd never stopped since that morning outside Aaron's room.

He sank into a solidly built chair at what looked to be a new kitchen table and stared at the new tile floor. One of those slate floors—he sort of dreamed about them sometimes, because his floor had a hole in the tile that grew a little wider every day. He hid it meticulously with a rug—Aaron and Kirby had been moving Kirby's bedroom set in before they kicked the rug aside and saw it. Aaron had cheerfully put "tile floor" on his list of spring things to do, and when Larx had rolled his eyes and said, "Hello, kids in college!" Aaron had reminded him that they were splitting expenses now.

And then he'd kissed Larx while the kids had finished moving Kirby in.

For this quiet moment, in a stranger's cold kitchen, a yawning pit opened up at Larx's feet, and he fought to stay on the edge before it.

"Are you really dirty?"

Larx pulled his attention to Shelley, who stood uncertainly at the entrance to the kitchen.

"I sort of need a shower," he confessed. "But I spent last night in the hospital because someone I cared for got hurt. Why? Can you smell me from there?"

Shelley giggled. "No—because my mom said you were dirty. Nasty dirty. Like what Braun did in Candace's room."

Larx swallowed. "I'd never do those things to a child," he said, meaning it with all his heart. "Somebody should have protected Candace. That wasn't right."

Shelley looked away. "Mom said she was lying. All women lied, and Candace was wicked like all women."

"That's not true," Larx said reflexively. Part of him was thinking about his daughters, about Aaron's daughters—about how even when they weren't perfect, they were as honest as they could be—but only part. Part of him was remembering his sister, when she'd gone into remission, telling him that there were no guarantees. Most of him was appalled because he knew this doctrine, had heard a variation of it from students in his classes—and he was one person, one *man*, and he was helpless to combat it.

"Mom says so," Shelley said, eyes narrowed. Oh yes. The rebel. The only thing that had ever worked with Larx himself had been pure reason.

"Is that the same mother who just backhanded you?" Larx asked bluntly. "Because she's the one in a police car, not you."

Shelley's lower lip wobbled. "She... she said we had to do anything to keep Roy. Roy bought this house, he had a job, he bought us food. So we couldn't lie to make him mad, and... and she said Candace lied."

Crap. "Do *you* think Candace lied?"

Shelley shook her head, eyes closed. "Braun came into our room a lot. Candace told me to pretend I was asleep. He... he made her cry."

She looked ready to break—and Larx didn't blame her. "Here," he said gently. "You brought crayons. Come sit with me. Let's color and talk. You sit across the table there, and I'll sit here, okay?"

He wasn't a big man—five foot nine, maybe. But Shelley wasn't a big girl either, and he was pretty sure all men would be threatening at this point. She set the crayons in the middle of the table and handed him a piece of paper. He took it and waited for her to pick the first crayon before picking turquoise blue.

The color of Aaron's eyes.

He started coloring the sea.

"Is that other man going to come back in?" she asked. "The darkie?"

Larx bit his tongue. Literally. So hard he saw stars. "That's, uh, not polite. Eamon is black or African American. You can say that."

Shelley grunted. "I get afraid I'll say the wrong one. But you're right. That's a word Braun and Roy used."

"Well, if you heard them use it, maybe think about words that nice people use. But you may get it wrong. It'll be hard. Just keep trying."

Shelley bit her lip and kept coloring. "So, if I think girls lie just because they're girls, I should think about Roy saying that when he hit Candace last night?"

"Yeah," Larx said. He was using all the blue. He reached out blindly and grabbed the gray and the black. "So it was someone you didn't like, doing a thing you didn't like. Maybe his words were bad too."

"Huh." Well, hopefully she would have social workers, foster parents, teachers, *someone*, who would make her see the world in less awful terms. "So, you're not dirty, and the cop guy is black, and my sister wasn't lying." She looked at her picture—stick figures, doing what, Larx couldn't see.

Welp. "That about sums it up," Larx agreed. "And we're worried about your sister. Did Roy know Braun was hurt before he left the house?"

Shelley grabbed a red crayon and started to scribble all over her stick figures. "Yeah. He got mad, said he was going to fix the bitch who lied and got him dead."

"'Bitch' is another word you might not want to use," Larx told her, trying not to bang his head against the table.

Shelley wrinkled her nose and grabbed another crayon. "I really hate coloring," she said. "I do—and I usually use pens. I've got nice pens in my room. But... but I don't want to go in there."

"Why not?"

"The whole house is empty," she said, sounding like a child for the first time since Larx and Eamon came in. "These were on top. Is Candace okay?"

Big breath. "I hope so. I got really excited when you told me about how she lit a fire with grease in a can. Is her snow fort in the backyard still?"

He heard a soft noise at the door and looked up. Eamon walked in quietly and nodded, standing in the hallway and pulling off his stocking cap and gloves while Larx talked.

"Yeah—it's out by the big split tree. Do you want to go see it?"

Larx looked up at Eamon, who sighed and started pulling his gear on again.

"My friend Sheriff Mills is going to go see it. We don't need to go out into the yard again. Let's just sit here and color for a little while, okay?"

She sighed and put her scribbled-on picture to the side and then pulled a clean piece of paper and started to color again. This time she grabbed a green crayon from Larx's pile, and he let her. The red and black had been disconcerting, and he was hoping the color choice had been one of convenience, not psychosis.

"Fine," she muttered. "Are we going to talk about Candace some more?"

"Just one more question, then we can talk about anything you want."

"I *want* to talk about my birthday," she said mutinously. "Mom said we weren't celebrating our birthdays anymore because Roy said it was too expensive, but I was supposed to get a doll on my birthday, and Candace said she'd try to do that."

"She did?" Larx saw his opening. "Dolls cost money. Where would she get money for that?"

"Her friend," Shelley said casually. "Mom said we needed to keep to ourselves so we could come home and study the Bible. Do *you* study the Bible?" She eyed him with suspicion.

"Not so much." Honesty. It had worked for him so far.

"Good. Some of the stories are fun, but most of the time it's all about how women lie, and I'm bored with that." And then, maddeningly, she just kept coloring.

"So, which friend did she have who was going to give you money for your doll?"

"A girl in her class. I forget her name. But—" Shelley lowered her voice. "Do you know what she'll do if she doesn't get enough?"

"Not a clue," Larx whispered back. "Are you going to tell me?"

"She got a card from Braun's wallet on Saturday—when he came into her room. She told him she'd scream if he didn't give it to her, so he did. She told him she needed a… to do a thing. She just kept saying 'it.' And he needed to pay for it. So he did. When I asked her what for, she said it was to get me a doll."

Shelley smiled benignly. "I would really like a birthday party too, but a doll would sure be nice. One of those firefighter dolls? With the big thing to play on with the elevator and the policeman friend and the soldier friend—Mom would *never* let me get one of those."

Larx pulled out his phone. "That's a shame," he said, thinking fast as he pulled up a website. "I think every little girl deserves the doll of her choice." He knew those action figures—and this little girl had just given him and Eamon a ginormous clue. Screw new tile, he was getting this kid a doll for her birthday.

Eamon came in a few minutes later and gave him a look. "CPS is here—should I let them in? Two women."

Larx nodded.

"Shelley? There's some nice people here who want to take you somewhere safe. They're women, so we're going to let them help you pack so you can take your best things and your good clothes with you. Do you want to go start getting your stuff?"

Shelley looked up at him and smiled and yawned. "Sure. Are they going to feed me? Mom gave me oatmeal for breakfast, but it was a long time ago."

"Sure," he answered, smiling faintly. "It was really nice talking to you, sweetheart. You told me so much good stuff."

She shrugged. "You were nice for someone who was supposed to be dirty. I'll try to not use those words they used anymore. Only people who are nice to me get to give me words."

She strode off to her room then, and Larx rubbed his temple with his fingertips.

"That kid is going to rule the world someday—we need to be really really careful what we teach her in the meantime."

Eamon stared after her. "Word. Now tell me what you got."

Larx pressed the final key on his phone for Pay-Pal and took a deep breath. "She's not going to Dog-patch—she's got her stepbrother's credit card, and I'm going to take a big leap here, so bear with me."

"Shoot," Eamon said soberly.

"Braun was abusing her for months—the little girl confirmed that. I have no idea when her mom got married, but it was probably this summer, judging by the girls' grades and their complete lack of anything of note on their school records. So Mom marries funda-mentalist scumbag Roy Furman, and his son moves in on his fourteen-year-old stepsister."

They both paused to shudder.

"And then?" Eamon prompted.

"I think she's pregnant—Yoshi guessed it, be-cause she'd been gaining weight in the right places, and because where's she going to get birth control in Colton where the whole world wouldn't see her, right?"

"I don't even want to…. God."

"Yeah."

Two women entered at that point, both of them dressed practically in jeans and boots and parkas, but with visible accessories as kid-friendly as possible.

One woman had ducks on her scarf and the other a big bow in her hair, and both had average, sweet faces with real smiles.

"Where is she, Eamon?" the shortest of the woman asked—the one with the scarf. She had a bobbed blonde haircut and a brusque attitude, and Larx had worked with Carlene Collins before. He stepped forward with his hand extended in honest friendship.

"Carlene, Sandy—she's in her room packing. She may need some help—she seems really levelheaded, but every now and then she remembers that her house is empty, and it freaks her out."

Carlene nodded at Sandy, who set off for the bedroom.

"Anything else you can tell us?"

Larx recounted what he knew of Candace and Braun and what they'd seen the mother do.

"We've got some damage to fix, then," Carlene said when he was done. "Okay. Good to know. I'm going to go help them—will there be officers out front when we leave?"

"Yes, ma'am," Eamon said. "Larx and I need to go find the sister—she probably managed to survive the night, but we're not sure how much more luck she's got."

A look of weariness crossed Carlene's middle-aged face. "I hear you. Go, be careful. We'll wrangle this one."

"Uh, Carlene?" Larx said, not sure if this was even allowed. "If I bring a birthday present for Shelley to your office, you could give it to her, right?"

A sudden grin split Carlene's face. "Larx, you make my job a joy. Yessir—even if you send it our way, we'll make sure she knows someone sent her a birthday present."

Larx nodded, and then he and Eamon left quickly. Larx realized he'd never taken off his snow gear, not even his gloves when they'd been coloring, and the snow was a welcome, refreshing smack in the face to wake him up from the cranky doze he could have fallen into.

"So she's got a credit card and a mission," Eamon said as they got into the SUV again. "Where do you think she's going?"

"Foresthill," Larx said with as much certainty as he could muster. "She's going to want the train to Auburn so she can get an abortion—as soon as she possibly can."

"I don't blame her," Eamon said softly. "Jesus. Poor kid. That shelter in the backyard was really something. Sleeping bag, a bunch of those cans with the grease all burned out. I wonder how often she went out there just to get away." He put the SUV into gear. "Now call your kids, and then settle in for a nap. We've got two hours to Foresthill in the snow, and I need you fresh."

Larx grunted. "And food," he said. "When we get there, at the very least. Police hospitality is for shit."

Eamon chuckled. "You help us get this kid to child health and welfare without getting dead or getting to Auburn, and I swear to God, I'll buy you steak. And Aaron too."

Larx yawned and pulled out his phone. "That's a deal," he mumbled. "Christi? Yeah, hon. How you doing?"

"Good, Daddy. We're all sort of hanging out and eating—I hope that's okay."

"It's what snow days are for," he said. "How's Jaime?"

"Sad," she told him softly. "He really misses his brother."

"Tell Yoshi. Maybe he can do something about that. I just wanted you to know that Eamon and I are heading for Foresthill to check something out, okay? It's going to take a little while because of the snow, so don't expect me until later. And even then, when I get back, I'm—"

"Going to the hospital. Don't worry, Daddy. We know. Thanks for telling us. Yoshi's ordering pizza for everybody. He says he doesn't care if that's okay or not, that's what you get for stranding him in the house with five thousand teenagers."

Larx chuckled. "Tell Yoshi I love him too."

"Sure. You tell Aaron we love *him* when you're there. Be careful, Daddy."

Of course he would be.

SNOWSCAPE

LARX AWOKE and found that Eamon had parked the SUV in the shade and was nowhere to be seen. After a bit of frantic looking around, Larx realized they were in a small section of strip mall, which was sort of an unromantic phrase for the historic clapboarded businesses that made up much of Foresthill.

About the time he figured Eamon must have gone inside for food, he saw the man himself coming down the stairs from the raised boardwalk to walk across the parking lot with two big white bags in his hand.

And two coffees, because he was a man with his priorities straight.

Larx greeted him warmly when he slid in and took the hamburger with supreme gratitude. "Nobody's seen her?" Larx asked needlessly, mouth full of burger. Mm… this wasn't a frozen patty either.

"No—but we sent dogs from the shed out toward Foresthill, and they picked up her trail. About five miles through, overland, they found a snow shelter a lot like the one in the backyard. She made it through the night, Larx—she'll make it here."

Larx smiled, some of the tension in his back easing. "And I think her life science and geography teachers should get medals for that. Just saying."

"You make that happen," Eamon said with a smile before biting into his own hamburger. They ate in silence for a moment, and then Eamon spoke again. "I want Aaron to run for sheriff next year."

Larx took a hard swallow on the burger in his mouth. "You've said."

"I still want it. Even with the getting shot. Can you deal with that?"

Larx closed his eyes and let his body yearn. Yearn to be next to Aaron again, yearn to see him, even pale in bed, respirator working, telemetry beeping softly.

Aaron, in this job for another fifteen years, maybe twenty.

But then, Larx was here, working when he wanted to be with Aaron. Larx had gotten shot that fall—he'd been the one taking the risks.

"I hope so," he said softly, taking a sip of his coffee. "Maybe don't ask me right now. Ask me in two weeks, when he's home and driving me batshit and I need him to go to work before I kick him in the shins."

"Fair enough." Eamon took another sip of coffee and then stiffened. "Whup—there's our girl."

The town was little more than two hundred yards of businesses on either side of the street, with a train track in the middle, and their girl had just emerged from the shadows of the two buildings across the street. She had to be theirs—fourteenish, medium build, dressed in survival gear, and limping just a tad from boots that probably needed extra socks to fit.

Other than that, she looked a damned sight better than Larx would if he'd spent the night in the woods.

Yoshi had pulled up the girl's picture for them, and Larx had remembered seeing her in the halls. Appearance-wise, she was like her sister—brown-haired, blue-eyed, average chin, average cheekbones, no outstanding features, no super extra animation to make her memorable in a crowd.

But Shelley had been young and—relatively—untouched by the awfulness her sister had endured over the last few months.

Candace had purpose now. She didn't move like a little girl who had been lost in the woods for the past night. She moved like a survivalist who had *camped* in the woods, broken camp, and was heading for her intended destination and, to her mind, a better life.

God help anyone who got in her way.

Larx remembered what he'd said about her being armed against her stepfather—and took it back. "I'm going to talk to her," he said quietly. Eamon had gotten him two burgers, and he pulled the second one out of the bag, securely wrapped in white paper, and put it in the bag with the fries. "She knows me—I might not be trustworthy, but I'm certainly nonthreatening."

Eamon side-eyed him. "Yeah, Larx. That's what I think when I see you. Totally harmless."

"I know you think you're being sarcastic, but seriously, I don't see how."

Eamon just laughed, and Larx shook his head. God spare him. He was just trying to keep his kids alive.

"Watch my back," he said sourly. "If Roy Furman sees her, things could get weird."

He didn't slam the door as he swung out of the SUV, and he kept his stride nice and easy. Nothing to see here, just a guy who drove two hours through the snow to wander the boardwalk of a little ol' gold rush town. As he was wandering, he saw the train station across the road—and figured that's where she was going.

Traffic on the highway was pretty light, so he took his life in both hands and ran to the train platform, then over the tracks and across the other side of the road. His boots skidded a bit on the icy pavement, and he tried not to wipe out in the middle of the highway, because that would be a terrible way to die.

She'd disappeared into the train station just as he crossed over, and as he mounted the steps to the boardwalk, he heard the sounds of a car fishtailing into the almost empty parking lot he and Eamon had come from. He looked over his shoulder and saw a battered SUV, black, skidding to a halt in the middle of the lot. It must have done a donut because he was facing away from the Colton County Sheriff's unit, which Eamon had parked in the back corner, in the shade.

Eamon had shown Larx Roy Furman's driver's license picture—square jaw, narrow eyes, blocky build—and the guy reaching into his car, profile to Larx, looked very familiar.

Larx hurried to the train station and pulled out his phone in time to see Eamon's text: *Backup is on the way. Keep her inside.*

Awesome.

Larx entered the small historical station and looked around. The whole room was paneled in lovely stained wood, beveled to look vintage, and photos of the old train station as well as various antiques showing the elegance of traveling during the steam era dominated the room.

The teacher part of his brain was thinking Oh, I'd like to see the period clothing and the preserved china at another date.

Most of him was thinking C'mon, Candace, don't hate me because I'm your principal.

He heard her before he saw her. The office was tiny but thickly cluttered by the displays of the old-world train station. The rusty, trembling voice was obviously right by the counter, but the bearer of it was sheltered from view by a wardrobe of antique clothes. Listening to her, part of him was reassured. She'd done an amazing thing, and she had a strong will—but she was still a fourteen-year-old girl in need of help.

"Ticket," she was saying. "I'd like to purchase a ticket to Auburn. When does the train come?"

"Oh, honey." The elderly woman had salt-and-pepper hair pulled into a ponytail that curled perfectly, and she smiled benevolently, like this poor dear had just wandered away from her parents and needed some cookies before she went back. "I'm sorry—the tracks are blocked up by Donner Pass. The train's not coming from that way until tomorrow."

"But…." She took a shuddery breath and pulled the lapels of the oversized army surplus parka around her shoulders. The army/navy store was about a mile from school—he wondered if she'd cut class to go buy it. "I need to get out of here. Is the bus working?"

"Candace?" Larx said gently. "Candace, honey?"

The face she turned toward him was wary and exhausted.

"I'm not going back, Mr. Larkin," she rasped.

"There's nothing to go back to," he told her. "Your mother backhanded your little sister in front of the sheriff this morning—"

"Shelley!"

"She's going to be fine," Larx said, his mouth twisting. "CPS has her—nice women. I told them I'd send her a birthday present—"

"She doesn't want dolls like girl dolls," Candace said hurriedly, panic in her eyes. "She wants the—"

"Action figures with the kickass play structure." He let a grin slip out. "Your sister's sort of awesome. But your stepbrother was killed last night as you were getting away—"

She let out a little moan, and he thought her knees were going to give out. She propped herself on the counter. "Roy's gonna... oh God, he's gonna flip—"

Larx nodded and met eyes with the alarmed ticket saleswoman. "Ma'am, do you have a place we can, uh, hide?" He took his gloves off and shoved them in his pocket. This might take a few, and the office was pretty overheated.

The woman's eyes widened. "Hide?"

"Yes, ma'am—we need to be out of the way while the policemen do their thing."

"There's, uh, a little break room in the back here...." She opened the counter and gestured them behind it. Once there, a small hallway led to a restroom cubicle to the left, and following it back took them to a tiny room that reeked of cigarettes and held the circular stains of a thousand cups of coffee. Larx looked around hurriedly, seeing a broom closet, a metal table with a computer on it, and a counter with sliding cabinet doors underneath.

"Is it going to be dangerous?" the woman—Marion, by her name tag—looked at Larx unhappily, and Larx felt a little bit of guilt. Was this how Aaron felt, having a firefight go down in Berto's front room, with Berto weeping in the corner?

"Candace, has Roy even been to the high school? Any of the town meetings? Does he even know what I look like?"

Candace frowned. "No—he heard you were...." She swallowed. "Uh, gay, and sort of ranted a while. He and my mom got into a big fight over home school and then, well, he made her shut up about it and that was all, I guess."

"Awesome. Marion, you and Candace go back in the room and—"

The little bell on the front door tinkled violently as the door was thrown open. "Candace? Candace, are you in here? Did you think getting away was this goddamned easy?"

Larx shed his coat and pretty much shoved it and Marion in the room and mouthed, "Get in the closet!" to Candace. Then he shut the door calmly and walked toward the counter, a determined smile on his face.

"Hi, sir, can I help you?" He scanned the ledger in front of him and the antiquated computer and hoped fervently that Roy Furman did *not* want to buy a ticket.

"Where is she?" The man in front of him didn't look sane—his eyes were glassy and bloodshot, and his whole body reeked of whiskey the way the back room had reeked of cigarettes. In his arms he cradled a shotgun—Larx wouldn't recognize the make, but it looked old and it looked deadly, and that was all he needed to know.

Larx let his eyes get really big as he feigned ignorance. "Where's who?"

"That lying little bitch that got my son killed—where the fuck is she?"

"Sir, I, uh, haven't seen any women come in—"

"*Don't fuck with me!*" Roy Furman roared, and Larx took a frightened step back before he could decide if it was in character or not. Furman wasn't tall—maybe Larx's height—but his shoulders were incredibly wide. He had a brutal build—a wife-beater's build. He probably had a weight set that he used, every day, so he could do to Marie Furman what Marie had done to Shelley.

"I'm sorry, sir—I'm going to have to ask you to leave—"

Furman lunged forward, grabbing for Larx's collar, but Larx took another quick step back. "Get back here, asshole—you're gonna tell me where the fuck she is—"

Larx danced out of his reach again, thinking that if only Furman would overreach on the end, at the lift-up partition where there was no counter to catch his body and balance up against, Larx had him.

"I don't know who"—he dodged—"you're mad about"—he dodged again, heading toward the part of

the counter that lifted up. "But you really need to—"
Almost there. "Get hold of your temper!"

And Roy played right into his hands. He threw
himself forward, overbalancing on the end of the
counter, and Larx leaped forward, shoving at Roy's
shoulders hard until he toppled completely over, land-
ing on his head while his shotgun hit the floor with
a clatter. He was lying there, dazed and floundering,
when Larx picked up the gun and held it like he'd seen
them held in the movies.

"Stay right there, asshole," he snarled just as Eamon burst in the door, gun drawn.

"Took you long enough," Larx panted, aware that
his arms were shaking with the weight of the weapon. The bell tinkled again, and Deputy Hardesty came
through, weapon drawn.

"Everybody freeze!" he shrilled, and Larx
rolled his eyes. Percy—thirtyish, sharp cheekbones,
and thinning beige hair pulled back from a widow's
peak—was probably his least favorite Colton County
law enforcement officer, and Larx really wasn't in the
mood to deal with him now.

"Are you going to shoot me?" Larx snapped. "Or
could you maybe draw on the wife-beating motherfucker on the ground so Eamon can cuff him?"

"Mills, you gonna let him talk to me like that?"
Percy whined, and Eamon gave him a disgusted look.

"You are pointing the gun at the guy who just
risked his life to help us," he ground out through gritted teeth. "Can you show a little goddamned sense?"

Percy grunted and pointed his weapon at Roy instead of Larx. At that moment Deputy Coolidge came
in, weapon drawn as well, and Larx dropped the stock

of the shotgun, holding the barrel with one hand, perpendicular to the ground, and the other hand up.

"Warren, you want to take this weapon?" Larx asked wearily. "It's the suspect's."

"Thanks, Larx," Warren said with a vague smile. Warren—round-faced and blond with wide blue eyes—had always struck Larx as none too bright—which made Larx glad he was no longer partnered up with Aaron on a regular basis. But Warren did Larx a solid now and held out his hand for the gun, which Larx turned over gratefully.

Eamon cuffed Furman, who was still dazed and mumbling obscenities, and then pulled him to his feet and gave him to Percy.

"Take him to Auburn and put him in jail—file charges against him in Placer County."

"Placer?" Larx asked, crossing his arms in front of his chest to disguise his shivering. "Why?"

"Because it could be a big old jurisdictional mess," Eamon said grimly. "We're technically in Placer County, apprehending a solid citizen who was just looking for his daughter, and you know what? This guy could slip out of a loophole, given Colton County's resources to hold an extended trial. I'm giving him to Placer and keeping the girls so they can maybe go back to school with their friends. That way he's far out of their lives. You like?"

Larx couldn't follow it all. "I think it's a start," he said, shaking harder with adrenaline. "Eamon, is this… is this normal?" If he hadn't just thought the room was overheated, he could swear it was freezing.

Eamon grunted. "Son, you're going into shock. This has been one hell of a day for you, hasn't it?"

Larx nodded, still shaking. *I want Aaron*, he thought disconsolately. *I want him so bad.*

"Okay—go fetch your coat, fetch the girl, and we'll head back. I understand they're holding a cot at the hospital just for you."

Larx's eyes burned, tearing up and watering over. "Sounds awesome," he muttered. "I'll be right back."

Candace rode back with them in the SUV, devouring the extra burgers and fries that were still in the unit. She told them pretty much what they'd suspected between bites, including the extent of her outdoor training, which she recounted with justifiable pride.

"I stayed warm all last night," she said, mouth full. "I could have done it again tonight, but…." She bit her lip. "I got so hungry. Power bars may be good for you, but damn, they don't keep you full. Not when you're…." She looked away.

"Candace, I'm pretty sure they won't make you stay that way for long," Larx said softly.

She nodded, wiping her eyes with the back of her hand. "That would be…. I don't want it. I hate it. I hate how it got there. I just… oh God. Mr. Larkin, last year, I was so worried about going to high school. I wanted to go to a dance with a boy so bad. And now? Now I just… I want to go to bed at night and not be afraid."

She broke down then, and Larx had Eamon pull to the side of the road so he could sit in back with her and hold her as she cried.

She fell asleep on him, about an hour from Colton. Larx waited until he thought he could talk without sounding broken and called Yoshi.

"Yosh? We found her. She's… well, she's okay, but—"

"Not okay. I hear you. We got lots of that going around."

Larx closed his eyes. "Do you need me there? I...." *I want to go see Aaron.*

"No. Tane and Berto came by for five minutes—long enough for Berto to hold his shit together and tell Jaime he was okay. I sent them to the hospital with a change of clothes for you so everybody else could stay in their jammies. We've got pizza, milk, and green vegetables. We'll be fine."

Larx nodded. Good.

"I'll be at the hospital, then," he said gruffly.

"Good job, boss. Way to principal, since you can't adult."

Larx chuckled—for some reason, that was way funnier than it should have been.

"Larx?"

"Yeah?"

"You sound unhinged. Go sleep next to your boyfriend. It just... makes things better."

Larx couldn't argue.

He had a few more hours to go, though—it was dinnertime when Eamon finally left the police station to take Larx back to the hospital. In the interim they'd gotten Candace safely lodged with Colton County CPS, filed charges against Roy Furman for child endangerment, assault, and brandishing an unregistered firearm, and filed more charges against Marie Furman for child endangerment and abuse. The last Larx had seen of Candace and Shelley, they were holding each other tightly in the back of Carlene's little Honda, on the way to their house so Candace could get some clothes to stay with a foster family.

She'd hugged Larx before they'd taken her, and he'd hugged her back.

"Tell Mr. Nakamoto I'm sorry," she said. "I know he was trying to help me the other day, but I didn't think he could."

Larx nodded. "He's just glad to know you're okay. He was really worried."

She'd cried a little more, and Larx wished fiercely for his own daughters.

He'd get there.

Right now he was just as happy to plod through the hospital with a bag of takeout in his hand as a parting gift from Eamon, and find Aaron's unit.

Aaron was sleeping, blond lashes fanning against his cheeks, full mouth pursed like he was working out a problem as he slept.

Well, they were both too old to sleep like children.

Larx slid out of his jacket and unlaced his boots, grimacing at the smell. Long, long day in last night's socks. He found a canvas tote by the coat hook and blessed and cursed Yoshi at the same time. He'd been expecting to find his moccasins, because that made sense if you were sleeping in a hospital, right? Instead, he found *Aaron's* moccasins, two sizes larger than Larx's, and Yoshi's Christmas gift to Larx the year before—Garfield slippers, because Larx's inability to function without coffee in the mornings was legendary, even to his colleagues.

Well, hell. He'd take 'em and be grateful.

If you couldn't laugh at Garfield after a day like today, you might as well cash it in.

There were two pairs of sweats as well, and Larx looked about hurriedly for any nurses before changing into one of them and then shedding one hooded sweat-shirt for the one in the bag. A shower in the morning—but right now, there was one thing he wanted, and one thing only.

The cot next to Aaron's bed was about two feet shorter than the bed itself, and that didn't do Larx any good at all. With a sigh he swung his legs over and laid his head on Aaron's mattress, running his finger gently over the back of Aaron's hand.

Aaron moved, stroking Larx's hair back from his forehead.

"Long day?" he breathed.

"Yeah."

"Tell me about it?"

"Later."

"What're you doing now?"

"Staying here. With you." Larx closed his eyes against the weak tears threatening to slip through.

"Good."

He kept his eyes closed, but they escaped anyway.

They kept falling until Larx fell asleep, Aaron's hand moving gently in his hair the whole time.

FRAGILE BEAUTY

OLIVIA BALKED at putting Elton in her dad's bed, but there was nowhere else for him to go.

And nowhere else for *her* to go either.

"I'll change the sheets," Christi offered, bags of exhaustion under her eyes.

"Why would you need to change the…?" Sometimes Olivia felt really dumb next to her younger sister. Christi just regarded her with that little twist to her eyebrow that begged Livvy to catch up so she didn't have to say anything that would make her feel bad. "Oh. Really?"

Christi chuckled. "They're super quiet about it, and we all pretend we don't hear. But yeah. Happens more than you'd think."

Olivia thought about it—not the act, because ew!—but about her father. Over Christmas, he and Aaron had always touched—bumping hips, hands on shoulders, heads on chests. It hadn't freaked her out—even if Larx hadn't been very up-front about being bisexual and what that meant, her first year of college would have opened her eyes to a whole lot. In fact, she hadn't noticed the touching much or thought about it—until this moment.

"Does it ick you out?" Olivia asked, curious. Her family home had become an alien ship in the last year and a half. She was literally asking her little sister how she should feel about this newly co-captained vessel, because she had no reference for herself.

Christiana's look was all scorn. "Oh my God— Livvy! He's a grown man! Besides." She bit her lip and looked around. "It's… it's comforting. The two grown-ups love each other. It's, like, way better than he was with Mom."

And just like that, Olivia was smacked in the face with her greatest fear, the thing that had haunted her into gnawing depression, the thing that had dogged her every thought of the sweet young man currently dozing in front of the television downstairs.

All her memories of her mother and father inter-acting were unpleasant—Dad would come home and go for a hug, and Mom would recoil and say things like "Get off me!" or "Geez, Larx, really? Now?"

Olivia remembered the look on his face—muffled hurt—as he'd tried to laugh it off.

Dad would bring home dinner—and her moth-er would cry because she took it as a criticism. He'd wash dishes to help out, and she'd yell that he was doing it wrong.

He'd sit down to play with the girls, and she'd looked relieved and angry, like he should have been taking that burden from her shoulders all along.

She never hugged them after day care or school, didn't play with them or talk to them while she was getting dinner ready, and seemed to resent him for not being there, all the time, to do the thing she hated worst to do.

He'd so loved giving hugs.

She and Christiana would hang on him at night, sit on either side of him to watch television, sit in his lap and play on his phone. Sometimes he would fall asleep next to them after reading at night, holding them close.

Her father had taught her how to feel safe—how to make touch safe. Her mother could have made her afraid, but her father, larger than life, charmed by her and Christi's every burp, fart, and giggle, made hugs and held hands and ruffled hair a healthy part of her day. She hugged her girlfriends without a thought, kissed them on the cheek and didn't worry about what it looked like. Held hands with boyfriends and platonic friends and new friends.

Her first lover—the high school boy before Elton—had told her when they'd broken up that he'd miss the way she cupped his neck when they were talking. He said she made him feel important, and he would hold out for that, whatever his next relationship would be.

Larx deserved someone who would touch him.

The thought haunted her for the rest of the day.

She let Christi change the sheets and went downstairs and tried to be responsible about making sure everybody had eaten and there was food in the fridge.

Kellan and Kirby she knew—had grown to know better over Christmas vacation, when everybody mooched around the house and played Monopoly and held Destiny events on the game system.

They were both very different—Kellan bouncy and restless in his body and guarded in his heart, and Kirby self-contained in his body but witty and cheerful in person. Together they seemed like brothers who should have been. They left each other alone when they needed it but could very easily play a game, watch a movie, or even tussle with the ginormous dog pretty much at the drop of a hat.

They were spending some time outside with the dog—and with Jaime, her father's personal stray—when she went downstairs.

She grabbed a spare coat hanging on the pegboard by the sliding glass door and put her slippered feet into her father's galoshes, which were sitting on the porch. The cold smacked her face a little, digging underneath what was probably Yoshi's parka, but for the first time since the previous spring, she felt what it was like to be warm in the cold.

"C'mon, Dozer—gonna get it! Gonna get it!" Kellan yelled, his short, powerful body literally springing up and down in the knee-deep snow. He waved a ball on a rope in front of the big blond dog, who barked in ecstasy whenever it swung near his face.

"Dozer!" Kirby called. "Dozer—c'mon, buddy! You know you want it!" Kirby was standing about eight feet away, a big fake ham-flavored piece of rubber in his hand. The dog turned around and ran toward Kirby, tongue lolling, to see what new wonder *this* boy held for him.

Jaime, who had been throwing a ball for the dog before Olivia came out, came tramping back toward the porch, shivering in a snow parka a little large for him and boots that looked just as large.

"Warm up," Olivia told him, smiling gently. The boy—all limpid eyes and frightened glances—looked cold and tired and out of place. Her father had taught her to project kindness—because that's what he did as often as he could. "I think Christiana started some hot chocolate. We can go inside in a minute and have some."

"You're not gonna torment the dog?" the kid asked, a brief crinkle to his eyes to show that he approved.

Olivia shook her head. "I'm more of a cat person." She thought sadly of Delilah. Every night over Christmas, she'd looked around for her furry Siamese goddess and every night she'd remembered that Delilah had passed away over Thanksgiving, and everything changed.

"I like them both," Jaime said, shrugging. "But dogs—we lived in an apartment in the city. All the dogs are little and yappy. Not real dogs, you know?"

"Now that you're here, you should get a big one," she suggested. She never would have thought a big blond dog—but then, she never would have thought a big blond sheriff's deputy for her father either. Maybe these were things that some people needed.

Jaime nodded, still watching the dog. "My brother—I think… I think a dog would make him happy," he said softly. "He needs a thing—a thing he can just love that doesn't need him to do anything but love it."

"And food," Olivia said, thinking about the giant bag of kibble that Dozer seemed intent on plowing through in giant increments.

"That dog can eat," Jaime agreed. "But see? He's so happy with kibble and some water, some scratches on the head. Berto—he tries so hard."

Olivia heard the hushed pain in Jaime's voice.

She was used to being the one in pain, the one with the list of prescriptions, of daily mantras. It took her a moment—a long moment, like lungs full of water—to remember how to react to someone else's pain.

"Why's it so hard for him?" she asked.

And it was like Jaime grew, he was so relieved to talk about it. His shoulders straightened, and he bit his lip. "He got hurt, really bad. He was in a gang—we lived in a shitty part of town, and, you know. Him being in a gang, it kept *me* safe. But then one day, his… I dunno, captain, asked *me* if I wanted to stand watch while two guys went and knocked over a store. I…. Berto always told me to tell him if that happened."

Olivia stared at him, terrified. All the things her father had worked with when she'd been a kid— they'd sounded scary then, but they were worse now.

"What did you do?" she asked.

"I told him. And he stood up to Cameron, and they said he had to let me join or he had to get out. So he said he was through with them and they jumped him. Just… beat the hell out of him, left him for dead."

Olivia held her hand to her mouth. "Oh God."

Jaime nodded, swallowing quickly. "I found him, you know? He told me to run, but I hid instead. I called an ambulance, put pressure on his worst bleeding. But… but when he got better, it was like, every minute, he was still in that knot of people, beating him up. And it's hard—sometimes I'm still hiding, watching him get hurt, but I remember we don't even live there anymore and I'm okay. He never remembers. He spends his every day trying to remember how to breathe like he's free."

"That's terrible," she whispered, her heart racing with anxiety. This wasn't even her stress! This wasn't even her life—but it was his. This boy who had just played with a big dumb dog until his hands were chafed with cold and his cheeks looked slapped.

"Yeah." Jaime took a big breath. "He smokes his own, you know? Doctors said it's okay. But that guy, he just ran into our house with a gun, and your dad told me to stay put and I did. That's what I do, right?" He sounded bitter, and she didn't blame him.

"It's not your fault," Olivia said, her voice thin in her own ears. "You didn't… you might have been killed. Aaron was in there, and he had a gun and a vest, and *he* was almost killed." Her heart clenched at that. Aaron had been there. He might have been new to the stepfather gig, but he was like Larx—Dad to his bones. And he'd been so decent about finding Elton, about not interfering in her business, about protecting Elton from her if she was too flaky to make her shit her own.

She swallowed, her world widening a little. It wasn't just her and her pain, or her and the growing life inside her—and her pain. It wasn't Elton, chasing after her like Don Quixote after a windmill and then turning into a true knight in shining armor when the giant bad thing was a tiny baby that would derail both their lives.

Aaron had been hurt—and she hadn't really seen it. Her father had been lonely for so very long, and she hadn't seen his pain.

And this boy, fragile and young—younger than Christi, or the two other boys in the yard—was afraid for his brother and trying so hard not to be alone.

With a sigh, she put her arm over his shoulders, waiting to see if he'd recoil. He didn't, relaxing against her with a sort of boneless grace.

"It wasn't your fault," she said again.

"My brother's in a bad place," he whispered. "He wasn't doing great before, but he's... he's so scared now. He texted me about an hour ago, and it was, like, ''sup,' and that's all. He... he loves me. I know it. But all he's got around him right now are big scary monsters, and he can't see me at all...."

And this boy—this stranger—cried in her arms. She stood for a moment, stunned, and then pulled him into a hug, remembering all the times her father had done that.

Including not four days ago, when she'd crashed through the front door with all her things and said she couldn't go to school anymore and she was moving home and hadn't given a single word of explanation.

Her father deserved some explanation.

But not now. Now he was out... what? Saving another kid like this one? Lost and alone and betrayed by the world at large?

Yeah.

That's what her father was doing.

He was *her* hero—she'd always known that.

But standing here, holding this kid as he came unglued, she saw how her dad, who could be so goofy, so comically unprepared for adulthood, could also be a hero to the world at large.

He never closed his arms if he could possibly help it. He went out and did what needed to be done.

Elton had gotten hurt, and all she could think about was Elton.

Aaron had gotten hurt, and they'd both made themselves think about a bigger world.

The idea was terrifying. She couldn't make herself brush her teeth some days. How was she supposed to extend beyond herself and help somebody else?

But she couldn't just leave this boy. He needed her. He needed someone who would hold him and tell him it would be all right—even if that person didn't know for sure.

Just like her father had when she and Christiana had been small. For the first time, she remembered those early days when they'd moved to Colton, and he'd been a single father and trying to convince both of them that he wouldn't desert them—not like their mother had. He wouldn't neglect them, suddenly finding them distasteful and tainted. He had worked long hours into the night—because he'd spent all their waking time together being everything he could for them. He'd made a game out of everything from eating their vegetables to saving money on the heating bill so they could *afford* the vegetables, so they would feel this, right here, this safety in the world.

Olivia had spent so much of the last few months obsessing about her mother, wondering if she was going to be just like Alicia, cold, distant, so immersed in her own personal pain that she lashed out at the people she should have loved most, that she'd forgotten the basic, most important lessons her father had taught her.

It all started with this right here.

It started with a hug when someone felt bad. A soft voice when someone was afraid. A safe haven when the scary monsters threatened.

It started with touch.

EVENTUALLY SHE shepherded Jaime and the other boys in. Even the dog had been played out and was content to flop on his pillow in the entryway, watching the people move around the kitchen and prepare him wondrous leftovers.

Olivia tended to the chocolate Christi had started, using the Larx method of throwing in all the things that made it tasty. Cinnamon? Yes. Nutmeg? A dash. Pumpkin spice? Sure. Some white chocolate cocoa— the last little bit in the canister? Perfection. And, oh hey, there were marshmallows, so everything was hunky-dory, right?

Yoshi was the one who pulled out two giant tubs of Cool Whip so they could pour the concoction over big fluffy pillows of fake cream and pretend sugar shock wasn't a thing.

Jaime drank his cocoa with them in the kitchen, laughing with the rest of the table when Kellan tried to lick a big dollop of cream off his nose, and Elton pretended to explain how he got high on hot chocolate, no alcohol necessary.

Yoshi had ordered pizza—in spite of the fact that Christiana and the boys had already started a stew in the Crock-Pot, and there were sandwich fixin's in the fridge—and everybody dug in cheerfully when it arrived.

Yoshi's boyfriend, Tane, arrived about ten minutes into the pizza, with Jaime's brother at his heels.

Berto looked like Jaime—pale skin, dark hair, dark eyes—but he looked like Jaime would if somebody had beaten him with a lead pipe at some point in his life—probably because they had.

His nose was squashed and sideways, and his jaw sported two or three lumps as well. His arm hung oddly at his side, his thumb twisting out at bizarre angle, and he walked with the measured limp of a man who would walk in pain for maybe the rest of his life.

He looked like he'd been crying for hours, and he held on to his little brother like a man hanging on for dear life.

"Come in," Jaime urged him. "Berto, they've got a dog. Just for a minute. We've got pizza—you can eat pizza and feed the crust to the dog and…." His voice wavered. "Come see that it's not awful here, okay?"

Berto nodded weakly, and Olivia gave the boys their distance. Yoshi tapped her on the shoulder when she came inside.

"Hey—could you go upstairs and get a couple of changes of clothes for your dad and Aaron? Maybe take your sister? He's having sort of a busy day today, and I think he's going straight to the hospital afterward."

Olivia yawned, ready for her depression nap. "Wow. Poor Daddy—this has got to really suck for him."

Yoshi nodded and looked compassionately at Tane. Tane—thin, bark-colored from the sun, heavily tattooed, and as lean as old shoe leather—had the same sort of weariness around the eyes that Berto did.

With a shock, Olivia realized that Tane wasn't okay inside either. Uncle Yoshi—cheerful and sarcastic and so damned capable—had always worshipped

Tane, but Tane had never been part of their circle. Olivia had never even wondered why until now.

Now she knew why.

He'd been shattered too, just like Berto.

A little bit like her.

"Yeah," Yoshi said after a moment of communing with his beloved. "Bad day all round. So if you could go get him some sweats and some toiletries and slippers—they'll let him shower at the unit, and he can stay with Aaron tonight, make sure he's all good."

Olivia nodded. Suddenly, fiercely, she wanted Aaron to be all good not just for Aaron, or for his son, or even for herself, so she didn't have to endure the labor of grieving.

She wanted Aaron to be okay for her father, because Aaron was to her father like Yoshi was to Tane: the glue that held them together.

"I'll grab Christi," she said.

It was Christi's idea to put the Garfield slippers in the bag.

"In the hospital?" Olivia asked, sounding way too grown-up, even to her own ears.

"Livvy, if there's any place in the world that you need cheering up in, it's the hospital. Trust me. We spent, like, a week there in the fall when Kellan's boyfriend got hurt—people saw my purple Snoopy pajamas, and it was like they'd never seen the sun before. If it's quirky, keeps you warm, and is brightly colored, people need to see it."

"Ugh," Olivia said, looking at her father's hooded sweatshirt drawer. "That is the opposite of his clothes collection. You'd think now that he has a boyfriend, somebody would buy Dad some purple."

Christiana regarded her with deep disgust. "It's
like you've never met your own father."

Olivia eyed Christi dispassionately—her sister
could be a total stinker, and everybody knew it. "Don't
tell me you didn't think it. We've lived in Colton too
damned long for our thoughts not to have redneck
non-left-wing overtones."

Christi smirked. "I gave him purple socks for Val-
entine's Day," she said, smiling so hard her chipmunk
cheeks popped out. "I couldn't resist. It's like when
Schuyler bought me overalls for Christmas." She
sighed. "I'm gonna miss Schuyler."

Olivia swallowed. Sure, a high school breakup
wasn't the end of the world—but Olivia remembered
when it felt like it was.

"Sorry about the breakup," she offered tentatively. "I wasn't really… in a place to hear about it when
I got here."

Christiana reached around her and grabbed a stan-
dard gray hooded sweatshirt, two pairs of white socks,
and a couple of pairs of undershorts. "Well, when you
pull your head out, come talk," she said frankly as she
was stuffing the clothes in a canvas bag. "I miss you."

Olivia wouldn't let herself get defensive about
that—she figured she'd had it coming. "I promise."

Christi looked around the bedroom again. "Want
to grab some more pajamas for Aaron?"

Shrug. "Sure." It would make Larx happy. Olivia
was all about that.

BERTO AND Tane stayed for about twenty minutes, and Jaime managed to get him to eat a slice of
pizza and sit on the dog pillow while petting the dog

for a good long time. When they left, Berto was probably wearing half a coat of big blond dog on his jacket—and Dozer wasn't going to move until absolutely necessary. Ever.

When they were gone, Jaime gave her a beaming smile and wiped the back of his cheek with his hand before going to the kitchen to help clean up.

His brother wasn't okay—but he had help. He'd eaten pizza, he'd petted a dog—Jaime would take that hope and cling to it.

Olivia found she was in the mood to do the same.

Elton had gone back into the living room and was channel surfing dispiritedly in the recliner. She walked in to him and took his free hand.

"Hey," she said, keeping her voice quiet. "El?"

"Liv?" His smile was tentative and hopeful, and she realized with a pang that she'd rebuffed him pretty hard these last few months, while yearning equally hard for his kindness, his quirkiness, the way his blue eyes took in the world with unexpected wonder.

Had she become so selfish in her pain that she inflicted it on other people, like her mother had with Larx?

She sank to a crouch in front of him and took his hands. "My sister got Larx's bed ready for us. Don't get too comfy—I can see the snow plow on the forestry track from here, so we'll probably be moving into Aaron's house tomorrow."

"We?" he asked wistfully.

Oh. "Well, yeah." She brought his knuckles to her lips and kissed them, letting the affection she'd kept so bottled up escape. "I've missed you since Thanksgiving. If you… if you want me, after all this—"

"Oh, I do." He nodded earnestly, and she couldn't help it. She laughed.

"Good," she said softly. "I'm… I'm still sad inside, El. I'm still lonely. And I need to talk to my dad, and maybe to a few other people as well. But…."

"But?"

She allowed her legs to fold, and she sat, resting her head on his knees. "I care about you. So much. I care about this baby. I'm scared. And I hurt. But there are so many big things to be scared about—so many worse ways to hurt. I want to get help. But I want this baby, and I want you in our lives. Can we try that?"

"Come here," he said, his voice thick.

She climbed into his lap, because he was still bigger than she was, and she rested her cheek on his shoulder. His arm around her reminded her what safety was, reminded her that people could be kind, could fill in the empty places in your soul.

"I love you," he whispered into her hair.

"I love you back," she told him, and giving him the words felt liberating. She no longer had to trap them against her chest, afraid they'd die if she set them free.

They wouldn't die—they'd heal.

And Elton deserved healing too.

PATCHES OF SKY

LARX STAYED two nights in the hospital with Aaron, but on Thursday morning school started up again, and he was needed.

He kissed Aaron goodbye early in the morning, eyes bright and shiny and lips soft on Aaron's temple, promising to come by in the evening with kids in tow.

Aaron was looking forward to seeing the kids again—but dammit. He wanted some time with Larx, because the last two days felt like he was missing something—something big, important, life-changing, but Larx was the only one who knew what it was.

How did that happen? How did Aaron get shot and Larx get the life lesson to go with it?

The thought buzzed through Aaron's head most of the day as he read from the tablet the kids had brought by the day before and flipped dispiritedly through daytime TV. Larx had authorized him three new movies through the tablet, but he knew he didn't get to go home until Sunday, and he wanted to save them for a time he wasn't irritated and pissed off.

Something was wrong.

Eamon stopped by around lunch, and Aaron relaxed for the first time in two days.

"How you doing, son?" Eamon asked kindly.

"Peachy." Bitterness dripped from his voice and pooled around the bed, but Eamon only laughed.

"Pissed off yet?"

"Bored as fuck. I need to learn to knit."

Eamon tilted his head back and laughed, and something about the sound pricked Aaron's antennae. Eamon wasn't in a good mood either.

"What's up?" Aaron asked quietly.

Eamon shrugged. "I… I thought I was leaving you with a good house," he said after a minute. "Next year the election comes up, I shoo you in, and I leave Colton safe and protected. Georgie and I take a few vacations and come home to a good place."

"This is a good place." Aaron had to believe it, but Eamon shook his head.

With a sigh he ventured into the room, unzipped his jacket, and sat, knees spread, elbows balanced on knees, hat in his hand. "I… my house is not in the order I thought it was. I thought the town could deal with you as sheriff and it would be not a problem—"

"Second thoughts about me?" Until he said it, Aaron hadn't realized how much he wanted the job.

"Hell, no." Unequivocal, Eamon's denial settled Aaron's stomach a little. "I just… I guess this is a preemptive apology. I can't fire Percy Hardesty for you. Dammit—I looked at ways to try, and the most I could do was write an incident report and put it on his record. I can't demote Warren from deputy to… I don't know… paper pusher. I can't sway the next election so that miserable woman Larx has to deal with on the school board can go the fuck away. I… I wanted to leave you a good house. And it's sound—I believe it to my bones. But it's not what I wanted."

Aaron swallowed against the ache in his ears, the lump in his throat. "Nobody can unfuck the whole world at once, Eamon. You did your best. What did Percy do now?"

Eamon laughed a little, his eyes still fixed on his hat. "Your boy said almost the same thing, do you know that? Except Larx—he wanted to know which job would unfuck it quickest."

Aaron smiled, wanting Larx—the real Larx, not the super sweet, super competent nursemaid who'd been there for two days—next to him again. "That's easy. His."

Eamon's chuckle was a little richer this time. "That's what I told him." He sighed. "Right before Percy drew down on him."

Aaron knew better than to try to sit up quickly, but he did it anyway, and his whole body hurt. "The fuck? Why were weapons even needed?" He fell back against the pillows and caught his breath. "What happened?" he finished weakly.

The look Eamon shot him said important things about how much Larx *hadn't* been talking. "Did he tell you what happened the other day?"

It was Aaron's turn to frown. "He said you found the girl at a train station. Why?"

Eamon stood up and scowled, then whipped out his phone and texted rapidly. When he was done, he sat back down and gave a grim smile.

"Uh…." Aaron wondered what he'd just said to whom—because Eamon was not the semidefeated man he'd just seen. This man was grumpy and irritated and ready to go kick some asses and take some names. "What happened? You guys found her at the train station and took her to CPS, right? Why would Percy even have his gun out?"

Eamon's chuckle held an edge to it. "Oh, Aaron. Let me tell you the story of a man named Larx…."

Aaron took a deep breath—as deep as he could manage with his healing lung and the cannula, anyway. "I am not going to like this," he muttered.

"About as much as Larx liked you getting shot."

"Oh my God—what happened?"

Eamon shook his head. "Son, I don't know who you thought you were sleeping with when you took on your mild-mannered principal, but I'm telling you, you got a superhero instead."

Aaron closed his eyes. Superheroes were fun to talk about but had lousy love lives. If Larx's saccharine withdrawal over the last few days told him anything, it was that Aaron was hospitalized proof.

"Hit me," he said grimly.

Twenty minutes later the nurse came in because his respiration was elevated and his heartbeat was racing. And he had still not found words.

When he'd stopped gasping for breath, he managed to put a few together for at least one of the thoughts racing through his mind.

"Tell Percy—" Gasp. "—if he draws on Larx again—" Gasp. "—I'll kill him."

"Sure, Aaron. That's the takeaway here."

Aaron glared at him.

"Aren't you going to ask why he didn't tell you?"

Aaron shook his head. He knew why Larx wouldn't tell him. Aaron was *stuck in the hospital*, and Larx couldn't do a damned thing about it. Why would Larx tell him about battered children and an asshole with a gun—*two* assholes with guns—when there wasn't a damned thing Aaron could do about it?

Larx didn't tell Aaron about his day for the same reason Aaron hadn't told his wife about *his* days.

For the same reason Aaron had fallen apart when Larx's arm had been grazed back in October.

Because love should be a straightforward thing, but sometimes it was like a nautilus—a thousand chambers of pain and denial until you got to the heart of the love.

EAMON LEFT shortly after that, and Aaron fell into a restless, fitful sleep. When he woke up, his daughter Maureen was there, and so were Kellan, Kirby, and Christiana.

"No Larx?" he asked, disappointed.

"Told you," Kirby said, holding his hand out for money.

Christiana dug into her purse, saying, "It doesn't mean he wanted to see Larx *more* than you. It means he wants to see Larx *as much as* you."

Maureen chuckled weakly, looking strained. "As long as he wanted to see me," she said primly.

Aaron smiled. "Of course. What brings you home from school?"

"My father. Apparently he got shot. How you doin', Dad?"

I'm missing my boyfriend, which sounds stupid, because we're getting near fifty and too old for this boyfriend shit. "I miss home," he said.

"Well, I'd say home misses you, but mostly I think it's just Larx."

Aaron clasped his daughter's hand. "Larx has been here," he said. "I'm glad you came."

"You gotta be careful," Maureen said softly. "Can't take chances—Olivia's gonna make you a grandpa. And she's going to be right by—aren't you excited?"

Wow. His daughter. Of course, Christiana had dealt with getting two brothers in the span of a month—but still. Maureen's reaction to giving her childhood home over to Larx's daughter was more than he could hope for. "You okay with that?" he asked, crossing his mental fingers.

"Peace Corps," she said softly. "I think after graduation this year, I'm out of the nest for good."

That hurt. "I will so miss you." Tiff was the princess, Kirby was his sarcastic son. Maureen had always been his firefly—practically bright, whimsical, and necessary, a light in the darkness.

"Well, not for a week," she said softly, kissing him on the forehead. "I'm here to take care of you during the day while everyone else is out."

Oh. Aaron's chest felt tight, but in the good way. "I don't go home until Sunday," he said. "But God, I'll be glad to see you." Then he frowned. "Where will you sleep?"

"In my room, like Olivia did before she was Mrs. Wombat." Christiana's chirp made Maureen laugh.

"We're comparing fathers—it's become our new hobby."

"She got the best one," he said. "Sorry."

Maureen's green eyes got shiny. "We told Larx, and that's exactly what he said. We decided it was a tie."

Aaron closed his eyes. "Somebody say something not mushy. I'm injured. Take pity."

"Sure," Kellan said, sitting at the foot of his bed. "Jaime broke your dog."

Kirby chortled. "Oh my God, he so did!"

"You will explain that." But he knew it wasn't serious.

"So," Kellan said, bouncing just a little—but Aaron could take it today when the day before it would have been uncomfortable. "Jaime is… well, the dog is his therapy, and that kid has needed a *lot* of therapy. So Jaime spends *hours* playing with the dog—in the snow, in the living room, on the porch. They tussle, they wrestle, they cook, they bake—you name it. And Dozer—you think he's a dog, he can take it, right? 'Cause he's a baby and he's got, like, tremendous dog powers of energy, right?"

"Not so much," Kirby said, pulling a chair out and straddling it. Christiana took Larx's cot—still set up next to his bed—and pulled off her shoes to sit cross-legged. He felt like the queen bee at a slumber party as Kirby picked up the thread. "So, this is, like, Thursday—three days. This dog has been enduring three days of this shit, right?"

"Course," Aaron acknowledged.

"Anyway," Kirby continued, "Jaime got up early this morning and tore that dog up. I'm surprised Jaime could even stay awake in class, because I heard them at, like, six in the morning, and he was running circles in the backyard, and it's still up to his thighs back there."

"And we get down this morning," Christiana said, hugging her knees, "and Jaime is eating his oatmeal and the dog is, like, *passed out* in front of the door. He's so whipped he's even *in his dog bed*, if you can believe that!"

"That's amazing." It was—but this story, his children, was even better. Aaron wanted them to keep talking, keep spilling their energy over him.

"Right?" Christi bobbed without moving anything but her chin. "So we set him up with food and water, and Larx rounds us all up and takes us to school, and we get home and you know what?"

"Hasn't moved?" Aaron hazarded.

"We checked to make sure he was breathing," Kirby said—then shuddered. "That was a bad moment. I did not want to have to tell you that poor Jaime played our dog to death. Anyway, Maureen pulled in about ten minutes later, and he didn't even bark. Just sort of whimpered. Larx made him go outside to pee, and he did, 'cause he's your dog and he's good, but Jaime was, like, out in the backyard going 'C'mon, Dozer! C'mon boy!' and oh my God!"

"That poor dog, Dad," Maureen added, eyes twinkling. "I never thought I'd see a dog do this."

"What?"

"He said no!" Kellan burst out. "Jaime's going 'C'mon, Dozer!' and the dog shook his head, walked up the porch, pawed at the sliding glass door, and waited until Christi let him in. Then he found his bed and just *whumpf*. Like he was done with this crap, right? Peace. Out."

Aaron chuckled. "Poor Jaime."

"No," Christiana told him, sobering. "It was actually what he needed. Jaime's been… I guess *anxious* is the word. Olivia seemed to calm him down when she was there, but she moved out last night, and I don't think he slept at all."

"He didn't," Kellan confirmed. "He's on the floor in my room, and I got up to pee last night, and he just freaked out. I had to get down on the floor with him until he stopped shaking."

Aw. Oh man. Kellan—what a good kid.

"That must have sucked," Kirby said with feeling. "'Cause you still—"

"Had to pee." Kellan nodded. "Yeah. That wasn't comfy. I barely made it after he fell asleep. Anyway, he must have snuck up to go play with the dog this morning, because, you know—"

"No sleep," Christi confirmed.

"So anyway," Kirby continued, and Aaron had a moment to marvel. Larx called them his "haiku poem"—and they spoke a family language like they'd been born to it and hadn't found it the same way Larx and Aaron had found each other.

"Anyway?" Aaron prompted.

"Yeah, anyway, the dog comes inside and Jaime's a little sad, but he comes inside too, and he sits next to the dog. And we're all snacking and pretending not to listen but…." Kirby's voice dropped.

"This was sort of wonderful," Maureen said, her voice reverent too.

"It was." Christiana agreed. "He just starts… talking to the dog. He starts off saying he's sorry he broke poor Dozer, and then starts talking about being broken, and how hard it is to sleep when you're broken, and how you had to feel safe when you slept. And then he just kept going. We all just sort of sat down at the table and ate, and he just… just kept talking. And I don't know if he knew we were listening, but his voice got lower and lower, and by the time Larx came downstairs all changed, he was… you know."

"Asleep," Kellan continued. "Jaime had just fallen asleep. Crashed. Next to the dog. The dog bed's pretty big and Jaime isn't, so they fit. Jaime just spooned the big doofus, and they slept."

"Oh." Damn. "Wow." Aaron felt a little watery after that. "You're right. That's amazing."

"So Jaime didn't really break the dog," Maureen added practically. "It's more like the dog, you know—"

"Fixed Jaime," Christiana finished. "It was magic."

"Well, for right now," Kellan said, sounding resigned. "Unless Larx says the dog can sleep in my room…."

"Knowing Dad, he's probably already moved the pillow," Christiana reassured him, and Kellan brightened.

"Awesome! Now I just have to…." He grimaced. "You know. Not step on the dog."

They all laughed a little, and Aaron suddenly understood. "That's why Larx isn't—"

"Here," Maureen murmured, more comforting than he could have imagined. "He couldn't leave—he wanted to. We could all see it. But that kid was asleep on the kitchen floor, and happy. He was afraid the kid would freak out if there wasn't someone he recognized there when he woke up."

Aaron felt a yawn coming on then and sort of wished he could have the dog as a nap buddy too.

"Don't worry," Maureen said, squeezing his hand. "We're going home soon. We just had to visit." Her voice tightened. "I needed to see you were okay for myself."

Aw. Mau. "Be here tomorrow?" he asked, hopeful.

"Until Larx gets off." The kids all met eyes. "I think you'll need to see him as much as he'll need to see you."

He nodded, reassured. Larx had a lot on his plate—and he had a lot weighing down his heart.

But he still loved Aaron—that hadn't changed.

THE EARTH BENEATH OUR FEET

WHAT LARX would forever remember about the day Aaron came home was how stilted their conversation was in the car at the beginning.

It struck him as… odd. Because talking—give and take, banter—that had never been their problem. It had, in fact, been their strength—right up until Eamon had texted Larx to *Dammit tell Aaron what happened*, and Larx had realized he never had any intention of doing just that.

"So, Jaime's doing better?" Aaron asked as Larx piloted the minivan out of the parking lot. Aaron had waited impatiently to get checked out, but they'd needed to bring an oxygen tank with them in case he had problems breathing, and that had taken time.

"A little," Larx said guardedly. "He actually spends a lot of time over at your place with Olivia and Elton. I guess they bonded, and he's not so overwhelmed over there. But when he's with us, he seems happier."

"How's Berto?"

Larx sighed. "Doing better. He's apparently sleeping better, especially if he medicates. One of the reasons he's so big on the marijuana medication is that he has no health insurance. I'd love to take him in to a professional, but it would pretty much financially cripple him and Jaime. Tane says he's doing okay, though. He comes by every day after work and spends time with Jaime and the dog. He's almost said hi to me twice."

Aaron chuckled like he was supposed to, but Larx was aware that his voice had a hard, plastic cadence because, dammit, there was something he hadn't told Aaron, and that was just unnatural.

"Is Mau fitting in all right?" Aaron asked, and Larx wondered if he had a checklist.

"Of course. I told you that Friday. Your daughter is brilliant and amazing—I mean, it doesn't surprise me because she's yours, but she's really sort of perfect."

"Says the father of Christiana."

"Yeah, and the father of the pregnant basket case living in your house."

Aaron rumbled disapprovingly. "And how's—"

"Don't ask," Larx said, feeling like his hard plastic was crumbling. "I mean, she seems okay, but she still hasn't made an appointment with a doctor, and Wombat Elton says she's eating and opening up a little, but she was really bad for a while, and I just…." Deep breath. "You know. I'm going to worry until she gets this whole sitch in hand. She's not better yet. Just… not."

"And school?"

"Oh my God, you're relentless!" Larx snapped. "Do you have, like, a list of our lives and you're marking off checks?"

"Pull over," Aaron snarled, and it was a good thing Larx had both hands on the wheel.

"What?"

"Pull over! There's a turnout here—you know it!"

Larx did what Aaron said, because he was surprised, and because Aaron was mad, and because God, he'd missed Aaron putting a capper on his mouth and his anxiety and the way the whole world seemed to overwhelm him sometimes. But how right was it to ask a guy who could barely breathe to make you hold your shit together?

The minivan skidded to a halt, because it had snowed again Saturday and not much had melted since, and Larx turned to Aaron with a mix of relief and frustration.

"Why did we—"

"Kiss me."

"Wha—"

"I can't move—*kiss me*."

Larx undid his seat belt and fiddled with the end, suddenly shy. "Aaron, we're, you know, we have a house and a bedroom and—"

Aaron reached out and tilted his chin sideways. "And kiss me, baby. You keep trying to make everything all right, and it's not. Kiss me, and then let's get honest."

Larx nodded, feeling tears threaten for the first time in days. He twisted his body, since Aaron was still healing, and turned so he could move into Aaron's space. He paused about a foot away and tried to meet Aaron's eyes. They'd let him bathe that day, and he smelled like his regular shampoo and only a little like hospital, but mostly like Aaron.

"Now kiss me," Aaron whispered.

Larx nodded and closed his eyes, touching lips and tentatively sticking his tongue out to trace the seam of Aaron's mouth.

Aaron opened for him easily, and Larx pushed inside.

His whole body went limp, like a noodle, at the sheer comfort of Aaron's taste.

He groaned and pushed farther, breath catching as Aaron welcomed him. Aaron lifted his arms and pulled Larx closer, until their chests touched, and Larx held himself stiffly because he didn't want to let his weight fall forward.

Aaron tightened his arms and insisted.

For a moment Larx was leaning against his broad chest again, relying on his strength. For just that moment, some of the burdens seemed to slip from his own shoulders, and he felt strong enough again—strong enough to face life, strong enough to care for his family.

Aaron was here, and he was helping Larx carry the world again, helping to bear the burden of a busy house and too many kids and grown-up responsibilities that frightened him and rendered him powerless and weak.

Larx didn't so much pull back as fall gently out of the kiss. His body wanted more—but Aaron had another week to go, if not longer. His soul was fed, just enough for the hard plastic wall to grow softer, pliable.

To let himself be real.

"Hey," Aaron said softly.

"Hey." Larx leaned his forehead against Aaron's before shifting sideways so he could rest his head on Aaron's shoulder.

"You want to talk about it?"

Larx let out a strangled laugh. So much irony here. Larx, the communicator, trying to hold all his feelings inside. "No," he said, then laughed some more. Aaron just ruffled his fingers through Larx's hair.

"I can listen."

"You're *hurt*," Larx said bitterly, and then cringed. "I mean, you don't dump all your problems on someone in the hospital or recovering from surgery. You can't even take a walk for another week—how do I…?" He couldn't even finish the sentence. His throat locked up, and his neck was stiff enough to crackle.

"Eamon's waiting for you to try to kill me with a frying pan," Aaron told him reasonably, and Larx pulled away long enough to give him a weird look.

"Do you mean from too much oil? Because usually I'm very veggie-friendly." He tried not to think of that one day hunting down Candace when he'd eaten meat and grease almost constantly. It had seemed like a coping mechanism—like the sugar, salt, and oil had fed his exhausted self.

"No, like she tried to take his head off with it," Aaron said, rolling his eyes. "Because he was hurt, and she was left to deal with the house alone. And she didn't have three… five… seven? Oh my God. You had *seven* kids—"

"They're mostly grown," Larx said weakly, because his head had been spinning since Wednesday and he hadn't wanted to whine.

"Who cares. Seven relatives, period. But you had Olivia and Wombat Willie and Jaime, and then Mau showed up—I mean, Jaime's sleeping on the floor, for Christ's sake. I'd be pissed at me if I was just late from the market with all that bullshit going on—but it wasn't just that. I was *hurt*, and you had to leave me to deal with that!"

Larx grunted, the touch of Aaron's words like the touch of his tongue on a sore tooth. He knew—he knew the places that ached, but he wasn't trying to drive a spike into them either.

"It's like walking into a rabbit warren," he admitted. "They just keep multiplying. It's like, if Jaime hadn't broke the dog—"

"Still?"

"Well, it's not so bad after Dozer said enough that one day. But yeah—he's still being a therapy dog, which is fine. Anyway, it's a godsend because the dog isn't spazzing out." Oh wow. Was it only a week ago? A week ago Olivia had brought her problems right into Larx's lap, and the spazzing dog had seemed like the end of the world.

Life had a quirky little way of putting *that* shit into perspective.

"Are we going to keep Jaime?" Aaron wouldn't judge—but he only knew the kid by name at this point.

"Jaime and his brother need each other," Larx said, reluctance in his voice. "But… but I don't know where they'll live. Tane has brought Berto by every day to care for his…." He couldn't help it. He smirked.

"Garden. But they have to go in through the back way. We all went in and cleaned up the broken furniture and repainted the walls and used remnants to replace the carpet in the house—everyone helped, even Yoshi."

"He hates physical labor," Aaron said encouragingly.

"I know. He seemed to think it was a dire thing. But this morning Tane called. He said he brought Berto by again, and Tane had to go inside. Berto just sat in the car and hummed to himself."

Aaron grunted. "Well, I guess we could rent out the bottom half of *my* house. I mean, I'm not crazy about growing pot in the old chicken coop or wherever, but we could do it."

Larx looked at him, irritated and warmed at the same time. "He'd pay rent," he said, because that had been part of the discussion. "And you're a really nice guy—and I think he and Jaime have felt really cut off here. I think having… you know, cousins or whatever, that would make them happy. And eventually Berto might be able to get another place."

"But it's a painful situation, and I left you to deal with it alone," Aaron said perceptively.

"Augh!" Larx buried his eyes against Aaron's shoulder. The inside of the car was getting cold without the motor running, but this time, this absolute quiet time, was such a treasure, such a wonder for the two of them, that he didn't want to start the car up. Starting the car up meant plunging back into the whirlpool again, back into the raging surf of people who seemed to need them. "It's *irrational* to be angry at you!"

Aaron's rusty chuckle warmed his stomach. "Larx—love is irrational. Teenagers are irrational. Dog therapy shouldn't make a damned bit of sense. But it does. Don't fight it. You're pissed. You're going to be pissed. About the only thing I can do about it is—"

"Fight back," Larx said, hating the truth. "Because if you give me nothing but 'Yes, Larx, you're right, Larx, I love you, Larx,' I can't be held responsible for what I do to you."

"Hide all the frying pans," Aaron said gravely.

"Hide all the pointy objects," Larx shot back, voice grim.

"Okay—fine. You want me to fight back?" And Larx's stomach clenched, because Aaron sounded like he meant business.

"Hit me." Larx's eyebrows were knitting so hard his head hurt.

"The train station."

And suddenly they unknit, and his eyes were all big and butter couldn't melt in his mouth. "What about it?" he asked benignly.

And Aaron's eyebrows looked like they were making a sweater. "You gonna tell me?"

"Nothing to tell. Girl tried to buy a ticket."

Aaron pulled away from him. "God is going to strike you down for lying, you faithless heathen! Holy Christ! Did you think Eamon wouldn't tell me?"

"Well, if Eamon was going to tell you, why did you have to ask?" Larx snapped back. "And it's not like you've told *me* what went on in that room!"

"I got shot! Isn't that enough?"

Larx's voice pitched angrily. "You saved Eamon's life. You made the shooter aim at you instead of shooting in my direction. You saved *my* life. Did you know that? Because when he missed shooting at Eamon, he shot out your unit. If he'd kept aiming that way, one of the bullets would have hit me—I have no doubt. So you put yourself in harm's way being a fucking hero, and I might not like it, but God, I sure am proud of you for it. But no—you just laid in the hospital looking like death and said, 'Just doing my job, ma'am, just doing my job!'"

For a moment his words hung, hot and steaming, in the cold air of the minivan. Then Aaron took as deep a breath as he could muster.

"Assholes with shotguns, Larx. You behind a counter facing an asshole with a shotgun. And Percy Hardesty drawing down on you like you were dangerous. I won't be able to work with that man ever again."

Larx let out a breath. "That really doesn't bother me. Percy isn't that bright—I'd just as soon someone else have your back, truth to tell."

Aaron leaned his head back against the seat rest. "When Eamon leaves office, he's either going to fire Percy or leave him for me to fire. We'll have to see how Percy takes Eamon backing me. Percy thinks he's got a shot."

"Well, I'll give a testimonial," Larx said acidly, and then *he* leaned his head back against the seat. Conceding to the inevitable, he turned the ignition on—but he didn't take the car out of park. Not yet.

"Was this our first fight?" he asked, feeling raw and hurt but still okay. Aaron reached across the console and laced their fingers together.

"Closest thing to," he admitted. "I'm going to have to weenie out of the rest of it 'cause I'm tired. Who do you think won?"

Larx pulled Aaron's knuckles up to his lips and kissed them softly. God, for all the anger, all the resentment, Aaron was *here*, and Larx was so glad he was okay.

"We'll call it a draw and fight again tomorrow," Larx told him. Then he sighed. "When do… when do we stop fighting about this?"

"About my job?" Aaron turned to meet his eyes, and for a moment, Larx was pulled into the pretty blue of them, just like he had been that day Aaron had stopped him on the side of the road to insist that Larx run somewhere else.

"Yeah."

"Until I retire. Can you keep it up that long?"

Larx closed his eyes and felt a smile steal across his lips. He hadn't given it permission to be there, but, well, sometimes the heart healed what it healed.

"Can you deal with me being mad if you get hurt?"

"That depends," Aaron said, voice sober.

Larx opened his eyes again. "On what?"

"On whether or not you break out the frying pan."

Larx nodded. It was going to be rough. They both knew it. But there was something reassuring about buckling up for a bumpy ride. Didn't make the ride any better, but there was a certain anger in surprise. No surprises here—Larx and Aaron had some shit to work out, and they had the emotional gloves and gas masks to prove it.

"I'll keep the frying pan on the stove," he promised, "but you've got to…." He took his own deep breath. "You've got to let me talk about the train station in my own time, okay?"

Aaron nodded. "I love you, Larx. Don't forget that while we're working shit out."

"Love you too." He swallowed and smiled. "I don't think I'd be quite this pissed if I didn't love you quite this much."

Aaron smiled, a sexy, cocky smile, and Larx's stomach did an irresponsible little backflip based on smile alone. "My boy loves me," he said, like they were kids, and just saying the words meant they could frolic naked through a spring meadow of wild flowers.

"Of course I do," Larx said quietly. "Whatever happens, it's not going to be because there's not enough love."

"Then we'll do fine," Aaron said, and for that moment, in the warming car under the long afternoon shadows of the looming pine trees, Larx could believe him. Yeah, spring wildflowers were nice—but if they were going to endure the frozen ground of cold anger, they had to be tougher. Buttercups, crocuses, pinks—those flowers pushed their way through snow and gave people hope for a gentler moment in time.

Larx and Aaron were going to have to be like the crocus—lying latent right now, while they sent out feelers to each other's hearts, knowing that soon the ground would soften, the sun would warm them, and it would be spring again.

THERE WAS an initial flurry of kids and excitement when Larx got Aaron home, but eventually they got him upstairs, ensconced in bed, king of the remote control. Larx kissed his cheek and told him he'd be back after he fixed everyone dinner. But when he got downstairs, he was surprised to see Christiana and Maureen working side by side, quietly giving each other help about where pots would be and what they were going to make.

"Guys, I was going with french bread pizza," he said, smiling a little. Wasn't the greatest meal in the world, but the thought of it right now filled him with sourdough bread joy.

"Don't worry, Larx," Maureen said, competence in every line of her shoulders, just like her father. "You've got canned kidney beans and ground beef and all the spices I need. I'm going to make chili and cornbread, and then you can have leftovers for the week. How's that?"

Larx thought he could cry from the joy of not having to fix dinner. "Wonderful," he breathed. "Should I set the table?"

"I'll do it!" Jaime popped up at his elbow, like a gnome. "It's my turn to help."

Larx laughed. "Have you broken the dog yet?"

"Oh yes, sir," Jaime told him gravely, nodding his head. Dozer was, indeed, passed out on his pillow. If nothing else, that seemed to be a habit now, and Larx approved. "If I could, I'd come over and break this dog every day."

Larx smiled gently. Aaron had offered—and Larx would ask him again and again to make sure it was okay. But this boy was welcome in his home—and his brother too.

Olivia and Elton were doing finances at the kitchen table. Kirby and Kellan were playing a video game intently in the living room. Everybody had a job, a thing to do, a purpose.

"Well, fine." Nobody was having a crisis. The thought left him… off-balance. Bereft. There was nothing to do because Aaron was….

Upstairs.

Oh jeez. He was upstairs.

And in a rush, the relief of having him there hit Larx right in the solar plexus.

He turned back around and went up the stairs, pausing in the doorway to their room, remembering the tense, painful conversation in the car on the way over.

How long was he going to be mad?

It was a good question—and he didn't have a good answer to it. He was going to be mad until he stopped thinking Aaron was going to be in the hospital. He was going to be mad until he got his running buddy back. He was going to be mad until he stopped panicking if Aaron was even a minute late from work, or if he heard the *shwack* of the Kevlar as he was leaving the house.

His hands started to shake. Was he going to be mad the rest of his life?

He put his shaking hand on the doorknob, and it swung open. Aaron turned his head and smiled gratefully. "You going to keep me company while I sit on my ass and age?"

His smile—so golden. All the anger in Larx's heart swept away, just like it had when they'd kissed.

Larx stepped into the room and leveraged himself carefully onto the bed. Once he got there, Aaron draped the afghan on his lap over them both and pulled Larx into the crook of his shoulder so Larx could watch TV too.

Nope. No anger here.

"All the kids okay?"

"Our daughters are working on dinner, our sons are working on the PS4, and the parents of our grandchild are trying to work out finances to see if they can both work from home and pay rent, insurance, and food."

"Mm... what about the kid who wants our dog?"

"The... cousin, I guess, who broke your dog, is setting the table. I'm pretty sure they'll call us when they're ready."

Aaron's chuckle was breathy but still warm. "So you're claiming everybody but the dog."

Larx sighed a little in mock resignation. "Okay. *Our* cousin who broke *our* dog is setting the table."

The night Jaime had fallen asleep next to Dozer, Larx had sat at the kitchen table when he was supposed to be doing paperwork and just stared at that boy and his dog. Aaron had needed that dog in his life. He'd *thought* he was getting it for Larx, but the truth was, a man like Aaron should just come with a dog. It should be part of the package, like cars coming with seat belts. Big blond men with wide chests and twinkling eyes and kind hearts should come with dogs. No-brainer.

If the dog was Larx's, Aaron was Larx's. Larx had said "I love you" and meant it. Their family had merged.

There were no takebacks on forever.

Aaron hmmed, oblivious to Larx's constant state of epiphany. "God, I missed this moment. It's just... so normal."

It was. Right down to how angry Larx *wasn't* when he was in Aaron's presence.

And right there, his question was answered.

How long was he going to be angry? Well, as long as he was going to be worried. But he was going to worry about their kids—all their kids—for forever, and he was apparently going to worry about Aaron that long too. Those moments when he was with them and their lives were fine—those had always been like sunny days in the mountains. You were blessed by them—but you didn't count on them.

And you didn't take out your worry—or your anger at being worried—on the people you loved the most.

"Christiana had to stay in the hospital for a week after she was born," Larx said sleepily, more relaxed than he'd been in… well, a week. "So for a week, Alicia and I took Olivia to the hospital twice a day so Alicia could breastfeed and drop off her pumped milk, and everybody held the baby—and then went back to the house. The stuff was all there, the new crib, the new clothes. And it sucked. There was no baby to put in the baby places. We'd had the hoopla of the birth, but Christiana's immune system had been compromised and she needed antibiotics, so, you know, no baby yet."

Aaron shuddered. "Must have been—"

"Weird!" Larx burst out. "Was the weirdest thing! But finally—finally—she was cleared to come home. I let Alicia stay home and nap, and Olivia and I went to get her. And you know Christi—she's just so… so *good*. Even as a baby. She napped for hours, slept night to morning—and we got her home right in the middle of nap time. So we'd been promising Olivia a baby to play with, and here was the baby, in a car seat between us and the TV."

Oh, Aaron's chuckle should have been bottled as a cure for sadness. "How anticlimactic."

"Right? So we're looking at the car seat and… nothing is happening. She's not even passing gas. And Olivia yawns—'cause we're all exhausted—and leans on me, still in her jacket, and says, 'Cartoons, Daddy!' So I turn on cartoons and lean against the side of the couch, and the whole family just… took a nap."

"Sounds nice," Aaron murmured, dropping a kiss in his hair.

"This moment, right here," Larx said on a yawn. "This moment is just like that."

"God, I love you, Principal."

"I love you too, Deputy. Help me remember that in the next few weeks, okay?"

"As often as possible."

"Mm."

Aaron dropped another kiss on his hair, and he dozed off. The family let him, eating quietly downstairs on their own, and when he woke up, there was a tray by the bed. Aaron was sleeping by then, and Larx sat cross-legged on the bed and ate, watching television, feeling like he was taking an unplanned holiday.

Like a baby's nap, it was best to take his good moments when he could get them. You never knew when the next squall was on the way.

THE NEXT morning he slipped out of bed early, grateful for the first decent night's sleep he'd had in over a week. Leaving Aaron's warmth was hard—usually they did this together.

Aaron shifted in bed and grumbled. "Really?"

"Haven't run in a week and a half!" he protested, half-panicked and, yes, still mostly asleep. Oh God! Was there something he hadn't done? Was there a thing on his agenda he hadn't gotten to? He'd gotten used to splitting duties with Aaron—groceries, cooking, talking to the kids. But now they had more kids than ever before, and Aaron had been out of commission, and he wasn't going to just come back and *boom!* Be okay.

Larx was still on for a few weeks, and he didn't forget it.

"Mm… sorry. Have a good run." Aaron looked so sweet—so healthy and well. Larx sighed and leaned over, kissing his cheek. Usually it was Aaron leaving before he did on a call. Larx wondered if it sucked as much then as leaving Aaron did now.

"It'll be us together soon," he promised, closing his eyes and breathing in warm Aaron. His deputy wasn't making going out in the cold any easier.

"Better promise," Aaron grumbled, pulling the covers up under his chin.

Larx dropped a kiss on his forehead. "Course."

He managed to pull on his sweats and hooded sweatshirt, then grabbed his socks and stocking cap to put on down in the kitchen.

To his surprise, Maureen was down there already, sitting at the kitchen table and doing homework. She'd been a godsend these last days, helping him to wrangle kids and generally stepping up to help out where she was needed.

"Getting behind?" Larx mumbled, plopping in the chair across from her and pulling his tennis shoes on. At his back was the weird fireplace he never used because it opened up to two different rooms and thus provided no heat. In the winter mornings, it was particularly useless because it let a draft in that could freeze the balls off a neutered dog.

"Mm," she confirmed, looking up to give him a drowsy smile. "Running?"

Larx nodded. "Couldn't... I mean, I *could* when he wasn't here, but...." He frowned, too tired to put together how this solitary thing he'd done his whole life had become dependent on knowing Aaron was at least okay.

"You needed him home," she said, the corners of her mouth crimping in like she was holding back a deeper smile. "He said that's when you guys got to know each other."

Larx rolled his eyes and tied his shoelaces. "He made me. He sort of ambushed me when I was running by the school and told me I should run on the forestry track with him." He smiled. "It made sense. I mean, I had company, and the forestry track is safer."

"Mm...." And now her eyes danced, and he realized the jig was up.

"He had really nice eyes, and he wanted me," Larx told her, waiting for the impish wrinkling of her nose. "I don't know what to tell you. It was just... nice. Being wanted. By someone with eyes like your father's."

The smile blossomed completely. "You give me faith," she said, her own blue eyes twinkling. "I came here for me, mostly. I needed to see he was okay. But I knew you'd take good care of him."

Larx let out a sigh and cast a look upstairs. "I try. His job...."

She nodded. "Kirby did some sort of magic formula in his head. As long as he knows where everybody is, he doesn't worry. But me and Tiff, we'd stay up at night and plan what we'd do if something really awful happened, you know?"

He pulled in a deep breath, trying to figure out what that would do to a kid.

"What did you decide?"

"Well, I said I'd stay with Kirby and raise him with our Aunt Candy. She said that was bullshit and we should go stay with Mom's folks. I said I didn't want to wear a dress every day to school, and she said I was being willful, which was their word for when I wanted to bring my stuffed bear places and they didn't think it was appropriate."

Larx grimaced. "Awesome." He took a deep breath and tried not to judge. "I mean, old-school, you know?"

Mau shook her head. "No—they're sort of tight-assed judgy people. Mostly I just went to bed every night and prayed really hard that Dad would come home. Aunt Candy wasn't a bad option, but I just really didn't want to lose him."

"Hm…." Larx wondered briefly what it had done to Aaron's oldest, if she hadn't had any faith to go back on. "Maybe your sister just tried to guard herself in case she did."

Maureen's eyes grew really big. "Oh my God. That could be it! Do you think that's why she's been such a bitch these last few years? I mean, even before you, she was just… awful."

Larx nodded. "Usually kids who lash out like that—especially kids from really nice people like your dad and mom—they're in pain. Worrying about your dad after your mom died, that would be a lot of pain."

"Oh. Oh wow. Thanks, Larx. I mean, it won't make a magic fix, but if I can talk to her about it—man. It sure would be great...." Her lower lip wobbled. "I mean, Christiana is so awesome. And Olivia—I know she's depressed, you know? But they're both so nice to me. And it just... I miss my sister. And if she keeps being like this, she's going to lose us."

Larx stood and grimaced. "We'll try not to let that happen." He let out a yawn and headed to the counter where he kept his water bottle during the winter. He filled it up from the cooler and took a couple of swallows before he set the bottle down and pulled his stocking cap from his kangaroo pocket. He took a couple of steps toward the door before looking up for the dog.

He sighed when he realized Dozer was still up with Jaime, sleeping on Kellan's floor.

"What?" Mau asked, looking around.

"No dog," Larx sighed. "You know, Tane says Berto is functional now—he just can't go back to the house. If your dad doesn't mind renting out the house completely—"

"Oh!" Maureen said, suddenly looking wide-awake. "That reminds me—"

A tentative tap on the sliding glass door shot Larx's heart right up to his throat. He whirled around and confronted a pleasant, round face muffled by scruff.

"Elton?" he mumbled.

"Yeah. Sorry, Larx," Maureen said as he opened the door. "I told him you were planning to run this morning, and he said he'd jog over and join you."

Larx grunted and opened the door. Elton smiled winningly, which he seemed to do a lot, and Larx sighed.

"Hello—"

"Wombat Willie," Elton said with a sweet smile. "Yeah. I know. I looked up what a wombat is, and, you know… I did knock up your daughter."

Larx woke up enough to grin at him. "You're awesome. Let's go running. Try not to leave this old man behind."

He stepped out into the cold and closed the door behind him, taking a few moments to stretch so he didn't wreck himself. Elton stretched during the break, his breath smoking into the darkness.

"I used to hate running," he said. "But Olivia was going every morning last semester, and I sort of picked up the habit."

Larx frowned. "Where is she? We used to run together when she lived at home." Christiana had preferred bicycling or swimming or something that involved less of a sweat-to-distance ratio.

"She, uh…." Elton sighed. "She's real tired because of the baby and, uh…."

Larx tilted his head. "I didn't see her yesterday until last night. Was she in bed all yesterday too?"

Elton closed his eyes and nodded, and Larx started to growl, low in his throat. "I think we should run by your house, don't you?"

The young man at his side swallowed. "Okay, sir."

"I think there's something there we can't forget."

Aaron's old house was about two miles away. In their early days, Larx would warm up for the first two miles, pick Aaron up, run three miles around the service track loop, drop Aaron off at his house, and then sprint home. If he left an hour before he was supposed to get ready for work, it gave him room for a nine-minute mile, and he usually ran around seven or eight. Once Aaron moved in, he shortened their run to five miles, and they ran it a little faster.

Wombat Willie ran a six-and-a-half-minute mile without breaking a sweat.

Larx could do it—but he hadn't run in almost two weeks, and he was definitely sweating when they burst into Aaron's house.

The place looked much the same as Larx had seen it when Aaron lived there, except cleaner. The mail wasn't stacked on the polished wood table; the dishes weren't dirty in the sink. The kids had dusted the place on Saturday before they'd moved their few possessions in, and Larx took a look around as they walked in.

"There's a bedroom on the ground floor?" he asked, thinking hard.

"Yes, sir. And four up top. We think the ground floor one was used as a study."

Larx nodded. "Yeah—it's got a miniscule closet." But Aaron had left his furniture there, and even his desk. At Larx's place, Aaron used the small desk back in the corner by the fireplace in the dining room, and Larx worked at the table.

They'd managed to do a lot of work together, just knowing there was a friend, a companion, breathing nearby.

"What are you thinking?" Elton asked perceptively.

"I'm thinking that Jaime and Berto might move in. We'd ask Berto to keep the room on the ground floor and to medicate outside, but we could move the greenhouse back there for him, and Jaime could sleep up near you guys. Would that be okay? I don't know how long it would last—"

"Naw, man. Jaime's cool. Berto… well, he's hurting, but…." Elton looked up the stairs with a suddenly adult posture. "You know, it helped her last week, to be there for Jaime. I think, maybe, having people around whose life isn't all hunky-dory, it makes her remember how much she has to work for, you know?"

Larx nodded. "Stay here," he warned, and then trotted up the stairs.

Olivia was a tiny ball in the corner of the bed, and Larx shored himself up.

"Olivia, wake up."

"Daddy?" She rolled over and grimaced at him. "Daddy, it's early!"

"And you left our house at six last night, crawled into bed, and haven't been up to do more than pee in eleven hours. Get up."

"Fuck off," she snapped, and he didn't even flinch.

He yanked the covers off, leaving her scrambling and indignant in her pajama pants. "*Daddy?*"

"Go put your sweats on, brush your teeth, and grab your hat. We're running in five, and you need to hurry up so I can get home in time to leave with the kids. Move it, Olivia—I mean now!"

She glared at him, hurt and angry and miserable, and for a moment he thought he'd blown it. Oh Jesus, that part of her, the angry, resentful part of her, the part that said, "Fuck off!" when she'd never, ever, not even during the stormiest part of her adolescence, sworn at him, that would take over, and he would have broken trust with her forever.

Then she bared her dingy teeth and snarled, "Fucking fine! Fucking tyrant! I'll be out in five minutes!"

Larx started going through her drawers, comfortable with her organization because he'd taught it to her. Sweats, T-shirt, hoodie, socks, panties, bra—he hadn't flinched from these things when he was buying them at Walmart, and he wasn't going to flinch from them now.

When she came out of the bathroom, greasy hair scraped back into a muddled ponytail, he had clothes set on the bed.

"Downstairs, ASAP," he snapped. "We'll have saltines waiting."

"Why are you doing this?" she snarled. "Why can't you just leave me alone?"

"Because I love you, and we need a plan here. You and me, we used to plan when we went running, remember? So we'll plan now. Two minutes, Olivia. I mean it."

He stalked out of her room and slammed the door, taking the stairs with the speed of a skittish cat.

"You got saltines, right?" He'd given the kids food to start with when they'd taken their stuff to set up. Elton nodded, wide-eyed, and grabbed the crackers from the cupboard.

"Why'd you do that?" Elton asked as Larx set them on the counter next to half a glass of milk. It had been Alicia's magic formula for morning sickness; he was going to take a chance on it being Olivia's as well.

"Because you have to live with her," Larx said, checking the stairs. She wasn't there yet, but they could hear her thumping around. "We'll go on a run, she'll come home and tell you what an asshole I am and how she can't believe she thought I was a decent father to begin with, and you'll get her into the shower and maybe look up depression treatment nearby on my health insurance. And then you don't have to live with her being pissed, and we can help her call an end to this bullshit."

Elton regarded him soberly from those surprisingly sweet eyes. "That's a real good plan, Mr. Larkin."

"Call me Larx."

"Okay. So, Larx, now that we got a plan for this, do you think we can maybe find a way to tell my parents I left school? I talked to the administration, and my roommate's shipping my stuff, but that other thing…."

He shuddered, and Larx felt some of his irritation fade from his body.

"We'll talk about it when we run," Larx said softly. "I think maybe you come pick me up, we come back and get her, and we do this regular-like as long as she can. We'll have some time to talk then."

Elton's sweet smile flickered at his mouth. "You're a good dad. Don't worry. I won't let her tell me what an asshole you are."

Larx swallowed hard, because what he'd just done, yelling at his child when she felt like hell, that had been one of the hardest, worst things he'd ever done as a parent.

"It's good of you to say so," he said softly. Upstairs they heard a door slam, and they both looked up and watched Olivia take the stairs the same way Larx had just done.

She swanned into the kitchen, bolted the saltines and the milk, wiped her mouth on her sleeve, and grabbed her gloves from the pocket of the coat hanging near the door.

"Can we fucking go?" she asked. "I have sleeping to do."

Larx and Elton met eyes and nodded.

"Sure thing, my angel," Larx said, and together they went jogging out into the cold.

TIME OFF

AARON HAD been hurt on the job a couple of times before. Once he'd been hit by a car—fortunately not head-on—and once he'd been grazed in the shoulder.

Both times what had hit him the hardest was not facing his own mortality; it was facing his own *inactivity*.

He was off the job for six weeks. He knew that. Logically, it took him a week to walk through the house and out and around the yard without getting winded. The doctor may have said he was healing fine, but he could feel his dissolvable stitches right up until they dissolved, and the man might very well have had the finesse of one of those guys who carves images on the head of a pin with a feather, but Aaron could swear he felt his flesh knit and resolve itself into scar tissue.

And that hurt too.

So he knew going to work was not an option, and while Eamon kept him briefed—Percy, for example, had a verbal warning, a written citation, and two weeks off without pay for drawing down on their civilian asset and not backing off—he wasn't so much as tempted to go in.

But being inactive around the house was driving him batshit.

He couldn't go running with Larx in the mornings, and *that* peeved him to no end. Aaron thought it was great that Olivia's boyfriend had started going with him—Elton seemed to need some direction in his life, and hey, giving young people direction was the thing Larx did best. But Aaron was also jealous.

Supremely, stupidly, madly jealous of the young man who got more of Larx's time than Aaron did. Aaron had thought his inner twelve-year-old could be staved off by action-adventure movies and the dog, but apparently that brat was on full-on whine in his head, going "But he's *my* friend, not yours!"

The mandate was clear—no running in the icy mountain air for at least six weeks after a punctured lung, but Aaron was climbing the walls.

About two weeks after he came back home, the air was still frigid and snow was still dumping periodically in the Sierras. March didn't always look like spring in Colton, even two Saturdays before Easter. It would have been a great day to sleep in, to snuggle, to catch up on movies and maybe clean the fridge.

Instead Larx's alarm went off, and he literally fell out of bed. Aaron heard the *thump* and sat up, relieved when nothing in his chest or abdomen twinged beyond normal.

"Larx? Baby? You okay?"

"I'm your baby," Larx said happily from the floor. "I like it when you call me that. It's sweet."

"Well, *baby*, you were up awfully late last night. You sure you don't want to sit this run out? It's Saturday." Aaron longed for him to stay in bed, just this once. For two weeks Larx had been doing double Dad duty—taking kids places, planning their days, planning their meals. Aaron had been trying to help, but even though he'd gotten progressively stronger, he was still so limited. At this point even driving was purely theoretical.

In practice, every time the SUV so much as went over a pothole, he gasped and expected pain. Larx was jumping through hoops to orchestrate the family's day so Aaron didn't have to drive a fucking car.

It was humiliating.

And it was killing Larx.

The night before had been a school board meeting—nothing huge or earth-shattering, unlike the one in October—but still, important. Larx had gone and asked for a review of the district's process regarding CPS, to see if there was any way possible a situation like Candace Furman's was not repeated.

He'd been blown off—and his friend Nancy had to stand up and tell everybody at the meeting about Larx's heroics three weeks earlier. He'd gotten a smattering of applause, and that was about it—according to Yoshi, who was a more honest reporter than Larx in these issues, anyway.

Aaron was getting a commendation for heroism—and he'd been wearing a goddamned vest.

The whole thing made Aaron want to just curl over his lover like Dozer curled over his stuffed bunny, but dammit, Larx wouldn't sit still long enough to cuddle!

But it was Saturday morning, nothing was planned, nothing was pressing. They'd even talked about going to a movie after Larx poked around his winter garden—maybe taking Olivia and Elton so they could talk.

Because Olivia was working so hard—helping Jaime, making meals for him and his brother, planning the nursery, looking for her own online job. But reports about what was going on in her heart weren't good. That was maybe the only reason Elton had been so excited about running—it gave him a chance to talk to Larx about depression and triggers and the things that seemed to send Olivia screaming into bed to haul the covers over her head.

Elton himself had started consulting work for a video game company—he was making enough to cover expenses, and he'd signed up for insurance under the company he was consulting for. Wasn't permanent, but the pay wasn't bad, and Olivia's one source of joy was how much people seemed to want Elton's work.

But Maureen had left the week before, and she'd spent part of her time keeping Aaron company when everybody went to school and part of her time trying to help Olivia fix up the upstairs of Aaron's house—maybe they should start calling it his "rental property" now, since Jaime and Berto had moved in the week before—and getting Olivia into a better headspace.

"Dad, it's horrible. I remember her from high school, and she was so bright and shiny. She *knows* how she used to look at the world, how she used to feel, but she can't remember how to feel that way. And every time I talk to her about the baby—she just cries harder."

But Aaron never saw that. Olivia greeted him with a quiet smile and food or discussion of curtains or help picking out baby equipment, because Larx wasn't great at researching safety and Aaron was.

Larx's daughter was doing all the "things" people did to prove they weren't depressed.

Except feeling better—she was skipping that one.

And just this once, Aaron wanted Larx to not run off into the ether. Just this once, Aaron wanted Larx in his bed, to touch, to be Aaron's and Aaron's alone.

God. Even to pretend to have sex. Aaron's blood pressure had just been cleared—they weren't going to break any furniture or set any records, but finally they could talk about sex like it was a thing.

"You want me to come back to bed?" Larx asked, bewildered still.

Aaron scooted over to the edge and looked down. "Please, baby?" he begged. "For me? It would be really awesome if I got you to myself for a morning. Please?"

Larx's eyes focused and his expression softened. "Yeah? Just… a lie-in?"

"Yeah." Aaron felt his smile go lopsided. They were just gazing at each other, Aaron in bed, Larx on the floor. "I'd like to… you know. Touch you."

Larx's lips—usually sort of lean—made a plush little O as he thought about touching.

"C'mon, Principal," Aaron begged quietly. "Come to bed with me."

Larx pushed up and climbed back in, shivering with reaction to being outside the blankets.

"If you think so," he whispered breathily.

Aaron pulled his wiry body—thinner now than it had been a month ago—up against his own bulkier form. Oh! It felt so good to have his man in his arms. He loved Larx's hard, runner's muscles, his sleekness, the way he wriggled to be closer.

Aaron spanned Larx's chest with his hand and whispered into his ear. "Some days, you just belong here with me."

The sound Larx made was of total human surrender. "God. Yes. Can we... just today...?"

His phone buzzed, and he groaned.

"No!" Aaron protested.

"Let me tell him I'm bailing," Larx muttered. "Here...." He reached over and grabbed it, pulling open the text box. "Not today, Elton. I have a man in my bed—"

"You are not!" Aaron laughed, although at this point he wouldn't have cared. God, he missed their time together.

"Shit!" Larx sat up in bed, the change in demeanor so abrupt it was frightening.

"Shit what?" Aaron asked, sitting up too.

"Elton's parents just landed in Sacramento. They're renting a car, and they'll be here in two to three hours."

"Where are they going to sleep?" Aaron asked, shocked. "The *roof*?"

Larx let out a harsh bark of laughter. "That's about it. Good Lord!"

He texted frantically for a minute and then slumped back into bed. "Apparently it's news to Elton as well. They're here to convince him to come back to San Diego."

"Well, that's douchy."

Larx fell back against the pillows and gave Aaron a sideways look through long, dark lashes. "We have two options here," he said softly. "We can run around the house like headless chickens screaming, 'The in-laws are coming! The in-laws are coming!'—"

"Or?"

"Or we can go back to what we were doing, get up in an hour, and let Elton's parents come visit us while our entire menagerie is still in pajamas."

Aaron plumped down in the pillows next to him and regarded Larx soberly.

"I need this time with you," he said bluntly. "I miss you. I miss *us*. I get that we have kids and you've been running your ass off trying to be principal/dad/nursemaid, but I'm tired of missing you. I don't even care if it's selfish. Please, baby. Even if we just go back to sleep. Even if these people hate our pajamas. Please, just lie down next to me for another hour?"

Larx's eyes grew fond again, and he reached out with the hand not holding his phone and stroked Aaron's jaw softly with his fingertips. "How could anybody not like our pajamas?"

"Plaid's always in style." Aaron sure hoped so—he'd been wearing it an awful goddamned lot in the past few weeks.

"Mm…." Larx burrowed his hands under Aaron's T-shirt, where the bandages and the stitches had lived until the day before. His touch was light, exploratory, and he was blessedly ginger around the ridges of Aaron's scars, but his hands felt so good. "You know what would *really* be in style?" he asked, batting his lashes.

"Skin," Aaron purred, breathing the word softly in his ear. He reached down, shoving his hand under Larx's sweats and kneading that tight, solid ass. "God, this feels good. It shouldn't, 'cause it's all muscle, nothing plush, but—"

Larx kissed him to shut him up.

This was usually Aaron's move, but he wasn't going to object. This wasn't a kiss of comfort or a kiss of connection. This was a full-on, openmouthed, tongue-dueling, octopus-handed kiss of romance and sex and naked bodies that should be writhing on the bed if it weren't for all the goddamned clothes.

Aaron moaned and rolled over on his back, hoping Larx would take the hint. Supporting his weight on his elbows would hurt, but Aaron would lick, suck, nibble, and tongue anything Larx put in his way.

Larx apparently felt the same way. He started out by nibbling on Aaron's neck, on his earlobe, licking a line down his throat. Aaron gave a happy little sigh and reached down to pull his T-shirt up. Larx took over, shoving it gracelessly to Aaron's armpits and sniffing Aaron's chest and scars experimentally, like a cat on a new patch of grass.

"What are you doing?" Aaron chuckled.

"I want to see how my property changed." Larx sent him an endearingly grumpy look from under his brows. "I told you to take care of my property, and it got scuffed, and I want to see where the scuffs are."

"Mm. Here." Aaron twined their fingers together, keeping his index finger free. "This here—" He traced a puncture between his ribs where they'd put the valve in his lung to help with inflating it and keeping the fluid out. "—this is where they pulled the rib out of my lung."

"Ouch," Larx said softly.

"I was unconscious," Aaron reassured him. "But my chest still hurts when I walk outside, so I'll assume it happened."

Larx kissed the inch-long incision gently. "To make it better."

Aaron's whole body shuddered. "That worked." He pulled their twined hands to the incisions on either side of his abdominal muscles. "These," he said, "were to repair the things—spleen, kidney, lower intestine—that got torn by my ribs or burst by the impact."

Larx moved down and kissed those too. "Ouchie," he whispered.

"Yeah." Healing, sweet and blessed, flowed through him, and he pulled their hands to his left pectoral, flattening his hand and turning it palm up so Larx's was palm down. "This—"

"There's no scars here." Larx peered up at him, a smile in his eyes.

"You can't see it," Aaron told him, sober as a judge. "This is where my heart aches when I see you working so hard, taking all the burdens on your shoulders, and I can't help."

Larx's eyes grew bright and shiny, and he bit his lower lip as it quivered. "You're afraid to drive," he said baldly.

"It's scary," Aaron told him, and admitting that something so simple scared him wasn't as hard as he thought it would be. "I got knocked off my feet, backward. And it wasn't in a car, but... but I feel that weightlessness and it... it terrifies me."

"Mm." Larx kissed his chest, pausing to be distracted by Aaron's right nipple, and Aaron let the sheer sexuality wash through him again. He kneaded his fingers softly in Larx's hair and bucked his hips, because arousal was a luxury, and he wanted to savor it.

Larx let him go with a pop and smiled, tranquil in this moment as Aaron hadn't seen him in a month.

"What about you?" Aaron asked softly, heart in his throat. This moment was so lovely—he hated to trample on it by pushing too hard.

But Larx surprised him—as he often did—in the best of ways. "These," he said, dragging their twined hands to the corners of his eyes, "are from trying to figure out how to get Christi to her PSATs, Kirby to his college tour, and Kellan to his basketball game when we don't have that many cars."

Aaron chuckled. Elton had walked in while Larx was having that discussion. He'd calmly said, "My car's fixed. Livvy and I will take Kirby, Christi can drive Livvy's car, and you can go see Kellan play."

Larx's entire body had almost melted—Aaron had felt his relief on a visceral level from across the room.

"That's a scar," Aaron agreed, pleased when Larx smiled. Then he grew sober, and Aaron prepared himself. This game was really very serious.

"These," he said, using his index finger to outline the deepened grooves around his mouth, "are from yelling at my daughter and knowing she'll hate me for a moment, but doing anything—*anything*, to get her out of the house, get her blood flowing, get her appetite back, so she can make better decisions about her health."

Aaron nodded, his own heart aching. He'd known this was weighing Larx down—but not once had Larx told him. He used his free hand to rub his thumb along the corner of Larx's mouth. "That would leave a mark," he agreed.

Larx nodded, then swallowed and pulled both their hands to his chest. "And this," he whispered, just as downstairs exploded into chaos.

They both froze, locking eyes, Larx visibly shaking. There was a pounding at the front door, complete with a ringing doorbell, a barking dog, voices at the back door, and three teenagers bolting out of their rooms and running down the stairs yelling things like, "What the hell…? What the actual fuck…? For fuck's sake, what in the actual hell!"

"Front door!" Christi called, and Kirby yelled, "Back door!" and Kellan yelled, "Dog! Dozer! The fuck! Get down!"

Aaron struggled to get his breath, to pull his emotions from the wobbly place he'd taken them, and Larx was obviously doing the same.

"Everybody's here," he said weakly.

"Baby…." Aaron wanted that moment back. God*dammit*, he wanted that moment back. That precious, raw moment when Larx was still, his true heart on his sleeve, the words that would set them both free about to spill from his lips.

Larx shook his head and gulped in a breath with the same expression he used when he was running.

"No baby," he gasped. "Not now. Need to not be baby right now."

Aaron wrapped his arms around Larx's shoulders and gave him a hard squeeze, like he was literally pulling him back together. He released the pressure and kissed Larx's temple.

"Let's go deal," he said. Larx rolled out of bed in his sweats and T-shirt, hair a disaster, expressive brown eyes more lost than Aaron had ever seen them. Aaron was still struggling to sit up when Larx pulled on his hooded sweatshirt and a pair of socks before putting his feet into his slippers and heading for the door.

"Larx!" Aaron begged, sitting up at last. "Wait— we can go down togeth—"

A man's voice, raised in anger, echoed through the house, and the look they shared morphed into panic.

"I'll get the thermostat," Aaron said, because turning it up was the first thing they did when they got up. "Go!"

Larx took off, and Aaron managed to find his own zipper hoodie, socks, and moccasins so he could follow his boyfriend—shitty word. *Goddammit*, boyfriend was a shitty word for what he and Larx had been doing in that bedroom just now. But whatever the thing they were to each other, the huge, important, painful word, Aaron needed to follow him into the storm.

By the time Aaron got downstairs, headless chicken Armageddon pajama party was in full force.

Larx was standing in the middle of the living room with one hand on the dog's collar and the other extended out in placation to a middle-aged couple— probably Elton's mother and father—wearing the kind of leisure suits Aaron only saw in department store windows in the movies.

The kids were ranged around them, and Elton and Olivia were behind him, Elton standing with his shoulders angled away from the couple and toward Olivia in protection.

"I need you to contain your animal, sir!"

"This is his own goddamned house!" Larx snapped. "I need you to lower your fucking voice and stand down! You burst in here past my daughter and start yelling, and of course the dog thinks you're an asshole! Now shut up and tell me what crawled in your puckered asshole and died! Oh—and while you're at it, tell me *who in the hell you are!*"

Larx's roar echoed off the walls of the living room, and even Dozer quieted down.

"I'm Shawn McDaniels, Elton's father, and I demand to know why you won't let my son return home!"

Larx frowned at him, genuinely puzzled. "Elton is free to come and go as he pleases. His car was fixed a week and a half ago—he's staying here of his own free will."

"Bullshit," McDaniels snapped. "Nobody leaves a full ride in San Diego to shack up with some baby machine in the backwoods of Tahoe!"

"Dad, stop it!" Elton snapped back, putting Olivia behind him instinctively. God, Aaron liked this kid. "She's right here, and you're being an asshole. I tried to talk to you on the phone—I've been trying for weeks. You didn't like what I said, so you and Mom get on your high horse and come bother these nice people? That's awful. Do you realize how awful that is? Larx should let the dog *eat* you. You've violated their home, and I'm not talking to either of you until you lower your voices and calm the fuck down!"

Shawn McDaniels reacted as though slapped. "Who *are* these people, Elton? Did you even tell them we were coming?" He was a big, ruddy man with thinning red hair and the complexion of someone who liked a scotch or three after work. He was probably Aaron and Larx's age, maybe five or so years older, but he *looked* sixty-five.

"Yeah, Dad, this is what half an hour's notice looks like. Mom said you just got to Sacramento. What in the hell?"

"Sorry, honey," his mother chimed in, glancing nervously at her husband. "I had the text all written, and I didn't send it until Auburn, and then the reception was bad so I don't think it sent until... well... when you got it."

Larx tilted his head. "Wow. Just... wow. If you guys like, you can come into the kitchen and—"

"Are you going to put that animal outside?" Mc-Daniels asserted.

"No." Larx smiled when he said it, showing all his teeth. "I'd like the luxury of letting him eat your face if you get nasty again."

McDaniels gaped once or twice, and to Aaron's surprise, his wife gave a tiny smirk. "Mr. Larkin?" she asked hesitantly. "I'm, uh, Cheryl, Elton's mother. We're sorry about the time mix-up. And *I'm* sorry about my husband. We're just concerned. Elton hadn't even mentioned this girl—"

"My oldest daughter, Olivia," Larx said stiffly. As much as Aaron approved of Larx standing up for himself, he was a little alarmed by the way he held his shoulders, his chest. Having his emotions so close to the surface, being assaulted by all this—Larx was pretty fucking resilient, but Aaron thought this might be the place where he snapped. "Please speak of her respectfully."

"You, uh, certainly have a lot of children." While Shawn fumed, Cheryl sent a conciliatory smile around the front room. "I'm sorry we didn't get a chance to get introduced."

Larx made a visible effort to calm down. "This is Christiana, Olivia's younger sister, and—"

"Our brothers," Christi said, her voice as cold as Aaron had ever heard it. "Kellan and Kirby."

"Are you triplets?" Cheryl asked, agonized. "You don't look anything alike, but you're all… uh…."

Aaron stepped forward. "It's confusing, I know. I'm Aaron George—"

"My stepdad," Olivia said, speaking for the first time and giving Aaron a weak smile. "And his son, Kirby, and our foster brother, Kellan. He's got two daughters too, but they're grown and don't live at home."

"Wait," Cheryl said uncertainly. "If Larx is your dad, and Aaron's your stepdad, who's Aaron married to?"

Boyfriends. Married. Husbands. Duh! "Larx and I are together," Aaron said, and he realized he was edging forward so he could put himself between Larx, just like Elton had done with Olivia.

"Don't you see?" Shawn McDaniels spat. "Cheryl, they're homosexuals."

"But who had the children?" Cheryl asked him.

"A test tube? Who cares! No wonder they're so desperate for their kid to breed—but our son isn't getting caught up in it!"

Aaron threw himself forward to keep Larx from lunging for Shawn McDaniels's throat. "Larx! Larx! Dammit, he's an asshole, but don't—*ouch!*" In the scuffle, Larx's shoulder hit him directly in the chest, and Aaron wasn't quite healed yet.

Larx backed up, hand over his mouth. "Oh God. I'm so—"

"I'm fine."

"Aaron, I'm so sorry—"

"Baby, it's okay. It just twinged—"

Larx swallowed, and the thing Aaron had been waiting for finally happened.

He snapped.

"I've got to go," he said brokenly and headed for the door, bending to grab his sneakers on his way out. Dozer followed him, and Aaron took a few quick steps after them and stopped, leaning against the couch with stars in front of his eyes because he wasn't supposed to move that fast yet.

"Goddammit!"

Olivia and Elton were having a meeting with their eyeballs.

"I'll get him," Olivia said. "He's only going on the loop. Don't worry, Aaron, he won't be alone." She started for the backyard but paused at the door to speak to Elton's parents. "Your son's amazing," she said, her voice wobbling. "He's the kindest, most wonderful man. I'm not sure who you let raise him, but whoever it was, they did a really good job. You should tell them that."

Aaron watched forlornly as she disappeared and then turned to the shocked people in the front room.

Only to have Elton step in front of him. "Dad, leave. You're not welcome here until you apologize, and nobody's ready for your apology yet."

Shawn McDaniels gaped again. "What in the—"

"This is Deputy Sheriff Aaron George. The night I got here, I'd wrecked my car and bumped my head. Aaron picked me up on the side of the road, figured out where I was, *who* I was, and called Olivia. He didn't yell. He didn't threaten. He took a goofy—" Only the family could hear the pause. "—wombat and made him feel safe, and then called the girl I'd been searching for and convinced her I wouldn't hurt her. He's in pain because he got shot that night, in the line of duty, so maybe don't act like you're going to bully him, because the kids and I would have to hurt you."

Elton's father took a step back, a flush of shame washing his already red face.

"The guy you just sent spinning into a rage was Mr. Larkin, the high school principal. The night Aaron got shot, he was *dying* to stay with him, to worry. Mom, remember when Dad got sick and you almost got us evicted because you didn't remember to pay the bills? They shut the electricity off, repoed the car—"

"Yeah, honey," Cheryl murmured, and Aaron knew the mortification on her cheeks for what it was. "I remember."

"Larx left the hospital and found a kid lost in the snow. He faced off against her stepdad with a gun to get her back. And then he made sure Aaron was okay for the night and came and made sure *we* were okay. Not just us either. One of Aaron's daughters, two guys who got caught in the crossfire that night and aren't doing that well. He was taking care of the world—when all he really wanted to do was take care of his husband. So you guys, coming in here like your shit is the only shit in the world—that's *bad*. It's *dumb*. I don't care if you're the district assemblyman to the rest of the goddamned county, Dad—here, you're nobody. And you're not going to *be* anybody until you get your head out of your ass."

"Elton!" his mother yelped, but Elton shook his head.

"Mom, that girl who just ran after her father? She's carrying your grandbaby. You make sure he knows, he either acts decent or you two will never see that baby. Ever. And you'll never see me again either. Now go."

"Son—" Shawn McDaniels looked ready to parley. Aaron might have given him the benefit of the doubt.

"No." Elton shook his head. "No. Just…." And for the first time he looked as young and as lost as Aaron had first seen him. "You hurt my family, Dad. You hurt people I care about by being a pompous ass. It's going to take a while to forgive. Go find a hotel in town—I'm pretty sure Larx and Aaron would offer you a room, but they've got two houses full of people who deserve one more than you. Call me tomorrow."

Elton's eyes grew hard again, and he firmed up his lower lip. Aaron stood up to his full height so he could step in front of Elton.

"You heard him," Aaron said, trying not to breathe too hard. "You need to leave, Assemblyman McDaniels." The name vaguely rang a bell now—a district down south. Far, far away from Colton County.

McDaniels scowled, but his wife turned to him and gestured with her chin. "Shawn, if you fuck this up now, I'll never forgive you."

And for the first time, Aaron saw signs of redemption in the man. His face softened and he put his hand up, like he'd rest it on her shoulder.

"But, Cheryl—"

"We need to leave."

And then she turned and walked out of the house. McDaniels followed her, pausing at the entryway and looking around.

It was like he saw them, for the first time, as they were. A family, awakened out of bed, to have a hostile stranger try to take away one of their own.

He took a deep breath and looked suddenly older. "This was... badly done," he said after a moment. Then he sagged deeper into himself. "I'm sorry. I'll... I'll try again."

And then he left.

Christiana waited until the front door closed and turned back around to Elton. "Wombat Willie, I am pretty damned impressed!"

Elton smiled and turned his head—but Aaron saw the wobble of his lip too.

"Well done," Aaron said quietly. "Guys, since we're up, do you want to start waffles and coffee—"

"And hot chocolate!" Christi said, and although she sounded almost desperately cheerful, Aaron appreciated the effort. She paused on her way to the kitchen and gave Aaron a careful hug. "Don't worry. He's coming back."

Aaron closed his eyes. "I couldn't go after him," he confessed, needing that comfort more than he wanted to admit. "We... we started out running together, you know?"

Christiana's hug grew stronger. "Yeah. I know. He just needed some space."

Aaron nodded and kissed the top of her head. "Yeah."

"Here. You go sit down and talk to Elton. Me and the guys'll make waffles. We can all take a minute to wake up, because geez! It's not even seven yet? Holy Christ! Those people had better apologize with chocolate."

Christi stomped to the kitchen, and Aaron found the nearest chair at the kitchen table and sank down.

"I'm so sorry," Elton said, head in his hands. "So sorry. Larx has been trying to get me to talk to my parents, and I finally tried the night before last. Dad got mad and hung up and... I had no idea he could get that mean."

Aaron grimaced. "Well, I think it's a good thing they live a long way away," he said diplomatically. "You and Olivia seem to be getting your world together, you know?"

Elton nodded glumly, leaning forward to rest his chin on his hands. "We had plans today," he said, seemingly at random. "There's this... this outpatient depression clinic in Auburn. Since that's like an hour and a half away, we were thinking of getting, like... like a long-term hotel room there. It's a two-week course. We were going down to meet the doctors and stuff and check out options"

Oh. Wow. "Did Larx know about this?" Aaron asked, hurt.

"Only a little. He looked it up and suggested it to her so she could say, 'Jesus, Daddy, get out of my life!' Then I moved in a couple of days later and said,

'Babe, look! They've got classes on pregnancy and depression and what kinds of meds you can take!' And then we let her think about it."

Aaron couldn't help it. He had to laugh. "Jesus, Elton. You guys are pretty Machiavellian."

Elton rolled his eyes. "I think I flunked that class, whatever it was. But she was going for it. She… she wanted help. I was going to ask my parents for money—"

"We'll pay," Aaron said, absurdly moved. Going to his parents had to have been hard in the first place.

"Yeah, but, you guys. You've given me all the stuff. I wanted to give you something too."

Aaron gave into temptation and ruffled Elton's hair, seeing how Larx could love all the kids and still have a soft spot for his own personal few. "You… you should have seen yourself," he said softly. "I'm not sure about your dad, but I'm proud of you. Anybody who loves you should be proud of how you stood up for people you cared about. I see why Olivia's so smitten. Why she wants to try so hard. You're way worth it."

Elton gave a watery little smile. "Thanks, Aaron. I mean, I know you're, like… like my girlfriend's dad's boyfriend, but that's the nicest thing a dad has ever said to me, and I'm going to take it."

"Stepdad," Aaron corrected gently. "You said I was her stepdad. And Larx's husband. Let's use those words, okay?"

Elton looked at him and smiled gamely. "Those are good words. I like those words. Maybe you should say them to Larx, you think?"

Aaron frowned. "Has he said anything?"

"No." Elton looked away and started picking at a splinter on the unfinished table. "But I was thinking, you know. I kept trying to call the people in the mental health place, and I would say 'Olivia's boyfriend,' and I got no love. So I said 'the father of her baby,' and they talked to me some more. But if I said 'I'm her husband,' that would have got their attention right quick. And then, these last few weeks, running with Larx, I kept thinking of you as his husband. 'Cause—and no offense, but you guys aren't… you know. My age. I mean, boyfriend, right? Kellan has a boyfriend. You got something more."

Aaron regarded him with raised eyebrows, the ornery part of him wanting to protest. He wasn't too old to have a boyfriend or a girlfriend, was he? What about a man-friend? What about a lover?

But *lover* sounded too personal to say in front of his children, and man-friend too impersonal for the guy who'd spent the last few months being a stepdad to the same kids.

And a boyfriend was someone who could run out that door and never come back.

Larx would come back—Aaron had no doubts.

But he needed a better name.

SNOW FLOWER

DAMMIT! WHEN had Daddy gotten so damned fast?

Olivia struggled to catch up with her father, cursing everything as she went. She cursed her jeans, which chafed, and her tennis shoes, which *weren't* her running shoes, and her denim jacket, which bound up her shoulders. She cursed her pregnancy belly, because at four months it was like a hard grapefruit in her abdomen, and she could feel the way it sucked the wind from her body, and she super super cursed that all she'd had on her way out the door was a handful of saltines and a swallow of milk.

And then she thanked God for Elton, who had made her eat that much, because when his father went super fucking ballistic, she would have thrown up without them, and that would have really sucked.

But as much as she cursed, she kept most of it internal so she had all her air for running.

Right up until the two-mile split, with Aaron's house—which was now her house—on the right and the rest of the loop straight ahead, when she watched Larx and Dozer take the loop and disappear into the dark shadows of the predawn gray. God, she wasn't going to catch them—not running like this, she wasn't.

Making a sudden decision, she veered off to the right, through the old chicken yard, past the fenced-in pool, past Berto, who was smoking quietly in the early morning peace, through the sliding glass door, and up the stairs.

Once she got there, she started throwing her clothes off, pulling her running clothes from the clean clothes hamper and blessing Elton once again for doing laundry when she'd been taking her first shower in three days. God, without Elton this place would fall apart, and damn, if she hadn't been planning to become a more functional human being again.

She clattered down the stairs, pulled her running shoes on, and grabbed her soft poly zipper hoodie from the hook by the door. Realizing she probably had fifteen minutes to spare, she turned around and grabbed the entire package of saltines and a bottle of water, then trotted outside so she could stare at the forestry road with Berto.

Larx should be coming around the corner in fifteen, maybe twenty minutes.

She kept moving as she came to a rest by Berto, jogging to keep warm. Berto had turned on the space heater by the garage, and she appreciated the warmth it threw out as well.

"I didn't think you were running today," Berto said on a steamy exhale. Elton had bought a vaporizer and oil for him at a dispensary two weeks ago, so the house didn't reek of pot, and Berto was humbly grateful for the cannabis dosage that didn't get him high, just settled his nerves.

"Well, shit went down," she said, grimacing slightly. "Poor Elton—I thought he was exaggerating when he said his parents sucked." She shoved a saltine in her mouth because she didn't want to think about that.

Berto let out a soft bark of laughter. "That's too bad. I miss the crap out of my folks."

She regarded him curiously in the growing light. He and Jaime were, for the most part, quiet roommates. Olivia had, for the past two weeks, started making them breakfast in the morning, because they'd arrived with cold cereal and not-quite-spoiled milk. Jaime had started looking at her with worship in his eyes—not a crush, so much, but she apparently made his world better, and she was running with that. Berto had been grateful—but, well, quiet. She often gave them rides to her dad's house so Jaime could join the general chaos going to the high school, and Larx could drop Berto off near work. Tane brought him home, and something about the way he looked when he walked in the front door and Olivia or Elton were making dinner and Jaime was doing homework by the table made her think that being put into a housemate situation was one of the best things to happen to their little family of two.

"You said they moved back to…." She wasn't really sure—just "back."

"Colombia," he said with a shrug. "For a while things were really bad there—drugs everywhere, gangs. Then the government started paying people to grow food instead of cocaine. Weird how that fixed things."

Olivia nodded, surprised. "So they moved back?"

Berto shrugged. "They wanted us to come, but me and Jaime, we grew up speaking English." He gave a faint smile before inhaling. "Didn't say it was *good* English."

Olivia laughed, liking him. "So you stayed and took care of your brother. That's nice. Me and Christi—I mean, she's sort of perfect, so, you know—"

"Hate her," Berto said promptly, making her laugh again.

"No—love her. But…." She sighed. "Hard to live up to." Broodingly she ate another saltine.

Berto nodded and burrowed down deeper into the lawn chair. He'd managed to find one of her dad's old sleeping bags, and she felt bad, suddenly. He'd come all prepared to camp out and meditate, and here she was, intruding on him with her bullshit.

"I know what you mean," he said, after a silence that had her rethinking her plan to wait for Larx. "The living up to. Jaime—he's smart, he's good with books. I… I was nothing but a thug, you know? I stayed so I could be a thug." He let out a bark of bitterness and inhaled again. "But then my crew, they were all, 'Hey, Roberto, he's pretty smart. Maybe he's smart enough to work for us!' And I realized, you know? Me choosing to jump down the toilet, that's one thing. I wasn't going to bring him with me. This?" He gestured to his battered face. "If I have to look like this my whole life so Jaime can have a good life like he deserves? It's okay. As long as I didn't bring him down with me."

Olivia swallowed hard, thinking of all the reasons she'd put off therapy.

Pride—pride at being able to take care of her own shit, without help from anyone—*that* was the number one thing.

Olivia—she was the oldest. She'd helped Dad pull his shit together when the single-father thing had seemed too big. She'd kept Christi from losing her shit during the dark year, when it was just them and Mom, and Mom had only fed them sometimes. She'd been the one to make things less bad when they got to see Dad, because he wanted so bad for them to be okay.

Was that when she'd gotten into the habit of putting a good face on shit?

When their mom sent them to school in yesterday's clothes and no food and told them to pray really hard to see if God wanted them to eat?

And then Larx would pick them up from school on Friday and take them wherever they wanted to eat, and buy them clothes and bubble bath and fancy girl toothpaste so they could spend three nights and two days feeling human again before going to a place where their mother told them they were abominations and just didn't deserve to be loved.

There were so many things she'd never wanted her father to know.

He'd guessed—he'd guessed and he'd fought like hell, and he'd gotten them out.

She'd never thought about it before—not until word had trickled down about the girl who'd been lost in the snow—but she and Christi were lucky their dad was such a good guesser and such a good fighter for what was right.

Poor Dad. Fighting so hard to make her better. Fighting so hard to make his kids okay. Hurting Aaron must have seemed like the worst thing in the world he could have done.

"Pride," she said softly. "Pride can do horrible things to us, you know?"

Berto nodded. "Yeah. But being nice, doing the right thing—that's brought me...." She saw it start small and grow and grow—a great peaceful smile taking over his face as he closed his eyes and turned them up to the breaking day. "This," he said softly. "It's beautiful here. You and Elton are good people, and you care about Jaime if I fuck this up. I get to play with your dad's dog whenever I want. And I just watched a sunrise in the mountains." He opened his eyes and turned off his vaporizer. "That's pretty awesome."

"Berto?" she asked, feeling some of his hard-earned joy seep into her own soul. "You know, we could get a cat or a dog here too. Would that be okay?"

His smile was almost as sweet as his brother's. "Either one," he said, biting his lower lip. "I'd be happy with either one."

"Me and Elton might be staying down in Auburn for a couple of weeks. I've...." She took a deep breath. "I need to see a doctor, about my depression, you know?"

Berto nodded, no judgment whatsoever. "That's bad. Can't feel like crap when you got a baby on the way. Need to be there, you know?"

Her throat grew tight. "Yeah. And Elton deserves a better me and...." Oh, this was so true. "I sure would love to enjoy the sunrise like you do."

That smile appeared again. "It's a good thing," he said.

"It really is. When we come back, we can visit the shelter." She thought of a dog or a cat, of the four of them taking care of it, of Berto and Jaime being cousins, rejoicing in the baby too. Maybe not forever. She would want to go back to school eventually, and Colton really was a tiny town.

"That would be wonderful," he said, and impulsively she bent and kissed his cheek.

"We can be family," she said quietly. "Would that be okay?"

"Yeah."

And right then, before the moment could get awkward, she heard the dog bark behind the trees.

"I'm gonna go catch up," she told him, handing him the saltines. "Think about what kinds of dogs you like—if we see one in Auburn and he likes us, we'll bring one home."

"That's easy," Berto said, shrugging. "Good dogs. The kind that will get along with Dozer and play with Jaime. A dog you can run with when your dad can't go."

"The perfect dog," she agreed, and jogged off the porch. "We'll be home by ten, Berto, so we can get to Auburn by one—see you then!"

She caught Larx as he was rounding the bend, and he stopped abruptly, did a little dance-steppy thing to get his rhythm back, and kept going. His face was wet, and he paused to wipe his cheeks on his shoulders.

"You followed me?" he asked, voice clogged, more winded than he should have been.

"Aaron tried—he couldn't make it past the door."

"Shit." Dozer frolicked ahead of them, because the run was one of many of his favorite things, but Larx's word made even Dozer's happy snuffling into something dark and sad.

"It's okay, Daddy. You'll get home. He'll be waiting. He understands."

Larx shrugged and shook his head, for once out of words of encouragement or understanding or even just words.

Olivia owed him some.

"So," she said, pulling back her pace a little so she could talk. "So, when Mom just fucking bailed on us even though we were living in the same house, I told myself over and over again that it was okay. I could take care of us. I was twelve. If she bought rice, I could cook it. I couldn't do my own hair, but I could do Christi's, and we would be just okay, and it would be fine."

"Livvy—"

"No, Daddy. Let me finish. The thing is, I kept saying that. Even when I got depressed. I kept thinking I had to be okay. I had to make me okay. So when I came home last summer and it seemed all right, that was like... like a sign. If I could just do the things that made me okay, I'd be okay, and I'd have a handle on this and nobody needed to help me."

"Baby...."

"Yeah. I was stupid. We all need help." She was winded. She could admit it. "I'm walking."

He slowed to a walk immediately, no questions asked. Because he was just her Dad.

"Anyway—so there I was, being all 'Olivia is an island,' and then I got knocked up and...." She dragged in a breath. "All I can think, all day every day, is that I'm going to fail this baby as bad as Mom failed us. Every goddamned minute. It's…. It's my biggest terror. And today—today, Elton stood up to his dad, and you almost hit him—"

"Not a good moment," Larx said dryly.

"No—but you had someone. We had lots of someones. It wasn't just me in there looking at those people. It was this whole… menagerie you forged, because you're you. And then I came home, and Berto's there, and all he wants is a dog. Just a fuckin' dog—maybe a cat. And the sunrise. And I think, Berto knows where it's at. He accepts help. Every day. And he's grateful. And he gives back the best he can. So I need to accept help. I need to talk to someone about how it felt to… to have to cut off my hair because Alicia couldn't be bothered to brush it, or how she wouldn't let us bathe, and we were outgrowing our clothes. And not you. You were doing everything. *Everything.* Just like now. You've been doing everything. And just like I had to let Elton take my burden, let me heal, let me make my own decisions, you gotta trust Aaron, okay?"

Larx nodded, which was good, because she was on a roll. As their feet crunched on the icy road and the dog ran circles around them, a rush of hope hit her chest, so hard she almost gasped. The sun was peeking through the trees, and the sky was this incredibly Easter egg shade of blue—gold, blue, green, the red of the dirt under their feet—it was a beautiful day. Cold as fuck—but beautiful. And she'd made decisions. And she was going to make some more.

And this baby would never be all alone, never with just Olivia for love.

Olivia had backup.

She could do this.

"I… I could really use some quiet time with Aaron," Larx said in a small voice.

"Yeah." Olivia took a deep breath. "Elton called his parents to ask for money so we could stay in Auburn for two weeks for the depression clinic."

"Oh!" Larx smiled, some of the care falling from his face, from his shoulders. "Really? You decided to do that?"

"Yeah, Daddy. You and Elton—you're a good team."

He laughed brokenly, but he didn't deny it.

"I," he said slowly, probably because he hated to talk about himself, "would really, really like to not worry quite so much about you. I mean… I'll always worry about you, but since Christmas…."

He used to take her and Christi walking when they were kids—nature walks, science walks. Look at this tree with the red leaves shaped like stars—it's deciduous, do you know what that means? See that gray squirrel? It's not indigenous to this area, it's an invasive species, which is too bad because they're really stupid and the brown ones are smarter. And at first they'd be all "Run to the thing! Touch the thing! See the thing!" But in the end, it was less about the thing than it was about spending time with Dad. They always ended those walks, the three of them, hand in hand, Larx in the center, because he was the center of their world.

Now she had Elton, and baby-to-be-named-later, but Larx—Larx would always be her daddy. She would always want to take a walk—or a jog—with him. Like the little girl she used to be, she grabbed her father's hand. So cold—she had gloves on, but he'd run out into the morning without even his hat. Poor Daddy.

"I'd like that too," she said softly, reassured when he squeezed. "I'd like to enjoy the sunrise. To take my baby walking with Elton. To see what kind of dad he'd be."

"I'd like to see that," Larx admitted.

"He might even be as good as you," she said, leaning her head on his shoulder for a moment.

"He might even deserve you," Larx said, making her smile.

She didn't have anything to say to that, and they walked in silence for a while. As they drew closer to the house, he paused under a giant granite boulder that marked their property and tugged at her hand.

"Look!" he said, excitedly, kneeling near the base of the boulder. "Get aw—Dozer, you dumbass, go on!" The dog ran around the tree looking for a squirrel, and Larx stroked a dark green leaf tenderly. "I planted them three years ago, and they're still coming up! I had to add a fuckton of potting soil, you know?"

"Pretty," she said, looking at the shoots poking their way through the snow. "What will they be?"

"Pinks, buttercups, crocuses." His face had that sort of weary peace that came after someone had cried for a while and the storm had passed. "Snow flowers, you know? Means it's getting warmer."

"They come up every year?"

"Sometimes the snow kills them off. I'm just glad the bulbs survived."

Well, with her father's love and strength of will, anything would.

"Me too."

She squeezed her father's hand in the beautiful morning, and together they walked him home.

CROCUS

AARON WAS waiting for them outside as they approached. Larx regarded him with a sort of weary joy. Dozer barked happily and leaped forward so Aaron could assure him he was still a good boy, always a good boy, and he should go inside for treats.

Dozer took off to scratch woefully at the door, and Aaron walked toward Larx and Olivia. Olivia let go of Larx's hand, breaking the illusion he'd sustained that she was a little girl again. Instead she kissed Larx on the cheek, then stepped forward and hugged Aaron tight.

"Told you I'd get him," she said with a little smile.

"Thanks, honey. There's waffles and hot chocolate inside, if you want."

Olivia paused and put her hand on her stomach. "You know… that sounds amazing." She disappeared into the house with Dozer, and Aaron walked the last few paces to Larx. He took off his gloves first and wrapped his hands around Larx's chilled ones, pulling them to his mouth and blowing.

"Baby, you didn't even have a hat on."

Larx swallowed hard. "I'm so sorry—" His voice cracked on the *y*, and Aaron pulled him forward into a full embrace.

"No sorry," he whispered. "None. You don't have to be sorry to me for a damned thing."

Larx shuddered in his arms, hard, and again, and hugged him back and held tight. His head, aching and stuffed from running and crying for damned near five miles, was suddenly too heavy to move from this spot, right here, on Aaron's shoulder.

"Want to go inside?" Aaron asked softly. "The horrible parents are gone. Elton ordered them away, told them to wait a day before they tried an apology. You would have been proud of him, Larx. He's a great kid."

Larx nodded. "He better be. Olivia's pretty awesome."

"They'll be okay together," Aaron told him, and after Larx's walk with his daughter, he could nod his head and have hope that wasn't bullshit. He shivered again, and Aaron murmured, "C'mon. Let's go upstairs. Let's talk."

Larx shook his head. Then he reached out and twined his fingers with Aaron's, pulling their hands to his chest, over his heart. "This," he whispered. "This is sore. I needed you. I needed you so bad. And you were hurt. And all I wanted to do was be at your side. All I wanted to do was lose my shit, cry, stomp, and scream. Forever—you promised me *forever*—and I didn't think that was a real thing, but then there was us and then you got shot and I'm so *angry*. I'm so fucking angry, I lose myself in my own head when I'm driving, and I feel it, building. Just… just raw fucking fury, and I'm going to lose it. I'm going to come home and yell and say something awful, something unforgivable, and drive you away so I'll be alone, but at least I won't… at least I won't…."

Aaron just held him, letting him spill, not trying to soothe him, not even a little, which was the only reason he could say the next part, the unforgivable part.

"At least I won't *lose* you, won't have you ripped away from me. Sometimes I'd just rather *know* I'll be alone, know there'll be this big stupid blank empty space in my soul instead of dream about a future where there isn't one!"

Aaron's arms tightened. He didn't leave, he didn't let go, he didn't yell. "Why didn't you?" he asked, voice as raw as Larx's. "Why didn't you come home and yell at me and say the unforgivable thing?"

"Because…." Larx closed his eyes against this, but nothing was going to hold back the whole of it now. "I'd… I'd see you, and you'd smile and… and I'd stomp on the mad, and it would be all okay, because I *had* you, I *have* you, and what kind of dumbass kicks a perfectly good man out of his life because he's afraid that man is going to get killed on the job!"

For a moment, the air around them was so silent, Larx could hear Aaron struggling for breath. Then a magic sound happened.

Aaron's soft chuckle rippled under Larx's cheek.

"What?" Larx asked, feeling stupid and young and all those things he'd been avoiding feeling by not talking over the past couple of weeks.

"I don't know what makes you think I'm a perfectly good man. I'm sort of an averagely good man, really. I'm sure there are perfectly good men out there with less of a chance of getting shot—"

Larx scowled up at him. "Shut up."

And Aaron caught his cold cheeks between his warm, gloved hands and captured Larx's mouth in a sweet, brief kiss. When he spoke again, it was maybe the last thing Larx expected to hear.

"Marry me."

Larx gaped. "Wha—?"

"Marry me. So if I'm ever in the hospital again, I'm not just your boyfriend or the man in your life. I'm your husband. So when Olivia walks down the aisle and has that baby, whichever order it happens, I'm her stepdad. So I'm the baby's grandpa legally, and if Kirby so much as skins his knee, you can make decisions without me. So the whole world knows I love you, and if I leave your side, it's because I absolutely had no other goddamned choice. And if…." His voice caught here, leaving Larx with another wound. "And if you ever run out that door again because your heart's too full or too angry, I know, without a doubt, that you'll be back for more than your stuff."

Larx closed his eyes, thinking he'd say something vague, something that would put the question off for when he was less angry, less distraught, less raw.

"Yes." He gaped at himself and shut his mouth, wondering how that came out. "Yes," he said again, because apparently words were taking a shortcut from heart to mouth without stopping at brain so it could fuck them up. "Yes, I'll marry you. God, God yes. If I want to marry you now, as pissed off as I am right now, I'll want to marry you every other goddamned day of our lives."

Aaron gave another rocky chuckle and kissed him, hard, like they were each other's, like they would be forever. Larx responded hungrily, drinking in his generosity, his possession, his *life*, while the world was peaceful and good.

Aaron gave a little gasp, and then Larx felt him, grinding up against Larx's leg in frustration.

Oh man, Larx wanted him so bad.

He closed his eyes and pulled away. "I don't suppose our kids are all going to the movies, are they?"

Aaron groaned. "No! Oh God, I wish." He took a breath back, and they both tried to pull their brains out of their desire.

"Maybe," Larx said, desperate, so desperate for time just with Aaron. "Maybe if we just close the door, say grown-up time, and… I don't know. Leave the TV on. Is that a bad idea? We just…." He wanted to sob. "We were in a good place this morning. I… I want that place back. I want it so bad."

"Let's try that," Aaron promised. "C'mon. First, baby, let's get you inside."

THEY WERE greeted by excited kids wanting to tell an exciting story, and Larx let them. Nobody asked where he'd been or why he'd left—he wondered if Aaron had briefed them, or if they were just close enough to adulthood to exercise the ultimate in kindness.

Breakfast was still on the table for him, and the strawberries and waffles turned out to be the thing that had been missing from his life that he'd never known.

He demolished his stack, whipped cream and all, and then finished the dishes quietly while everybody went to change.

While he was washing, his youngest threw out a casual miracle.

"Daddy, I'm going to drive Olivia and Wombat Willie home—Princess is whining a lot about running in her jeans and needing a shower and whatever. It's actually set day for the drama club—you know, paint the flats, set them up, lights and stuff. We all know people who're gonna be there—we thought we'd go help." She was so insouciant about it, dark glossy hair scraped into a ponytail, bright, wicked brown eyes flashing up at him brightly.

And he thought, of course. Isaiah had been stage manager three years running—Kellan would know a lot of people in the play this year.

"Course. How long do you think you'll be gone?" he said, trying not to launch into the CW Frog dance, complete with top hat and everything. Aaron had sat quietly during breakfast, touching his knee, drinking coffee, and talking in low tones while Larx mostly nodded. He was out of words. Maybe tomorrow he would tell everybody that they were getting married, have a plan, set a date. Right now he was content just to know it would happen—that Aaron wanted it to happen, just as much as he did.

"Well, they should be done by four, and I think everybody's going out for pizza afterward." She gave him a coy little bat of the lashes, and he laughed.

"Would you like to raid my wallet so you three may, too, have pizza afterward?"

"Oh, Daddy, you're the best!" She said it with such unctuousness that he had to laugh.

"Just remember that I'm the best sometimes when I say no," he told her, and was rewarded by her arms over his shoulders and a kiss on his cheek.

"Have a good quiet day," she said, voice completely at odds with the impish little opportunist she'd presented herself as. "We'll text you before we come home—let us know if you want us to bring dinner, okay?"

Larx nodded, swallowing hard. His emotions were still perilously near the surface, and he thought again what a miracle his children were—Christiana in particular at the moment, but all his children, as a whole.

"Maybe offer to take Jaime when you drop off Livvy," he said, because the boy had a habit of showing up during quiet times so he could play with the dog. Two miles was a damned long walk to play with a dog.

"Way ahead of you," she chirped. "We already texted him, and he's up and ready."

Oh, God love them all.

"Thanks, honey. Just…." He couldn't even look at her. God, even if Aaron hadn't been there, his whole body hurt with the need for peace. "Thanks."

She kissed his cheek again, and the whole lot of them made a loud and noisy exit. Larx put the last plate in the drying rack and was unsurprised when Aaron stepped behind him, wrapping his arms around Larx's waist and kissing the back of his neck.

"Are we really all alone?" he said softly.

"We really are."

"I can't promise acrobatics and fireworks." Yeah, he said that, but he was nibbling on Larx's ear and tugging slightly, and Larx's groin was one big aching mass.

"I'll take you naked," Larx promised fervently. "Naked and an orgasm… I'm not picky."

Aaron laughed outright. "You're a cheap date. Which is good, 'cause we're both public servants and make diddly over squat."

Larx dried his hands on a dish towel and, blasphemy! Left it on the counter. Then he turned and kissed Aaron soundly.

And then pulled back and wrinkled his nose. "I… I've got sweaty parts," he apologized. "Pits and stuff. And…. God, I haven't even brushed my teeth!" In horror he put his hand up over his mouth as though he could suddenly take back all the necking they'd been doing over the last half hour.

"Ditto," Aaron agreed. Then he smiled, whimsical and playful. "Shall we take a half-hour break for hygiene and morning things and then, you know. Meet back in your bed, naked, like a date?"

"Sure." Then his eyes opened in horror. "Who gets the kids' bathroom—"

"One, two, three—"

"Not it!" they both cried, fingers to noses. Larx sighed. Dammit.

"You win," he said. "I'll go get my hazmat suit."

Aaron cackled. "Well, since Kirby is my son, and he learned his habits from me, I'll cut you a break. Half an hour?"

God, he was wonderful. "Your sports magazine is in the living room," Larx told him, grinning.

"And your science magazine is on the dresser," Aaron informed him. "One, two, three—"

"Break!"

USING THE bathroom in peace was a luxury, and so was a shower without a time limit. Larx was about five minutes later than the promised half an hour, and Aaron hadn't quite gotten there yet himself. Larx—clean, dry, naked—slid between the sheets of their bed and shivered with the sheer sensuality of it.

Then his carnal horndog took over, and he went rooting through his end table for a few select items they might want. Aaron wasn't ready to be penetrated yet, and he wasn't ready to pound Larx into the mattress either—but that didn't mean they couldn't have fun in other ways, with other things. Hell, most of their sex happened with the lights off, trying to be as quiet as church mice so the other mice in their church wouldn't know what was going on—just opening the drawer was a big naughty spot.

They'd already learned that being able to have sex as loudly as possible was one of the most erotic things they'd experienced in their lives.

He'd just set out his pitifully small assortment of toys when Aaron slunk in through the door with a towel around his waist. He looked over his shoulder sheepishly before turning the lock, and Larx covered his eyes with his hands.

"We're alone," he said, smirking.

"I am aware," Aaron said with dignity, draping the towel on the dresser. "I just… you know. The dog was giving me the eye, and I didn't want to explain."

"The dog?" Holding his face straight was incredibly difficult.

"We, you know. We cut off his balls, Larx. We cut off the dog's balls, and here we are. About to have sex. And he knows it. It feels like we're taunting him."

Larx lost it, rolling to his side and howling into the pillow. "Taunting him?"

"It's not funny!"

"Oh, it had better be funny! Taunting him?"

"He might have wanted balls! I mean, I know it was policy, and I even know why—"

"Aaron, sweetheart, your dog would have committed suicide by mountain lion. You know that. I love that dog, but God knows he's not bright, and he's a little lazy. He would have gone out into the wilderness to get him some tail, tried to fuck a mountain lion, and died. Animal control would have had to tell you, 'We're sorry, Mr. George, but your dog was trying to fuck a mountain lion and he died. We've had his wiener bronzed—would you like it for a keychain?'"

Aaron was openly laughing now. "A keychain?"

"Yes. Their wieners are little and ugly—a keychain at the most."

"His balls could have been fuzzy dice on the car, at least," Aaron said, and now he was the one holding a straight face.

"There goes Deputy George. He's got his dog's balls on his rearview mirror—don't mess with him. You know what we call him?" Larx was almost laughing too hard to finish.

"Don't. Please." Now Aaron had his hand over his eyes even as he was sliding into bed.

"We call him the—"

"If you say 'Castrator,' I'm leaving you."

"Fixer," Larx said, his smirk so broad it hurt his cheeks. "We'll call you the Fixer."

Their giggles quieted, but their eyes still twinkled as they looked at each other, the dance of light through their curtains almost as seductive as music.

"I can't fix everything," Aaron said breathlessly, and Larx slid his fingers through Aaron's still thick, blond hair.

"You fix my heart just being here." Larx closed his eyes as they kissed, losing himself in Aaron's touch and smell, in his presence, his body touching Larx's, their skin bare against the other.

"Mm...." He tilted his head back as Aaron nibbled down his neck, rubbing gentle teeth against Larx's collarbone.

"You brought out goodies," Aaron murmured. "Are you trying to tell me something?"

Larx looked at the largish plug he'd selected and closed his eyes again, suddenly embarrassed. "It's been a long time," he said, because "God, I need to be fucked!" was a little bawdy for all the sweetness in their bed at the moment.

Aaron just chuckled. "You are not fooling me for a second," he said. "You're a man with needs!"

"Yes!" Larx covered his eyes. "I have needs. And most days, you satisfy those needs just fine—"

Aaron sucked Larx's aching nipple into his mouth, and Larx gasped.

"But today...," he prompted.

Larx had spread his knees already under the covers, and the air was kissing along his naked flesh, tantalizing the tender bits that didn't usually get set free.

"Today I'm in need," he admitted.

Aaron chuckled and scooted down the bed, tapping Larx's leg so he'd lift it and give Aaron access to the treasures between his spread legs.

"Today I can answer your needs," Aaron told him and then disappeared behind the V of Larx's splayed body.

Larx felt Aaron's tongue licking up and between his testicles, slowly, methodically, digging into the base of Larx's cock, flattening, getting the underside with a full-court press. Larx let out a groan that probably rattled the windows, and he didn't care.

Ah, God, he really did need.

Aaron engulfed him, a carnal cave of heat, and Larx tried not to thrash on the bed, his body craved so badly. Aaron tightened his mouth, his tongue, his palate, and pulled up slowly, until Larx's whimper echoed in his own ears.

"Hand me one," Aaron whispered, and augh! Larx fumbled, for the plug, for the lube, picking in the end something longer, thinner, that could slide in and out and… and fuck him. He yearned for possession, and Aaron seemed to know that as he took the toy from Larx's hand and the tube of lubricant with it.

The coolness of the lube dribbled between Larx's asscheeks, and he let out a gasp of relief. Oh… oh yes. He wanted. So badly. Aaron's finger wasn't nearly big enough, but two fingers made a beautiful ache.

"So tight," Aaron murmured, his breath fanning Larx's sensitized cockhead. "Like it's trying to trap me."

"I'd rip your dick off," Larx threatened crudely. "God, Aaron, that's… perfect. That's wonderful. More. Just fucking more."

Ahhh…. Larx made his entire body go limp, because the thrust of the cool silicone toy was not nearly as organic as Aaron's body inside him.

But the fullness, the stretch, oh, that was needed, and then Aaron sucked on him again, and fucked him with the toy, slowly, both ends, rhythmically, slowly, slowly….

"Faster harder Jesus, Aaron, fuck me!"

For a moment embarrassment threatened to return, but Aaron pulled back and thrust harder, harder, the base of the thing stretching and popping from Larx's sphincter, and Aaron's mouth a treacherous heaven, hard and soft, brutal and sweet, again, again, again, again, overwhelming him, overriding the stress, the confusion, the anger, the ache of loneliness that had overtaken Larx's heart too many times in the past weeks.

His climax bore down on him like a freight train, and he knotted his fingers in Aaron's hair and gibbered, begging him to please, please, just… oh yes… just keep doing… oh God… yes… just… fucking *that*.

He allowed himself to cry out, his voice echoing in the space of their room, Aaron's mouth working him, milking him, as he poured all his frustration and worry from the past few weeks right down Aaron's throat.

Aaron took it all and pushed up to hold Larx as the trembling overtook his body.

"How you doing?" Aaron whispered after a moment.

"Nungh…."

Aaron laughed and kissed his temple.

"Did you forget something?" Larx asked, deliciously uncomfortable as he worked the plug in his ass.

"Nope. Thought you'd want the reminder while you were… uh, returning the favor."

Larx grinned lazily and pulled Aaron down for a kiss, tasting himself on Aaron's tongue. "My pleasure," he promised and then rolled to his side so he could kiss his way down Aaron's body, stopping at all the vital points. His collarbone, his nipples—oh yes, his nipples—and then down, with careful kisses on his scars and careful nibbles on his hip bones.

The whole time he was vibrating, aroused again by the pressure against his prostate, by the plug still in his ass.

By the time he was eye to eye, so to speak, with Aaron's generously sized body, he almost couldn't concentrate on his job.

"Larx," Aaron hissed. "Swing around so I can play."

Larx did, swinging his bottom so his hips were up near Aaron's head, almost weeping with relief.

Aaron's cock in his mouth was a sensual experience in itself, fat and long, precome salty on Larx's tongue, the head pushing against the back of his throat. Larx fell into his work while Aaron… fiddled. Played with the handle, pulled the thing out, slid it in, harder. Harder. Harder. And Larx kept sucking, harder, and longer, and faster, and—

He buried his face against Aaron's thigh. "I'm gonna come again," he panted, shaking.

"I'm gonna come once!" Aaron panted with a particularly hard thrust. "Let's see who gets there first!"

Larx laughed helplessly, then took Aaron into his mouth again, using his free hand to stroke delicately, his thighs, his balls, his taint….

"Oh!" Aaron cried out as Larx penetrated him gently, just a fingertip today, still working his mouth over Aaron's cock.

Aaron's spurt of come, silky, sweet, and salty, into the back of his throat was as erotic as the plug being thrust into his backside, more so, because it meant Larx had pleased the man pleasing him. When he buried his face into Aaron's thigh and screamed and spurted, it was with the freedom of orgasm, the ultimate joy of give and take, the amazing flight of holding his lover's cock in his mouth while his lover pleased him too.

This time Aaron pulled the plug all the way out and put it on the towel on the dresser to clean later, and Larx flopped around on the bed, coming to a rest with his head on Aaron's shoulder. Aaron wiped his thumb along the side of Larx's mouth, taking one last trickle of come, and then sucked it off, and the two of them regarded each other soberly, with the air of men who had accomplished a great thing.

"That was…." Aaron panted.

"So necessary."

"Like breathing."

"We need to do that way, way more."

They laughed then, relaxed, sweaty, and Aaron rolled over and took Larx into the safety of his arms.

"We'll get married," Aaron said, voice rough.

"Yes."

"Because this is forever."

"I promise."

"Don't leave me."

"Swear."

"And no more secrets."

Larx sighed. "I'll try. Sometimes, what's in my heart—"

"Complicated." Aaron sighed over his head. "I know. But trust me, okay?"

"Deal." Larx curled against him, ready for his man-nap before round two, and suddenly he let out a wholly inappropriate giggle.

"What?" Aaron asked, his own voice drowsy as well.

"Wait until I tell Yoshi."

Aaron's deep chuckle rumbled against his cheek and lulled him to sleep.

WILDFLOWERS

"MARRIED?" YOSHI demanded as they ate lunch in Larx's office. "*Married?*"

Larx shushed him, but Nancy, Tane's sister, was sitting with them this day, and she took up the cry. "Seriously? Married?"

Larx grimaced, a little embarrassed but secretly as thrilled as a girl in a romance movie. "Yes. Married. Like they do in the storybooks, right? It happens."

"Well, yeah," Yoshi said, rolling his eyes. "To *you*, maybe. But you get shot teaching science and subdue psychopaths with shotguns. I mean, just because *you* think getting married happens doesn't mean it happens to the rest of us!"

Nancy patted his arm. "Honey, Tane will ask you. Or, you know, show up someday with rings and say, 'Wear it or don't. I'm wearing it because it's how I feel.'"

Yoshi looked at her sourly and waved his left hand with the etched stainless steel band on it. "It's like you were there."

Larx stared at him. "That's a wedding ring? It's awesome!"

"It's a not-wedding ring, because we had a not-wedding," Yoshi muttered. "He helped Berto move into Aaron's old house and came back with the rings and that super not-romantic proposal she just mentioned and told me that I shared his goddamned pain so I should share his goddamned joy." Yoshi shrugged, and his cheeks heated. "Okay. So maybe it was a little romantic." Then he looked up from his egg-salad sandwich—which everybody was eating, because Easter Sunday had been last weekend and who had anything else?—and sighed. "But it's not a summer wedding in your backyard, with the sun setting and a white canopy and your daughters singing and your sons ushering people to sit and the whole town there, because Aaron's running for sheriff and why wouldn't you invite people—is it?"

Larx stared at him. "That's what we're having?"

Yoshi nodded. "Yeah. I won't let you settle for anything less."

"You guys, I was thinking some friends and some cake—"

"I'll do the flowers," Nancy said on a happy sigh. "I bet the girls will help me—"

"Don't count on Olivia," Larx muttered. "She's going to be pregnant through August, and she might just try to hurt you."

"How is she doing?" Nancy asked kindly. She'd had Olivia in her class, as had most of the teachers at Colton High.

"Better," Larx said simply. He wouldn't tell them about the two tearful, emotionally fraught phone calls he'd gotten during her two weeks in Auburn. Aaron had been there afterward to pick up the pieces, and they seemed to be all stitched together now. What mattered was that Olivia was coming home tomorrow afternoon, and on Sunday night Elton's father was going to try the family introduction thing again. Larx didn't have a lot of hope he'd fix things, but hey, it was a free meal. "That reminds me!" He was happy to change the subject. "Candace—her first day back at school is Monday. What's the buzz in the hallways?"

Yoshi smirked. "The buzz is, the heroic principal went up against her homicidal stepdad and saved everybody's life, hurray! And what was Yoshi doing when this happened? Yoshi was home, feeding teenagers pizza. Because Yoshi likes teenagers a little better than Yoshi likes guns."

"Okay, *Douchy*, you can stop talking about yourself in the third person now," Larx told him. "We all know the world would have fallen apart if you hadn't constipated three teenaged boys and caused my daughter to break out."

"That was the grease in the pizza, not me," Yoshi said with supreme righteousness.

"And it doesn't have a thing to do with"—Larx's playfulness faded—"whether or not anybody at the school knows about the nature of her abuse or the procedure afterward." He didn't even want to say the words in the high school environs. Candace's trauma was her own—Larx wanted to make damned sure she had control over who knew about it. If the whole school was buzzing about her, he'd make arrangements for her to go to school in Truckee—he wasn't going to subject her to the additional pain of having her private life on display.

"I haven't heard a whisper," Yoshi said, just as soberly. "I asked her geography teacher—the one whose class her friend attends—if her friend has said anything or is the type to gossip. She said the girl's life revolves around Candace as a friend. She's been sad and distracted since Candace left, and she's really excited that she's coming back. Period. So I think we're bringing her to a safe place."

Larx nodded. "Good. If we get even an inkling that it's not, we pull her out and we shelter her." If Candace could trek twenty miles across the mountains in the snow, sleeping in a snow shelter to stay alive, the least they could do was help her navigate the pitfalls of high school society. Larx was damned well going to try.

"Deal," Nancy said, and Yoshi nodded in agreement.

"How about Jaime—how's he doing?" Larx looked at Nancy because she usually ate lunch in the staff room, and she had more of the pulse of the teachers than they did.

"Great," she said, nodding. "As you very well know, he's stayed active in his clubs, has started hanging with the drama kids, and is signed up to take the PSAT practice courses starting next weekend. Your boy is doing okay; you can relax."

Larx rolled his eyes. "Never," he said, meaning it. "We can never relax. You think I relax about my kids? You are sorely mistaken." No finish line. There was *no* finish line. You just kept running the best race you could.

For a moment they were quiet, because *everybody* had been worried about Livvy, and then Yoshi spoke up.

"Seriously—you think we're going to stop badgering you about the wedding that easy? I mean, Larx—this is going to be Colton's social event of the year!"

Larx just shook his head. "Aaron runs for election in the fall—don't you think he'll have enough on his plate?"

"Nope," Nancy said smugly. "Just leave the details to us."

"I don't even believe this," Larx muttered.

"No, seriously. We'll take care of it," Yoshi reassured him.

"Guys, we haven't even told the kids!"

Nancy and Yoshi looked at each other in evil agreement. "You have a week," Yoshi said.

"That's fair," Nancy agreed. "A week. You said he asked you three weeks ago? You have a week to tell the kids, or we tell them you're both eloping to Tahoe."

Larx stared at them. "You're awful people." He meant that.

"We're awful people who are going to arrange your wedding," Yoshi said sweetly. "I think you should be nicer to us than that."

"I think he should bring us sandwiches," Nancy said thoughtfully. "Sub sandwiches. Because Jesus, egg salad is going to make me fuckin' puke."

Yoshi agreed, and then they both started talking about wildflowers in mason jars and who they knew who decorated cakes as a hobby, and Larx spent the rest of his lunch lacing his hands behind his neck and wishing for a teleportation device.

And trying not to dread Sunday, when the whole family had to face Olivia's in-laws for one more happy try.

COLTON HAD one "fancy" restaurant, a steakhouse, with tablecloths and limited seating and a waitstaff that sort of trickled down from Reno because Colton didn't have quite the amount of gambling despair. Aaron and Eamon ate there sometimes for dinner when they were discussing administration, because Eamon liked the place. He'd treat Aaron, usually, because the price was pretty steep, and Aaron was always grateful.

Elton's father had made reservations there for ten, which meant they pretty much took up the floor, and Larx brought Jaime because, in his words, "This guy fuckin' owes us big."

Well, not that Jaime ate a lot, but Aaron wasn't going to argue.

The dinner started awkwardly, plastic smiles and the obscenely loud clatter of utensils. All the boys were dressed in button-down shirts and sweaters, and Christiana had busted out with a full-skirted dress and heels. The black skirt had a tiny white print of Jack and Sally from *The Nightmare Before Christmas* on it, and Aaron heartily approved.

Olivia was dressed in a sapphire-blue tunic and leggings, her baby bump just barely visible when she sat down. Elton wore a suit, like his father, and Cheryl was wearing slacks and a sweater with sparkles.

Larx had even managed a sport coat over his sweater, and Aaron had too. Aaron had been a little

dismayed at how much alike their sweaters looked—
but there was nothing they could do about it now. It
was like they were all hoping the awkward finery
would make people forget about the couple invading
Larx and Aaron's home and saying nasty things three
weeks before.

But then, it had been a big three weeks.

"So, Olivia," Shawn McDaniels said cordially, "I
hope your, uh, treatment went well?"

Olivia laughed. "It's not like they pumped me full
of drugs and zapped my brain, Mr. McDaniels. We just
went over medication I could use while pregnant and
nursing and talked about regimen and meditation tech-
niques. It was just that we had to journal every day and
practice everything we were taught, so, you know, by
the time we got home, it was habit." She rolled her
eyes. "Lots and lots of habit."

"Will you be able to take that habit and go back to
school after the baby's born?"

Aaron and Larx both sucked in a breath, because
Olivia had talked frankly the day before about how
much she needed her people right now.

"We'll see," she said, with a confidence Aaron admired. "Right now there's colleges in Reno which are
closer, and online courses that I can complete without
leaving home. I really would rather take things slowly,
sir. Taking care of myself, taking care of my people—
the degree in biology will come."

"Biology?" Cheryl McDaniels said, fascinated.
"I had no idea that was your major. What made you
decide to go into that?"

Olivia smiled slightly. "My dad's a science teacher. He spent a lot of our childhood taking us into the

world and showing us that it was full of wonder. I mean, scientists are going to save the world, right?" She smiled brightly. "I'll join them when I can."

Oh! She was lovely. Charming. Quirky. She was Larx's daughter down to her toes. Aaron didn't see how anyone wouldn't love her as a new daughter— but the McDaniels family tried.

"I'm not really sure scientists are going to save the world," McDaniels intoned, and Aaron barely refrained from rolling his eyes.

"Well, it's not going to be the politicians," Kirby muttered to Christiana, and she snorted, drawing the attention of the rest of the table.

"Really, young man? Who do *you* think is going to save the world?" Oh God. He was one of those people who condescended to teenagers. Aaron was supposed to be running for an elected office, and he could hardly sit at the same table as this guy. Not good, not good, not good!

"The teachers, sir," Kirby said boldly. "I've never learned anything from a politician, but all my best decisions come from information and a working brain. It would be great if the politicians paid them more thought—just, you know, in case you want to take that into your day job."

There was general laughter at the table, and McDaniels retreated long enough for the family to order. Larx had told Aaron that his order would depend on what kind of asshole McDaniels would be beforehand. He'd been civil but unsubtly trying to show up pretty much the entire family. Larx ordered the steak and lobster, and while Aaron ordered the fish on diet principle, he admired Larx's decision greatly. Aaron was reasonably sure the meat wasn't going to be the only thing being grilled while they waited for their food.

However, McDaniels's first targets had proved to be unexpectedly resilient in the poise department—he chose his next victim with an easy kill in mind.

"So, Jaime—"

"*Hai-me*," Jaime corrected. "You don't say the *J* in Colombia. It's pronounced *Hai*-me."

Elton's father swallowed and tried again. "Jaime—are you and your brother going to be living with my son for long?"

And for a moment, Jaime looked bewildered. "We're renting the rooms from Deputy George, sir. It's like people in an apartment complex, except we all went in together and got a dog." The smile that popped out on the young man's delicate features could have made angels swoon. "We gotta live there together for a little while at least, sir. It's a real good dog."

"As long as you and Berto need to," Aaron reassured.

"It's actually a lot better than living at the dorm, Dad," Elton intervened. "We take turns making dinner, Olivia makes breakfast for everybody, and we clean the house twice a week. It's nice having a family there."

"But these people aren't related to you!" Shawn McDaniels burst out, and Larx and Aaron both hid their smirks behind their hands.

"What?" McDaniels demanded.

"We were just wondering how long it would take you to get there," Larx said dryly. "Elton's the father of my grandson. He's family. And even if he wasn't, we like him. We'll keep him as long as he wants to be here."

"Thanks, sir," Elton said, holding his hand out for the five.

"My man." Larx gave back. "Now seriously, *Shawn*, are you done poking at us? I thought we were here to get to know each other, not be deposed."

"Good word," Kellan said from Aaron's elbow. "I was trying to think of something that meant 'grilled like a trout' but sounded like a grown-up would say it."

Larx regarded him with mock severity. "Aren't you going to be eighteen in a couple of months? I mean, won't you be a grown-up then?"

And Kellan shook his head with horror. "Hey, I was promised a two-year addendum to my childhood when I moved in. I'm not claiming grown-up until I'm twenty."

"Addendum." Larx winked. "Nice word!"

Everybody laughed except Shawn McDaniels, who managed to suck all the light out the world as he was sucking down scotch.

"I'm just trying to get a feel for who my son will be spending his time with!" Shawn protested. "You have to admit, your... *lifestyle* is somewhat unorthodox."

"The working-parent lifestyle?" Aaron asked drolly, figuring it was his turn to take a hit. "Because my wife worked—she had to. We needed the money. Or did you mean something else?"

McDaniels regarded him with an unfriendly glare. "You know very well what I mean."

"No, sir," Christiana said, dimpling evilly. "Spell it out for us."

And now McDaniels was on the receiving end of eight very unfriendly sets of eyes. "I'm sorry, I'm just old-fashioned—"

"Why is it people use that word as an excuse for doing something really awful?" Christi asked, like they were having a different conversation. "Right before someone does something really racist or dumb, they're like, 'I'm just old-fashioned, but I think children should be beaten and not heard!' Or, 'I'm just old-fashioned, but I think women should vote like their husbands do.'"

"Wait!" Kirby said, like an excited student. "I've got one! 'I'm just old-fashioned, but I think girls are too dumb for science!'"

"Or athletes shouldn't be in drama!" Kellan added.

"Or I'm just old-fashioned, but I think Mexicans should go home," Jaime said, disgusted. "I'm not even Mexican. Do people think that's the only country south of Texas?"

"I'm just old-fashioned, but I think a father should give cows to his in-laws so they know how much his daughter is worth," Elton said pointedly, and Olivia smacked him on the arm.

"Twenty. I am a twenty-cow woman."

"And an entire coop of chickens, my love," Elton said, smiling sweetly.

"Hey," Aaron said, eyes twinkling. "Old-fashioned isn't always bad, you know?"

He watched Larx's eyes widen across the table, because Larx could read his mind.

"Examples, Aaron," Christi demanded—but she trusted him, so her smile never dimmed. "We need examples."

"Okay," Aaron said, watching as Larx shook his head in panic. They hadn't said anything to the family— not once—about their conversation three weeks ago, about the tremendous monumental thing they'd agreed to, about the direction their lives were heading. "How about, I think when two people are really in love, and their lives join seamlessly, and they want to be together even when they're super pissed at each other, that if it's important to them, they should get married."

Olivia and Christi caught on first.

"Daddy?" Olivia asked hesitantly.

Larx mouthed "You asshole" at him before turning to the kids. "Yes. Aaron asked and I said yes."

The table erupted into applause and whistles and good wishes, and Aaron watched as Shawn McDaniels conceded defeat. Nobody here was going to let him make them feel small—not a soul.

"Congratulations, gentlemen," he said when the hubbub had died down. "Do you have anything planned? A date? A venue?"

"Venue should be our front yard," Aaron said, smiling. "I'm pretty sure there's flowers in the spring and summer, and we can barbecue in the back."

"But when?"

"Sometime not winter," Jaime burst out. "I'm sorry—I know you people are all, like, 'Okay! It's spring! Hurray!'—but there's still snow in the shade, and I think you all are full of it!"

More laughter, and the food arrived just then, but Aaron winked at Larx's glare from across the table and knew he'd be in for it later. There'd be kids in the back of the minivan, though, so Larx would just have to wait until they got home.

"THAT ENDED better than it began," Larx said as he was getting ready for bed.

Aaron was already under the covers, and he watched Larx's trim body in the light from his reading lamp and smiled. "You think that's the end?" he baited.

Larx looked at him sideways before hanging up his sport coat and setting his belt on the dresser. "Feeling frisky, Deputy," he said primly.

"Hey, I've been cleared to run with you," Aaron said. "I think that means we can do the other thing too. The big thing. The thing you're dying to do, and don't deny it."

"Wouldn't dream of it," Larx said with a wink. Then he sobered. "One more week at home—will you live?"

Aaron shrugged, resigned. "I'm on desk duty for another month, and Eamon wants to ride with me for a week or two to make sure I, you know…."

"Stop flinching," Larx said softly.

Driving—it was still a problem. So far the kids had missed it, but Aaron felt Larx's hand on his knee whenever they got within fifteen feet of another car, no matter which one of them was driving. Larx knew.

"Yeah." Aaron leaned back and massaged the knot forming between his eyes. He had plans for this evening, dammit, that didn't include worry. "But that has nothing to do with what I want from you tonight."

Larx laughed and then crossed his arms in mock irritation. "After dropping that bomb on the kids, you think I'm going to put out?"

"What did you think we were going to do, Larx? Run away to Tahoe and elope?"

Larx scowled. "Have you been talking to Yoshi?"

"No! I just know you—you don't want the ceremony for yourself. Well, tough."

The tension bled from Larx's shoulders, and he took off his slacks and folded them before hanging them up. "Good luck with that," he muttered. "Nancy and Yoshi have plans for us. You have no idea. I mean, I think they've picked a date and everything."

"Well, good. Have them coordinate with the kids—seriously, all we'll have to do is hire a house-cleaner and show up for the ceremony."

Larx guffawed. "My God, you have no idea what you've done, do you. Do you have any idea how ba-nanashit this whole thing is going to get?"

Aaron shrugged. "As opposed to our lives during the last six months? And hey—Kellan and Kirby grad-uate in a couple of months, and there's going to be a baby in August, and—"

Larx threw his hands in the air and stalked to the bathroom to brush his teeth. Aaron used the time to remove his boxers and take off his T-shirt, stashing them neatly under his pillow. Larx might talk a good game about getting too irritated for sex, but once he got in bed to find Aaron naked, the whole world would come to a halt.

Aaron was really looking forward to that happen-ing tonight.

Larx came back into the room and shut off the light, not even looking at Aaron before sliding into bed. Aaron rolled to his side and pulled Larx into his arms, finding his mouth even in the starry vision of the new dark.

Larx groaned in total surrender, just that quickly, and ran his hand down Aaron's flank and hip, gasping slightly.

"Wow, Deputy," he teased. "It's like you're in the mood to do the thing."

"Not the thing," Aaron whispered in his ear. "The fucking thing. I'm in the mood to do the fucking thing."

And oh, Larx moaned again, responsive, giving, all his irritation turning to passion in a flash of desire.

Aaron took his time, seduced him, used his mouth, his teeth, his hands, his tongue, brought Larx to wanton, begging submission, and Larx urged him on.

"Yes! Oh... there. Kiss... oh please, touch... let me touch you—please, Aaron, let me suck you—"

Aaron's cock grew hard from Larx's words alone.

And when he followed words up with touch, Aaron's need amped up from hard to unbearable, to swollen, aching, throbbing with arousal.

He'd wanted to spend an hour, but he needed much sooner than that. It felt like moments, heartbeats, a few cries in the night before he had Larx where he wanted him, thighs spread, ass lifted on a pillow, slicked up and dripping and waiting for possession.

His body welcomed Aaron like the cave welcomed the dragon—hot and moist and ready for invasion.

And passion.

And tumult and frantic chasing after glory.

Larx found his first, arching up, tightening around Aaron's cock, spewing, thick and urgent onto his stomach as Aaron watched in the faint light. Aaron's own climax rippled through him, clenched his stomach, knotted his chest, exploded outward into sound, even as Larx gasped under him, hand shoved in his mouth to muffle his cries.

Aaron never wanted to leave the haven of Larx's body.

He fell forward, feeling his recovery in every sinew, regretting nothing.

"Oh God," he groaned into the hollow of Larx's shoulder. "I needed that. Did you need that? I needed that."

"I so needed that," Larx panted, wrapping his legs around Aaron's hips, his arms around Aaron's shoulders. "I needed that more than air."

Aaron rolled to the side and grinned at him, and Larx grinned back. His narrow face relaxed as it so rarely did.

"Did you need it as much as our family needs our wedding?" he asked, making sure.

Larx groaned, a totally different kind of groan than he'd let out a few minutes ago. "Oh, fine. I get it," he admitted. "It needs to be big. They all need to know. It needs to be a deal."

Aaron closed his eyes, relief and orgasm making him weak. "Good. Because us being in love? In spite of all the chaos of our lives? That's a big deal to me."

He felt Larx's kiss on his shoulder as Larx rolled to his side so he could rest his head there next. "Me too. We'll make it a big deal to the world. I promise, Deputy."

"I'll hold you to that, Principal."

"Mm...." Larx was falling asleep, naked and despoiled, and Aaron thought he'd wake him to dress in a few minutes. Right now Aaron could hold everything that had been missing from his life for so long in his arms, against his chest, next to his heart.

He knew—they *both* knew—what a rare and strange thing happiness was. They knew enough to grab on to it with both hands and carry it with them into an ever-changing future.

BONFIRES

AMY LANE

Bonfires: Book One

Ten years ago Sheriff's Deputy Aaron George lost his wife and moved to Colton, hoping growing up in a small town would be better for his children. He's gotten to know his community, including Mr. Larkin, the bouncy, funny science teacher. But when Larx is dragged unwillingly into administration, he stops coaching the track team and starts running alone. Aaron—who thought life began and ended with his kids—is distracted by a glistening chest and a principal running on a dangerous road.

Larx has been living for his kids too—and for his students at Colton High. He's not ready to be charmed by Aaron, but when they start running together, he comes to appreciate the deputy's steadiness, humor, and complete understanding of Larx's priorities. Children first, job second, his own interests a sad last.

It only takes one kiss for two men approaching fifty to start acting like teenagers in love, even amid all the responsibilities they shoulder. Then an act of violence puts their burgeoning relationship on hold. The adult responsibilities they've embraced are now instrumental in keeping their town from exploding. When things come to a head, they realize their newly forged family might be what keeps the world from spinning out of control.

Running in the Sun

AARON GEORGE adjusted the collar of his uniform and checked his graying blond hair in the rearview mirror—and then felt foolish. He was forty-eight years old, for sweet Christ's sake. But Larx was running down Cambrian Way again, and he'd taken his shirt off in deference to the afternoon heat, and something had to be done.

His shoulders gleamed sleek and gold in the late-September sun, and his body—lean and long, although he was around Aaron's age—moved with a longtime runner's grace.

Aaron had been working hard to keep off the fifty pounds that had hit his waist when he turned thirty. He was about halfway successful, because diet and exercise weren't as easy when you drove an SUV up and down mountain roads as they had been when he was flatfooting around the city.

But Aaron's wife had died ten years ago, and he'd had three kids—two of them out of the house now. It had felt easier, somehow, to take a deputy position in Colton. The city—even Sacramento, which was a small city by most standards—was a young man's game. Colton, population 10,000 or so, was a little more laid-back and suited for raising a family.

Which had apparently been Larx's idea too, since he'd brought his daughters to Colton after his divorce.

Or that's what Aaron had heard. Mr. Larkin— Larx to his students and staff—had moved to Colton seven years earlier. Aaron's youngest two had taken Larx's science class and pronounced him "way cooler than anyone else in this hick burg." When the older administration retired, Larx had put up quite a fight to not be the principal.

Aaron hadn't been there, of course, but his youngest, Kirby, had been an office TA his junior year. He'd heard the battles raging in Nobili's office, and the staff room, and once, he'd told his father salaciously, in the middle of the quad.

In the end, Larx had conceded to be principal on three conditions.

One was that he got to teach AP Chemistry during zero period in the morning, before school, because he'd worked for five years to make the AP program flourish and he was damned if he'd give the class to the two-year rookie who was the only other teacher at the school qualified to teach the class. (Kirby told his father there had been much rejoicing with this caveat, because Mr. Albrecht was, by all accounts, a power-hungry little prick.)

The second condition was that his best friend, Yoshi Nakamoto, be promoted to the VP's spot. Yoshi was in his early thirties and had taught English at John F. Colton High School for six years. As far as Aaron had heard, he was a solid teacher and a nice guy, and probably the exact person a new administrator would want to have his back.

The third condition was that Larx still got to coach the track-and-field team year round.

It was the one condition he hadn't been granted, because (and, again, with Kirby as his source) Mr. Nakamoto had insisted Time-Turners were only real in Harry Potter books, and Larx just didn't have the hours in the day.

Which was when Larx had started fucking with Aaron's nice orderly life in a big way.

Because every day at 4:45 in the afternoon, Larx would appear on this stretch of road, right when Aaron was wrapping up his rounds of the county. He would run from the school down Cambrian, turn right on Olson—which was barely more than a tractor road—and cut through to the highway, which was squirrely as shit and had no shoulder. He'd run the highway for a mile, turn right on Hastings, which was *also* squirrely as shit and had no shoulder, and then turn right and run back to the high school on Cambrian.

The first time Aaron had seen him do this, his heart had stopped. Literally stopped. Because he'd seen the headlines scrolling behind his eyes: *Local Principal Killed by Own Stupidity. Entire High School Runs into Road Like Wild Ducks in Protest and Mourning.*

And then, just when his heart had started beating again, he'd seen—really *seen*—Larx without his shirt.

Aaron was forty-eight years old. He'd known he was bisexual in high school, but it had been easier to date girls than boys back then, so he'd gone with it. He'd loved his wife with all his heart, hadn't looked back once from the day they'd met, and had been busy as hell over the past ten years trying to raise his children.

Aaron's libido had mostly closed up shop since his wife died, with occasional openings during tourist season when the kids were at their grandparents'. One glimpse of that glistening, tan back, those rangy shoulders, the sweat-slicked black hair, and his libido woke up and started to pray to Cialis, goddess of horny middle-aged men.

He'd gunned his motor that day and passed Larx in a haze of confusion. He was desperate to get the hell out of there before Larx caught him staring openmouthed at a guy trying to be sweaty, glisteny roadkill in the red-dirt shade of pine trees up near Tahoe National Forest.

The next day his libido told him he'd been a fool to pass up that chance to watch Larx run, and that if he passed him again, he should slow down a tad and take in the view.

Aaron had done just that, slowing down a little, giving Larx a wide berth, smiling and waving as he passed. They knew each other from parent meetings, board meetings, community events. If given a chance, Aaron would gravitate to talk to Larx in a crowd, because he was funny and smart and a born smartass. So it was only natural that Larx waved back, friendly-like, and Aaron tried not to spend the next few hours of paperwork and gun and fishing permits grinning like a teenaged girl.

He'd had two of those. They weren't rational creatures, and he had no intentions of turning into one.

Larx had a narrow, mischievous face, a rather sharp nose and chin, and wicked brown eyes with deep laugh lines at the corners. He looked more like a hell-raiser than an authority figure, and when he grinned and waved, he gave a couple of dancy little steps to help keep in rhythm on the side of the road.

It made him look like a perky little lemur, except human, and with glisteny tanned shoulders and laugh lines and a nearly hairless chest and an ass you could bounce a quarter off, barely covered in nylon running shorts.

But no. Aaron was in no way turning into a teenaged girl.

That hadn't kept him from making sure he adhered religiously to his own schedule, the one that had him driving by Larx just when he started to sweat the most. Today, though, was going to be special. Today, Aaron was actually going to *talk*.

What could it hurt? Larx didn't have to know about Aaron's little crush. And even if he *did* think Aaron was hitting on him (which he most absolutely was positively not), Aaron knew for a fact that Larx had not only allowed but encouraged the GSA on campus. So even if he *thought* this was a come-on, and was not, in no way, absolutely not interested in men, hopefully he wouldn't go screaming for the hills, holding his shirt to his magnificent chest in maidenly horror.

Or that was Aaron's thinking, anyway.

He pushed his mirrored sunglasses up his nose, rolled down the passenger window, and slowed to a crawl, grateful the road was long and straight enough to give any car coming up behind him a chance to slow down.

"Good afternoon, Principal," he said laconically, trying to keep his smile genial.

Larx turned enough to salute and kept up his steady jog. "Howya doin', Deputy? Everything quiet, I hope."

"It is, it is indeed. But I gotta say, you been giving me a lotta bad moments, running on the side of the road these days. You never heard of a *track*?" Ooh—good one! The friendly neighborhood PSA, because nothing said come-on like irritating the fuck out of the object of your interest.

"Well, sir, I have heard of a track," Larx told him, his voice tightening. "However, the football team is running practices out there, and I really hate being the old man running laps."

He was lying. Aaron knew it.

"And the cross-country track that wraps around the back of the school's property?" Aaron knew for a fact Larx used to run with his cross-country kids, even during the off-season.

"Yes, sir, I may know a thing or two about the cross-country track as well." Stubborn shit wasn't even winded.

"Well, I'm glad you're so well-informed," Aaron sallied. "May I ask—and humor me here—if you are aware of other routes on which to run besides places that routinely turn the local wildlife into street waffles, then what in the holy hell are you doing on the side of the goddamned road?"

In response, Larx sped up.

"I'm *driving*, jackass!" Aaron hollered.

"What's that, Deputy? I can't hear you! Old man going deaf here!"

Larx held a hand up to his ear even as he poured on the speed. Ha! Guy thought he could out-stubborn Aaron? Two. Teenaged. Girls.

Aaron had this down.

They were nearing Olson, which was mostly a forestry service road, and Aaron stepped on the gas just enough to pass Larx up and turn right. He pulled up short and hopped out of the SUV.

When Larx rounded the corner, Aaron was leaning against the side of the unit, arms crossed, head turned toward the road.

"You gonna be civilized about this discussion," he asked, "or are you going to make me try to keep up with you? I warn you, I was slow in high school, slow in the military, slow in college, and I ain't got much faster since."

Larx scowled and kept running. "Try."

Aaron had lied, actually. He ran every morning. He wasn't as fast as Larx—or for as long—but he was ready for this, even in his boots.

He locked the SUV, pocketed his keys, and caught up with Larx.

"You're faster than you think," Larx muttered after a few uncomfortable moments.

"Well, I do run myself," Aaron panted. "But usually in the morning, on the old forestry service track out beyond Highway 22. You know that one?"

"Yeah?" Larx sounded impressed. "Yeah. I live out near there."

"I know you do." Three years ago Larx's oldest, Olivia, had gotten a flat tire driving home from a drama rehearsal. Aaron had helped her change the tire and followed her to make sure she got home. Olivia had since graduated—she was a year behind Aaron's middle girl, Maureen—but she'd been sweet. A little scattered, like a ladybug in a windstorm, but sweet.

"So maybe, now that you've proven your point about having enough time to coach the team, you could give an old man a break and run on the home track instead of out here where everybody can see you."

Larx stopped dead and stood, hands on his hips, scowling. "Is that what you think I'm doing?"

Aaron stopped gratefully and rested, hands on his thighs. "Isn't it?"

Some of the iron seeped out of Larx's body, and he shivered. Without self-consciousness, he pulled at the T-shirt around his neck and put it on. On the one hand, this relieved Aaron considerably—he was standing just close enough to smell Larx's sweat and become supremely aware that his bare skin was a reach-out-and-touch-me distance away.

On the other, the shirt was soft and comfy and was almost more intimate on than the bare skin.

"I just… needed to get off the property," Larx said after a moment. "I didn't want that fuckin' job."

Aaron had never heard a school official swear before.

He couldn't contain his grin. "That's the most amazing thing I've ever heard," he breathed. "Do you say the other swear words too?"

Larx rolled his eyes. "Please. Our staff room sounds like truckers and fishwives—the English teachers get really creative. You'd be surprised."

"Well, not anymore. You've plum taken the mystery out of it for me." Aaron winked, and Larx shook his head.

"Do I have to?" he asked plaintively. In those four words, Aaron heard the weight of the job on his shoulders. "I've got a shit-ton of messages on my phone right now, and if I don't get off campus, I am morally obliged to answer them."

Aaron took off his Colton County Sheriff baseball cap, smoothed back his blond hair, and tucked the hat back on again. "There is no law that says you can't put your life at risk, Larx. That's not what this is about."

"Then what's it about?" Larx stood, hip cocked now, and Aaron wondered if he'd been a resentful and rebellious teenager back in the day. And if anyone had told him it wasn't "in the day" anymore. Larx still had a kid in high school too—a junior, but in the AP class. Maybe he took lessons from her on how to be rebellious. In any case, Aaron had always thought Larx must have been a fun dad—and a good one. His ex-wife lived down in Sacramento, if Aaron remembered right, and Larx had the kids up here in the hills. Whatever their reasoning, Larx had custody, and that was a big deal.

He was a good man.

Aaron cleared his throat. "It's about your friendly neighborhood deputy wondering if he's going to have to tell his son that they need to hire a new AP teacher this year."

"Argh!" Larx ran his hands through his hair and stomped his foot. "I just… you ever want a grown-up to talk to who *doesn't* work with you?"

Aaron blew out a breath. "That's what my wife was for," he said apologetically.

Larx grimaced, probably in sympathy. "I'm sorry about that," he said, from reflex.

Aaron was tired of sympathy. "It was a long time ago, and you didn't drive the car. And it's beside the point."

"Yeah, I get it. The point is, you'd rather not have me set a bad example by running on the side of a shitty road. I get it."

"Well, the point is also that you could run on that forestry track, and that if you give me fair warning, I could run with you!" A part of Aaron was aghast. *Retreat! Retreat! Retreat! His gaydar might engage, and then you're fucked!* But a part of him was exhilarated. *Ballsy move, Sheriff George. That might just get you laid!*

Larx squinted at him. Aaron usually saw him wear sunglasses outside, but apparently he didn't feel the need when he was sweating. "Really?" he asked skeptically.

"My property is right off the back of it too," Aaron said, not sure if Larx knew this. "I'm about two miles away, if you follow that track."

"I did not know that." Larx confirmed his suspicions and scratched the back of his head. "You do seem a bit faster than you claimed to be."

"Well, I do run a few times a week. Only around three miles, but if you loop around, you could go longer after you pick me up and drop me off. It's better than running here." That was nonnegotiable.

Some of the starch and defiance seeped out of Larx's posture. "Yeah. Sure. That's… nice. Nice of you to ask. Thank you."

"So I usually leave the house at six thirty for work. We could meet at five?" That would give him half an hour to eat a granola bar and shower. And an hour to run if he went an extra two miles with Larx. It would be cold, so he wouldn't get to see Larx's glisteny chest, but he would get the man's company. Those brief conversations at football games and board meetings lingered in Aaron's mind. When he wasn't fighting the system, Larx was damned funny, a thing Aaron had appreciated even before noticing his muscular shoulders and tight, stringy glutes.

Larx nodded. "I've got headlights," he said, which was a good idea, because the days were getting shorter and running in the dark was a good way to get lost—or twist an ankle.

"Well, good. I don't. I usually go in the evening before dinner."

Larx cocked his head curiously. "So why are you changing now?"

Crap. "Kirby likes you," Aaron said. "Would hate to tell him I had to shovel your body off the pavement."

Larx tilted his head to the exact opposite angle. "You sure do believe in keeping your population safe. One person at a time, even."

Aaron had blue eyes and fair skin, and he fought against the heat building in his face. "Well, it's a small town. We'd feel it if you became roadkill—can't deny it."

Larx pulled a corner of his mouth back in a cynical smile. "Then don't try."

His eyes were brown, and his mouth wide and mobile. Aaron stared at that mouth just long enough for the moment to become uncomfortable.

"Tomorrow morning, Sheriff?" Larx asked, breaking the silence.

"You want a ride back?" Aaron asked courteously, pretty sure that would be the worst thing ever at this point, given how acute the attraction.

"No, sir. I think I'm going to finish my run."

Aaron nodded and repositioned his baseball cap. "Suit yourself."

He turned then and strode back to the SUV, resisting the urge to look back and see if Larx was gazing after him. He was pretty sure he felt eyes boring into his back, but he damned well wasn't going to turn around and check.

He managed to keep the little encounter to himself as he returned to the county office and filled out his dailies. He briefed the chief on his activities—how he was pretty sure the mom-and-pop weed operation they'd spotted a month ago had escalated and they might need to call the DEA, and how the high school's request for a sidewalk lining school property should be backed by the sheriff's office as a matter of general safety. He *didn't* mention Larx, but Larx wasn't the only idiot who thought he was immune to traffic.

Sheriff Eamon Mills nodded, asked if Aaron's report had been filed, and then, just as Aaron turned away, stopped him. "Uh, George?"

"Yessir?"

"I know this isn't your shift, but there's a home game coming up in two weeks. It's from one of those schools out of county—you know...." Mills grimaced. "We're a small town, mostly, and this is a big-city school. I'm sure *their* kids are going to be just fine, because I know the coach, and Foster runs a tight ship. It's *our* parents we need to worry about, you understand?"

Aaron grimaced. Yes, he did. Kids these days, with the internet and cable—they had a view on diversity and the wider world that was both boggling and gratifying. The adults in the family? Well, that wasn't always the case. Two years before, a school bus driver from a city school had gotten freaked out by a snow-flake. Terrified at the prospect of driving in the snow, he'd left his students stranded in front of Colton High after they'd won a playoff basketball game. Aaron and Larx had managed to round up sheriff's vehicles and parent volunteers to get the kids back to their home school, but Aaron could still remember how afraid those kids had been, huddled together against the gym, surrounded by a hostile population of rednecks who were *not* happy to lose to a big-city team.

"You're looking for some more uniforms at the game?" he asked, not reluctantly. Not at all. Larx would be at the game. Game nights were part of a small-town officer's duty, and Aaron had worked his share. When Larx had been teaching, Aaron had seen him occasionally, because it *was* a community event, but not always. The principal *had* to attend the game, though.

Larx would be there. They'd have over a week of running under their belts. Aaron would drag Kirby there, Larx's youngest daughter would probably attend—it would be fun.

Platonic, single-parent fun.

Uh-huh.

"Yeah, son. That would be helpful. Maybe you and Larx could spend some time in the opposing team's bleachers laughing, giving out free concessions, letting our people know we're all friends here. That okay?"

Eamon was African American and in his sixties, probably ready to retire. He'd spent a few years in the military, a few more in 'Nam, and a few more "getting lost in New York," as he liked to say. He was both as homegrown and redneck as they came, and surprisingly educated and cosmopolitan in his own way.

Aaron loved him like the father he'd wished he'd had. "That's fine," he said, smiling a little. "I'll bring Kirby—nobody can be mean to that kid when he bats his brown eyes at 'em."

Eamon nodded. "I appreciate it. And definitely bring the whippersnapper along. That kid needs to spend more time here filing. Last time he went into the archives, he actually solved two cases."

Aaron grimaced. "Yessir, well, I'd just as soon he not get quite so excited about law enforcement as a career. He's a danger to himself *without* the firearm." Caroline had been sort of a charming klutz too, and that kid did take after his mother.

Eamon chuckled. "We'll keep the cabinet locked, don't you worry. But maybe don't actively keep him away, Aaron. You know kids. The more you say no, the more the kid wants to find ways to make that a yes."

"Two teenaged daughters," Aaron said grimly. Eamon had been there. Hell, Eamon had been there when Aaron's oldest, Tiffany, had to be taken home in a squad car when she'd been busted having sex with her boyfriend under Cofer's Bridge. He'd been there when Maureen had been busted getting drunk with the other drama kids after they'd taken down the stage of their senior production. Name an embarrassing moment in a parent's career and Eamon had been there to give advice, his hand on his deputy's shoulder.

"I remember," Eamon said now. "How *are* Tiff and Maureen?"

"Well, Tiff is on track to graduate in two years, because she just changed majors at the last fucking gasp and needs to take almost her entire four years over again."

Eamon whistled. "Pricey."

"It is indeed. I told her she'd have to work through part of that, and she called me a tyrant. I told her the only reason she didn't have to earn *all* of it was that her sister was on track to graduate a year early and join the Peace Corps so she could go teach children to read in India. Tiff called her sister a name, which I will not repeat, and Maureen called Tiff another name, which I will not repeat, and by the time they both went back to school, neither of them was speaking to the other."

"Or to you?" Eamon asked kindly.

"Well, Maureen was speaking to me. Which only cemented her identity as an 'ass-kissing little pussy'— in her sister's exact words."

Eamon grunted. "Son, you can't take that to heart. Kids…."

Aaron sighed and scrubbed his face with his hand. "I know. She'll get over it. She almost always does. I just… I have a brother I haven't spoken to in years. He just lives on the other side of the country, is all. I wanted so badly to have the kids grow up and give a damn about each other."

"Aaron, you've done your best. And you know, you've got Kirby. That kid can bring those girls together in a heartbeat."

Well, truth. Kirby had been sending the girls a letter a week over the past six weeks, each one on a little note card, each one updating the other on what her sister was doing. If anyone could play peacemaker there, it was Kirby. "I'm hoping so," Aaron agreed. That sounded like a good place to leave, so he turned away, only to be brought up short.

"Aaron?"

"Sir?" Aaron turned back.

"I almost hate to ask this, as a meddling old man, but I *am* old, and I haven't made it a secret that I may decide not to run in the next election. And if I don't, you know I'm going to ask you to step up and run."

Crap. This. "Yessir—and I'm honored." Aaron did know how Larx felt. There was not much he hated more than the thought of being the only grown-up left for other people to look to.

"Well, don't be. It's a shit job and you get no sleep. But it sure is easier with a helpmate on the home front."

Aaron grimaced. "Yessir. I have been aware of that for the last ten years."

"I know you have. And yet you've never looked for another Mrs. George."

Oh God. His whole body washed in a prickle of sweat at the prospect of lying to Eamon—or even dodging the question. You just did not *do* that to a man whose wife had cooked for your family once a week on the pretext of "just making extra." You didn't do that to a man who had kept cookies at his desk for ten years in case his deputies' children should be forced to do their homework in the police station. It wasn't right.

"Or Mr. George," he said, lungs feeling like they were being pressed between a Volkswagen and a sheet of steel.

Eamon's eyes opened wide, and he gaped a few times.

Aaron smiled weakly.

Eamon snapped his mouth shut and shrugged. "Is that so?"

"It's a toss-up, sir."

"Well, a missus would be easier, but that's not my call to make. I'm just saying that you don't have to do it alone."

Aaron closed his eyes to try to keep the burning behind them from getting out of hand. "Thank you, sir," he said quietly. "I should get home now."

"Gail's making cookies tonight, son. She'll have some ready for Kirby tomorrow."

Aw, dammit. Aaron had to turn away, because he was not at his manly best at the moment. "That's right sweet of her, sir. I'll have Kirby draw up a thank-you note."

"We look forward to them every time."

Kirby tended to draw cartoons on his thank-you notes. The last one had featured a pig rolling around in hearts and daisies, snuffling with happiness over a steaming plate of cookies.

"I'll tell him that."

Aaron kept walking. He just could not handle another hit in the feels this day, and that was the truth.

When Aaron got home, Kirby was at the kitchen table working dutifully on his homework, some sort of chicken/veggie/Thai disaster cooking in the small kitchen behind him.

"You're late," Kirby said without looking up. He was a stickler for things like that.

"I was talking to my boss." *I was coming out to my boss in case I could possibly maybe someday bang your principal.* Nope. That last part was staying subtext.

Kirby looked up as he walked in from living room, and the familiar shock of seeing Caroline's brown eyes, surrounded with a thick fringe of lashes, peering back at him zapped a little path of sweet pain through Aaron's heart. "What about?" Kirby worried. He had an active imagination, and in the same way Aaron couldn't watch Larx jogging down that horrible road without picturing the worst, if Aaron was so much as five minutes late, Kirby imagined him dead.

"About going to the football game next Friday night."

Kirby grimaced. "You're on redneck patrol, aren't you? To make sure we don't embarrass ourselves because we haven't ever seen big-city folk before."

"Pretty much. Want to come make some new friends?"

Kirby perked up. "People who have spent the last ten years of their lives somewhere that hunting season isn't considered a legit excuse not to go to school? I'm there."

This was Kirby's last year of high school, and Aaron could sense that need in his boy to get the hell out of this tiny town. Not that he blamed him—Aaron would miss him is all.

"Thanks. Eamon asked about you. He's sending cookies tomorrow." Aaron strode into the kitchen and poured himself a glass of protein juice to fortify himself for his run. Stuff tasted like shit, but Kirby had mixed it up for him the year before, and it really worked. Anything to keep him from eating cookies after his shift.

Kirby grimaced. "Dad…."

He walked back toward the battered wooden table so he could let Kirby see his actual sympathy. "Yeah. I know." Gail was the loveliest woman, and her casseroles and side dishes were amazing. But her cookies….

"We have chickens who will love them," Aaron said diplomatically.

Kirby shook his head. "That's why I drew the pig last time."

"Well, if it hadn't been so darned cute, maybe she would have gotten the hint. How's dinner?"

"Ready when you're done with your run," Kirby responded promptly. "So maybe get out of my hair and let me finish my chemistry. Larx'll be pissed if it's not perfect."

"Deal. But I'm going to start running with Larx in the mornings from now on, so however that fits into your plans."

Kirby squinted at him as though he had sprouted another head. "You're going to *what*?"

Aaron fidgeted with his empty glass. "I, uh, you know. Me and Larx are going to go running. In the morning. So he doesn't have to run on the side of the road. That sort of freaked you out."

Kirby blinked slowly. "Yes. Yes, it did. But I didn't expect you to go out and invite him to run. That's like, super deluxe up close personal service there, Dad. I'm not sure you can go above and beyond for every citizen in town—even this town."

"Well, Larx isn't just everyone," Aaron said, soldiering on. "He's the principal."

Kirby's face had been sweet and round as a child, but he'd developed a strong jaw and high cheekbones as he'd grown. He had dark blond hair like his father, and he'd be a fine-looking man someday, but right now he was a *beautiful* adolescent. The kind you thought angels modeled their own faces after.

Right up until his "bullshit" line arced between his eyebrows.

Like it was now.

"There are secret adult machinations at work here," he pronounced. "I'm not sure how or why, but this does not bode well for any involved."

Aaron fidgeted with his empty cup and then walked back into the kitchen. "Uh, watching a lot of science fiction there, son?"

"Yes, Dad, with you. So don't pretend you don't know what I'm talking about."

"Not a clue. Gonna change and go running. Back in half an hour. Bye!"

It wasn't pretty, but retreats seldom were.

That night he fell asleep remembering Larx squinting at him in the dusty sunshine, the iron out of his spine and some sweetness in his smile.

He dreamed he'd moved forward, taken a step, until he could feel the heat from Larx's exertion, until he could feel Larx's breath on his face.

He dreamed of their lips touching in a simple kiss.

AMY LANE is a mother of two grown kids, two half-grown kids, two small dogs, and half-a-clowder of cats. A compulsive knitter who writes because she can't silence the voices in her head, she adores fur-babies, knitting socks, and hawt menz, and she dislikes moths, cat boxes, and knuckleheaded macspazzmatrons. She is rarely found cooking, cleaning, or doing domestic chores, but she has been known to knit up an emergency hat/blanket/pair of socks for any occasion whatsoever or sometimes for no reason at all. Her award-winning writing has three flavors: twisty-purple alternative universe, angsty-orange contemporary, and sunshine-yellow happy. By necessity, she has learned to type like the wind. She's been married for twenty-five-plus years to her beloved Mate and still believes in Twu Wuv, with a capital Twu and a capital Wuv, and she doesn't see any reason at all for that to change.

Website: www.greenshill.com
Blog: www.writerslane.blogspot.com
Email: amylane@greenshill.com
Facebook: www.facebook.com/amy.lane.167
Twitter: @amymaclane

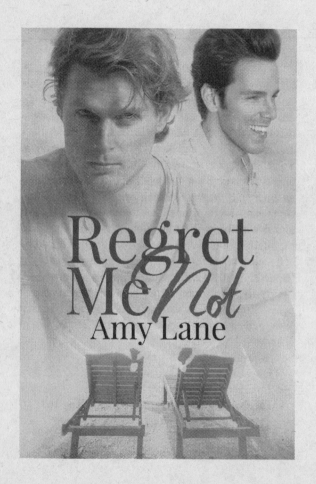

Regret Me Not
Amy Lane

Pierce Atwater used to think he was a knight in shining armor, but then his life fell to crap. Now he has no job, no wife, no life—and is so full of self-pity he can't even be decent to the one family member he's still speaking to. He heads for Florida, where he's got a month to pull his head out of his ass before he ruins his little sister's Christmas.

Harold Justice Lombard the Fifth is at his own crossroads—he can keep being Hal, massage therapist in training, flamboyant and irrepressible to the bones, or he can let his parents rule his life. Hal takes one look at Pierce and decides they're fellow unicorns out to make the world a better place. Pierce can't reject Hal's overtures of friendship, in spite of his misgivings about being too old and too pissed off to make a good friend.

As they experience everything from existential Looney Tunes to eternal trips to Target, Pierce becomes more dependent on Hal's optimism to get him through the day. When Hal starts getting him through the nights too, Pierce must look inside for the knight he used to be—before Christmas becomes a doomsday deadline of heartbreak instead of a celebration of love.

www. dreamspinnerpress.com

The
plays
that matter
don't
happen
on the
field...

Winter Ball

Amy Lane

A Winter Ball novel

Mason Hayes's love life has a long history of losers who don't see that Mason's heart is as deep and tender as his mouth is awkward. He wants kindness, he wants love—and he wants someone who thinks sex is as fantastic as he does. When Terry Jefferson first asks him out, Mason thinks it's a fluke: Mason is too old, too boring, and too blurty to interest someone as young and hot as his friend's soccer teammate.

The truth is much more painful: Mason and Terry are perfectly compatible, and they totally get each other. But Terry is still living with his toxic, suffocating parent and Mason doesn't want to be a sugar daddy. Watching Terry struggle to find himself is a long lesson in patience, but Mason needs to trust that the end result will be worth it, because finally, he's found a man worth sharing his heart with.

www. dreamspinnerpress.com

DREAMSPUN
DESIRES

THE VIRGIN MANNY

Amy Lane

The Mannies

*Growing up and
falling in love...*

The Mannies

Growing up and falling in love…

Sometimes family is a blessing and a curse. When Tino Robbins is roped into helping his sister deliver premade dinners when he should be studying for finals, he's pretty sure it's the latter! But one delivery might change everything.

Channing Lowell's charmed life changes when his sister dies and leaves him her seven-year-old son. He's committed to doing what's best for Sammy… but he's going to need a lot of help. When Tino lands on his porch, Channing is determined to recruit him to Team Sammy.

Tino plans to make his education count—even if that means avoiding a relationship—but as he falls harder and harder for his boss, he starts to wonder: Does he have to leave his newly forged family behind in order to live his promising tomorrow?

www. dreamspinnerpress.com